THE CURSE OF BLACK MOUNTAIN

MOUNTAIN

C R DEMPSEY

CRMPD MEDIA LIMITED

CONTENTS

For Mena and Poppy

CHAPTER I
THE MORNING AFTER

E unan awoke to the sound of rain pattering on the roof of his tent. His leaden limbs lay like disobedient, lazy dogs that refused to meet the day and unite with the surge of energy that burst through his hazy brain as the dreams faded away. Sitting up caused a sharp throb in his head. Was it from last night's celebratory ale or exhaustion from battle? He inhaled deeply, only to fold in two under a coughing fit. The rancid smell of sweat and dampness filled his tent; unfortunately, he recognised it was coming from him.

The rhythm of the rain stopped. Eunan heard the clang of armour outside and the groans of the men. Then it dawned upon him. Yesterday was the greatest victory ever for the clans of Ireland, and Dublin lay before them. The enemy was beaten but not destroyed. The ultimate victory lay before him, but only if he could get out of bed.

He dragged his bulky frame through the various debris on the tent floor — bloody rags, a broken mug, and various trophies picked off the dead to earn him bragging rights — careful not to place his knees near the exposed blades of axes. He undid the flaps and stuck his head out into the crisp morning air. His red hair was immediately recognisable.

"So glad you could join us today," said his uncle Seamus with a toothy grin as he poked at the fire embers, trying to eke out some heat without getting more firewood. His grey, matted hair was slung over his shoulder, and though he was dressed only in a dirty white shirt, he seemed immune to the cold. Eunan joined him by the fire. Seamus smirked.

"Look at us," he said wryly. "We have just won the biggest victory known on these shores over the English, yet we sit here like a pair of beggars." Eunan gave Seamus a wide smile.

"I'll certainly need a wash and to put on my fineries before I pose for the tapestry they'll hang on the Enniskillen castle walls."

Barely had contempt formed a sentence for Seamus's riposte when a young boy sprinted up to them, heaving for breath.

"The O'Neill has summoned all the commanders to his tent," the boy said between breaths.

"Thank you, son. Now, go quench your thirst before you return to your master." Seamus pointed towards some barrels on a nearby cart.

The boy grinned. "'Tis a grand day indeed! Everyone is celebrating!"

Fearing the boy wanted some other reward, be it a tale or a coin, Seamus gestured towards the barrels as if that was his only reward. "Go quench your thirst for there is enough water today to go round for all."

He punched Eunan in the shoulder. "Come on, now's not the time for frivolities or dreaming of fancy tapestries they'll make when you're dead. You've got to think like a commander if we're going to stop the O'Neill from squandering this victory."

Eunan and Seamus knew they needed to be presentable before meeting the O'Neill, so they found a stream where Eunan washed off the most visible excess mud from the battle the day before. He stood in the river, using one hand to ladle water over his body while scrubbing with the other. Seamus took a more cautious approach, sitting on a rock with much of his clothing still on and delicately pouring water while keeping an eye out for approaching people.

"Eunan! Come here!" Eunan turned around, making sure that his private parts were still beneath the surface.

"No one wants to see that," Seamus said with a smirk, "but they might if you use these." He held out a bunch of wildflowers he had collected. "Rub these all over your bits when you're finished washing, and you'll smell lovely for your father-in-law and uncle-in-law. It will really impress them and show them what a great husband you are to Sorcha."

Eunan averted his eyes from his uncle's glance. "Keep them for your own wife. You'll need them to apologise for being away for so long."

"Dervella will be fine," Seamus sneered. "I'm sure she's glad to see me go every time I leave."

"Don't be so sure," Eunan responded as he climbed onto the bank to dry himself off. "That woman is the dearest person to me in the world; far more of a mother than my own. Her only mistake was choosing you as her husband."

"Ha! She should count herself lucky. She could have married one of my brothers!"

The last sentence caught Eunan's attention.

"You never told me before you had any other brothers besides my father," he said.

Seamus swore, knowing it was his fault for stirring up Eunan's curiosity.

"Now, don't you go blaming me for not telling you," Seamus said, wagging his finger. "As a commander, you should get all the pertinent facts before making decisions. Don't inquire after my other brother. We'd be better off if he was in a much lower pit of hell than your father, as he truly deserves it."

He picked up Eunan's shirt and threw it at him; luckily, Eunan dove to catch it with enough time to prevent it from getting wet.

"Get changed and drop the subject of my immediate family. Bath time is over; we must ensure the O'Neill makes the most of his victory."

The path to the centre of the O'Neill's camp was covered in planks of wood, for it had only taken a smattering of rain for the many feet to convert the paths of the camp into mud. The air was heavy with the smells of roasting cows, smoke, and the stench of sweaty men. Most of them were in good spirits, though some faces were gripped with pain due to injuries sustained during the battle. They all waited anxiously for a physician who could help them save their limbs.

Eunan shared in the jubilation of those who survived the battle relatively unscathed as he followed Seamus through the camp. Seamus retained his demeanour as a commander and shook hands with those men along the way who he considered would not make it to the end of the day. He promised them prayers and more victories in their names.

The O'Neill's galloglass surrounded an open area and carried his chair into its centre where he could address the subordinate clans. Eunan and Seamus were pointed to the right-hand side and were invited to stand behind the Maguire. The men exhibited an array of emotions — some were still celebrating their victory the day before, others showed signs of disquietude, shifting uncomfortably as if debating whether or not to voice their inner qualms.

As soon as the O'Neill entered, surrounded by his bodyguards, a thunderous cheer erupted from every throat present in deference to him. However, Eunan noticed Cormac walking solemnly at his heels, head bowed. Without further ado, the O'Neill took up residence on his throne-like seat, face stoic and as if cast in solid stone.

Seamus sensed the mounting tension and huddled closer to Eunan. "I get the feeling we won't be here for long," he muttered beneath his breath.

A deafening silence descended on the sea of people as the O'Neill stood. They all anxiously held their breath as they waited expectantly. He quietly rocked back and forth before finally addressing them.

"Yesterday, we won a great victory that will be remembered throughout the ages. As we speak, my agents are at sea to tell the Spanish King of our great victory, hoping that it expedites his army's arrival. But contrary to the songs I heard around the campfires last evening, I still believe the Lord Deputy to be a powerful foe. There is still a strong chance of an English army landing behind us. No O'Neill can countenance being out on campaign while his wife and children get murdered at home. Therefore, there will be no march on Dublin, and we shall wait in Ulster, where the Englishman fears to tread until the Spanish King sends his army. Congratulations to you all. Return home and take in the harvest, sons and daughters of Ulster!"

The shouts of disagreement rumbled like thunder through the crowd. But before anyone could act on their fury, O'Neill was ushered away by his body-guards, flanked by his Galloglass entourage.

"Come on," Seamus said to Eunan as he signalled him to leave. "There'll be no persuading the O'Neill today."

Eunan followed and worked his way through the crowd. He felt a slap on his chest and looked down to see a hand with a letter.

"From a rebel in Munster who hopes to see you soon," a voice said.

Eunan looked up and saw a figure melting back into the crowd. He quickly tucked the letter into his pocket, resolving to read its contents when alone.

The letter felt like a death sentence in Eunan's pocket. Its cruel mystery threat-ened to unravel all he had worked for, and with Seamus's suspicious eyes upon him, he doubled his efforts to lose himself in the throng of commanders. Even-tually, he returned to his tent, shut out the world, and entered the stale air that was almost suffocating in its intensity.

His breathing quickened, and his hand trembled as he pulled the letter out, barely managing to keep his grip on the paper. Images of Sorcha flashed before him — lying immobile on her bed surrounded by white sheets, her arm reaching slowly towards Eunan as though it drained all her energy; Cara's smiling face framed by windswept curls on Devenish Island, her cheeks flushed with life. Tears stung his eyes, and exhaustion gave way to guilt. Then came a vision of Sorcha pregnant with their child; her body barely rising from the bed. Should he discard the letter unopened outside the camp, where it would be drowned in mud kicked up by a thousand marching feet? His breath hitched in his throat, but he knew he had no option but to open it. He had to be brave enough to accept whatever awaited him.

He ran his fingers over the creases and lines of the letter, which carried the potential evidence of a conspiracy against him and his strongest hope in weeks. He shut his eyes tight and silently prayed before desperately prying open the paper. The parchment shook in his grasp as he read through it quickly until finally, there it was, at the bottom of the page: Cara. The name alone was enough to bring raging flames back to life inside him.

"Eunan? Where are you?"

The voice startled him out of his trance. Seamus's voice echoed through the tent's thin walls, but Eunan did not move. He clenched his fists hard around the remnants of the letter so tightly that his knuckles turned white, then he shredded the letter into tiny pieces and stuffed the remains into his pocket with determined rage. With one last deep breath to steel himself, he stood up straight, marched out of the tent, and cleansed himself of emotion.

"There you are," Seamus said. His eyes narrowed. "What have you been up to? Your cheeks are all red."

Eunan made a feeble attempt at a grimace.

"I may have got too much sun yesterday being spared rain for so long. What has you so interested in my complexion all of a sudden?"

"I have commanded men for too long not to know when someone is up to something. But that is a question for another time. Gather your men. There is a column of the enemy retreating towards Fermanagh. We are needed to ensure your homeland is safe."

Eunan pulled his shirt straight and thought of his sick wife in bed with her slightly elevated belly.

"To Fermanagh. Let the people know we are their protectors."

CHAPTER 2

THE SPREADER OF DESTRUCTION AND DEATH

T he remnants of the English army retreated from Armagh in defeat, their officers attempting to keep a semblance of order as they streamed away like a broken river. The majority of the Irish soldiers had either fled to the rebels or returned home, leaving only those who were bloodied and mud-splattered behind.

Taaffe stood near a campfire, his blanket draped over his wide shoulders in an attempt to protect himself from the cold, screaming curses at a silent sky as he recalled how he had been torn away from Eunan Maguire before he could make the kill.

Suddenly, Shea Óg appeared from the shadows, his pale complexion hinting at his inner pain caused by Seamus MacSheehy's vicious attack on him that set him on the downward path to sitting here with Taaffe. With its extended cheek guards, his helmet covered the facial scars Seamus had given him that day, and Shea Óg's madness for revenge surged within. Nevertheless, Shea Óg still expected Taaffe's gratitude for saving his life and now he looked expectantly at the man.

"At least you're still alive," Shea Óg said. "I expect you to settle up with me if we make it back to Dublin, as I expect the rebels not to be far behind. Then we can see who the winner is likely to be and if the Queen will send another army which will be equally as badly led."

Taaffe threw off his blanket, stood up and thrust his face into Shea Óg's.

"We're in this together." Shea Óg felt the rush of air from Taaffe's nostrils jabbing into his chest. "I'm just as Irish as you are,, and you are going nowhere without me."

"Then what are we supposed to do besides rejoin the retreat to Dublin?" Shea Óg said.

Taaffe turned away and spat.

"I can't go back there empty-handed. I owe too much money."

"Then what are we to do?"

"I will go to Munster. I still have friends, and my creditors would not hire men to pursue me there."

Shea Óg shrugged his shoulders.

"Then what am I to do?"

"You know where Eunan Maguire's lands are, and we know he will not be there. Burn his lands, and kill anyone you come across. Then follow me to Munster, where I will have everything prepared." Taaffe turned and grabbed Shea Óg by the shoulders. "Don't let me down. Think of all our comrades we left on the field today. Get some revenge for them."

Shea Óg shook off Taaffe's grip.

"Why don't you want to come with me if you want your revenge so much? It is not like you to be afraid to get your hands dirty."

"I need to get back to Munster to use my contacts before news of this catastrophic defeat reaches them first. Go, and I will wait for you. I'm sure you can handle it. There should just be women and children because all the warriors should be here."

Shea Óg smirked.

"All the better that you come. What will make Eunan Maguire follow you to Munster more than if you kill his relatives and create a blood feud? He is an honourable fool and will be compelled to follow, and then you can spring a trap. His uncle will accompany him because he has always harboured dreams of reviving clan MacSheehy."

Taaffe stroked his chin.

"His uncle is a MacSheehy?"

"That he is."

"Never has foolish pride caused the needless death of so many in the one clan than in the MacSheehys. The combination of a blood feud and the chance to redeem his clan's honour will be too much for both of them. They will be foreigners in an unknown land. Easy to kill."

"Then it is settled?"

"I have no more important place to be than the home of Eunan Maguire. Let us mount our horses and ride into the dark unknown."

"You have the luck of the devil, Taaffe."

Taaffe laughed.

"Luck? Many people say I am the devil."

The sky was an ashen grey, smothering the world in a thick blanket of smoke and ash. Eunan's eyes burned from the sulphurous fumes and piercing beams of the harsh sun breaking through the clouds. His gaze moved to the lake shore, where a thick smoke column snaked into the heavens.

"I can't be sure if it is O'Cassidy house, but it points in the right direction," Eunan declared.

"We must move quickly," Seamus urged. "It might be from another village, but we must get there before they attack our own."

Eunan commanded scouts to rush forward as most of the men were on foot and desperate to return home and protect their families. They scavenged for any food scraps they could find and refrained from aggressively attacking the enemy due to their dwindling ammunition supply and hopes for peaceful negotiations. There was no need to slaughter those who marched past them either, for their Irish comrades were deserting in droves from the English army. They wanted only to fight against those who dared threaten their homes.

The roads were clogged with people fleeing to or from the northern lords, their victory ringing loudly in their ears. Eunan had a heavy feeling in his gut that boded ill. His own village was burned in the past by these same rebels. He had never been responsible for its protection in such a crisis before, and he could feel the burden of guilt pressing on his chest.

He felt a wave of dread rising as he saw the scouts returning pale-faced. The messenger stuttered out his news that a small band of men had passed through — just a whisper of destruction — but it reverberated like thunder around him.

Eunan's thoughts flashed to the burning of his childhood home and the death of his parents, and he was filled with an unbearable rage. His hands curled into fists as he remembered his duty to protect his people and their families from this same fate.

"How bad?" His voice trembled, barely recognisable in its weakness.

The messenger replied softly, "It was only a small group of raiders, my lord. It appears they didn't leave any destruction in their wake."

Eunan's brow furrowed as he fought against his rising frustration and anxiety. "Then why did we hear tales of such devastation?" he demanded.

"With the mass desertions to the English ranks, many men passed through Monaghan and south Fermanagh. I cannot deny there was destruction and harassment of the local population. However, the systemic destruction seems to have targeted your lands."

Eunan's face contorted with rage.

"This can only be the work of Taaffe. I should never have let him leave the battlefield alive. How long until we get there?"

"Half a day on foot."

Eunan looked away but pointed behind him.

"Fetch me, Seamus, and Fáolán, and we'll ride in front of the men."

The messenger shifted on the back of his horse.

"Is that advisable, lord?"

"Taaffe is nothing if not a bully and a coward. He will flee as soon as he hears we are coming."

The messenger bowed.

"I shall get the constables to hurry along the men."

With that, the messenger bowed and galloped off.

Eunan felt his heart race as they drew closer to O'Cassidy house. As they rode closer, Eunan felt a heat wave radiating from the billowing smoke as it enveloped them in its smothering grasp. His heart pounded against his ribcage as he drove his horse forward. His muscles coiled as he dug his heels into the side of his horse while testing his own balancing skills and the agility and strength of the beast beneath him. Seamus signalled Fáolán to draw back for fear that their reckless leader was galloping them straight into a trap.

As the house crumbled under flames, a swirling mass of black smoke billowed high into the sky. The sight that greeted Eunan made him sick to his stomach: bodies were strewn across the ground, some charred beyond recognition, others still oozing blood from fatal wounds. Gasping for air, he staggered through the destruction, searching for familiar faces amongst the bodies that littered the grounds. His heart shuddered as he recognised some of his faithful farmhands; his lip quivered as he frantically searched for more. Tears welled up in his eyes as he continued to turn over body after body until Seamus and Fáolán arrived, their faces etched in shock at the scene before them. His stomach turned as he flipped over yet another mangled corpse. He swallowed back his grief and kept searching as fresh waves of despair coursed through him as his gaze settled on a particular body.

"No!"

Large chunks of the clothing were charred beyond recognition, but what could be seen seemed to be the simple garb of a farm worker. The hair had been burned off, revealing a much shorter length than it had been before. Although severely damaged, the face still resembled its former state when the person was alive.

"DERVELLA!"

Dervella's face was covered in dried blood, bone jutting from her right cheek. Her right eye was swollen shut, her lips busted open, and her teeth scattered on the ground around her.

Seamus ran up behind Eunan to see what he had found. Seamus howled like a wounded wolf. His heart felt like it would rip out of his chest as he threw Eunan off her body. He scooped Dervella up gently in his arms and staggered a few yards before collapsing on one knee, finally crumpling to the ground and laying her tenderly on the grass. He knelt beside her with his back to his companions, his shoulders shaking with heavy sobs. Eunan slowly moved closer, arm outstretched, an empathetic response ready to flow from his mouth as soon as his trembling hand found its way onto Seamus' shoulder. But before he could move another step, Seamus noticed something from the corner of his eye that sent fear coursing through his veins. He recognised the wiry shape of a body beside Dervella. His fingers trembling, he reached down and turned the body over. His stomach churned as the tragedy was revealed.

"ARTHUR!"

Eunan's eyes blurred with tears as he knelt beside Arthur's body, slumped and still against the grassy ground. He reached out a shaking hand to brush away the matted hair from Arthur's shattered face, barely recognising the beloved figure through his grief. His great friend, his last link to Desmond, his mentor, was dead., He looked into the sunlit sky, the previous gloom having departed and leaving smoke alone to pollute the air. He raged at God for allowing such a beautiful day to exist while two of his closest companions were dead and defiled. His chest ached with anguish as he felt the pain of both their physical deaths and the emptiness in his heart where they once resided. His soul floated above him, reaching out to touch the ground where his loved ones lay in cold repose, yet the distance between them felt like an unbridgeable gulf. Tears ran down his cheeks as he cursed the wickedness of those responsible. Bitterness filled Eunan's heart as he looked upon the evil that had taken away two of his most cherished family members. In his delirium he heard their lifeless bodies cry out.

"Why did you abandon us? If you were here, you could have defended us. You abandoned us just like you abandoned your parents."

"Hey. Are you all right?" Fáolán said.

Eunan looked up and saw the thick branches of an old tree. Along its arms shone the sun, nurturing life radiating from the centre of the tree to the green leaves that hung at the ends of the branches that were about the size of the palm of his hand. His head hurt, and his mouth was dry. His eyes could not focus because of the blinding sun.

"Water. Please."

The water sparkled in the sunlight as it left the top of the flask and fell into his mouth. His throat was not positioned for the rapid water intake, and he jackknifed forward all coughs and splutters. He rubbed his eyes. Seamus sat across from him, shoulders slumped, his head leant to the right as if he had lost the will to hold it upright. The body of Dervella lay to one side of him and Arthur on the other.

"So it is true?" Eunan said at last.

"I never thought I'd see the day," Fáolán said, "but the mighty Eunan Maguire fainted."

The withering look he received in reply told him this was no time for any attempts at humour. Eunan twitched as he ran his hands through his hair.

"She was like a mother to me, and Arthur like my greatest friend. They both gave their lives toiling for me."

With that, Seamus stood up as rigid as a ramrod.

"We must bury them, then we need to find out who did this and seek our revenge," Seamus said matter-of-factly.

"We don't have to look far to see who did this," Fáolán said. He walked over to the oak tree trunk whose branches sheltered them. It was the same oak tree under which Caoimhe O'Cassidy was to marry the son of Connor Roe Maguire, where Seamus killed the groom during the ceremony. He pulled out a dagger from the trunk and caught the piece of paper the dagger held to the bark. He handed it to Eunan. Eunan read the message and looked away to hide his tears.

"What does it say?" Seamus said. He was in no mood to be kept waiting.

"Cormac O'Cassidy wants his lands back — signed the Sheriff of Sligo."

"Taaffe!" Seamus spat. "This is a blood feud of the type we cannot let go unanswered. No doubt this is supposed to be a trap, but he has made a fatal mistake murdering my Dervella."

"He has written the letter in blood," Eunan said. "I have no wish to guess whose, but he did it in case there was any doubt it was a blood feud."

"We must have the burials first, take some time to rest and then locate Taaffe and have our revenge," Seamus said. "Where did you bury your first wife?"

"On the islands near my village," Eunan said.

"Fáolán, get a cart and bring us to Corradovar," Seamus said. "From there, we set off to Desmond's island. It holds pleasant memories for everyone concerned, and their spirits have far less chance of being disturbed than they do here. For I fear this soil will absorb lashings more blood before it is still."

No arguments came to Eunan's lips, just a tear to his cheek. It was a fitting resting place to lay them both alongside Desmond, where they would be at peace.

CHAPTER 3

THE CURSE

They wrapped the bodies in cloth and placed them on the cart Fáolán had retrieved from the village.

"The villagers say they are sorry for your loss," Fáolán said, in harmony with the mournful air.

"It's about time they showed us some gratitude for all the protection we have given them," Seamus growled.

Eunan opened his mouth to defend his people, but Fáolán signalled to him to be quiet, and Eunan kept his peace. They drove the cart to Corradovar, with Eunan's men forming an escort. As the funeral procession entered the village, the residents came to pay their respects.

One woman recognised the hardened features of Seamus and stood beneath his horse.

"She was a good woman, that wife of yours," she said. "She looked after us and would allow us to dip into the O'Cassidy-Maguire store of grain if we were short. 'Tis a novelty for us, a master that would look after us so well."

Seamus's chest heaved.

"Eunan Maguire will follow her good example and look after you as well as she did."

"Where are you going to bury her?"

"On the islands where she should find some peace."

"She was a Munster woman, wasn't she? Would her passing not be easier for her to be buried in her own soil?"

"I wouldn't want to plague her soul with the bad memories of her youth in Munster. Too many of her relatives were wickedly taken, and I fear their blood would have polluted the very soil that should comfort her. She had some of her happiest times on the islands, albeit not her own soil. But she will be content there. Now, thank you for your kind wishes, but I must get on with loading the boat."

"You'd not be wise to take to the lakes at this hour," the woman said. "With only a couple of hours of sunlight at best, you'd not get far until the dark surrounded you. If you were lucky, you'd run into the Maguire's men, and you'd have to plead your case that you're not bandits. If you were unlucky, you'd run into the bandits and have to plead your case that what is in your sacks is of no value to them. If you could utter a word before they slit your throats."

She signalled for them to follow her. "Come stay in the rebuilt chieftain's hut. Let us repay some of the kindness your wife showed us."

Eunan looked at Seamus, and to his surprise, Seamus nodded for them to follow.

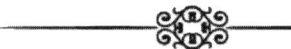

The morning was bright and crisp, and the blue of the sky was reflected in the blue of the lake. The wind blew from the north, creating wispy white horses on top of the rippling waves. The entrance to the shore of the village was protected on both sides by thick beds of reeds protruding from the water, shielding boats beginning or ending their journeys from the worst vagaries of the open lake. The woman who had hosted Eunan and Seamus stood with them by the shore and pointed to one of their best boats.

"She'll see you right for the passage to the lower lough," she said. "She's as sturdy as they come, a fitting vessel for the saint's last passage."

Seamus juddered in a double take.

"She was never referred to as a saint in her life," Seamus said.

THE CURSE OF BLACK MOUNTAIN

"Well, she was a saint to us, and the priest would like to say a few words to help her on her passage to heaven if you don't mind."

A crowd of well-wishers had gathered, and the priest stepped forward. Seamus gestured to him to give his blessings. The boats, Eunan, Seamus, and Fáolán were blessed, and the priest then blessed the bodies and led the villagers in prayer. Seamus stepped back, for he felt like a fraud. He had not been to church since he fled Munster as a youth and had treated priests with suspicion ever since.

Once the blessings were over, the bodies were gently lowered onto the boat. It was the perfect size for the small party, for one person could sit up front and guide the boat, the bodies could rest in the upper middle part and there were two benches and two sets of oars in the rear. Seamus directed Eunan to the front as they climbed into the boat.

"Don't be away from us for too long, Eunan," the woman called after them. "We will fix your fields as best we can, but there is a limit to what the women, children, and the old can do."

Eunan stood in the boat and saluted them.

"You will always be in my heart and under my protection."

Seamus grunted as he dipped his oars in the lake, and Fáolán pushed the boat off the lakebed.

The monotonous splashing of the oars in the lake as they journeyed towards Enniskillen did nothing to break up the tension in the boat. Eunan distracted himself by taking in the rolling hills on either side and looking for openings in the woods that hid small villages populated with fishermen in tiny one-man boats eager to find any bounty to feed their families. He took note of the thickness of reed beds lining both sides of the lake, but it was all for nought. Seamus had a knack for crushing any joy from any situation if he chose, and today, he seemed determined to do just that.

The boat jolted as they hit something.

"Hey," Seamus shouted, "if you can't avoid the mud banks in the middle of the lake, give Fáolán a go. Get back here and take the oars."

Eunan and Fáolán negotiated around each other and the two bodies to swap positions in the boat without capsizing it. Eunan sat and grasped the handles of the oars. They were warm and damp from both the friction of the constant movement and the water dripping down the oars. Eunan soon found Seamus's rowing rhythm. But he found the silence eerie. Here they were, all three of them in the boat together and without a word from any of them. Both of them studied the shore awash with melancholy with every wave that broke on the bow of the boat.

Eunan spoke to Seamus's back.

"So why don't we bury Dervella in Munster, as the woman said? Rumour has it that the O'Neill will raid down that way soon. I thought it was always your dream to return to Munster and revive the MacSheehy."

Seamus sneered and spat in the water and carried on rowing.

"If you want me to join you, you need to tell me sometime."

Sitting as he was, Eunan couldn't see the emotions boiling beneath Seamus's face.

"She has the curse of the Black Mountain," Fáolán explained.

Eunan turned and faced front, for he felt he would get a better answer from Fáolán.

"She had survivor's guilt, as do the both of us. If you witness half your clan turn coat on the other and you run with only your lives, that is the survivor's guilt. We do not talk about it. We only plot revenge. Now row towards Enniskillen and not another word about it. I fear Seamus would rather club you on the head than discuss the Black Mountain."

Eunan glanced back at Seamus and saw Fáolán was right. He dipped his oars back into the water.

CHAPTER 4

RETURN TO THE ISLANDS

T hey rowed until dark and pulled their boats onto the shore in a gap in the reed beds.

"We'll stay here for the night," Seamus said. "Get your feet wet and find us a secure mooring."

Seamus threw the end of a rope over Eunan's head for him to catch. The daylight was fading fast, but Eunan saw Seamus's mood had not improved. He would have to ask Fáolán about the secret of Black Mountain that cast such a shadow over their heads.

Eunan jumped out of the boat and stood on the shore, waiting for Seamus's instruction.

"The bodies stay in the boat," Seamus said. He jumped out of the boat and walked straight past Eunan. "Make a fire. Fetch some rabbits. We leave first thing in the morning."

Eunan looked to Fáolán and nodded for them to go into the woods.

The woods devoured Fáolán completely as he moved forward, the shadows stretching towards him like malevolent claws. The eerie cooing of owls echoed from within the depths, almost as if warning him to turn back. Fáolán readied his bow, taking his aim with a steady hand and a silent breath. As he released the arrow, two rabbits emerged from the depths of the forest — time was running out if they had any hope of dinner that night. The arrow flew like lightning, only to thump against a gnarled tree root at the last second.

"If you are going to shoot, don't frighten everything else away," Eunan said as he smirked.

Fáolán scowled and drew another arrow. There was a rustle in the bushes, and another arrow was loose. This time, it was met with a squeal. Eunan dove in with his throwing axe and finished the beast off. The pig twitched as the last of its life drained into the soil.

"That'll be enough to see us to any of the islands and beyond," Fáolán said, and he broke into a wide grin flush with success and as if he had been freed from melancholy by leaving Seamus's company.

Eunan found a strong branch from which to hang the pig. They placed either end of the branch on their shoulders and walked back towards the camp. He heard Fáolán whistle and decided now was his chance.

"You know how Seamus wants me to become a MacSheehy?"

"Yes."

"Then, should you not tell me about the Black Mountain so I can share your secret?"

Fáolán immediately lowered his part of the branch and turned to face Eunan. All the joy drained from his face.

"If you weren't there, you cannot share the secret. You cannot feel the pain. It was the last stand of the Great MacSheehy Galloglass. My father, Seamus's father, your grandfather. Traitors cut all down. Returning to Munster opens up the grave of all those feelings and hopes. Seamus must face it, but not now. He is not strong enough to face the curse of the Black Mountain and deal with the death of Deirvella. Drop these questions until you see Seamus is in the right mind to deal with it. Now pick up the pig and come back to the camp."

Eunan did as he was told, but his curiosity burned even stronger than before.

Finally, the island of Desmond emerged in front of them after a gruelling day of rowing through the turbulent lake. Eunan had never been so relieved when he saw the familiar reeds rustling around it and the minuscule pebble beach they would have to drag their boat onto. A thick blanket of silence had descended over them ever since Eunan had brought up the dreaded Black Mountain. Without looking back, Seamus leapt from the boat and left Eunan struggling knee-deep in the water, knowing he would soon have to haul the lifeless bodies from the boat without his help. His gaze was firmly fixed on the island, and Eunan watched Seamus's back with rising apprehension.

"Maybe a few gulls have broken into the house?"

Seamus scowled at him and walked to the south side of the island, where Desmond, Eunan's beloved mentor and the man whom the island was named after, was buried. Eunan scurried after him. He found Seamus beside Desmond's grave, stamping on the turf and kicking away the stones.

"You can dig down to a reasonable depth quite easily," Eunan said softly.

Seamus grunted and looked out across the lake. The sun was sinking behind the hills, and a quick decision was required.

"Do we have suitable equipment in the house?" Seamus said over his shoulder.

"Yes, and with three of us, we should make short work of it."

"Then we dig, we drink, we get revenge."

Eunan soon found himself in a shallow grave with only the stars for light. Seamus had made steadier progress with his grave already up to his waist.

"This will do for my Dervella. She didn't want to be halfway down to hell but would rather join with the soil, albeit only adopted soil." Seamus climbed out of the grave, and his shadow loomed over Eunan. "Go and fetch her with Fáolán, and I will finish your friend's grave. If I left it to you, we would still be here in the morning."

Eunan smiled and clambered out of the grave. Seamus was in no mood for backchat.

Eunan returned after a while, holding Dervella's ice-cold legs while Fáolán carried her by the shoulders. They navigated their way around the unsteady terrain of rocks and divots, searching for a place to rest her body. Seamus emerged from Arthur's grave, the spade heavy in his grasp. He cast his gaze downward as

Eunan and Fáolán lay Dervella alongside the fresh mound of dirt. His heart felt heavy with sadness as he realised that this really was goodbye.

"I'm no priest," Seamus said when he lifted his head. "Nor am I the master of emotional speeches. But I do know this. I loved you, Dervella, as much as this hard heart can love anyone. My heart turned to stone as we watched our families get murdered on Black Mountain, but you gave me the hope and energy to carry on. I was never the best husband. I was cruel and selfish and disrespectful, all the bad things a man could be to his wife, yet you still stood by me and loved me. You remain inside me, in my heart, in my soul. I will not talk of vengeance for taking you away from me or vengeance for Black Mountain, for they are the pursuits of the living, and I wish for your soul to find the rest and comfort that was denied to you in your life. God, or whoever, may they bless you and lead you to a comfortable place. They can give all your sins to me, for they would make little difference to a man with a soul as black as mine. Goodbye, my love."

Seamus got into the grave, and Fáolán lifted Dervella's head and gave it to him. Eunan took the legs, and they laid Dervella to rest. Eunan made no effort to hide his tears. It would be a long night.

Eunan emerged from Desmond's house, his hair tousled, his clothes dirty, and his head still clogged with the lingering effects of sleep. He reached into his pocket and pulled out his fishing string. The steady diet of fish was becoming tedious as the weeks on the island had long ago begun to drag. But he stayed for Seamus, for he had taken the death of his wife very badly. He had slipped into a deep depression after they had buried his wife and Arthur on the other side of the island alongside Desmond. He stayed on the island for he knew if he left, Seamus would fall into drink and probably end up with a knife in his belly at the rear of some alehouse, either by the blade of one of the numerous enemies he had made or as the result of taking on someone less drunk than him. Eunan remembered how Seamus had been good to him on occasion in the past, so he stayed with him so he would not come to harm.

Seamus lingered around the house most days, not bothering to shave, clean himself or change his clothes. It was no different from when he was out on a campaign, but he took to spending long periods alone, which was very burdensome on Eunan, considering that only the two of them were trapped together. He had a mood like salt, causing friction and irritation whenever he rubbed himself into a conversation. Eunan took to reading his face from a distance and avoiding him as much as possible on such a small island when he was most abrasive.

Eunan took up swimming whenever he noticed that Seamus had slipped into a deeper depression and packed a knife into his bag, which he slung over his back as he swam from island to island. When he got onto dry land, he could explore and, if lucky, obtain some other foodstuffs to break the steady fish diet. It was a relief to step off their island, giving himself freedom from Seamus's moods and providing exercise, as being cooped up in such a confined space drained his energy and soul.

When he returned from his foraging trips, he tried to make dinner for them every evening. His culinary skills were passable—mostly learned from watching Arthur and Dervella—since every soldier out in the field had to learn one meal they could forage from the fields and forests to survive. His efforts did not always get an appreciative reply.

"Fish again?" Seamus said, scowling. "How can you live on these islands if all there is to eat is bloody fish?"

"I'm sure you've put up with equally bad while trapped in the Wicklow mountains for months?"

"The food was good. It's the company I complained about. But I can't speak ill of the dead lest I join them before my time. Not that I'd care. What is there to live for now? My Dervella is gone."

He flopped down at the table, swept away the dishes with a swing of his arm and made a pillow of his inner elbow.

"As the last of your family, I have to be everything to you now. Remember, you could be a great-uncle soon."

Seamus raised his head.

"Then why do you spend your time with me when you have a pregnant wife to look after?"

"She has plenty of people attending her, and you have only me. You're the last of my family, too, and I'd prefer you not to drink yourself to death. She'll understand when I explain it."

"I wouldn't bet on that, nor would her father be so understanding."

"Let me sort out your life first before I sort out my own."

Seamus's dry lips hurt as he cracked a smile for the first time in weeks.

"How the worm has turned. Never in all my time did I expect you to look after me, including being wounded or my unlikely arrival at old age."

"I'm glad I can still spring a surprise upon you. You do the same for me by eating what I prepare you without complaint."

Seamus sprung back and raised his hands in fake shock.

"What!? Are you going to cut out my tongue?"

"I'm glad you can still make a joke, albeit at my expense."

"If I couldn't find a joke out of you, I may as well drown myself in the lake."

"Endless ridicule or your death by drowning. You know how to present me with a difficult choice."

They were interrupted by the crack of feet on the pebbles of the shore. They both went for their weapons. Eunan went to peer out the window, and Seamus hid behind the door.

"There are three of them," Eunan whispered. "We could take them if they were hostile."

"We'll have a lot of graves for such a small island," Seamus said.

"They will have to deal with the vagaries of the lake's tides. Their bodies will not sully the sacred soil of Desmond's island."

"I come seeking Eunan Maguire," came the cry from the cove.

"Who comes looking?" Eunan shouted from the window.

"Your master, the Maguire. Your wife. Your master, the leader of the Mac-Cabes. The south Fermanagh shot. How many more would you wish to appear on your list before you show yourself?"

"I recognise that voice," Eunan said. "It is my young constable, Odhran."

"I bet he is only a couple of tufts behind you in growing a decent beard." Seamus laughed at his own joke, and Eunan smiled, for it was good to see his uncle jolly again, even if it was at his expense. "But can you trust him?"

"If they were to send anyone from the MacCabes, it would be him. He may lead us into a trap, but he would not do so knowingly. I don't see we have any choice."

"Of course, we have a choice. What have I to live for anymore? I can go out with my axe swinging."

"We can easily find someone more worthy to stand in front of your axe. Now, I am going to open the door. Promise me you will not perpetrate any violence unless provoked?"

"That still leaves me with a lot of scope, for I am easily offended."

Eunan threw his eyes to the heavens and opened the door, concealing his axe from view. He covered his eyes for Odhran, who had the setting sun behind him.

"The Maguire sends his condolences for your loss and the ravaging of your lands. He will amply compensate you for your losses if you return to your former role."

Eunan's pupils blossomed.

"He wants me to lead his Galloglass again?"

"Alas, no, but the south Fermanagh shot is one of his ablest units, and you are one of his best commanders."

Eunan grinned.

"Are you hoping that such flattery will make you my second in command again?"

"It is an honour to serve, no matter what the role."

"Why does the Maguire want me to return now? I have an obligation to my uncle, who suffered a worse loss than me."

Seamus shoved Eunan out of the way and stood in the shadow of a tree so his vision would not be obstructed.

"Don't make me sound like I've been enfeebled in front of the men. I am still the warrior I once was."

"But the Maguire and the O'Gallagher will be glad to hear that," Odhran said. "For they both have a debt to repay to you. The invasion of Munster begins in a couple of weeks, and they would like you to lead it."

"Why didn't you say earlier?" Seamus said. "To the boats, for at last the MacSheehy get to wreak their revenge."

Seamus went into the house and picked up his axe and nothing else. Eunan scurried after him, for he worried Seamus was not in the right frame of mind to return.

CHAPTER 5
IN THE BELLY OF THE BEAST

The night was dark and silent as the spectre of the rebel siege loomed over the city of Dublin, sending fear into the hearts of its citizens. Those who could leave had already done so. Those who could not cowered in their houses. Some were forced to stay to defend the city because they had not found a way to desert, and some chose to stay either for loyalty to the Queen or to protect what their families had managed to claw out of this hostile land full of opportunities. Cormac O'Cassidy saw this impending doom and chose to defy it, throwing a lavish party for those who stayed and could not escape, gathering merchants, powerful military commanders, and personal minions to witness his last stand of defiance. He purchased the finest wine and the tastiest delicacies, celebrating this last stand against imminent death.

Taaffe extended his mug so that Cormac O'Cassidy could refill it.

"Don't you be making me throw this wine down the drain just like my money," O'Cassidy said. He pulled the jug away just before the level that most would interpret the mug as being full.

"I'm very grateful for all you've done for me." Taaffe nodded in acknowledgement. He owed O'Cassidy a lot. He was only back in Dublin because O'Cassidy had stated to his creditors that he was under his protection and paid off the debts to those who were least forgiving of Taaffe. O'Cassidy had become a rich man in a comparatively short time through his deal with Captain Williamson. Supplying the army with food, clothes and weapons proved extremely lucrative, partly because of the preference of the Irish recruits to drop their weapons on the field when fleeing the battle. With Williamson's protection, he had become one of the major merchants of the city.

"Don't forget that Shea Óg and I devastated Eunan Maguire's, sorry, your lands, to deny the enemy their use, of course. Seamus MacSheehy's wife is dead, along with many of those traitors who sided with Eunan Maguire."

"That is the kind of repayment I want," Cormac said, waving his finger in Taaffe's face. "But I don't consider any of your debt repaid yet."

Taaffe scowled.

"After all the effort I put into making a blood feud with Eunan Maguire. Remember, all debts may go up in smoke with O'Neill at the gates of the Pale."

"Pah! If he were going to attack, he would have made his move by now. I'm not afraid of him. He and his ilk took everything away from me, including my beloved daughter, and the only reason I am still on this earth is to avenge myself upon Eunan Maguire and Seamus MacSheehy."

"Well, we did our best, given the circumstances." Taaffe took another drink and savoured each gulp, thinking about what he just escaped from. "Now, we may as well pack up and leave while we still can."

Captain Williamson was standing on the other side of the room at this gathering of merchants and military men organised by O'Cassidy. He wound his way through the crowd and put his remaining hand on O'Cassidy's shoulder. He grinned at Taaffe, and Taaffe gulped, for he knew it was never good to get the captain's attention.

"Oh ye of little faith," said O'Cassidy. "This defeat has brought even more money to Captain Williamson and myself." His finger prodded every point into Taaffe's chest. "With one army destroyed, they have to create and resupply another army, which means enormous profits for us, for they are so desperate they will almost pay any amount for arms and equipment. We'll soon need a man of your abilities to acquire us large tracts of land when you have cleared them of the troublesome natives. I look forward to you returning to me, my beloved south Fermanagh."

Taaffe grimaced and blushed at the same time.

"I'm so glad I can be your toad."

Captain Williamson stepped between O'Cassidy and Taaffe and put his arm around Taaffe's shoulder.

"I know this can feel humiliating to you, but that is how it is. Men are judged here on how much they are worth now, not on their past reputations, which even you must admit you have done so much to trash."

"I am a man of the times," Taaffe protested, his cheeks red and knuckles white. "Men like him are nothing without me to be the muscle."

"I know that, and you know that, but to the money men, you once more have to prove yourself. But do not worry about that. I have the restoration of your reputation all in hand."

Taaffe threw the captain's arm off his shoulder.

"Oh, but I am worried about being so indebted to you. O'Cassidy is easy to read, but you are the most cunning snake, always coming from a different angle. I do not know whose interest you are operating in half the time except for your own."

"That is why we get on so well. We have so much in common. It takes one to know one, as they say. No, I have arranged another posting for you. You are out doing the dirty jobs of the war but on a mission that will greatly enhance your reputation. What do you say?"

"Do I have a choice?"

"You always have choices, but they are not necessarily good ones."

Taaffe's shoulders slumped.

"Let me have at least this night to enjoy a drink, for tomorrow I may die."

"Embrace the risk. On the edge is where you live your best life. Don't get sentimental or overdramatic. Your utter ruthlessness is your greatest asset."

"And my greatest downfall. Why can't I lead a simple life, be a farmer, till the land, and cease to be a victim to anguish as God stirs my fate."

"You have long ago made your pact with the devil; the sooner you accept that the sooner you will be at peace. Now, I have someone to introduce you to."

The captain put his right hand once more on Taaffe's shoulder and guided him across the room. They stood behind a man in a white shirt with ruffled cuffs and a sturdy build. The captain tapped him on the shoulder.

"May I introduce Sir Warham St Leger, a long-time veteran of the Irish Wars?"

St Leger turned around. The remains of his white hair were tied into a long ponytail, and his wiry frame held up well to his seventy-two years. He sneered at Taaffe.

"Don't tell me you must resort to Bingham's cast-offs?"

"I take it you have met before?" The captain looked to Taaffe, who hung his head and sighed.

"Oh, it is a small world in the wilds of Ireland," St Leger said. "I can find any number of cutthroats who will kill on command. Why should I take one in who I know will stab me in the back at the first opportunity he gets?"

The captain looked at Taaffe for an answer. Taaffe turned his head.

"I only went to court on the captain's instruction here."

St Leger turned to the captain.

"Is this true?"

"He may be a dog, but he bites who you tell him to."

"I am standing here," Taaffe protested.

"Unfortunately, your reputation proceeds you, which forces me to have a frank discussion about your nature while also emphasising your strengths. Such is the long rocky road to redemption."

St Leger scowled as he looked Taaffe up and down.

"So what do I get for taking him on?"

"Besides my eternal gratitude, a unit of twenty horse and thirty shot as ruthless as they come. When the Queen finally prevails, you will get the choicest cuts when her butcher chops up the land he has cleared."

"I have heard about his auctions and know he is one of the most notorious men in Dublin, who owes everyone and is only here because of your protection."

The captain smiled.

"He is a little misunderstood. You must remember that he was Bingham's right-hand man for years, and their land-selling operation was the envy of all the governors of Ireland."

"Who had all their dirty secrets revealed when they ended up in court."

"Bingham had become a liability for the crown. But you can rest assured that he will never desert."

St Leger laughed.

"Such is his reputation with the Irish as well." St Leger looked upon Taaffe once more and sneered. "I will take him on one condition."

"What is that?"

"I can execute him if he steps out of line."

The captain slapped him on the shoulder and smiled.

"You will find him to be a great asset to you," the captain said, turning to Taaffe. "Won't he?"

"Do I have a choice?"

"With all that I have had to pay out so you could show your face in Dublin again, no."

Taaffe curtsied to St Leger.

"At your command."

CHAPTER 6
SEARCHING FOR THE RIGHT EXCUSE

Eunan gulped as he found himself at the bottom of a hill. This section of the road always transformed him into a nervous little boy, for it rounded the woods and brought the looming shadow of Augher Castle into view. He slowed his horse to a trot as he most often did and wracked his brain for what he thought were acceptable excuses for being away for so long while his wife was pregnant.

The first excuse was for general consumption, which concerned the war and his importance in it. It usually went along the lines of he wished to come back but the Maguire needed him and insisted upon him staying. The second excuse was similar, designed for a whisper in his father-in-law's ear. It would appeal to his sense of duty that Eunan could not abandon the line and, therefore, his men, and he had to sacrifice himself for the overall good of the rebellion and his clan. The third excuse was for the bedroom, exclusively for his wife. It was the natural progression of the other two, where he was forced to stay, and his heart was wrenched in two. His wife would tell him how proud she was and how much she missed him, and Eunan would feel a pang of guilt for his wife believed his every word, and he regretted his exaggeration tinged with lies.

But this time was different. This time, he had left the ranks of the rebellion, albeit with the permission of the Maguire, and attended to his own business without informing his father-in-law. Normally, he would act independently and have no such contact with him, but after such a glorious victory and Dublin at their mercy, it was no time to leave the main rebel army. His father-in-law would not accept his excuses about the fragility of Seamus's mind, having seen so much death and also living with such a sickly daughter. But he was out of time. But he was out of time.

"The lord's been looking for you."

Eunan turned toward the voice, and his hand automatically went for the throwing axes tied to his belt. Two men he recognised came out from the woods with dead rabbits slung over their shoulders.

"Is he in a good mood?" Eunan said.

"You'd be blessed to catch him in a mood better than this. There is no need for you to dilly-dally while you round the bend. He'll welcome you with open arms no matter what you've done."

Eunan saluted the men and drove his ankle into the side of his horse. Sorcha would soon be in his arms.

Cormac flickered with emotion when his son-in-law stepped into the room. Some would have been wary of such a welcome, but Eunan knew that for Cormac, this was him being positively ecstatic. He welcomed him with a handshake and slid his arm over Eunan's shoulders. Cormac turned his attention to the servant who escorted Eunan to his room.

"My son-in-law has returned from another successful campaign. Select a cow whose loss will not impinge too much on milk production for the winter, and let us celebrate."

He ushered his son-in-law into his sparse chamber to converse in private.

Eunan had seldom been in this room, a secluded haven tucked away from the rest of the castle. The air was thick with the scent of burning pine and oak, and the licks of flame sent waves of heat towards him. Weapons and trophies from battles long since fought hung on every wall. A chair sat beside the fire, well-worn from years of use. The desk behind it was covered in papers, some elegantly handwritten while others were haphazardly scribbled upon. His father-in-law gave him the most generous smiles, eventually making Eunan suspicious as if such an act was the prelude to bad news. But his father-in-law made one of his servants bring another chair, a jug of fine wine and some wood for the fire. As they sat and drank together, Eunan couldn't shake off the feeling that something important was about to be revealed. But the sound of wood snapping and popping filled the otherwise silent room as the flames danced higher. Cormac must have something important to say if he was keeping him away from Sorcha. She must have miscarried again. Eunan shuffled awkwardly in his seat as his imagination filled in the blanks of the silence.

"Sit, Eunan, sit. We never had the chance to celebrate the glorious victory of the Battle of Yellow Ford together, and I mean to rectify that this evening."

Eunan turned to move his seat as a ruse to hide his confusion.

"I would be honoured to raise a mug of wine with you and salute all those brave men who gave their lives."

Cormac nodded his head.

"And so you should. A commander should value the lives of his men. Never throw your men into anything you would not do yourself; always show that you value them. That is how you must build loyalty."

Eunan smiled, for he always wanted to talk to his father-in-law about such matters and was in two minds about changing the subject. He might offend him, and this opportunity may be gone forever. On the other hand, Cormac may respect him more for showing concern for his daughter. But how could he be a commander without taking a risk?

"May I inquire when I can see my wife?" Eunan said, hesitant to see Cormac's reaction. "The last I saw of her, she was pregnant and well, but given her history, I can hardly take anything for granted."

Cormac drew his eyebrows together.

"I share the same concerns, yet have a different point of view. When her heroic husband comes home from such a glorious victory, it may raise the passion in her. The aforementioned husband, who, throughout the dangers, periods of idleness, drink, and other temptations camp life may offer, has remembered his loyal wife and left the camp follower prostitutes alone, may see fit to indulge his passions. When these two passions collide, that of a stallion dragging his hoof down the door as his full sacks sag towards the ground and a young woman who wishes to welcome back her hero, a grandson precariously wedging himself in the womb may be caught in the middle."

"I would do nothing to endanger my child," Eunan protested.

"I said nothing of malice, only two young people caught up in their passions."

"I didn't know there were three people in my bed."

Cormac turned his head to pour some more wine.

"There are, and I will grant you the doubt that you meant one of those people in the bed was me."

Eunan could sense his father-in-law had reached his limit. He bowed his head.

"No one more than me wishes my wife to give birth to a healthy baby boy, and I will do whatever it takes to ensure that happens."

"I am glad to hear that. I hope we can converse again as warriors one day, but you have made it clear you have no time for that now. So, I will not step in the way of my daughter's happiness. She is in her room and knows you have arrived."

Eunan turned and extended his hand, hoping to think of something to clear the air before he touched Cormac's flesh. But Cormac had turned to his papers and left Eunan's hand hanging.

"May we continue our soldier talk soon, father-in-law?"

Cormac nodded and returned to his papers.

"My daughter's health permitting."

Eunan closed the door behind him.

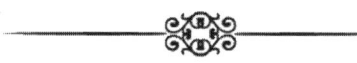

Eunan was greeted with a look and a nod from most of the castle residents as he passed on his way to Sorcha's room. The nods were cordial and curious, and the eyes followed his back, and they wondered what would happen when he reunited with his wife. Outside her room, the physician spoke with Sorcha's female attendants and finished giving instructions when Eunan caught his eye. He nodded his head as Eunan came to Sorcha's door.

"Good evening, Eunan," the physician said as he put his hand on Eunan's shoulder. "You look slightly gaunt. You must eat well before you are called back to the war."

"I plan to eat heartily, so don't you worry about that. How is my wife doing? I hope you have been taking good care of her?"

The physician smiled and looked away.

"I will leave her to tell her own story and not spoil it for her. She has a couple of months to go before the child is born. I fear I will be fully employed until the year is out, but I hope I will attend to both mother and child."

"You have my gratitude and trust, and please ask if you know how I can ever repay your kindness."

"To see Sorcha give birth to a baby boy would be repayment enough for me. I'm sure Cormac has already warned you off, but try not to overexcite her. I am hopeful that if she can give birth to one child, she can give birth to another."

Eunan grinned.

"What does everyone think I am going to do?"

"What young men just back from war always do. But your wife is more fragile than others. Remember that."

Eunan slapped him on the back.

"Both mother and child will be invigorated by seeing me alive and well when I leave. Now,, to overexcite her."

He winked, but the physician did not share his humour. Eunan knocked on the door.

"Come in."

Eunan gently pushed the door and peered around it. Sorcha lay in her bed rosy-cheeked but otherwise as pale as her sheets, her belly a mound in the middle of the bed. Her broad smile absorbed the energy from her face.

"My husband." A croak became a cough, and she leant over the side of the bed to spit the contents of her mouth out into a bowl on the floor. Any dreams a young stallion may have had fell with the spittle into the bowl. He picked up a cloth hung over the stool beside the bed.

"Let me wipe your face for you, my love. The war you fight against nature is far greater than my fight against the English."

Sorcha took the cloth from him and wiped her mouth. She started to cry.

"I am sorry you find me in such a state. As you returned, any proper wife would have been waiting by the door for you."

Images of his mother flashed before his eyes as she lay in her bed and growled at him, the supposed cause of her affliction. It was a constant weight on Eunan's mind as his mother blamed him for her inability to have children after she gave birth to him. His wife now lay helplessly before him, but the contents of the mound of her womb would be the future for both of them.

"Don't worry, my love," he said as he helped her into an upright position, propped her up with pillows, and made sure she had access to her bowl and a cloth to wipe her mouth. Once you give birth to a healthy boy, then you can concentrate on getting better yourself. How much longer do we have to wait?"

"The physician says around two or three months. Are you going to stay here and look after me? It would be wonderful if you could be here for the birth." Sorcha attempted a smile but could not expand her powers of persuasion beyond asking him to feel sorry for her.

Eunan sat up straight-backed and resolute.

"Damn all of them and their war. I will stay here and hold my wife's hand until she has a baby."

Sorcha smiled and took his hand.

"Shall we start now, then?"

Eunan sat on the side of the bed, and she handed him one of her books. He placed it on his lap and read to her, turning the pages without letting go of her hand. Sorcha nuzzled into his armpit. Eunan smiled at his wife, burying deep the nerves that she looked as ill as ever and destined to lose another child.

The weight of Eunan's dread grew exponentially with each step he took closer to Cormac's room. The moment eventually came when he ran out of steps and had to steel his nerves to enter the chamber. The door creaked ominously as Eunan opened it. His father-in-law was hunched over his maps, silently beckoning Eunan in. He could feel the air thickening as he crossed the threshold, bracing himself for what awaited him. The silence was broken.

"Do you think we should march on Dublin?" said Cormac over his shoulder.

Eunan did not know whether this was small talk or a continuation of the warrior talk they had when he first arrived. He decided on caution because he knew his father-in-law was proud and did not want to provoke his wrath unnecessarily.

"I have been away from the front for several weeks and would not want to question the great O'Neill after his glorious victory. The risk of the English landing behind us in Lough Foyle is great, and he is right to watch our rear."

Cormac turned to him and curled his lip.

"You are as timid as he. There is no quicker way to squander a victory than to cower and hide instead of sweeping your enemy off the field. We should be having this conversation over plundered wine in Dublin Castle. But alas, as you say, he is the O'Neill, and I am merely his brother living here in this draughty castle."

Cormac waved his hands, daring Eunan to agree with him. He had the rough end of the deal, to end up in this castle and his brother to be the O'Neill. Eunan had no interest in climbing onto such rocky ground.

"I am more comfortable with an axe in my hand than bent over a map."

Cormac scowled at Eunan's attempts to avoid the conversation.

"You need to aspire to command as my daughter's husband. Warriors do not always spawn warriors, much to my regret. So you must expand the pool by getting your daughters to marry well."

Eunan felt a bead of sweat on the small of his back. He wished for his father-in-law to get to the point so he could leave, for he felt the burn of his father-in-law's inquisitive eyes on him as he tried to catch him out.

"What are you doing here, Cormac, if the opportunity to sweep into Dublin is still alive?"

Cormac shook his head.

"My brother sent me here to look after his rear." Cormac pushed his maps away from him but resisted the urge to throw them on the floor, for he would only have to pick them up again. "But he gave me a message for you."

Eunan hesitated. Why would the O'Neill have a message for him? He paused and looked at Cormac's inquisitive eyes, but waited for him to speak.

"You are to lead your men into Munster. I arranged this for you, and the Maguire agrees with this plan." Cormac stared at Eunan, waiting for him to express his gratitude. Eunan worked out what was in it for Cormac before he remembered to smile.

"The O'Neill means to stir Munster into rebellion so that all of Ireland," Cormac continued, "except the Pale, will be in flame. He has entrusted this responsibility to you, as per my recommendation. It is a wonderful opportunity for you to win back your command. There is no need to thank me, for I would do anything for my daughter."

"When do I leave? My wife will give birth soon, and everything will be well."

Eunan made a fist behind his back, knowing he was powerless. His mind flew to Sorcha's room, where she lay ill with child. Would this be the last time he would see her alive? Eunan tried to banish such thoughts but kept his hand behind his back as it shook.

"You leave tomorrow morning for Enniskillen to collect your men there."

"But what about Sorcha? I need to be here to support her."

"All the more reason to have a good campaign and be back in a couple of months. Anyway, she will be better off without you here to get under her feet. If it is not an argument, you'll think of other ways to get her overexcited."

"What if..." But the words died in the back of his throat. What if he refused? It would probably be the quickest way to a divorce and disgrace in Fermanagh. He knew he was cornered.

"Yes?" Cormac said.

"What if the campaign goes on longer, and she goes into labour?"

Cormac slapped him on the shoulder.

"Look at how well I look after your wife with the most expensive physicians in the land. But don't you worry, I will keep you well informed. Now go and enjoy your night with your wife, but not a word of this until the morning. Remember. Don't get her overexcited and have her lose another child."

Eunan nodded and gave a faint smile. He closed the door quietly behind him.

CHAPTER 7
THE SHADOW OF BLACK MOUNTAIN

Seamus's mouth twitched, a murmur of what could be the beginnings of a smile. But as his mind's eye drifted to the distant silhouette of Black Mountain, an oppressive dread settled in his heart and quashed any sense of joy. He rode out at the head of his men who sang their fevered rebel songs of hope for freeing Munster, and yet all he felt was an uneasy disquiet. His thoughts went back to his father and the fear in his eyes before his life was taken from him. But what stuck was the overwhelming look of defiance. His father spat when asked to renounce his former loyalties, and his spittle barely nestled in the mud before his head joined it. He promised to protect his brother during the demise of the rebellion and then swore they would return to free it all again when they were exiled. Memories resurfaced of Dervella, whom he promised a perfect future together away from the chaos; she had laughed at his romantic notions, yet here he was now, marching back into Munster with a conquering force. His mind wavered between hope and dread as they approached the Munster border.

He had met O'Gallagher at Enniskillen Castle and was given charge of two hundred Munster men, a mixture of shot and swordsmen. They had some modern weapons, but the O'Donnell had deemed it too risky to send new weapons south and have them lost. The O'Neill had been more generous and gave Captain Richard Tyrell five hundred men armed with pike and muskets. Seamus felt jealous when he saw such well-equipped men march by. But he did not need them. Everyone would come flocking to them as soon as the MacSheehy returned to reinstate the Earl of Desmond. That is why his men carried all the weapons they could, even though some had never been so obsolete. He also sent word for Uaithne to join them so he could arrange a supply route for all the weapons he thought he would need.

He brought Fáolán with him as he thought he would need him to go off to find what MacSheehys of old still hid in the province and rally them to his cause. Fáolán also held the anxiousness of his master in his heart, for the march down to Munster had opened up long-buried but not forgotten wounds from the Black Mountain that surprised him with their ferocity. He noticed Seamus's grim demeanour and how far away it was from how Seamus normally acted when he took over a new unit of men. Sure, he could be harsh, his tongue biting, but his current attitude was hostile. Seamus rode alone in front of the men, leaving discipline and general instruction to the constables, and Fáolán rode not far behind him, wondering what was going on behind that granite face.

They stopped for the night in the territory controlled by Uaithne O'More and his older half-brother Brian. Seamus unpacked the officer's tent in silence and erected it in the middle of the camp with the help of some of the constables. The officer's tent was large enough to fit Seamus's bed, some of the more valuable items they carried in their baggage train, and a table small enough for up to six people to talk comfortably around.

"Can I be of assistance, lord?" Fáolán said as he put his hand out to take the spare tent pegs from Seamus's hand.

"You can. You can make sure I am not disturbed until Uaithne arrives. Then I will speak to him and only him. The only other reason you can disturb me is if we come under attack."

Seamus waved him away, but he ignored the gesture and lingered.

"Is there anything the matter, lord? Anything I can help you with?"

"I have given you your instructions, yet you hang around my tent like a lost dog. If you cannot see to it to obey your leader, then I will be forced to have you flogged."

"But, lord—"

"Do not test me. You are to me as the other men are."

Fáolán could see that he was not for moving, so he nodded and mumbled and went to watch for Uaithne. Seamus retired to his tent to battle his memories.

"Sweet Dervella." Seamus felt a deep sadness contorting his chest. His eyes moistened, and he constantly raised his hand to wipe the tears away. The shadows of the night danced on the roof of the tent, taunting him as he sat up in his bed. Whenever he closed his eyes, he was back at Black Mountain, desperately trying to save her. But now, on the eve of his return to Munster with an army by his side, was no time for sentimentality or tears.

"Lord," came a timid voice from outside the tent.

"Say what you must with intent, or do not say it at all," Seamus said. He was simultaneously irritated by being disturbed and being able to rid himself of Dervella and the ghosts of his ancestors from his head. He coughed so he could speak in a steady voice. Fáolán stuck his head between the flaps.

"If you are ready to resume, Uaithne is here."

"Send him in, but retire yourself for the evening. I have not the patience for your sarcasm."

"I shall do as you request and save my insightfulness for the morn."

Seamus shook his head and poured himself a drink. He smiled gratefully when Uaithne brought the insatiable spirit of youthful exuberance into the tent.

"I smell the midlands burning, and I have before me the chief arsonist," Seamus said as he opened his arms to give Uaithne a warm embrace.

"It was dark, but even the clouds could not suppress the glint of fire on fresh swords," Uaithne said.

"They will soon be dulled with the blood of the English settlers who stole our lands," Seamus said as he handed Uaithne a drink.

Uaithne grinned.

"The O'Neill has seen fit to match his promises with swords."

Seamus proudly placed his foot on the nearest of a collection of locked chests.

"He has done more than that. When we march through Munster to declare the new Earl of Desmond, the people will flock to us. We will fill their hands with the weapons and means to free themselves, and the earldom will be restored, but this time, it will be free. I will return to the old MacSheehy lands and take back the castles of my forefathers. Then I will return to the mountain where Ormond murdered my father and the pride of the MacSheehy Galloglass and build a church for them in the shadow of Castle Matrix and rebury them in consecrated ground as they deserve."

Uaithne butted mugs with him and nodded.

"A man with a plan. All shall cower before him."

"It is not for my glory that I do it, but to restore the earl, so things return to the way they were before."

Uaithne raised his mug once more.

"No better man to do it."

Seamus growled to himself, for these youngsters could not appreciate his pain even though they may have heard the tales. He had to forgive their disrespect, for they knew not what they did. Fáolán understood for he was there. Dervella understood, but this boy did not. He raised his mug to Uaithne and forgave him. He would be a useful ally.

CHAPTER 8

BURNING SKIES

The next day, Seamus and Uaithne joined forces for the foray into Munster. Their plans were fluid, depending on how much resistance they met. Richard Tyrell was not far behind them with another substantial force should the opportunity present itself to drive a wedge deeper into Munster. Fáolán followed the restoration of Seamus's mood and rode alongside him. They paused on a hill before they made their descent into Munster. Seamus savoured the air as he inhaled through his nostrils.

"Can you smell that fresh air, Fáolán? How long has it been since you smelled it? Since you were a boy?"

Fáolán gave a weary smile.

"It would stretch the bounds of my memory, that's for sure."

"Well, you just try to remember which fancy castle your ancestors used to live in, and we'll hang whatever English lord saw fit to steal it from you from the nearest tree."

Fáolán grinned.

"What if I cannot remember which one it was?"

"A best guess will do. I won't be asking for deeds or anything."

Seamus sighed as he took one last gulp of air.

"It's a shame we must subject something of such beauty to such destruction."

"Yes, but we didn't start it, did we?" Fáolán said.

"But we are here to finish it."

Seamus and his allies marched into Munster, and the opposition melted away. Richard Tyrell joined them, and their joint army found itself in the middle of Munster, with the Queen's forces cowering behind the walls of their castles across the province. Seamus invited Uaithne and Richard to meet in his tent to decide how to pursue their campaign.

The two young men were ebullient. They wore their smiles with pride as if they were already the masters of Munster. Seamus could not help but smile himself, but tried to suppress the swell of excitement and thirst for revenge that rose from the pit of his stomach. Images of the face of dead Dervella and the beheading of his father kept randomly flashing in front of his eyes. They raised their mugs and butted them together.

"Here's to victory," Uaithne said. "Now, do you want me to track down the cattle herds so you can redirect them northwards?"

Richard raised his eyebrow to Seamus and returned his attention to Uaithne.

"Direct the cattle to us by all means, but we are here to stay. The O'Neill instructed me to find James Fitz Thomas Fitzgerald and declare him the Earl of Desmond. Once we have an earl, all the Catholics of Munster will rally to his cause."

"Where is this earl to be?" Uaithne said. "Is he a rebel in the mountains or a soldier of the Queen who has joined the rebellion?"

"No, apparently, he has a farm on the south coast. Do you know this man, Seamus?"

"I am not familiar with him," Seamus said. But declaring yourself the earl is a quick way to lose your head. You would want to be pretty sure of yourself, for every couple of years, someone is publicly executed on the charge of declaring themselves the Earl. Seldom is their sanity considered in their quick trial."

"Is he, or was he, a military man?" Uaithne said.

"I think the O'Neill is looking for a puppet prince," Richard said. "Someone he can control, but we, his commanders in Munster, will really be in charge."

Seamus shuffled in his seat as if it had just caught fire.

"The earl, or at least the earl who is in the people's memory, was and should be a great man. He was the prince of Munster, one of the most powerful men in Ireland, backed up by the MacSheehy Galloglass. The people will not stand for a puppet prince."

Richard gave a sideward glance to Uaithne, who hurriedly raised his mug, thinking of a salute along the way to distract Seamus from whatever provoked his temper.

"To the Earl of Desmond. May the people rise behind him, and we all shall be free."

Seamus's mug slowly rose to meet the salute, his mood sapped by the memories flooding back at the mention of the Earl of Desmond.

"To the Earl," Seamus mumbled, "and may all remember him fondly."

Richard glared at Uaithne, who now realised he wanted him to steer the conversation away from the Earl, but Seamus's head sank.

"I grow tired now," Seamus said as he turned away from his guests. "I no longer have the stamina of youth and must be well rested if tomorrow I am to meet the new Earl of Desmond."

Richard signalled to Uaithne that it was time to leave.

"We shall see you in the morning when I shall return with directions to the man of destiny," Uaithne said.

All he earned was another stern glare from Richard.

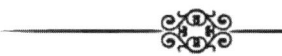

They split into three columns upon Seamus's suggestion and agreed to make an example of any English landlords or settlers they came across before they were to meet up on James Fitz Thomas Fitzgerald's land and declare him the new earl. They were to create a great spectacle to rally the people of Munster to their cause. Seamus took the central column with the most direct route to where the earl lived. Fáolán rode up beside him as they climbed to the top of a prominent hill.

"When I was a boy, this used to be O'Callaghan lands. Look at it now."

The sun blazed down on the country house below, scorching its white stone walls until they shone like a beacon. The fields overflowed with barley and wheat, dancing in the wind like thousands of miniature flames. Tiny huts with thatched roofs dotted the rolling hills, each appearing as an inky blot against the landscape, their grey stone walls seeming to soak up every last bit of light from the blazing sun above. Seamus gulped, for the lands looked prosperous and had not fallen into decay as the stories the exiled MacSheehy told themselves since they were not there to protect the earl, his people and their lands. But the MacSheehy had to have a purpose. There must be a fault in this idyllic picture.

"I remember when the earl's cattle used to roam free upon these lands. The MacSheehys were the masters in the local castle, and food was abundant for all."

Fáolán did a double take on Seamus. Who was this sentimental old man whose head swam in the past? The Seamus of old would have been coming up with a battle plan or left the looting to the Kern while the main body of men continued their mission. But this old man dithered and dreamt of the past.

"We need to move on, lord, in case the English work up the nerve to attack us. We can come back for these estates when we have the earl. It will be all the more impressive if the earl comes to liberate them."

But Seamus turned and ignored him.

"I will have the people toil no more under their blasphemous oppressors. For now is the moment of their liberation."

Before Fáolán could protest, Seamus had jumped off his horse and raised his axe to signal the men to follow him. Seamus marched across the fields, the sharp glint of his axe reflecting the mischievous grins of his men. Most of the tenant farmers fled before Seamus and his men. Some ran to protect their families, some ran to the woods to hide, and some ran to the master's house to spread the warning and to seek help. A red-faced man rushed out of the house, the sound of his laboured breathing filling the air as he struggled to propel his enormous belly towards Seamus, sweat pouring from his forehead in rivulets. He stopped a couple of yards before Seamus and raised his finger.

"You cannot—"

Seamus swung his axe across his body, catching the man below his chin, and sliced straight through.

"I can."

The man's body fell to the ground and twitched until his soul departed. Seamus strode on before halting at the barred doors of the house.

"I am only here for the master and his English tenants," Seamus called out. "Give them up and accept your freedom. The land is yours, but heed the call when the Earl of Desmond comes through your lands and seeks your help."

Seamus's men gathered around him, and the smell of sweat and fear filled the air.

"Search the area," Seamus said as he pointed to the places he suspected of harbouring his foes.

"Wait," came a voice from the house. "How do we know you are not a pack of bandits who come to rape and murder us all?"

"The O'Neill sent us to liberate all good Catholics of Munster. As a Mac-Sheehy Galloglass and a fellow Munster man, I give you my word that we are friends to all Catholic tenant farmers and mean to free you."

"What if we are none of these?"

"Stay in your house and burn in its embers, or come out and face us and pay for what you have done."

The voice trembled and wavered as it spoke, thick with fear.

"What if I did nothing and purchased the land from someone I considered a reputable seller?"

"Then come out and state your case, and your tenants will state theirs."

"I will be out momentarily. I need to gather my things."

Once the tenants realised Seamus and his men were not there to massacre them and steal their belongings, a crowd gathered around the entrance to the house. The more they waited, the more confident they became. The first stone struck the house.

"Come out and face us," came a cry from the crowd.

With a creak, the door was pushed ajar, and stones clattered against the outside.

"Stop," Seamus said, raising his hand. "Let him come out and say his piece. Anyone who throws a stone without my permission will stand in his place."

As the man stuck his head around the door, he saw the hostile stares of the silent crowd. He reached behind him and dragged forward a large chest. He identified Seamus as being the one in charge and dragged the chest over in front of him. He waved to his wife and two daughters, and they emerged from the house, forming a tight circle of protection around him. He fixed his stare at Seamus for he knew he was his only chance of getting out of there alive. He fiddled with the lock and opened the chest. Inside, the coins glinted in the light, and Seamus could make out the outlines of various other items of value.

"This is all I have," the man said. "I lay no claim to be a good man, but whatever you accuse me of, my wife and daughters had nothing to do with it. Do with me what you will, but take what I offer for their lives, and I will put myself in your hands."

Seamus smirked.

"You are deluded if you think you are not already in my hands."

Seamus turned to the crowd and pointed at the man.

"This man stole your lands. State your accusations and let him be judged before God and man."

The crowd needed no more encouragement to state their grievances.

"He evicted my family when we could not pay our rent last winter."

"He cut off my finger for stealing food as my family starved."

"He never paid me for work that I did for him."

The man dipped his head, his face flushing red as he tried to hide his embarrassment.

"It seems the people have spoken," Seamus said.

"Please spare my family," the man said as he gathered them close.

Seamus pointed to the woods.

"Hang him off the nearest tree. Set his family on the road to Dublin. Kill all the English settlers and redistribute the land."

Seamus armed the crowd, who set upon the man and dragged him away to the appointed tree. Their blood up, they then set off on a rampage across the countryside, searching for anyone they perceived to have wronged them. The mother and the two daughters barely made it past the woods and onto the roads before they fell to the wayside as more casualties of war.

CHAPTER 9
A MAN ENFEEBLED

Seamus ordered his men into formation on the grassy plains in front of Connihy Castle, tucked away in Killnataloon, Cork, Munster. The walls were modest and could have been quickly demolished by a cannon if they had one. He had been entrusted with commanding five hundred men, mostly shot, comprising mainly Munster men who had made their way north and supported by one hundred Scottish swordsmen mercenaries, all of whom were eager to go to battle. As Seamus and Captain Richard Tyrell, sent by the O'Neill, led the way, the men followed behind, their breath visible in the cold air. Seamus felt a chill run down his spine as he was surprisingly overwhelmed by nerves. His voice was unsteady as his hands trembled, and he harshly scolded any man he believed was not meeting his expectations. His mind flew back to the Battle of Monasternenagh, the greatest battle in the history of the MacSheehy, a heady mix of pride and folly.

Seamus looked along the ranks of his men. They appeared a ragtag of rebels, farm boys and mercenaries, none of which would have the moral purity or courage to stand beneath the banner of the Pope or the Spanish King, going off to an unknown foreign land to fight for God like a crusader of old. Never mind any of them being able to aspire to be a member of the MacSheehy Galloglass of Rory MacSheehy or his father. His face flushed as he contemplated how best to present these men to the Earl of Desmond as his army. But that was his mission, what he had dreamed about ever since he left Munster, how he would throw off the dark shadow of the Black Mountain. It was his destiny.

Uaithne and Richard exchanged confused glances as they watched Seamus's strange behaviour as if he were conversing with ghosts. Their patience had now run out, for it was just another inauguration to convince another distant relative of a once great clan leader to become a puppet of the O'Neill. Uaithne thought it was time to break the cycle of Seamus's endless pacing up and down.

"If he is not going to come out, I suggest we go and knock," he said, pointing to the castle door. No one appeared to be on the ramparts they could call up to.

Seamus muttered a curse and felt the warmth of his blush radiating from his cheeks.

"If anyone is to get the Desmond, it shall be me."

Uaithne and Richard glanced at each other and stepped aside. Seamus bowed his head and butted the end of his axe on the door.

"Oh, great Earl of Desmond, the MacSheehy have returned to restore your lands."

Uaithne and Richard met each other's gaze, their faces filled with bewilderment. Seamus was always the most cynical for these inaugurations. Usually, he would find something else to occupy his time, for he found that the easiest way to contain his sarcasm. Seamus gulped as the door opened.

An old man stood in the doorway, quaking before Seamus.

"James Fitz Thomas Fitzgerald?" Seamus could not hide his disappointment.

"No, my master does not wish to come to the door. When the sun appears from behind the clouds, it does so as a deceiver. He is a landlord of modest means, a faithful Catholic, and good to his tenants. Please take what you can find, as we have no means to stop you, but we have no pot of gold hidden anywhere to justify you going on the rampage to find it. Then, when you have had your fill, kindly leave us at peace."

Seamus grimaced and raised his axe to pass it on to the would-be earl to raise the blood in him.

"This is destiny calling for your master. Some of us are born into service and cannot avoid our obligations. Send him out and let him be declared the earl."

The old man scowled and hid further behind the door as he was too afraid to shut it in Seamus's face.

"My master does not want it. You declare him earl, return up north to the O'Neill, and then the earl hangs from the nearest tree when the English return."

Seamus's cheeks reddened, for this is not how it had gone in his dreams.

"May I suggest we have this conversation inside and not in front of the men?"

"My master declines your invitation."

The old man went to close the door, and Seamus swung his axe. The blade buried itself in the side of the door so the old man could not close it.

"My blade insists."

The man disappeared momentarily. He returned, opened the door, and gestured for Seamus to enter.

"Only you may enter if you leave your weapons behind."

Seamus pulled his axe out of the side of the door and threw it on the ground, signalling Uaithne and Richard to follow him.

They were brought into a back room in the castle, where several men armed with old swords lined the walls. Seamus could see them twitch and sweat as they stared straight in front of themselves, the best pose they could strike to look intimidating. Seamus knew he had to act fast before one of them mustered up enough courage to make a move. He devised a daring plan to disarm the most fearful-looking man of his sword and use it to slay the other two assailants. It was an impulsive plan formulated out of adrenaline rather than reason.

James Fitzgerald turned around. He was skinny and pale and avoided eye contact with his guests. He was a man in his forties with a pleasing complexion, and Seamus thought his looks would surely draw the people to him if he proved to have any backbone. He appeared unwilling to engage in conversation, and Seamus's patience was wearing thin.

"We are here to declare you the Earl of Desmond," Seamus said. "It is time to lead your people to freedom."

"What if their freedom impinges on mine?" James said.

"What is that supposed to mean? We are your MacSheehy Galloglass. We have come to follow the earl once more. It is your duty."

"If I am the earl, do I not define what duty is?"

"I am not here to debate with you nor play semantics. Come out and be declared before the men."

"What if I have no wish to play the rebel? I did not summon you here from the north. A man of my credentials could easily seek the protection of the crown, get declared earl by the Queen, and put down the rebellion."

Seamus could see James's guards' faces turn pale, for they would have to enforce the prospective earl turning coat. Then Seamus remembered what little he knew about James.

"We could just offer the title to your brother if you are not interested?"

James felt his body tighten as he whipped his head around, trying to conceal his face. He felt what was rightfully his and what he had yearned for all his life slip away.

"That won't be necessary. The people need a leader, and he is not it. I will lead. I will reluctantly be the earl."

Seamus smirked.

"I knew you'd come round. Now, prepare something inspiring to tell the men. They have cut a swathe through Munster to get here, and the rest should quickly fall if the people know we have restored the earl."

"I will meet your men, but I have a mission for you in return."

"If you are the earl, then I am your Galloglass. Speak it, and it shall be done."

"Wait here while I get dressed. I cannot go out as the earl unless I look my best."

CHAPTER 10

SEAMUS THE MATCHMAKER

Seamus led the ranks of Fáolán's men, their weapons gleaming in the morning light as they marched to the edge of the farm. Their objective lay ahead, towering atop the hill, and as he surveyed it, Seamus's eyes smouldered with determination and a touch of dread.

"He wants you to take the wife?" Fáolán said. "Why?"

"Why question the Earl?" Seamus snapped.

"Because I do not know the man nor ever heard anything positive about him. You wouldn't start carrying out random raids for any other tin-pot chieftain we declared on the way here."

"That's because none of them were the Earl of Desmond," Seamus barked. "Can you feel it in your blood? Are your ancestors calling you? The restoration of the earl means the restoration of the earl."

Seamus turned to Fáolán in what was interpreted as a slightly crazed look.

"The only time you spout this nonsense is when you've been on the ale, and any time you have, you've denied all knowledge the next day. I've never heard you talk like this sober."

Seamus gritted his teeth, refusing to look at his companion.

"If you cannot appreciate the moment, how does MacSheehy blood flow through your veins? Can I rely on you, or do I need to remove you as one of my commanders?"

Fáolán clenched his fist until his knuckles turned white.

"I also witnessed my father's death on Black Mountain. We have a shared bond of pain and shame. Yet, we have not learned from the past, as restoring the earl is foolish. He will be no better than the previous one. Surely the blame for the falls of the houses of Desmond and MacSheehy lay at the previous earl's feet?"

Fáolán's finger jabbed the air in what he thought was the direction of Black Mountain to show his affinity with Seamus. Seamus looked past Fáolán, refusing to budge from his point of view.

"This Seamus is tired of your questions and insolence, like we are equals. You had better acquit yourself well today to stop me from reconsidering your position."

Fáolán rubbed his nose in a half-hearted attempt to hide his sneer. But he knew it was best to keep his mouth shut when Seamus was in this mood.

"It does not look well defended," Seamus said, his mind having returned to his mission. Fáolán, you circle to the rear, and I will approach from the front. Kill anyone who resists you."

Fáolán gave a resentful nod and signalled for a group of men to follow him.

Seamus stormed up to the farmhouse, his axe held high and a look of unhinged fury in his eyes. As he approached, those in his path quickly scattered in terror. He slammed the butt of his axe into the door in repeated strikes, the thuds reverberating throughout the land.

"Sean O'Callaghan, get out here," Seamus shouted. "Get out before I burn you out. You've got to answer to the Earl of Desmond for what you've done."

"What have I done?" Sean asked as he hurriedly barricaded himself in. "There is no Earl of Desmond, so how can I have done anything to him?"

"By God's blood, there is," Seamus said as he hurled his axe blade against the door.

***

The farmhands exploded from the barn, their tools raised like weapons. Seamus unleashed a brutal swing of his axe, catching one of the farm boys in the side and felled him like a sapling. He turned and brought the butt of his axe down hard onto the leader's face, splitting his nose and sending a spray of blood into the air. The force of the blow sent him reeling back, and Seamus swung his weapon to the other side, at which point they dropped their tools and ran for their lives.

Seamus returned to battering down the door, and his men joined him. The door juddered on its hinges, and chunks of wood and metal flew everywhere.

"I will come out. I will come out," came the cry from inside.

Seamus stood back and heard the barriers behind the door being dragged away one by one. The door opened, and a red-faced, rounded man with a pointy beard stood in the doorway with a rusty old sword shaking in his hand. He stepped back and away from the door and lowered his sword in a gesture of peace.

"Take what you wish, but please spare my family," the man said, his face bowed to the ground.

Behind him stood a tall, statuesque brunette, her pleasant features contorted by fear. Seamus grew suspicious of the nature of his mission, but he thought back to the glory days of the MacSheehy and how they ruled these lands under the direction of the earl. It was not for him to question the earl's wisdom.

"Step outside and let us discuss our business together," Seamus said. "Your family can stay in the house nice and safe under the protection of my men."

"I have no wealth to speak of except the crops in my barns, the cows in my field and the land itself. Take it, take it all. Set me on the road to Cork, and you will never have to deal with the likes of me again."

Seamus put his hand around the man's shoulder.

"The Earl has business with you, irrespective of your wealth. I have an axe, and you have nothing to bargain with that I could not take."

The man went pale, and Seamus shoved his rigid body away from the house. The woman screamed.

"Be gentle with her, boys. The Earl wants her in one piece."

Seamus led the farmer down to a sheltered area by the brook. Shaded by trees and a dry beach eroded by seasonal swells, it was out of sight of the farm. Seamus began poking the branches overhead with the butt of his axe so he could find the sturdiest.

The farmer broke into a cold sweat.

"What am I to hang for? What have I done to deserve this? I offered you everything I own, yet I still face the rope?"

Seamus lassoed the rope over the selected branch.

"Don't try to appeal to my sentimental side, for it died long ago when you drove my people off the land."

"I did nothing of the sort." The man went red-faced as he pleaded for his life. "I bought the land for what I considered a fair price. I drove no one off the land but took back those who had been driven into the woods and a life of poverty and banditry. You can ask my tenants how I treated them. The least you can do is tell me who the earl is and what I am accused of?"

Seamus held out the noose.

"The earl is James Fitz Thomas Fitzgerald, and I have no idea what you are accused of. I accept the least I can do is tell you why you are being hung today. The Earl instructed me to do so as he said you were an enemy of the people, and I should bring him your wife, who will not be harmed."

"What?" The man hid his head in his hands. "Are you a man of honour?"

"What is that supposed to mean? Why waste your last breath protesting when you can say a prayer for yourself before you put the noose around your neck?"

The man threw an accusatory finger towards Connihy Castle.

"That man is unworthy of any title, especially that of the Earl of Desmond, which seems to dazzle you so. He has always lusted after my wife and swore revenge after she spurned his advances. Ever since then, the animosity has just built. Now he has got a naïve fool to follow him and execute me because he has to cower before a title."

Seamus thrust the noose in the man's direction.

"Put that around your neck. You'll get nowhere by insulting or goading me."

"Why? Are you afraid of the truth? You'll hang me without a second thought, so I know I am already dead."

Seamus looked at the man and saw the defiance in his eye.

"Look, I've been ordered to kill you. It is not up to me to ask why. Your death could be the spark that frees the whole of Munster, maybe even Ireland."

"I care not for your delusions. I could just as easily be the martyr whose tale of wrongful murder turned the province against you and get you and your tin-pot earl hung."

"I am prepared to take that risk. Now, put on the noose before I drag you over by the hair."

The man walked over to Seamus and maintained eye contact. He took the noose from Seamus's hand and placed it around his neck.

"Hang me if you must. But my innocent blood and the harm that you will cause to my family will be on your soul forever, and you'll account for it at the gates of heaven."

"I would be surprised if I was allowed even that far."

Seamus pulled on the end of the rope, the anger and humiliation of all the MacSheehy ghosts in his head pulsating through his veins. The man rose and kicked his legs.

CHAPTER II
A GHOST FROM THE PAST

S eamus rode ahead of his men and prisoners, for he could no longer bear the wailing of Ellen Butler and her recently bereaved children. He felt faint and vacant inside. It was not the first time he had had to execute a man, but normally, the victim had done something directly to him or his men. But he did not know what the man had done in this case. On the other hand, many a landlord and English settlers had stolen the land of the earl and were hung and killed, so why should this man be any different? It was the way the man had pleaded with Seamus. Somehow, the execution did not feel right. He looked at the dead man's wife, and through the red puffed-up eyes and cheeks as she wailed for her dead husband, Seamus could still see the beauty. Should he get to know the man's character he followed, or would this be a dereliction of his duty to his MacSheehy ancestors? They followed and obeyed the earl through thick and thin. Therefore, so should he.

Fáolán noticed the uncharacteristic silence of his master and that he was deep in thought. Nothing good usually comes when Seamus ponders something for a long time. He decided to break the trail of thought and rode up beside him.

"By God's ears, she has a pair of lungs on her? I wouldn't fancy having to guard her cell."

Seamus fixed him with an icy glare.

"Sorry," Fáolán said. "You can guard her if you feel that strongly about it."

Seamus leaned over.

"Can I trust you?"

"Of course you can. There's no need to ask," Fáolán said, his concern soon trumping his surprise at the question.

"Do you trust me more than the memory of the earl and the duty you feel towards your ancestors?"

"I have a clear head if that's what you are asking. You normally do, too. But something seems to have happened to you since Dervella's death. If you need me to do anything, all you have to do is ask."

Fáolán saw Seamus make a fist and that he tried to conceal it.

"I need you to look into this so-called new earl of ours. I am beginning to doubt his character and his worthiness to hold the title Earl of Desmond."

"Of course, but it is most unlike you to fall for all this clan head and inauguration nonsense you have seen so many times before. Remember, no matter what kind of man he is, the earl is only a tool of the O'Neill. It is your mission to ensure that is all he remains."

Seamus shook his head.

"It matters to me who we follow. If the MacSheehys are ever to rise again, they must follow someone honourable and worthy of the title. If not, the MacSheehy as the Galloglass of the earl are nothing and do not deserve to be resurrected."

"I will make my inquiries, lord, but be prepared to be disappointed, for I will not sweeten my answer."

"That is why I am entrusting you with the task. But not a word to anyone."

"Of course, lord. I shall begin at once."

Fáolán turned to hide his smile, for he thought Seamus was finally seeing sense.

They rode up to Connihy Castle past the newly constructed camp of the army from the north and noticed a smaller camp in the shadows of the castle. The new earl appeared to be gathering supporters even before he was officially declared.

Seamus pulled up his horse, dismounted, and was met by the sharp points of several axes.

"Who goes there?"

"I could ask you the same thing," Seamus said as he tried to brush past the blades. But the wall of axe points reformed as resilient as before.

"Who are you?" asked the guards.

"I am Seamus MacSheehy, and I have been off performing the requests of the earl. As you can see, I have a prisoner who the earl will be delighted to meet."

"How can you be a MacSheehy? We are the MacSheehy," a guard claimed.

"MacSheehy?" Seamus laughed. "There were no MacSheehy here when I left. Please do not insult me with your preposterous claims to be of my clan. Who is your leader, and where did you come from?"

"They are all good Munster men, and they follow me."

Both Seamus and Fáolán cocked their ears as they were drawn to the voice. As the imposing figure of a man stepped out of the castle gates, Seamus felt his stomach drop and his heart stop. The man's face seemed worn and weary as if he had been through many good and bad tales. His well-chiselled face still gave hints of a once handsome youth, a look that would have enhanced his prospects. He wore his hair long, its youthful colour long since faded. His broad shoulders showed years of practice swinging an axe, the muscles defined and robust. He carried himself with confidence and authority, aided by his highly decorated battleaxe, gleaming in the sunlight. Despite his dented breastplate and tattered shirt, there was something unmistakably formidable about him. Seamus could feel his palms sweat with fear at the sight of this fierce warrior. When their eyes met, Seamus felt himself stiffen, sensing the stern, cold gaze that seemed to pierce right through him.

"Murrogh? Is that you? What rock have you crawled out from under?"

"I still answer to that name, but I am not the man you remember, Seamus. I have held the remains of the MacSheehy clan here in Munster to my bosom and nurtured them, biding our time until we could return."

Seamus fixed him with an icy stare.

"You are no Galloglass for what you did and certainly no MacSheehy. The Earl is a fool if he takes you on after what you did."

"I think you'll find that I am both. These are my Galloglass pointing their weapons in your face, and the new earl has declared me the head of the reinstated MacSheehy Galloglass. You may join us if you wish, but you must bow down to me, kiss my hand and give me your undying allegiance."

"We both know I would sooner chop it off and stuff it down your throat before I finish you off in the most cruel way that would present itself. No one but Ormond himself, the enemy of your father, your brothers and your clan, has done more to destroy the MacSheehy clan than you."

"Do my men have to arrest you because they consider you a threat?"

Fáolán had stood to the side and watched while the conversation went south. It was time to step in.

"What would your new master think if you arrested the commander of the army sitting on his doorstep? That the ensuing slaughter of so-called MacSheehy would rival that of the submission of the MacSheehy?"

Murrogh backed away and tried to laugh it off.

"How men lose themselves when they get a bit of power. Please, bring your guest to the Earl and let us share an ale to celebrate the ensuing nuptials."

Seamus furrowed his brow.

"What wedding? No one mentioned anything about a wedding to me."

Murrogh smirked.

"No? That is strange. I thought you were important. You have escorted the Earl's new bride here. The Earl must marry a Butler and unite the main Munster houses. I hear you also ensured she was available for the wedding. Well done. We can always rely on you when there is a lynching to be done."

The veins on Seamus's throat bulged as he tried to contain his temper. Weak, small-minded fools had used him, and he was the worst fool for falling for it. Seamus turned and headed back to his camp.

"Tell me when the inauguration is, and all instructions for the men of the north are to come through me."

Murrogh smiled and ordered his men to bring the wailing Ellen Butler to greet her soon-to-be husband.

CHAPTER 12
UNMASKING THE WITCH

E unan found himself once more at the gates of Enniskillen. His horse bore the stripes of mud as they had ridden down from Augher Castle as fast as the wind could carry them. He gulped as he shouted his name to the gate tower guards. As if they would not recognise him? He was one of the most recognised faces in Fermanagh, if not the most notorious, after Connor Roe. His heart sank in trepidation at entering the castle. The more time he spent there, the worse his memories of the place became. He would have to smile and lie about the closeness of the relationship with his father-in-law. The Maguire would want to know that his alliance was still strong. He would have to bow his head to his new master, Feargal MacCabe, who was probably plotting to have him killed. Nor did he trust Fachtna Óg, the Maguire's adviser. Desmond's island never seemed so attractive, even with Seamus's moods.

He dismounted and walked through the castle courtyard to the main tower. It was a hive of activity with carts being loaded with weapons, food, tents and other supplies which meant the Maguire was planning a major raid. But Eunan did not flinch, for the Maguire was always planning a major raid. Some men saluted Eunan, for they were old comrades. Eunan embraced some but nodded to most, for no one wanted to delay his meeting with the Maguire. He climbed the stairs with Odhran shadowing his footsteps. The guards announced him and opened the doors to the great hall.

The Maguire was bent over a map, his face lit up by the elation of planning a new campaign and the numerous candles on the table. The title of the Maguire sat a lot easier on his shoulders these days. His charisma and ability to lead his warriors meant that his personal standing now eclipsed that of Connor Roe. His principal rival for the title was now demoted to a minor ally of the O'Neill. Connor Roe's men, who had not already defected to Hugh Maguire, followed in service to the main O'Neill army. Irial MacCabe, the Maguire's primary military adviser, stood beside him, pointing at various places on the map. When Eunan entered, he raised his head, gave Eunan a cold stare, and returned to his map. There was never to be any forgiveness for Eunan crippling him and ending the active service element of his military career. The Maguire raised his head, and his face creased. He smiled at the sight of one of his greatest warriors.

"Eunan," he cried as he walked over and threw his arms around him. "How goes it in Augher Castle? Are you a father yet?"

Eunan gave a faint smile.

"My wife did not do me the convenience of giving birth before I was recalled to go out on campaign."

The Maguire slapped him on the shoulder.

"Don't worry, it happens to the best of us. She'll be well looked after where she is." He leant into Eunan and whispered, "You're probably better off. You don't want to get under her feet when she has a baby to look after."

He winked at Eunan, and Eunan smiled back, for he did not aspire to be seen as rude. Feargal MacCabe walked over from the fireplace. The warmth did not follow him over. He extended a cold handshake for appearances in front of the Maguire.

"I trust you are well rested after the Battle of Yellow Ford? We expect you to replicate that success in this campaign."

Typical Feargal, everything was a political game of chess.

"We shall do what we must to win," Eunan said. He turned to Cearbhall MacCabe, with whom he had always had a much closer relationship.

"May our plans today bring victory and glory," Eunan said.

"Through the actions of brave warriors such as yourself, it will," Cearbhall said.

"Now that the greetings are over, for Irial has still not forgiven you for breaking his ankle," the Maguire said as Irial glared at his back, "let us return to our maps."

The Maguire smiled and slapped Irial on the back. Irial strained every sinew in his body to prevent himself from howling in protest. He made do with jabbing his finger into the middle of Munster.

"Here's where we want Eunan to go," Irial said.

Eunan glanced over his shoulder and was grateful the finger prodded dry land, for many a demonic sea monster lurked amongst the waves.

"Are you coming with me?" Eunan said to Irial in a playful tone.

"No," said Irial, his voice seething in resentment. "You crippled me, remember?"

"Oh, I thought you'd forgotten about that."

Eunan laughed and was grateful Irial's glare did not turn him into stone.

"Don't mock him," the Maguire said. "You get to return to the field, and he doesn't. Let him tell you the plan."

Irial ground his teeth and once more prodded Munster.

"Your mission is to go there and cause as much chaos as possible. The province is about to fall. Get as many of the population to support the O'Neill's earl as possible, and when you are finished, bring as many cattle back as you can reasonably herd."

"My uncle left for there several days ago," Eunan said.

"Then you will be in good company," the Maguire said. "You will take your own men, the south Fermanagh shot, and I will join you as soon as Feargal has replenished the MacCabe ranks."

Feargal threw a glare at Eunan.

"Give the man a break," the Maguire said. "This land will take much more blood before anything is resolved."

The pause in conversation told Eunan his time there was done. He bowed and went to assemble his men.

Eunan rode through one burnt-out village after another in the middle of Ireland on his way to Munster. What roads there were carried people to the Pale or the woods, for they did not know where the war would break out next. But all Eunan could think back to was dead Dervella's face. He held her in his arms, cried out and wept, but she would answer none of his pleadings. Her head rolled back, and her mouth fell open, but no words of kindness or reassurance came out. A fresh tear rolled down his cheek to be absorbed by his sleeve, just like all the others. Arthur was close to his thoughts, but either his mother or Dervella, his surrogate mother, always occupied his mind. His mind turned to his wife, and life renewed itself with the birth of his son. Why was it he who was out on the back of this horse? If the mission was to bring death and destruction, this could have been anyone out here. Was this the work of Irial and Feargal? Sending him away to deny him witnessing the birth of his son? Did they want him out of the way so they could consolidate their power? Eunan thought back to his mentor Desmond and what he would have done. Maybe Irial and Feargal had done the worst thing they could to a man with a troubled mind. Give him some free time on the back of a horse on a boring journey and let the devils do their work.

Eunan marched through eastern Munster, along the borders with the Earl of Ormond's lands, along a route that Seamus, Richard, or Uaithne had not travelled. He had one ear out for news of Taaffe, for it was rumoured he was nearby. It was relatively peaceful compared to where he had just come from, and town after village surrendered without a fight and let him march through. They approached another village, and a scout rode up to him.

"There is a disturbance happening in the village square."

"Are we to expect resistance?"

"They are trying to execute some rebels."

"Then we must ride swiftly and save them."

Eunan signalled to Odhran, and they rode into the centre of the village with ten select men.

A large crowd was gathered in the centre of the village — by reasonable estimates, the population of the village and most of its immediate surroundings.

They were all gathered around in a circle, their attention on a pyre stacked high in the middle. There was a platform at the top, as yet unoccupied. Eunan halted the men and looked at Odhran to see if he was of the opinion they should interfere. Odhran shook his head, and Eunan held his men back. The crowd paid little attention, for they were fixated upon the largest house in the centre of the village. Eunan ordered one of his men to fetch him something to stand on so he could get a good view. The house door opened, and several burly men reversed out, obviously struggling with someone. A woman was at the centre of the melee, struggling to free her limbs so she could then free herself. Her head was shaven, her face covered in bruises as the men who tried to drag her to the pyre continually threw punches. The violence ignited the crowd.

"Kill the witch."

"Burn her."

"Kill the rebel witch."

Eunan glared at Odhran, who mouthed 'no'. Eunan pointed towards the men waiting outside the village. Odhran shrugged his shoulders. Eunan stormed over.

"I am your commander and telling you to get the men."

"Why are you intervening for this woman? As long as the village pledges, we normally leave them be. What do you care if they burn her or not?"

"They said they were going to burn her for being a rebel. We will not tolerate that. Fetch the men or go home. Your choice."

Odhran cursed under his breath but turned and left.

"Come with me, men," Eunan said to the remaining men. "It is time for stout hearts."

Eunan elbowed his way through the crowd, and his men followed. He grabbed the first guard, manhandling the woman by the shoulder, and yanked him backwards.

"Unhand me," spat the man.

Eunan lifted the butt of his axe and rammed it into the man's nose. Blood spewed everywhere. Some other men peeled off and became embroiled with Eunan's men in a fistfight. Eunan waded through the crowd, swinging the butt of his axe to clear the way. Hands grabbed at him from the mob, and the occasional fist connected with the back of his head. The hostile crowd now surrounded Eunan and his men, but Eunan had the woman in his sights and was determined to save her. He struck a man on the back of the head, and he collapsed down in front of him. The woman now faced him with a villager tugging on either arm as she struggled. Eunan punched one man in the face and removed the other with the butt of his axe. His men now formed a circle as the villagers closed in. Eunan grabbed the woman by the hand.

"Oh, Eunan," she said. "You have come to save me."

Eunan froze. There was something familiar about that voice. He looked at her again, her hair ripped out in patches and shaved in others, covered in mud and bruises, with blood flowing from her cheek. Yet there was something familiar about the glint in her eye.

"Cara?"

Cara threw her arms around him and kissed him. It was hard to tell who was more confused, Eunan or the crowd now baying for his blood.

CHAPTER 13

MORE BLOOD FOR ST JUSTIN'S DAY

E unan peeled Cara off him with his free hand and shook his head. A chorus of voices rose from the crowd, shouting, "Look, the witch has bewitched him!"

"She has done no such thing," Eunan shouted back. "Who here suggested that she be burned?"

"Well, the allegation that she put a curse on the village proved to be right," said a voice. "Look, she conjured up you."

The crowd edged closer, but Eunan kept them back by his threatening stance backed up with his axe. A portly man entered the crush until he stood in the front rank. The large shiny brooch that held together the red cloak wrapped around his shoulders signified he must be the well-to-do farmer or merchant of the town.

"Let us have no more bloodshed on St Justin's Day," the man said. Release the girl, be on your way, and let no more be said."

A drop of sweat rolled off Eunan's brow as his eyes darted from face to hand of all those who faced him in the crowd.

"We have not come to cause trouble but to liberate you from your English overlords."

"It looks the opposite to me the way you wield that axe."

Eunan shook his head without taking his eyes off his opponents in front of him.

"Let us go before my men arrive. I do not aspire to be known as the perpetrator of the St Justin's Day massacre, but I will not let you kill this woman."

"Then she has cast a spell on you, oh liberator."

The people of the town looked to their leader to see if they should all charge and damn the consequences. Surely God would protect them if they went on such a heavenly pursuit? But murmurings came from the back of the crowd, and they parted as Odhran and the rest of the men from the north marched to Eunan's rescue.

"I suggest you all go home and lock your doors until these demons have gone," said the man. He stood and waved his arms towards the village houses and the farms on the outskirts, and the crowd gradually dispersed.

"Do we need to negotiate terms, or will you leave now that you have retrieved your witch?"

Eunan strode towards him, his index finger jabbing the air.

"My terms are the same as always, these lands given back to the clans and the English settlers on the road back to the Pale. We can do this peacefully, or else I can make an example of your village and the next one will welcome me with open arms."

"The lands prosper way better than they ever did now that the English landlords run them. Your offer is a return to the past of constant infighting and having Galloglass live off your land. How would this appeal to the common man living in relative peace now?"

"He would know that the one true God blessed these lands. With that blessing, those blasphemous priests who desecrate the mass and the Bible with their heresies have been sent back to the heretical queen."

"So says he who cavorts with a witch."

A hiss stole through the air, and an arrow lodged itself in the man's eye. He clutched for the shaft to pull it out. An axe came down and put him out of his misery.

"No one speaks to the agent of the Maguire like that," Odhran said as he wiped his axe blade on the man's shirt.

Eunan was incensed. He grabbed Odhran by the arm.

"As you correctly stated, I am the agent of the Maguire, and I say who lives or dies, not you."

"I'm sorry, lord. I did not fire the arrow; I merely put him out of his misery."

"Then who did?"

The Maguire men shook their heads. Cara stepped forward with a bow in her hand.

"You can see on my face what he did to me. If ever there was a cruel English landlord, he lies before you. Do with me what you will, but Odhran did him a mercy."

Eunan shook his head and hid his face from the men.

"Clean this up, make a camp, and we'll discuss this in the morning." He stormed off, leaving Cara with Odhran.

Eunan took up residence in the house of the dead merchant as the village was as good a base as any for his mission in east Munster. It was a small stone home with room enough for a few tables and chairs. It had a large fireplace that kept him warm and a hearth good for roasting meat or baking bread. Just before dusk, a knock came upon his door. With shadows stretching, Eunan picked up his axe and placed it beside the door, should he need it.

"Who goes there?" Eunan said through the door.

"It is me, Cara."

"Are you alone? Where are my guards?"

"Don't worry that I am alone. I am neither a witch nor an assassin. Your men surround the perimeter of your house. I can provide valuable information about the village and surrounding countryside and provide you with my company."

"What if I have no wish for company? I am a married man, after all. How can I be seen taking into my house after dark a woman accused of being a witch?"

"You answered your own question. I have no torch, and if you trust your men to be discreet, open the door."

The door opened with a creak.

"You can come in only to tell me how you got here, and then you must leave. The men would earn a pretty coin from my father-in-law for the tale of me harbouring you at night."

The candles of Eunan's lodgings illuminated Cara's face. She beamed from ear to ear.

"You still took me in, though?"

Cara came and stood before him. She had found herself a new sky blue dress, which would have complemented the long, curly black locks if she still had them, that haunted Eunan's memory. She had washed her face and rid herself of the cake of mud. Unfortunately, this only accentuated the bruises on her face, black, purple, and red pools that hurt the eyes of the beholder as much as they must have stung the woman who possessed them. Eunan ached to touch those bruises, to caress them. His hand reached out, but thoughts of his wife and father-in-law immediately intercepted it. He turned his head away, hoping to hide his feelings so he could suppress them in the shadows of his heart.

"You can stay until you are safe and then go north if you wish."

"Or I could stay and be your war wife," Cara said as she smiled and looked away. Eunan's face went in the opposite direction, an eruption of red upon his cheeks.

"The old ways are dead. I only have one wife, and an important alliance is attached to her. I could not disappoint her, for she is with a child."

"If you were so concerned about her, you would have mentioned her first and been at home with her for the birth of, I assume, your first child."

"No wonder they had you down for being a witch," Eunan muttered.

Cara slapped him so hard in the cheek that it stung. Eunan held his cheek, which stopped his hand from flying back in retaliation.

"If I am a witch," Cara said, "then you are a wizard, and you would burn on the pyre with me."

"How come?"

It was Cara's turn to go red as she advanced towards him.

"The easiest way to slur a woman is to say she is a witch. I came here because my family used to live here many years ago until they were sent on the road north as their lands were given to English settlers. I came back when Seamus sent me away from you on the day you were to be married. Broken-hearted though I was, he wanted to send me away with a mission so I would not dwell on losing you. He told me to go spread the word of the rebellion, for it would not be long before he would follow me down with an army. I travelled down and found what Irish I could. Most were small farm holders renting from absent English landlords. I found some sympathetic ears until one man gave me up to the local mayor and major landholder who I killed tonight. He put me on trial for being a witch, saying my words were poison in men's ears and all listening to me would bring was famine and death. They were about to burn me until fate threw me in your arms."

Eunan looked at the ground, familiar with calling a woman a witch. Why else would the crops fail if a man had done his best to toil the land and listened to the word of God on the Sabbath? A man could only follow the instructions of the priests as best he could, or circumstances would allow. But for such a calamity to occur, there must be some other source of evil. But he looked at Cara and remembered how she had saved him by being his companion on the island during his trial.

"I could be accused of being a wizard myself for all the death and destruction my actions have caused. But before I was to depart with my wife, I tried to look for you, but Seamus told me that he planted you there to distract me from thinking about my trial."

"It worked, didn't it? But do not feel sorry for yourself or wallow in self-pity. It also unintentionally worked on me, and my feelings are true. I even wrote to you encouraging you to come but omitting my feelings in case the letter fell into the wrong hands. Your wife is across the other side of Ireland, and there is a whole island of war between you. Take me to be your war wife. You could die tomorrow, as could I. I know you have your obligations, and I will keep our actions a secret, and once you leave the confines of Munster, you are hers."

Cara threw her arms around him and looked into his eyes. Eunan tilted his head downwards to avoid her gaze but did not break her embrace.

"What say you then? Do you take me to be your war wife?"

Eunan raised his head with an objection on his lips, which was smothered under Cara's lips. He lifted her off her feet and towards his bed.

CHAPTER 14
THE GATHERING OF THE CLANS

N ews of the earl's return spread far and wide across the province. Soon, the English landlords and settlers in the region were either slaughtered or set upon the road to the Pale. The English army and their allies were not strong enough to directly oppose the men sent by the O'Neill, so they retreated into their castles and walled towns. They knew they would be relatively safe behind their defences as the rebels had no cannon. The Earl of Ormond, whose lands were next to the province, was too busy organising the defence of the Pale to intervene.

Since he was now the provisional master of all the old lands of Desmond, the new earl of Desmond called all the various factions of rebels together in a conference. Through this conference, he hoped to stamp his authority and persuade the wavering clans of southwest Cork and the Kerry mountains to join him. However, the total defeat of the last earl several decades earlier still lived in the memories of the people. Seamus was tasked with setting up a show of military strength with the soldiers from the north to assure them they would not be standing alone.

The Connihy Castle camps had grown considerably as men gathered to the Earl's cause. However, there was a tinge of disappointment as most of the men were not local but those who had either been banished from the province or were bandits in the woods. Still, Seamus kept his camp in order and sat with Richard Tyrell after they had finished a rabbit stew lunch as the representatives from the various clans began to arrive. Fáolán approached and flashed his usual cheeky grin.

"Greetings, lords. Are you ready for the big wedding today? I never took you for a matchmaker, Seamus?" Seamus cringed, but that did not stop Fáolán. "I'm sure your beloved earl will let you stand beside him with your ceremonial axe just in case she says I don't?"

Seamus cast him a withering look.

"Sometimes your biting wit is a bit too biting."

"But that's why you keep me around." He smiled until Seamus caught the humour and gave a faint smile back.

"I can't think of another reason."

"Maybe I can. For what information I can glean from my contacts?"

Seamus slapped his knee.

"That's my boy."

"From what I have heard of the good earl so far, he is the perfect puppet for O'Neill, and I cannot argue with his selection. But I have Richard's relative youth beside me, and I don't want to strip him of his illusions, him being invited to such a fancy wedding and all."

"Please don't," Richard said as he wiped fake tears from his cheek. "I need something to hold on to when the wind blows through the tent on a rainy night and freezes my balls off."

"Bah, God damn the pair of you if you don't want to hear the fruits of all the labour I have put in for you. The lowlifes I've had to go drinking with to get this information for you."

The practised pained expression on Fáolán's face was wasted on Seamus and Richard.

"Spit out whatever you found out so we can get back to feeling sorry for the bride," Richard said.

"Well, let's go back to the Desmond rebellion."

"Ah, sure, why not?" Seamus said. "Let's rake through that well-hoed ground once more. If you please, try not to make the MacSheehy look too much like the fools they were. I realise what a delusional fool I have been, but the earl and the MacSheehy are good sirens for support."

Fáolán put his hand on Seamus's shoulder.

"Aw, I didn't know you were so sensitive."

Seamus brushed his hand away.

"Just tell your story."

"A long, long time ago, back in the day when the MacSheehy were great—"

"Shut it."

"All right," Fáolán sniggered. "When Ormond and his men hunted us down up some godforsaken mountain, his lordship's father fought against us in the Desmond rebellion. The crown supported him in becoming the replacement earl."

Seamus shrugged his shoulders.

"So what? The O'Neill fought with the crown during the Desmond rebellion. That the earl is a turncoat and will support whichever side will make him the earl is not a revelation. Do you have anything better than that?"

Fáolán's face fell, and he looked crestfallen. Seamus's hand met his back in a solid slap.

"If it's any consolation, I couldn't have a lower opinion of the Earl after he made me kill the poor bride-to-be's husband. I'm sure you can come up with some other gossip to amuse me, but for now, the wedding is about to begin, so I will leave you to wallow in your failure."

Seamus stood up and straightened his jacket.

"Today may be a sham, but no one will be let down by the spectacle of the O'Neill's men."

Seamus and his men marched through the fields and pastures of the earl's lands. The crops and trees yielded in the face of their armour and shields. They seemed to part like a sea, opening up before them and closing after them like a curtain.

The air was heavy with the smell of damp earth and filled with the distant sound of birdsong. Seamus felt a profound sense of peace as he led his men forward, revelling in the simple beauty of the surrounding landscape. In moments like this, with all of nature's splendour around him, Seamus felt a connection to something larger than himself, giving him a sense of purpose. It was not to prop up the earl.

Before them lay the church where the ceremony would take place. It was nestled between a small wood and a cliff that overlooked the white horses riding on the Atlantic Ocean. The church looked small and quaint, an old place of worship made of aged wood and stone. Its red roof tiles, black shingles and mossy stone added to the rustic appeal. There was a field outside the church and Seamus lined up his men on both sides of the path. This would allow the Earl to impress his guests with the military support his allies from the north had lent him.

The wind carried the smell of rain and fog that blanketed the sea. Seamus smiled at the scent of the sea air. It reminded him of home. He turned his gaze to the line of men and heard the boots stomping on the ground. Each soldier wore a steel cap on his head and swords and daggers hanging from their belts. His men stood in two rows, one on either side of the path. Their weapons were slung over their shoulders, and the sun glistened off their leathers. The leathers were the same colour as the faille they wore under their tunics. Seamus and his men stood and waited for all the guests to arrive. Fáolán noticed Seamus was getting agitated.

"Do you want me to see where they are?" he said.

"I feel that now is the part of the day I am doomed to enjoy most, so why ruin it?"

No sooner had the words left his mouth than he saw Murrogh and the re-constituted MacSheehy Galloglass round the corner of the road that meandered through the woods. Seamus's knuckles turned white as he squeezed the shaft of his axe.

"Ego incoming from the north," Fáolán said.

"I told you my day was about to get worse," Seamus said.

Murrogh stormed out before his men and strode straight towards Seamus and Fáolán.

"Happy day to you," Fáolán said. "Nothing like a brisk walk before the ceremony begins."

Murrogh gave him a withering look and turned to Seamus.

"I demand to know why you are forming the guard of honour for the Earl. That privilege is exclusively reserved for the MacSheehys, the earl's own Gallo-glass."

Seamus stepped forward, toe to toe with Murrogh, and their eyes locked.

"I don't take orders from either you or the earl. I am here to represent the O'Neill. The O'Neill wants the earl to impress all the other clan chiefs into uniting with him against the crown. Your collection of farm boys and old men just doesn't cut it."

Murrogh snarled at him.

"Once everyone sees the MacSheehy are back, the old clan members will flock to rejoin."

Seamus gave him a steely stare.

"You must be a victim of the ale if you think no one remembers what you did in the past. The last I remember of you was when you were killing your own clan and taking orders from Ormond. Your plans will come to nothing, for if I remember, they will remember too, and you will hang from a tree for your crimes."

"I demand you vacate this land to give the MacSheehy the pride of place for the Earl's wedding."

"If your MacSheehy are so great, they'll move us off. Alternatively, you can occupy anywhere where we are not. We have liberated your land for you, so you can move around as you please."

"The Earl will hear about this," Murrogh snarled. He signalled to his men to move back where they came from.

"I thought not. I look forward to my discussion with the Earl about this."

Murrogh cursed but signalled to his men to move along. He lined his men up between the woods and the lines of men from the north so at least the Earl would see them first when he came around the corner.

They all waited patiently with blue skies overhead and a cooling sea breeze. The air was fresh and crisp and drifted the smells of salt water and sweet grass, of drying seaweed and dead fish. They heard the sound of the waves washing onto the shore below. The rustle of the many trees in the wind. The birds squawking. The other sounds of impatient men shuffling on the spot, knowing that when the moment came, it would be one of disappointment, but at least it would be over.

The Earl finally came around the corner like the ringmaster at an amateur fair. His red cape billowed behind him as his white stallion galloped down the muddy road. He wore a bright red cap atop his head, its glimmering feathers swaying in the wind.

As he reached the line of MacCabes, he pulled back on the reins, and his horse stopped. He thrust his chest out and surveyed the bustling crowd with his head held high. The Earl's entourage followed closely behind, all dressed in their finest attire. Their freshly polished armour glinted beneath the sun. Murrogh, in an impressive display of reverence, bowed deeply and presented him with a sealed letter.

"The O'Neill supports your claim to be the Earl of Desmond," Murrogh said with a flourish. "If you would be so kind as to follow me, I shall escort you to the church to unite the Fitzgerald and Butler families."

The Earl's lips curled up into a playful smirk, and he gave a curt nod of agreement as he tugged the reins of his snow-white steed. His retinue followed close behind, their regal robes exuding an air of superiority and arrogance. The crowd of onlookers cheered and parted as the Earl made his way through the guard of honour and to the church.

Seamus's hands clenched in a white-knuckle grip, and teeth gnashed in his fury. Murrogh had the gall to try and take credit for providing the earl with the legitimacy and power to claim the title when it was Seamus and the O'Neill's men who had done so.

When the Earl arrived at the church, he was met with an enthusiastic crowd of people from all around the region. The sea of well-wishers parted for their beloved lord and gave him a wide berth, allowing his horse to pass unhindered. The Earl remained atop his horse as he looked over the crowd with a satisfied smile. He raised his hand slowly, and, in turn, a hush fell over the sea of people before him.

The Earl cleared his throat and began to speak in a powerful voice that echoed throughout the churchyard. "Today marks a momentous occasion for us all," he said. "For too long, our two families have been embroiled in a senseless fight between one another. We have lost loved ones, friends, and family members to this conflict...but no more."

The earl paused as murmurs ran through the crowd. He continued, "I am proud to stand here today as your unifying force, to restore peace between the Fitzgeralds and the Butlers once more." The crowd roared with enthusiasm.

"For centuries," he said, "bloodlines and politics have divided the Fitzgeralds and Butlers — but no more. Today, we are united under one banner — my banner."

Seamus laughed.

"I think he started on the ale a bit too early," Fáolán said.

"Yes, but it sounds like he is taking all of this too seriously and getting too big for his boots," Seamus said. "We may have to intervene before he gets us all killed."

"Let's go in for the wedding ceremony," Fáolán said. "I don't think the laughs are over yet."

Seamus and Fáolán walked up to the steps of the church with the other guests, only for the axes of the Galloglass on the door to come down in front of them.

"No armed mercenaries in the church."

"Get out of my way," Fáolán said as he grabbed the shafts of the axes and tried to push them away. "I've got more MacSheehy Galloglass in my little finger than you'll ever have in your whole body."

Seamus went for his axe, but Murrogh heard the commotion and came out. "Let them in...as representatives of the O'Neill."

They brushed past Murrogh and entered the church. But again, Murrogh had taken over the ceremony by placing a ring of MacSheehy Galloglass around the church walls and his Galloglass constables on the altar dais. It was supposed to give the ceremony a sense of historical authenticity, but it only gave it an air of menace to have so many armed men in a claustrophobic church. The other attendees, some of whom had travelled from great distances to witness the occasion, had entered the church with awe and reverence, but as they took in the sight of so many armed men, that feeling was quickly replaced with a sense of unease.

The Earl made his entrance in his most splendid clothes, his chin aloft to fit his new social status. Behind him came the bride, dressed in her spotless white gown, her head held high despite the veil that hid her face. Though it was impossible to tell what thoughts and feelings were contained beneath the fabric, one could guess that a few tears had been shed on this day. Murrogh and the priest waited for them at the altar.

The priest began the ceremony, and the Earl and his bride stood together, illuminated by the soft light of the candles. The words were loud and clear, and despite the presence of Murrogh's Galloglass, a stillness descended as the ritual was solemnly carried out. A gentle sobbing broke the silence. The front ranks of the crowd looked around to see where it was coming from. Fáolán elbowed Seamus and pointed at the bride and then at the throbbing vein in the neck of the purple-faced Earl. Murrogh gestured to the priest to hurry up, and the priest moved on to the binding of the hands for which Murrogh stepped in to hold Ellen's limp hand up. Fáolán sniggered, but Seamus turned away. How could he have facilitated such a farce? Once the ceremony was over, the earl led his bride to the front of the stage.

"Now the FItzgeralds and Butlers are united, no one can stop us."

He held his bride's hand aloft, which set off a loud bout of wailing and tears. Murrogh came forward once more and whisked her away. The Earl stood alone on the altar, looking around and shifting from side to side, wondering what would happen next. Murrogh returned to the altar, the bride having been sent away. He extended his hand in invitation for the Earl to take centre stage. The Earl shuffled forward, looking back to Murrogh for reassurance. He received a smile back. Murrogh stood beside him and looked at the crowd to draw their attention. He lifted the Earl's arm as a sign of triumph.

"May I present the new successor in a long line of earls. The prince of Munster, crowned by his own Galloglass, the new Earl of Desmond."

The crowd cheered, and Murrogh placed a crown upon James's head.

"The earl never wore a crown," Seamus said to Fáolán in disgust. "Now he is just making things up."

Seamus pushed past the MacSheehy Galloglass and stormed out.

CHAPTER 15
AN UNCLE'S ARM AROUND THE SHOULDERS

F ires had been lit outside the church, and the smell of roasting cows and pigs filled the nostrils of those outside and those still in the church. An assortment of bards had been assembled, but they were mainly from the ranks of the Northmen, for the Earl did not have the finances for a lavish wedding as he lived on an impoverished farm. Munster provided poets, and they waxed lyrical about the Earl, his airs and graces and his ancestors. Most were glad of a good meal and the chance to show their craft out in the open, for they had been exiled to the forests as the forces of the Crown cracked down on Gaelic culture. The cattle and pigs had been stolen, and the dregs of Munster's renegades made their way to the event, hoping to be granted some legitimacy.

The musicians filled the air with old victory songs, and the people cheered. The Earl emerged alone from the church and raised his hand to acknowledge the reception he thought was his due. Murrogh rushed out behind him and got his men to form a guard of honour to escort the Earl to his seat at the top of the specially laid-out feasting area. Seamus and Fáolán pushed their way past the objections of the MacSheehy and occupied the seats to the right of the Earl. Here, they could observe what happened, but more importantly, they could get served quickly.

As the Earl settled into his seat, men of shabby appearance approached him, each claiming to be the leader of a minor clan in Munster. Throughout, Seamus barely lifted his head from his food until a youthful man, tall in stature and muscular in build, came to make his assertion.

"Earl, I am pleased to make your acquaintance and pledge my loyalty and that of my men to your cause. My name is Donal MacCarthy, and I claim my deceased father's title of MacCarthy Mór."

Seamus stopped chewing and put down his knife. Finally, someone worthy of paying attention to. He had heard the most prominent clan in south Munster was now up for grabs since the patriarch had died. This was someone he needed to know. He got up off his seat to approach Donal and the Earl. But Murrogh saw him coming. He leapt out of his seat.

"The MacSheehy support your claim in principle and by the sharpness of their axes. The Earl welcomes you, Donal MacCarthy Mór." The Earl glared at Murrogh for acting in his name but declined to contradict him.

"Yes, welcome to our alliance. We are supported by the might of the forces of the O'Neill, and we extend their support to you."

The Earl smiled, for he considered he had reasserted himself. Now, it was the turn of Seamus.

"If you pledge allegiance to the O'Neill, he will support you and consider inaugurating you as the MacCarthy Mór when he arrives," Seamus said.

"Nonsense," Murrogh said with a laugh. "Seamus jests, for he forgets what just happened. Too much life out in the field and not much in the halls of lords, perhaps? The only person who can perform an inauguration in Munster is the earl himself. Go, Donal. Sit and enjoy yourself. Leave the arrangements to me, and MacCarthy Mór and the Earl of Desmond will once more be reunited in Munster's fields and halls of politics."

Fáolán hooked his hand in the crook of Seamus's elbow.

"Leave it, lord. Give the Earl his day. Bide your time, and we'll take care of both of them."

Seamus growled and returned to his plate. He tipped it over for the dogs, for it had now gone cold. He clicked his fingers for more food. He sat and ate until a large body of men appeared between the two sets of woods. A wave of trepidation came over the crowd. Murrogh sent his men to investigate.

"Eat, everyone," Murrogh said to the crowd. Bards, strike up another tune to the glory of the Earl. I'm sure these are more men to celebrate the Earl's wedding and join our rebellious ranks."

The atmosphere dipped and Murrogh stood up from his seat to gesticulate to the bards to play louder. Several minutes later, the scouts returned and bowed before the Earl.

"Lord, the Maguires have arrived and apologised for their lateness."

Seamus rose and threw down his napkin.

"A queen's shilling it is Eunan leading those men."

He walked towards the Maguires as they were being directed where to camp.

"Do I have to be on the other side of all your bets, no matter the odds?" Fáolán said.

He stuffed the remains of the beef into his cheek and followed Seamus.

Eunan was a mess of mud and damp when he arrived. His whole body itched, and he could not wait to throw off his armour and wash his clothes in the nearest river. That is, if he could not obtain a new set of clothes and, given the looting he had seen so far, that should be easy. But he had barely thrown his bag onto the ground from one of the baggage carts before he heard his name. He turned around and saw Seamus with his outstretched arms. His heart jumped when he saw his old uncle once more, who had climbed out of the pit of despair brought on by his recent bereavement. He ran to embrace his uncle. Seamus would not fully let go and held him by the shoulders at arm's length.

"Welcome to the land of our forefathers," Seamus said.

Eunan winced and pulled away.

"You can't still be sensitive about your father, Cian, after all you have seen and done? He haunts me in this place, but I know he is just a ghost."

Eunan sighed and turned away.

"Until I know the mystery of Black Mountain, I will never truly be my father's son. May we meet on a more pleasant topic, or shall I say you look much better than when I saw you last?"

"You learn quickly to press the thumb into a bruise."

"Let us not dishonour her memory with talks of bruises."

"We must practise our greetings and settle on a more mundane topic to break the ice. For example, have you been in any good bogs lately? Or, my, is your axe sporting many a shade of blood this weather? I will give it a moment's thought when I have the time."

Seamus's eyes furrowed as his attention was drawn over Eunan's shoulder.

"Is that a ghost I see? Come forth, girl, and show yourself."

Cara gave a coy smile as she swaggered forward in exaggerated steps. She settled her head on Seamus's chest, and he wrapped his arms around her.

"You have many questions to answer," Seamus said. "I see you have been getting up to mischief in Munster, for nothing else could explain that drastic haircut or the extensive bruising on your face."

Seamus took her chin and rolled her head to examine the bruising.

"I assume there was more than one by the depth of colour on these?"

Cara took her face back.

"And they were cowards, one and all, to treat a woman like this. Eunan should have burned the village, but he let them pack their belongings before sending them back to the Pale."

Seamus's face dropped as he turned to confront Eunan.

"Your forefathers had to run from these lands like rabbits, with even the shirts torn off their backs. They only made it because their foes were too busy wetting their axes with their families."

"I thought the MacSheehy were the greatest Galloglass in the land and would always stay and defend their families?" Eunan said, angry that he thought he had Seamus cornered in a lie.

"Sometimes, we have to sacrifice so that others may live. I hope you never have to find that out. But we veer away from the subject. Surely you are not too queasy to spare a village the torch when they deserve it?"

"They declared Cara a witch."

Seamus furrowed his brow.

"Almost every town in the land has declared me an outlaw at some stage. I have never paused momentarily to contemplate it when something needed to be done."

"If I burned the town, it would have proved that Cara was a witch, and all she had brought was death and destruction as they predicted."

"Yes, but surely you would have killed all of those who harmed Cara, so everyone who thought that would be dead."

"The men believed it."

Seamus's eyes darted from Eunan's solemn face to Cara's coy smile.

"You didn't."

Cara's eyes darted to the side.

"You did." Seamus hooked his arm into the crook of Eunan's elbow and dragged him away.

"It is not his fault," Cara said to their backs.

"His father-in-law won't see it that way."

Seamus dragged Eunan out of earshot and spun him around so he faced him.

"What the hell do you think you're doing? The other men can take women when they are out on campaign, but you can't. In case you haven't worked it out, these prestigious marriages have a downside. You have to be discreet, if at all. The family get offended if you flaunt it around that you have other women. Their daughters are humiliated. Relations between the two parties that hoped to gain anything from the marriage go sour. Your men are five hundred spies with their ears to the door, hoping to earn a coin by telling tales about their master. You certainly guaranteed them a payout by lying with a witch."

"She is not a witch," Eunan growled, his face red as his lank hair.

"Once the rumour starts, there's no stopping it. He was a clever one, that Scottish mayor. There is no better way to douse a rebellion than by saying it was led by a witch who would bring death and destruction. The death and destruction are guaranteed either way, so it is a self-fulfilling prophecy."

Eunan turned his head and scowled.

"The men would never tell tales about what went on on campaign."

Seamus laughed.

"What about the local village cripples? Poor sods who had their limbs chopped off or have had injuries that mean they can't work? They tell stories for a living, and a story like yours could keep them in food for life."

"I could take care of that."

"No, you can't, and stop telling yourself you can."

Eunan spun around.

"You put us together. It was your plot for her to seduce me."

Seamus raised his hands in apology to placate Eunan.

"I did, I did. But I thought you were going to get hung, so I sent her to distract you. I didn't know she would fall for you. I did all this for you so you would be a better man than me and your father."

Eunan looked at the ground to give himself time to think. He grimaced and raised his hand in invitation for Seamus to clasp it.

"I will do what is right, and I will do it soon."

"Do it today so the seeds of rumour do not grow to be weeds. Now let us attend the Earl and see what is happening."

They walked back to see a line of shabby-looking men queuing up to kiss the hand of the new earl and offer hostages to him as a sign of their loyalty. Murrogh stood beside him, his legs astride and arms folded, pride stuffed into a breastplate and morion helmet. Seamus gestured to Richard Tyrell, sitting on the Earl's table, eating but not paying much attention to the proceedings, to follow him. Seamus strode up the line towards the Earl with Eunan and Richard behind him in support. Murrogh ordered his guards to stop them. Seamus halted at the tips of the MacSheehy axe hooks.

"Nobody pledges without pledging to the O'Neill," Seamus shouted towards Murrogh and the Earl.

Murrogh smirked and turned to the crowd.

"I think our friend from the north has got a little lost. He seems to still think he's floating around, the lord of his little boat on the lakes of Fermanagh and not in Munster in the lands of the Earl of Desmond."

Laughter rippled through the crowd.

"Your beloved Earl will hang from the nearest tree if my men and I return north and he finds no men of substance to support him. I would advise the Earl to consider on what side his bread is buttered."

Murrogh threw an accusatory finger at Seamus.

"Hold your tongue, for only the Earl gives orders here. I suggest you and your men avail themselves of the Earl's hospitality and not let the free ale go to your heads. I will see if he will grant you an audience tomorrow where you can discuss the terms of your stay in Munster."

Seamus stood and tilted his head. Eunan stood and watched Seamus's handshake, and his face became possessed by red.

"We need to go back to the camp," Seamus said.

Eunan and Richard frowned in unison. It was not like Seamus to back down.

CHAPTER 16

A CACOPHONY OF PLEDGES

S eamus stormed ahead of Eunan and Richard.

"Where are you going?" Eunan said, trying to get Seamus's attention.

But Seamus did not turn around. He strode ahead of them and marched through the camp to his tent, reached in and pulled out his axe. His constables dropped what they were doing and crowded around him.

"Get one hundred armed men out here before me, now," Seamus barked at them.

"What for?" asked one accustomed to Seamus's temper.

"Just do it."

They all turned and barked at their own men to assemble, for they knew there would be no debate about Seamus's orders.

Eunan and Richard caught up with Seamus. He glanced at them but did not pause long enough for them to make any argument.

"Follow me."

Seamus strode out before the men and led them to the wedding celebrations. The crowd cleared out of the way. The Earl leapt out of his chair to flee, but Murrogh pressed his hand down on his shoulder, forcing him to sit and await his fate.

"We are in this together now, Earl," Murrogh said. "Form a line to defend your earl," Murrogh shouted at his men. The MacSheehy looked at each other and then at the fury on Murrogh's face. No one was brave enough to openly disobey their leader, so a line was formed by default. Seamus marched up to the line of MacSheehy and put his face into that of the man who stood opposite him.

"Get out of my way or feel the wrath of my axe."

The man cowered behind his shield, but his comrades pressed together to force him to stay in line.

"There is no need for violence," Murrogh said. Don't forget you are guests of the Earl, and the Earl is O'Neill's ally."

"The earl is nothing without the O'Neill, no matter how much you pretend otherwise. You are outnumbered two to one. Do not think that I will hesitate to massacre you all. I can easily find someone else to be the earl."

"Would you massacre your own clan?"

"You did. I was there. It would be a fitting end to the insults you have bestowed on our family name."

Murrogh's axe lowered as he saw his line falter.

"We must remember we are all allies on the same side. Men, stand down and let them pass."

The MacSheehy parted like the Red Sea, and Seamus and his men piled into the vacuum. However, Seamus was well aware of falling into a trap and did not consider that Murrogh would think such defiance strategically stupid. He made sure his flanks were guarded before going up to confront Murrogh and the Earl. Murrogh waved to two of his men to watch the Earl and ensure he stayed in his place. Murrogh stepped forward and mirrored Seamus's aggressive stance.

"What are we to make of such egregious threats to the earl by our so-called liberators?"

Seamus walked straight up to Murrogh until they were nose to nose.

"Don't try to be something you are not, Murrogh. You're not clever enough for all the political nonsense. You are both nothing without the O'Neill. Therefore, everyone who wishes to be our ally and leader of their clan swears loyalty to the O'Neill. They also give appropriate hostages. If you want to kidnap a load of boys, then that is up to you, but the prestigious hostages go up north to the O'Neill."

Murrogh backed away and shrugged his shoulders.

"But the people have risen for the Earl, not the men from the north."

"We can turn back around and go home if you wish. Your old friend, the Earl of Ormond, will be straight in after us to hang your earl, but you may survive since your friendship goes back a long way."

The Earl gulped and felt his neck.

"No, I don't think so," the Earl said. "Stand down, Murrogh, and pay proper tribute to the O'Neill who has given this opportunity. We'll soon stand on our own feet, but today, we are grateful to him."

Seamus grinned, for he knew this fool would never stand alone, but he refrained from telling him as long as it was to his advantage.

Murrogh invited Seamus to follow him and pointed to those who had already been taken as hostages.

"Take your pick."

Seamus laughed.

"How am I supposed to know what any of these are worth? Start the ceremony again. No one has pledged to the O'Neill, and the new chieftains need to convince me of their hostages' worth before I accept them."

Murrogh gritted his teeth, but the Earl nodded in agreement. Seamus pulled up a seat and sat beside the Earl.

"Murrogh," Seamus said, "you may begin. Send the first prospective chieftain."

Seamus signalled to Eunan and Richard to come and join him. A line of shabby men now formed before Seamus. The first man in line bowed before both the Earl and Seamus.

"I am here to claim the title of the O'Begley, my lords. The title was taken from my family at the time of the Desmond rebellion, just like yours was taken away from you."

The Earl tried to look severe, but Seamus smirked as he could see his cheek twitch.

"That is a sad story indeed," Seamus said. "I like how you tried associating the Earl's apparent loss with yours. The only thing this earl lost was his pension from the Queen."

Everyone except the prospective O'Begley glared at Seamus, who replied with a smug grin.

"But so far, you have failed to convince us you have any legitimate claim to the title. If I were to stand up now and shout, 'Is anyone else claiming the O'Begley title?' What would be the response?"

The man lowered his head and gritted his teeth.

"Many would raise their hand, but there is no truer claim than mine."

"I would not expect you to say anything else. Why do you have the best claim? Is it because you made it to the front of the queue? No, this will not do at all. Fetch my secretaries. Get everyone in this line to state their claim as to what clan, what the basis for their claim is, how many men they have pledged to them, and what else they can bring the O'Neill. Only then will we hear these claims. We shall meet here tomorrow morning and assess the claims clan by clan, largest first."

Seamus got up and walked off, and Eunan and Richard followed in his wake.

The claimant for the O'Begley clan stood red-faced and motionless.

"But I already pledged to you," he said to the still-seated earl. The Earl threw back his chair and stormed off. Murrogh, followed him like a little dog.

The next day was breezy, and the clouds darted across the sky, casting shadows that danced across the land. Despite their appearance, there was no threat of rain. Seamus strolled over from his camp to the site of yesterday's wedding feast, confident that his authority had been reasserted. However, as with the day before, one hundred of his men marched behind him, along with the secretaries the O'Neill had sent with him. They had their junior assistants run after them, carrying the ledgers that captured the truth, lies and everything in between they had gathered the day before. Eunan and Richard again trailed in Seamus's wake.

Murrogh stood waiting for them, the chairs of Seamus and the Earl both empty. Murrogh gave a sheepish nod to Seamus, who ignored the pleasantries and sat straight down.

"Where is the Earl?" Seamus said as he glared at Murrogh. "We have news that Ormond has entered Munster, so we have far better things to do than settle squabbles over fields barely filled with cows."

Murrogh gave a signal, and the Earl appeared. His movements were stiff and hesitant as he adjusted his shirt, his embarrassment palpable. He had hidden himself when he saw that Seamus had not arrived in the vain hope that he could re-establish some gravitas over Seamus that had cruelly been taken away the day before. He knew he had failed when the smirks of the northerners showed they had seen through his plan. He took his seat and waved to Murrogh to commence. Seamus glared at Murrogh, daring him to start without his permission. Murrogh felt a chill down his spine as he saw Seamus's men positioned around him. He backed into the shadows, desperate to escape, but there was none. Seamus perched himself like a king, satisfied he was now in charge and arrogance radiated from his smirk. Eunan joined Seamus's side with one beckoning gesture, leaving Murrogh alone in the darkness.

"You take charge of the order of the clans. Largest first. I won't sit here all day, for I have the men to prepare. Watch what I do, and you can take over. Richard will come with me."

Eunan nodded and took the list of clans from the chief secretary.

"First up, we have the MacCarthy clan."

Seamus rubbed his hands together.

"Good. One of the biggest ones first. We'll soon see where we are when this one is sorted. Read the details before we see the candidates."

Eunan studied the notes of the scribe, his brow furrowing halfway. He whispered a summary in Seamus's ear.

"I remember the MacCarthys well," Seamus said. Opportunistic turncoats, if ever there were any. But you are telling me they are in an enfeebled mess. As much as I loathe helping them, for all I can think about is how they turned on the earl, I must do so. The key to unlocking southwest Munster and the old clans is the MacCarthys and O'Sullivans. So, who have we got in front of us today?"

"Donal MacCarthy, the illegitimate son."

"Perfect. He is already a rebel and has fighting men. Why are we taking so long to decide when the answer is in front of us?"

Murrogh poked the Earl, but he folded his arms and sank back into his chair. Murrogh would have to do this himself.

"Florence MacCarthy Reagh has the better chance of uniting the clans," Murrogh said as he stepped forward. "'Tis strange such a conniving worm should carry a woman's name". He shook his head in disapproval. "Only the heavens know what possessed his parents to bestow such a name upon him as they poured the holy water on his poor head in front of God. Despite being an English dandy, he has the most substantial claim among those who would join our cause. "

Seamus turned to stare down Murrogh.

"Where is this Florence MacCarthy Reagh? Is he in your pocket? Is he also presenting his case?"

Murrogh backed away.

"The last I heard, he was in Dublin or London. But a man like him will return when he hears there is a chance of getting his lands back."

"That's no good to me. If he can make a decent case, may I suggest we go with what is in front of us? Anyone would think you were arguing with me because I usurped you."

Murrogh looked away.

"No one has any cause to think that."

"Good. Send for Donal MacCarthy, and let us hear his plea."

Donal MacCarthy stood barrel-chested, legs astride like a man mountain before the Earl and Seamus. Donal's skin was weathered and his hair sparse and grey, but his eyes twinkled, revealing that there was more beneath. On top of a large frame was a face that oozed quiet confidence that he could do whatever was necessary to get his own way. Donal stood like a statue. It was hard to fathom that mischief and mayhem lay under that calm surface. Donal was a hard man.

A life of being a rebel out in the mountains, exposed to the winds that blew in from the Atlantic Ocean, had made him into a colossus, a statue out in the hills.

Seamus smiled, for he liked what he saw. Donal was the type of man who would take to the hills and fight a guerrilla campaign, tying down many an English soldier and leaving the plains to him. The MacCarthys may have been weakened, but they could still have their uses.

"I take it you are Donal MacCarthy?" Seamus said.

"That I am."

"Why should the O'Neill use some of his valuable weapons to arm you and send his men to help you?"

"Because I am his best hope to restore the clans of Munster."

Seamus signalled to Eunan to lend him his ear.

"This one looks more of a doer than a talker," Seamus whispered. "I like him, but you may wish to give him a bit of a hand."

Eunan fixed a stare on Donal.

"How many men can you pledge?"

"All the free MacCarthys that are not under the English yoke."

"Can you put a number on it?" Seamus said. "We need to show how many men you can raise to prove to the O'Neill what a worthy ally you would make."

Donal stroked his chin.

"Maybe three hundred swords, five hundred Kern? It depends more on whether we are going to war."

"And you would be willing to pledge to the O'Neill?"

"If he could rid us of the English and restore the one true church, the whole clan would pledge to him."

Seamus's eyes lit up.

"Sign him up as the MacCarthy," Seamus said to Eunan before turning to Richard. "There is your army to train. Munster could soon find its feet again." He turned once more to Eunan. "You take the rest of the clans. I need to talk to Richard and Donal."

CHAPTER 17
CANDLELIT PLOTS

T he pledges were made, hostages taken, and Seamus had sewn together the bottom blanket of a rebellion without pricking his finger. He now found himself in charge of an army of men he had brought from the north, Murrogh's MacSheehy, and a ragtag group of rebels drawn to the new earl. Richard was sent to the MacCarthy lands to see if he could build an army in southwest Munster with Donal's men. This was partially to set up a counterweight to Murrogh's MacSheehy and partly to start a rebel movement that did not necessarily support the Earl.

Seamus rode ahead of the men connecting with the scouts as they returned with information regarding Ormond's whereabouts. Eunan was confused by Seamus's unusual behaviour, though he hadn't yet had time to ask him about it. It differed from when he was grieving on Desmond's island and seemed detached. It appeared that Murrogh had some power over him since if Seamus had locked horns with anyone else, he would have gotten rid of them long ago. He didn't want to travel with the Earl and Murrogh, so he excused himself and rode after Seamus, who was alone. Eunan slowed his horse beside Seamus, who glanced at him and then fixed his gaze on the road ahead.

"Uncle, have I missed something? What has happened to you since you arrived here? I thought you would be jumping for joy at the newly resurrected MacSheehy Galloglass, overjoyed at the sight of the new earl. Yet you seem at war with their very existence. Why?"

"Have you sent the witch away?" Seamus said, not taking his stare off the road ahead.

"Her name is Cara, as you know, for she was once your agent. No, I haven't had a chance, as I've been busy with you the past few days. She's not riding with us if you're worried about that."

"My concern is your standing with the Maguire and your father-in-law. You must end it at the first opportunity and hope your men were otherwise occupied so they forget your indiscretion."

"I will sort it, uncle, but I did not ride here to be lectured by you but to inquire how you are."

"Oh, I'm wonderful — just dandy!"

Eunan sighed.

"Please do not deflect, for it is a simple inquiry," Eunan said sternly. "You ought to have everything you ever wished for, yet you are more miserable than ever."

Seamus turned his head and met Eunan's gaze with a sharp intensity.

"Is it a surprise to you?" Seamus said bitterly. "Munster used to be the place where I met my wonderful wife, but now that she has been taken from me, the land feels sour, as if her loss taints the very air I breathe and the water I drink. The Earl is a mere puppet, and the MacSheehy clan disrespects our name with their cruel and self-serving deeds. All my dreams have been shattered, yet here I stand in Munster, unable to deny its beauty as a land. No matter how bitter it tastes."

Eunan placed a hand on Seamus's shoulder, but it was shaken off immediately.

"Now is not the time for emotions," Seamus said sharply. "It is a time for hardened hearts, for no matter what we think of what we do now, it will shape the future. I want the future to contain my past."

"What would Dervella have thought of your hardened heart when you stand in your homeland with an axe in your hand?" Eunan asked quietly.

"Don't sully her name by using it to get emotional leverage over me," Seamus snapped. "You can't trick a trickster."

"I only mean to talk you down from what I know you do not want to do," Eunan persisted.

"Do not pretend to know my mind. You may be my only kin, but do not test the limits of my patience. We are here to complete a mission, and I have no intention of letting my feelings hamper the execution of it."

"Just like you provided the Earl with his bride?" Eunan said with a chill in his voice.

Rage flashed across Seamus's face.

"Fáolán has a big mouth," he said, shaking his head.

"Only to those he trusts — and he did this with the best intentions," Eunan countered.

"Many a conundrum was born out of the best of intentions."

"Let me help you, uncle — for Dervella, for the past kindnesses you've shown me. I owe you that much."

"The only help I want from you is to get rid of the witch and smother any rumours before they spread. Now, leave me be, for your words already bore me. Do not let boredom turn to irritation."

Eunan opened his mouth to respond, but Seamus had already turned towards an approaching scout who waved his arms furiously; something important had happened. The scout pulled up his horse before Seamus and caught his breath.

"Kilmallock Castle has fallen to Ormond," he said. "He has eight hundred men and is waiting for the Earl."

"Damn," Seamus cursed. "The castle is the key to his lands and is right in the middle of the MacSheehy holdings. However, I have been instructed to avoid open battle at all costs. We will try to lay siege to the castle, but that is it."

Eunan clenched his hand into a fist.

"I don't know why you came down here," he said, "but I came to fight."

"Fight we shall," Seamus replied, "but we must pick our moments. It's useless to light a spark only to have it extinguished by the first bucket of water."

Eunan scowled at him.

"Excellent," said Seamus. "My dress rehearsal of denying the Earl and Murrogh their victory of northern blood for southern glory has passed the audition."

He spurred his horse and motioned for Eunan to follow.

A month of cat-and-mouse ensued as the Earl systematically eliminated all English settlements in western Munster. He accepted the submission of minor clans that emerged from forests and fields after they were freed from English rule. Ormond chased them around Cork and Kerry, but as the first earl had done in the Desmond rebellion, he declined to engage in battle. They eventually found themselves in the same deadlock as before, with the Earl besieging Kilmallock Castle.

With the swelling of ranks came the swelling of egos and the swelling of confidence unmatched by a rise in abilities. The Earl summoned his captains to his tent after nightfall.

In place of the usual array of maps of the area and a map of the castle based on scout reports, fine continental wine imported through Cork harbour was on the table. The servants filled mugs, and rebel leaders reached down to take one—all except one.

"The O'Neill," Seamus said, "the provider of the bulk of the forces and the only ones worth their salt, has forbidden me to engage in pitched battles and sieges. I won't disappoint him."

A cloud descended on Murrogh's face, but he concentrated on the more easily persuadable members of the alliance.

"Surely the Maguires are familiar with taking castles and aren't averse to capturing this one? You came here for glory — glory achieved by taking the rock atop yonder hill."

Eunan took a sip from his cup, remembering how Feargal and Irial would have their spies watching him. Nothing would make them want to remove him quicker than a pile of dead Maguires.

"The Maguires are here to support the O'Neills. Whatever Seamus says, we'll do."

Seamus grinned at Murrogh, who slammed his mug upon the table.

"It is an insult to the Earl to have his arch-enemy reside in one of his principal castles. If this rebellion is ever to succeed, we must drive him from the province."

"Or you could look at it another way," Seamus said. "You have him trapped where you know he is and cannot escape without alerting every rebel in the province. We can do whatever we like for there is not another Crown force of substance between us and the Pale. One option would be to head west and drive out the English settlers. This could also help us gain support by bringing together the local clans. Another option would be to launch a massive raid into Ormond's lands. Can you imagine his face if he heard this? He would surely sally forth from the castle and you could easily lay an ambush for him — two infinitely sounder options than throwing blood against the castle walls."

"That is cowardly talk," Murrogh said. Nothing will show the people of Munster that the Earl is here to stay more than Ormond's utter defeat."

"You should know; you were his lapdog for years."

Murrogh moved with unnatural speed and thrust his face towards Seamus. "I did what needed to be done so my family could survive. You ran away with your monstrous brother, covering up his crime. Yet here you are to grace us with your presence again. Have you brought any MacSheehys back? A couple of renegades, maybe? Your brother's bastard son born from his evil deed inflicted upon a poor woman?"

"Do not disrespect my mother!' Eunan tried to shove himself between Murrogh and Seamus as they spoke.

Seamus stood back and gave a cold smile.

"It is not yet time to air our grievances. You will know when it is. Though you may think yourself better than Cian and me, the evidence before us suggests otherwise. If you wish to attack the castle, by all means, go for it—you are O'Neill's allies, not his subordinates. However, no northern men will partic-ipate in the assault but can provide support."

Murrogh grinned victoriously as if he had found Seamus's Achilles heel. He lifted his mug with one hand and saluted the Earl. "The MacSheehy will launch the assault; it will be the third charge of the Battle of Monasternenagh that would have quashed the English lines if someone had alerted our clansmen about their musketeers hiding in the woods."

He winked at Seamus when nobody else noticed. Seamus gritted his teeth and called Eunan over. "Stay here and try to guide their plans in a suitable direction. I am no longer wanted here."

Eunan tried to grasp Seamus's sleeve, hoping he'd remain, but he had already disappeared.

CHAPTER 18

NORTHERN BLOOD FOR SOUTHERN GLORY

E unan stood at the edge of the woods, watching the assault on the castle unfold. In the far distance, looming ominously over the peaceful landscape, was the castle. It was a formidable fortress of grey stone, built to withstand the test of time. Its impenetrable walls were like sheer granite, appearing even more impressive in the brilliant sunlight. The vast fields of wildflowers that engulfed the area seemed to be in direct contrast to the craggy mountain of stone, as if nature intended to mock it and defy its power. The sweet scent of freshly cut grass and flowers and the pungent aroma of the nearby river filled the air. But something else made the tranquil atmosphere uneasy — an aura of protection and security emanating from the castle's mighty walls. No ladder could hope to scale them, and no battering ram could hope to breach them, and yet they still provided a sense of safety for those who lived beneath them.

Despite this, breaching them was precisely what the MacSheehy meant to do. With no cannons, few muskets and newly made ladders constructed from freshly felled trees, the MacSheehy meant to pursue their assault. Murrogh appeared before his men, bearing a traditional leather shield and sword with matching breastplate and morion helmet. He raised his sword to the sky and bellowed, "WE ARE THE MACSHEEHY, AND WE WILL BE VICTORIOUS!"

With that, all the Galloglass roared in approval and ran towards their goal.

Seamus had dispatched Fáolán to watch Eunan to ensure he did not become overexcited and join in. Eunan suspected this, but they only exchanged meaningful glances without saying a word. But once the charge began, their blood rose.

"Do you wish you were out there?" Eunan asked.

"No," Fáolán replied. "I have no desire to spill my blood for a granite rock that will never be taken. How about you?"

"I'll give Murrogh one thing — he has courage," Eunan said.

"He may have courage, yet soon enough, he won't have any men," Fáolán stated.

"What he had were not worthy of being called Galloglass; at least the few that remain have a chance at meeting expectations."

"That's optimistic of you," Fáolán said. "These men are your kin too, what is left of a once great Galloglass clan. If Murrogh falls on the battlefield today, who will lead the MacSheehy? You have the youth and the leadership skills to take over from him."

"Oh, you flatter to deceive, Fáolán. Either you or Seamus are better placed than me to become the leader. I've sworn myself to the Maguire and have my own kin to look after. Besides, the battle continues, and here we are, dividing out the spoils of our own side."

They looked out onto the charge of the MacSheehy, and the only thing going for them was the limited number of muskets Ormond could fit on his walls. What muskets could be deployed on the walls were more of a threat to the fields of wildflowers than the charging men.

The only sound was the bass thump of the drums, marching in time with the men's steps. Their progress was marked like a death clock, which chased behind them like a black cloud, ready to envelop all before it. The young men laughed as they marched, their voices ringing through the air, cheerful and bright. The bright sun beat down on the young men as they marched forward. Their few breastplates and morion helmets reflected the molten light, creating a glow around the edges that gave them a wraith-like appearance as if they were already in the afterlife.

The grass crackled with a deafening cacophony in the wake of the MacSheehy charge, the crack of gunpowder cutting through the sweet smell of summer. The air reeked of death and danger, the castle defenders' heavy muskets loaded and ready to strike. Hellfire erupted from each barrel, releasing an acrid smoke that clung to the men's clothes and skin alike. No one could ignore the carnage they left in their wake as the MacSheehy advanced, the graveyard stench of blood, sweat and ruined corpses carried by the wind merging with the pleasant aroma of wildflowers. The voices of war rose up like wild dogs as the men thundered forward, urged on by rallying cries and shouts of encouragement from their officers. A cacophony of curses and imprecations bellowed from the fields as its occupants howled out their rage, bitter with defeat, helpless against their enemies' onslaught.

The vast sea of wildflowers and grass had become a killing field. The castle walls were lined with muskets pointed outward, the safest place on the field. Soldiers' heads popped up on the wall like tall grass in the summer sun. Eunan and Fáolán's jaws dropped at the sight of the young men falling to the ground who had no protection from the barrage of bullets. Nevertheless, the constables held their ground and ordered their men forward, ladders hoisted up by eight men onto their shoulders, making them easy pickings for the musketeers.

"Retreat!" Eunan screamed from his hidden position in the trees, but all his efforts were futile. He saw Murrogh and a group of his men huddle together under their shields, edging their way across the field. But their shields were ineffectual, for the scant protection they offered from the bullets was negated by the large target they made.

"What can we do to stop this madness?" Eunan said. Fáolán could see the temptation to order his men to charge grew within him.

"Hold the line and remember your orders," Fáolán said, an uncharacteristic air of strictness in his voice. "You have got to let this play out. Trust that Seamus has a plan."

Eunan bit his lip as he watched the battle. The MacSheehy had become disordered, running away from the musket fire and being chased by their constables to rally for another charge. When the volleys of musket fire subsided, single shots were aimed at scattered figures in the field. Suddenly, the castle gates creaked open, and Lord Ormond's pike and swordsmen, accompanied by cavalry, charged out onto the battlefield. The MacSheehy ran out of their hiding places in terror.

"I can't watch this anymore," Eunan said before snatching his axe and rushing out onto the field. Fáolán tried to stop him, but couldn't.

"THE CRY OF THE MAGUIRE!"

Eunan lifted his axe above his head and heard the thunderous roar of his comrades behind him in the woods. He dashed out into the open field towards the advancing English. Taking advantage of the distraction, the MacSheehy rushed to get away. They had had their fill of battle for today. As the man of Ormond raised his shield, trembling at the oncoming Eunan, Eunan smashed his axe into the side, and it shattered into two pieces. Struggling to release his weapon, the man thrust his sword at Eunan's face, but Eunan parried it and hit him on the back of his head with such force that he fell like a sack of potatoes. With no time to go in for the kill, two other men immediately confronted Eunan; one with a pike aiming towards his face and another with a sword attempting to circle him and jab from behind. Out of the corner of his eye, Eunan could see the swordsman coming for him, and any time he moved, he felt the threatening jabbing motion of the pike pointed at his face.

"Damn you, get it over with and stab me in the back," Eunan cried.

He heard a chilling cry and the sound of something heavy striking somebody's head. The pikeman went pale, so Eunan hooked the pike on his axe, reached for one of his throwing axes, and let loose. The pike fell to the ground.

"You didn't think I was going to let you come out here by yourself, did you?"

Eunan whirled to see Fáolán's grinning face standing beside him. But there was no time to congratulate each other as more enemies came upon them. Eunan and Fáolán were now entangled in battle again. Odhran had managed to call for help from the South Fermanagh shot, who lined up behind the attacking foes. They both got off two volleys before the musketeers on the castle walls fired again. Ormond's men then retreated towards the castle, and Eunan raised his axe to signal their own withdrawal. They retired in good order into the woods alongside the remnants of the MacSheehy.

That evening, Eunan was summoned to the Earl's tent. As he entered, he noticed the interior was sparse, far from the desires of the Earl as he knew them. It consisted of a table resting on the ground and a solitary bench shoved into a corner. A chest lay discarded haphazardly beside a weapons rack which held several ancient swords and shields. The torches that illuminated the space flickered in unison with the gentle breeze outside. Ashen smoke sifted through any gaps, exiting through the tent flaps while flames from a fire outside crackled and hissed.

Eunan wore a bandage on his arm through which his blood had seeped. Exhaustion began to set in as adrenaline drained from his system—dizziness washed over him, and his wounded arm throbbed ceaselessly. Tension hung and mingled with the smoke as Seamus and the Earl loomed before him. Seamus's face contorted with anger while the Earl cowered like prey in the corner.

"I see you have a memento of your foolishness today," Seamus said, pointing to the bandage on Eunan's arm.

"My northern blood was a small price to pay. If I had not charged out today, all would have been lost, and your beloved MacSheehy would have been wiped out again."

"They are not worthy of the name," Seamus muttered. "It may have been the best thing they were wiped out, for it would have brought forth a professional army, not foolish farm boys."

Murrogh stumbled into the tent, his face ashen and smeared with congealed blood. Wrapped tightly around his head was a red-soaked bandage, a painful reminder of the gruesome events on the battlefield. The stench of death was everywhere — the acrid smell of vomit mingled with the metallic aroma of blood, infesting every corner of the room. Hanging his head in shame, Murrogh knew everyone present was aware of his failure. The Earl shifted nervously as they waited for Seamus to pronounce his verdict.

An oppressive silence muffled the room while all eyes rested upon Seamus. Murrogh's heart thudded loudly in his chest as he braced himself for what fate would befall him. Suddenly, it was disrupted by Seamus's thundering voice.

"Why were you such a fool as to throw away the lives of your men when I specifically told you not to?" he asked in a voice that was controlled but laden with twenty years of anger.

Murrogh was at a loss for words. He tried to say something, but the shame and guilt of his actions rendered him speechless. The anger and revulsion in Seamus's eyes clearly showed that he had let him down.

At last, with a guttural groan, Murrogh forced the words out.

"My actions were foolish and rash," he began, voice trembling with emotion. "I am sorry and take full responsibility for what I've done. But let me tell you this — my men will be all the better for what they've been through!" He turned to face the Earl, sweat pouring down his face. "Please forgive me, my lord," he pleaded, desperation cracking his voice. "I can only hope you will allow me to fight again at your side."

"Forgive you?" Seamus declared incredulously. "If I could not have you hung before, then I should have you hung now for disobeying orders. The blood of your men is on your hands, and you should ask their widows and orphans for their forgiveness, not me for mine, for it will not be forthcoming."

The Earl stood up and placed his hand on Murrogh's shoulders.

"Murrogh is my man, and he shall lead my Galloglass again. Many a man has to die in pursuit of freedom and glory. Go forth and replace those you lost and train them up to be true Galloglass."

Seamus gave a bitter laugh.

"As long as neither of you two has to die, then that is fine. This siege is over. We will allow Ormond an escape route back to his lands and work on consolidating Munster and creating a proper army. From now on, Richard and I are in charge of military operations in the province."

Eunan's face dropped, but he knew it was best to hold his tongue, given Seamus's current mood.

Seamus threw an accusatory finger at Murrogh.

"If I catch you insulting my family name again and recruiting any more farm boys to take the place of men, I'll hang you all from a tree."

With that, Seamus stormed out.

CHAPTER 19

THE SHADOW IS CAST

Seamus strode into the night. His shadow cast long in the pale moonlight. The camp was quiet, the mood subdued, and the fires were low, for whatever confidence the rebels had was shattered that day. But questions and doubts pecked away at Eunan like crows swirling around a dying man.

"Oh, to hell with it." There was no point in being afraid. He needed answers from Seamus, and now was as good a time as any. He ran after him and tapped him on the shoulder as he strode back towards his tent.

"What happened in there? Why was I not named as a commander? Am I being punished for my actions today? I saved many allied lives."

Seamus stopped in his tracks, grunted at the barrage of questions, reached into his pocket and handed him a letter.

"No, not at all. You have been summoned up north. I expect your departure tomorrow."

Eunan opened the letter, and his expression changed again: shock, elation, sadness, and anger swirled across his face.

"We'll leave as soon as the men are ready," he said as he straightened up and shoved the paper into his pocket.

Seamus raised an eyebrow.

"What did your letter say, if you don't mind me asking?"

"Sorcha is likely to give birth any day now."

Seamus smiled and grabbed him by the shoulders.

"You could be a father the next time I see you."

But Eunan shied away from Seamus's grip.

"And you could be dead by the time I get back, be it an axe in your belly or a knife in your back. What is it between you and Murrogh? I know there is something, for if he was a nobody, he would be dead in a ditch by now, for the Earl has no power to defend him."

Seamus's face dropped, and he turned and continued walking back to his tent.

"There are some things buried in the past you are better off not knowing. I will have taken care of Murrogh by the time you return."

Eunan ran and hooked Seamus's arm to pull him around. Seamus automatically whipped his arm out of Eunan's grip, leaving him to stumble in front of him.

"I'm sorry," Seamus said when he saw the anger in Eunan's eyes. "I have a warrior's reflexes, which have always served me well."

But Eunan was not for pacifying.

"Answer my questions. You so desperately want me to become a MacSheehy but refuse to tell me all it entails. If I joined with Murrogh and what he calls the MacSheehy, would I be a MacSheehy then?"

Eunan stood solid, directly in his way.

"I cannot put it off any longer," Seamus said, bowing his head. "Follow me to my tent, and I will tell you everything."

Eunan scurried after Seamus as they strode back to the tent. Several men were warming themselves around a small fire in front of the opening.

"Leave us," Seamus instructed them. "Go and make sure no one is within earshot, for whoever I catch that has heard my tale will have their ears chopped off and thrown in the fire."

The men went pale, nodded and ran off to tell anyone they ran into to move away.

Seamus held his hand out.

"Sit and make yourself comfortable."

Seamus went into his tent and retrieved a bottle.

"Here, drink this. You may need it to see the world differently after you hear my tale. It feels so distant, a spirit world that haunts my dreams. I barely recognise myself with all that has happened since then. But brace yourself, for it is the tale of the submission of the MacSheehy at the end of the Desmond rebellion. A tale that banished once proud warriors into the woods to quake in their boots and not to appear in daylight in the lands they once ruled. This is the tale otherwise known to those there as the curse of Black Mountain."

CHAPTER 20

THE CURSE OF BLACK MOUNTAIN

S eamus felt the aching in his knees as he knelt in the dank mud puddle. His body was battered from battle. The numbness spread like a heavy fog throughout his limbs and lingered down in the depths of his soul. The lank strands of his hair clung to his face as the relentless downpour from an angry grey sky assaulted his bruised skin.

He raised his head as he heard the groans of his comrades around him. They also knelt and looked to the ground as the victorious MacSweeney Galloglass searched for vengeance for the long guerrilla war the MacSheehy under the Earl of Desmond had waged against them in the Kerry mountains. They were the apprentice MacSheehy Galloglass, the clan's youth, the next generation of the MacSheehy Galloglass.

He looked for his brothers, the sons of Raghnall MacSheehy. The three of them were the story of the MacSheehy encapsulated in the lives of three young men. The eldest was the pride of his father, a great warrior, obviously going to be the leader of men, and it was heavily rumoured he was going to be the youngest ever leader of the clan should the incumbent, Rory MacSheehy, be killed. This was always possible, given the never-ending feud with the MacSweeney Galloglass clan. The youngest was Eunan's father, Cian, a great prospect for a warrior but always with a bent for cruelty and spite. A frequent disobeyer of orders, he was the wild element of the clan that specialised in self-sabotage every time they seemed to be getting somewhere. Then there was Seamus, the middle son, in awe of this father and the other Galloglass. He was as great a distance from the man he would become as it is to walk blindfolded from Fermanagh to Munster. Seamus could not see his brothers, so he gritted his teeth as he fought against despair and searched desperately for an escape route, only to receive the damp thwack of a stick on the back of the head.

"Eyes forward," came the command.

Seamus bowed his aching head and muttered a prayer. Whatever remained of his belief in God or the church had not quite extinguished and burst into a small flame, for Seamus would now put his faith in anything that may save him.

Sweat and rain merged on his back like icy tears as he contemplated what fate may serve him next. A gust of wind brushed against his cheek, reminding him he was alive. Within his chest beat the heart of a Galloglass with the tempo of a battering ram attempting to break out from beneath his ribcage. The wind also carried a bitter aftertaste, the heady whiff of fear and defiance. He again scoured the faces of desperate men, hoping to find his brothers.

Across from them, in ragged lines at sword point on the plateau of a Kerry mountain, were the senior Galloglass of the clan, all kneeling with heads bowed in front of the Earl of Ormond. The pounding rain on the backs of their heads forced them lower in submission. Ormond sat on his chair and gave them an arrogant smirk as he lorded over them. Seamus noticed the tattered shirt and long locks of hair belonging to his father. He knelt as part of the leadership of the MacSheehy Galloglass, kneeling in line facing the Earl. One of the Earl's men pulled out a severed head from a sack and paraded it before the conquered Galloglass, inciting ridicule and laughter from their captors.

"Everyone move forward," came a harsh voice from behind. "The Earl wants you all to witness the submission of the MacSheehy."

Seamus's hands trembled, locked in a knot behind his back.

He received another whack to the back of the head, and the pain bounced off the inside of his skull, for the blow landed in the same place as before. He struggled to his feet as his head throbbed, his motivation the point of a weapon in the small of his back. He was marched to the edge of the kneeling lines of senior Galloglass. His head hung low so as not to gain any unwanted attention.

"Kneel."

A stick across the back of the calves sent him crashing into a mud pool. Despite the pain, he lifted his head, for he did not want to end his days in the humiliation of drowning in a shallow pool of muddy water. He lifted himself to his knees, the wind as biting as any whip on his wet, raw skin. But he was now in earshot of Ormond, as his captors intended.

Ormond launched himself from his chair and raised his arms to the sky, demanding his guard throw the head of Earl of Desmond into his waiting hands. With a triumphant swipe, he volleyed the head through the air, not caring about the thick droplets of mud and blood that flew in every direction and speckled his pantaloons. It landed with a sickening thud in a mud pool before the Mac-Sheehy leader. He walked steadily towards Rory MacSheehy, never breaking eye contact, until he stood over the bound leader of the rebels.

"Rory MacSheehy," said Ormond, throwing up his hands once more as if the grace of God had granted him his triumph. "I always knew this day of reckoning would come — I standing victorious and you kneeling at the Queen's mercy!"

Rory spat a defiant globule of blood and saliva from his battered lips as Ormond called for his chair to be brought forward. Sitting squarely between them was the severed head of the Earl of Desmond. Ormond leant back in his chair and tipped his head back boldly, revelling in this moment of ultimate victory.

"So, where did following your master get you?" Ormond sneered down at Rory. "Sure, you got lands and castles, but they were all built on the glories of the past, and they were all burned to the ground because of his incompetence. The once great MacSheehys, even though they outnumbered their enemies, followed their master into the hills like obedient dogs to live out their glories as bandits." Ormond smiled and wrapped his arms around the landscape of forest and hills. "Look at all of this and you in your rags. You gave up your ancestors' honour, pride, and legacy to live like beggars because you followed a fool who would not fight."

Rory raised his bruised and battered head, his long hair caked in mud and blood.

"You have won. Be respectful to your fallen foe, and do not gloat. We may be defeated and have executed some of your men, but we never disrespected your men or the MacSweeneys."

Ormond rocked back in his chair and laughed.

"Respect! Ha!" Ormond turned to his men, who stood armed and thirsty for revenge behind him. "He, the man on his knees, with the blood of your innocent relatives on his shirt, has the gall to talk about respect." Ormond stooped and thrust his face into Rory's. "Munster burns. Your families, those who do not already hide with you in the hills, have been evicted or already lie dead on the roadside, their eyes picked out by the crows. But has their sacrifice all been worth it? As long as you have your pride."

Rory shook his head.

"Taunt me now if you must, Ormond, but grant me my dying wish to speak with a priest before I am taken from this life."

Rory's voice quivered with contempt as he looked upon the face of his enemy. His knees trembled with fury and pain, yet still, he forced himself to kneel straight despite his suffering. The only way to end his pain was for death to come quickly. But Ormond only gave a contemptuous laugh.

"Did you send priests before you when you raided my lands and when you killed the Queen's subjects who were given grants to settle her land? When you made the people under my and the Queen's protection homeless and destitute? What did you do to help them, or was their misery more fuel for your foolish pride?"

Rory shook his head and laughed.

"Don't pretend that you are any better than me or Desmond. You came and burned the lands of Desmond, murdering and evicting his people. The only difference between us is that you won. Now, take your victory and humiliate and kill me. But set my men free so they can live their lives even though it is to till your soil."

Ormond sat back in his seat.

"With all the bad blood that has flowed between us, there are certain men amongst your supporters I could not trust, and by leaving them alive, I would only be storing up trouble for myself in the future. Therefore, on this windswept hill with the Atlantic Ocean lapping below on the rocky shore, I will bury our differences once and for all and deal justice to those who harbour resentment in their souls. On this day, our feud ends forever."

Ormond sprang up and glared at Rory. He barked out orders, gesturing to the summit of the hill.

"Bring me the executioner! Have him sharpen his axe so that the blood of those who defy Her Majesty the Queen can flow into the sea below."

Ormond slowly turned and lowered himself, slowly extending his arm authoritatively.

"Let us begin. Men, bring me Desmond's head and his lackey, Rory Mac-Sheehy."

The MacSweeneys seized Desmond's hair, laying his severed head on a chair next to Ormond. Then they seized Rory's arms and kicked at his legs as he attempted to move, tossing him roughly before Ormond. He painfully tugged himself onto his knees while being beaten by the guards on either side of him, trying desperately to keep him still.

"Rory MacSheehy," sneered Ormond. "I have been waiting for this opportunity for many years. I have kept the image of justice snatching away your life with its sharp blade close ever since you came here today. But I must fulfil my duty as an emissary of the Queen and ensure that justice is served."

One man stepped forward, ledger clutched tightly in hand, ready to read Rory's crimes against their kin and friends. But Ormond halted him mid-sentence, raising a hand in refusal.

"No need." His voice was void of emotion as he rose. "Let us not allow our hearts to become callous by reciting the wrongs this man has done to helpless innocent people." Gazing into the distance, he seemed to seek mercy within himself, but his men knew it was just a facade.

"Justice may be harsh but must not be carried out with a hard heart."

Standing tall, Ormond wiped his face clean of all feeling.

"Have you anything to say for yourself, Rory MacSheehy, before the Queen's justice is dispensed?"

Rory raised his head with firm resolve, determined to face death with dignity. His body felt numb from the relentless cold, yet he marshalled his strength, determined to grit his teeth until his last breath. With a flick of his tongue along the back of his teeth, Rory gathered the last bit of saliva in his mouth before propelling it at Ormond's face in one last act of defiance. He may not have hit his target, but this was all that a battered and bound Galloglass could do. The scene blurred as his life and legacy flashed before him. He looked to the right, to the young apprentice Galloglass, who stood as captive. Seamus MacSheehy stood there in his twentieth year: a stout, dependable Galloglass, a future leader. Behind him, his troubled brother Cian. He, too, would make a good warrior if only he could get his head right. The other brother knelt, his expression weary, but the twitches gave away the calculations beneath. Their father knelt behind him, one of the most dependable and loyal constables who served Desmond through thick and thin. Rory embraced a flood of emotion, for he no longer had the fortitude to contain it. Should he further defy his captor, risking the lives of those men, or succumb meekly to a submissive death? No, this was not what his men deserved.

"I beg you, show mercy!" Rory shouted as he turned to his men. "If I must live with the blood of those I have slain, then let me take that burden alone! Spare my men and their families, for they have served me faithfully and not a death can be laid at their feet. If they are shown clemency and allowed to return to their lands, I'm sure the passage of time will heal wounds and dim memories. May there only be two heads rolling in the mud today and the seeds of peace sown."

Ormond gave a slow clap and spoke.

"What a speech! Any soul listening to it would think you are an angel wronged by all around him. But do tell me, how many lives have you taken? How many warriors did you slay with your own hands? And after contemplating that, how many lives of the wives and children of my men did you take? If you have not lost count, you could consider the number of lives of all those who were innocent. What kneels before us is not a wronged soldier but a cruel and calculating murderer."

Rory hung his head in shame. Every pair of eyes burned into him like red-hot coals, seeking justice from one who had caused so much suffering.

"No answer?" Ormond surveyed his men. "Since he takes responsibility for his own actions and those of his men, have any of you lost a friend or loved one to this man?"

A man stepped out from the front rank, his eyes smouldering with hatred as he trembled with restrained fury. "Rory and his men devastated my village. They slaughtered my brother and father without a second thought, and I can't even imagine what they did to the rest of the villagers."

"Then take your revenge," Ormond commanded. "Pick someone from Rory's disciples, make sure they were adept at using an axe, and lop off their hand so they could never wield it in anger against the Queen again."

Ormond snapped his fingers, and a soldier hastened forward, setting a blood-soaked block on the ground beside Rory. The man scoured the second rank of MacSheehy before finally selecting his target by standing behind him and pointing to the nape of his neck.

"Good," Ormond said to the constable standing near him. "Get him."

Two guards rushed into the ranks of quivering MacSheehy and seized the chosen man, who began kicking and begging for clemency. They searched for any special marks on his right hand that would show it was his weapons hand before laying it on the chopping block. The axe came down sharply, making contact with a nauseating thud, flinging droplets of hot blood across the ground as his wrist gave way beneath its keen blade. The man screamed, writhing in anguish as blood spurted from the gaping hole where his hand had been moments before.

"Now pick up the hand and return it to its leader," Ormond bellowed.

The soldier followed orders without hesitation, lifting the severed hand dripping with scarlet liquid, giving one final glance of contempt at Rory before hurling it at him full force. The crimson-faced man staggered back into the throng, gagging on sobs of shock and rage.

Another man stood forward.

"They killed my wife and son."

Another lowly MacSheehy was selected, and his hand was thrown in the face of his former leader.

"I lost my whole family when they set fire to my house."

"Five of my comrades died in one of their ambushes."

Rory was soon covered in blood and surrounded by hands. He shook his head to stop the blood flowing into his eyes and raised it to face Ormond.

"I could turn to my men and ask them if they had also been wronged and get the same answers."

"You could," said Ormond, "but all you can give them is pain as you lost."

"Then be off with my head, and may you kick it along the road as my headless body is dragged to hell. Let us spare the soil of Munster the blood of excessive vengeance. Do what you like to me, but give my men and their families a chance of a second life."

"I grow weary of your pleadings and pretence at amiability when your sins blacken your soil. For all the chaos and death you have brought to these green and pleasant lands, I condemn you to death, and may the devil hold you accountable when you meet him in hell."

Ormond gave a hand signal, and the blade flew into the air. Its velocity carried it straight through Rory's neck, cleaving it effortlessly in two. A line of blood-drenched the ground as his head and body swiftly followed.

Ormond grinned.

"Now, who's next?"

Ormond sneered at the cowering MacSheehy Galloglass constables and spat derision.

"No volunteers?"

Ormond hunkered down to taunt the nearest constable.

"Lost your nerve, have you? How you brave warriors have become meek little lambs."

A single voice of defiance rose from among the sea of bowed heads.

"We would gladly fight you one-on-one, but your offer holds no honour. Kill us, jail us or set us free, but do not degrade us with your gloating."

"Ah, Aonghas MacSheehy. You always had aspirations for Rory's role. I think you can fulfil that today."

Ormond went and towered over the kneeling Aonghas.

"Now, here you are atop this mountain, and your greatest ambition is granted to you. As the leader of the MacSheehy, do you pledge allegiance to the Queen and renounce all titles to your former lands until you can prostrate yourself before her, beg her forgiveness and ask for your lands back?"

Aonghas met Ormond's gaze with a heavy sigh.

"Just swing the axe, then. You know I'll never agree."

Aonghas looked past Ormond's shoulder towards his family, his young son Fáolán hiding behind his mother's leg. He sighed deeply and returned his gaze to Ormond's cold face. Ormond waved his hand, and his guards dragged Aonghas to the block. With a swift strike of the axe, Aonghas's head was severed from his shoulders. Ormond grabbed the decapitated head by its hair and tossed it into the crowd of the MacSheehy families he had taken prisoner. Fáolán's father's head landed in front of his wife as she knelt in terror. Fáolán locked his hands onto her kneecaps and cried into the back of her knees.

Seamus and Cian averted their gaze as, one by one, the heads of their clansmen were lopped off with a swift stroke of the executioner's blade. The impossible request of subservience was posed to whoever Ormond considered a threat, and Ormond systematically butchered the best and brightest warriors of the clan until the core was destroyed. Ormond then turned his attention to the young, methodically removing the hands of anyone he deemed may one day attempt to take revenge.

Seamus and Cian were taken from the crowd as yet untouched by the blades of vengeance and lined up to be questioned by Ormond. All those who dared bellow their rage after witnessing the murder of their fathers or family members or showed any insolence were immediately slain. Those who bowed their heads were singled out and made to stand in front of the remains of the clan and hung their heads in shame. Irrespective of this, their ranks swelled with those who wished to live. Cian's hand shook as Ormond advanced towards him. A boy several places in front of them pissed himself, and he was made to join the ranks of those who had submitted and was forbidden to hide the large stain around his groin. Cian could now smell Ormond's breath and feel the presence of the MacSweeneys behind his back. Seamus reached over and took hold of his brother's hand to stop him from being branded a coward.

Seamus's elder brother was two people closer to Ormond than Cian. He looked down the line and saw Cian's distress. A voice broke the tension.

"I will do it. I will submit and lead the MacSheehy. I accept the Queen. Rory was my uncle so I can take his title."

Seamus looked past Cian's bowed head. He was right. It was his brother's voice. But Seamus's throat went dry before he could plead with him not to disgrace the family.

"If you are to lead the MacSheehy, then you know what to do," said Ormond.

The man knelt where he stood, not pausing to clear the spot of debris.

"I swear allegiance to the Queen..."

"I am the Queen's agent," said Ormond. "You must lay prostrate and pledge before me."

Seamus's elder brother did not raise his eyes nor show any emotion. He placed his hands in the puddle before him and eased himself into the cold water.

"I swear allegiance…"

"You what? I can't hear you. There's the wind up here, and the Queen is in her palace in London. How is she supposed to hear you?"

"I PLEDGE ALLEGIANCE TO THE QUEEN. I RENOUNCE ALL CLAIMS TO THE FORMER LANDS OF THE MACSHEEHY AND WILL LAY MYSELF BEFORE THE QUEEN AND ASK FOR CLEMENCY FOR ME AND MY CLAN."

Ormond laughed.

"What is your name?"

"Murrogh MacSheehy, lord. Son of Raghnall MacSheehy."

"Well, son of Raghnall, my mission here is not complete. As the Queen's agent, you must first prove yourself loyal. Finish purging your clan of all undesirable elements and present me with a core of the clan by the end of the day that is prepared to fight under the Queen's banner by the end of the day."

Murrogh began to lift himself from the puddle, and when he was on his hunkers, Ormond thrust his face into his.

"If you fail me, I will kill your family, all your relatives, and decimate the remains of your clan. Do we have an understanding?"

"Yes, lord. It will be done as you ask. You will find me worthy of your trust."

"If you are so worthy," Ormond said slowly, "show me how you would deal with a troublemaker."

Murrogh felt his heart pounding rapidly as he glanced at the dissenters amongst his clan members. His anger boiled over, and he grabbed one of them, who stood between Cian and Seamus and threw him to the ground.

"This man was a heinous murderer of your men. A coward hiding behind his bow. Many a man did he creep up behind and shoot in the back," Murrogh declared as he looked to Ormond for approval. He was met with a raised eyebrow as if his job was only half done.

"I will chop off both his hands so he can never carry a bow again," Murrogh said. "Then I shall set him on the road to wander Munster. His stumps will be a lesson to any man that may be tempted to rise up in anger against the Queen."

Ormond smiled and signalled to his men.

"Don't let me stop you. But to prove yourself to me, you must carry out any retribution yourself."

Murrogh felt his heart drop as the colour drained from his face. Ormond's men placed the bloody stump beside Murrogh with the unguarded axe resting on top of it.

"I cannot hold him down and cut his hand off at the same time," Murrogh pleaded.

"We can help you. Select a hand, and my men will hold it for you. But you must chop it off."

Murrogh wrestled with the man until he held up his right hand.

"This one," Murrogh declared through gritted teeth.

At Ormond's silent command, his henchmen pulled the man's arm down and held it upon the block before him. Murrogh picked up the axe and sized up the trajectory to the man's wrist. His hands trembled as he imagined taking aim at Ormond instead of the man's wrist.

"Focus on the task at hand," Ormond said with a smirk.

Murrogh bit his lip until it split. He settled his mind, and the axe descended. The man howled, but his wrist was still held to the block.

"And the other hand," Murrogh ordered.

The left hand was dispatched with much less fuss.

Ormond smiled, for he knew Murrogh was his. Seamus turned and threw up behind the line of boys that trembled like leaves in a gale wind.

CHAPTER 21
THE CLAN ENDURES

Seamus stared into the fire, his eyes transfixed on the flames as tears streamed down his face. His voice quivered when he broke the silence.

"It weighs heavily upon me to tell you Murrogh is my brother. My chasm of shame knows no bottom, and so far, I have only shared this truth with those acquainted with the tragedy of Black Mountain."

Eunan's face hardened upon this revelation. Although he had heard many stories before, nothing could have prepared him for this.

"But uncle..."

Seamus cut him off, feeling the pain of his burden swell in him again. He lifted his head and sniffed back the tears.

"I struggle every day against the memory of that event. My own brother was complicit in killing many of our people, Fáolán's family, and the Galloglass warriors. Now, he tries to revive the very same clan he slaughters and puts himself forward as a leader of the Munster rebellion. Though the myth of the earl still holds power among our people and Murrogh is his right-hand man, I cannot escape what has been done and neither can anyone else."

"But he murdered his own clan," Eunan said, compressing his anger into a whisper.

Seamus continued, his body shaking and his fingers jabbing the air.

"The guilt of all those lives lost lies heavily on me for why did I survive when so many didn't? Did Murrogh do this so we could both live or so he could take over as leader? Why did he leave me with such an unbearable burden, where those who died were slaughtered in front of me instead of letting me lie down with them?" Seamus's voice trembled as he asked these questions aloud. "Can you understand why I am so consumed by bitterness now?"

Eunan placed a hand on his uncle's shoulder.

"I can only see from his actions that he has set out to be your foe."

Seamus rubbed his cheeks and dragged the palm of his hand down his chin and neck.

"He has tried to revive the clan, with those he did not help slaughter. Justice is deaf, but family is blind. I cannot see how any relative of mine, never mind my brother, could have ever carried out so heinous a crime."

"Judge him like you would any other prospect for the leader of a clan," Eunan whispered.

Seamus gnashed his teeth, and his hands became anguished fists, so he dragged them down his chest.

"But you don't understand the nature of my curse. I have the guilt of the souls of the dead on my conscience and am blinded by not being able to see the perpetrator."

"Let me be your eyes, uncle. Let me free you from your curse."

Seamus shook his head slowly and looked away.

"Leave me to wallow in my guilt. Go to Tyrone and be a father. That will be my best revenge for the time being. That the next generation of MacSheehy has been born, and my father's blood still lives on."

Eunan rose but turned to look at his uncle.

"I may go, but I have not forgotten our conversation."

"Go. Things will be different when you return."

Eunan reluctantly nodded and clasped his uncle by the hand before disappearing into the night. Conflicted emotions rolled within him like the rolling hills that led back to Fermanagh.

CHAPTER 22
THE BEGINNING OF A LONG WALK

The Earl of Essex stepped off his ship, his head swirling with conflicting emotions. He was proud of his appointment as Lord Deputy of Ireland, seeing it as a well-deserved stepping stone in his successful career. On the other hand, he was disappointed by what he saw: small buildings and puny plumes of smoke instead of the magnificence of London. But he reminded himself that the Queen needed someone with his abilities, and he would be amply rewarded once he quashed this petty rebellion. He knew he would only be here temporarily. It would be over soon if he knuckled down.

The Earl's clothes were made of the finest English cloth, his doublet and hose a matching deep green with gold accents. The gold buttons on his doublet were embossed with the Earl's Griffin crest. The gold trimming and buckles on his shoes glinted in the pale sunlight. His boots made a thunderous noise on the cobblestones as he walked. The Earl's walk was deliberate and purposeful. His shoes of fine leather and hard leather soles made a sound like a slow rolling thunder that preceded the man and echoed in the ears of those in his wake. The Earl's frown was as deep as the sea, his eyes like a cold grey sky. His skin was a healthy tan, kissed by the sun. He surveyed the dock and tried not to gag on the foul-smelling tanning shops near the port. He was accustomed to the sights and smells of a seaport but was more familiar with London, Portsmouth, Southampton, and Plymouth, and this port was clearly not in the same league.

A salty sea breeze blew through the Earl's nostrils, bringing the smell of fish and rotting wood. As he walked, he rubbed his eyes and nose and, through the tears, noticed the desperate faces of the officials who had come to greet him as if he were their saviour. He could not help but smile at the thought of his own power and imagined himself as a returning king, welcomed by a cheering crowd.

The Earl examined the harbour, surrounded by small buildings and littered with debris, apparently from a recent storm. Some stone and wood structures were in danger of crumbling or burning, adding to the feeling of decay in the city. A few buildings had already caught fire, casting a sickly red glow on the wet cobblestones. Wafts of grey smoke blew across the harbour, causing the static dignitaries to break into coughing fits. When the smoke passed, they returned to stand and wait with solemn faces and hunched backs.

The officials bowed low, murmuring gratitude and respect as he walked past. He nodded slightly in acknowledgement, not wanting to appear too proud, and continued until he reached the harbour gates. The Earl could feel the awkwardness of the officials, their fear as if he were royalty that might be insulted by the state of their city.

At the end of the line of officials stood the Earl of Ormond, along with all the senior army officers in Dublin and surrounding districts who were not required for active duty. Ormond moved his weight from side to side, for he considered himself too old to take to the saddle, which was a young man's game. He propped himself up with a stick as the new Lord Deputy approached.

"Greetings, Sir Robert. We are honoured to have one of the Queen's most prestigious soldiers here to lead us."

Essex smiled, then felt something soft upon his shoe. The smell of cow dung hit him, and he looked at his foot in disgust.

"The pleasure is all mine, let me assure you."

Ormond snapped his fingers, and one of his servants ran to clean off the Earl. Ormond knew the Earl from the Queen's court and was familiar with his lofty expectations, which applied to everyone else except himself. But ever since he became a national hero after the success of the raid on Cadiz, where he defeated the Spanish navy, he was untouchable. If anyone could save Dublin, it was him.

Ormond extended his hand to greet Essex, but one of Essex's men had retrieved a new pair of shoes from the earl's baggage as it was unloaded from the ship. The Earl paused to change his shoes before accepting his welcome.

"I hear it is a bit like Scotland, but with more rain?" Essex said to Ormond.

"There are some similarities, but—"

"Good. Then we shall march from Dublin around the country, make a few examples of the rebels, get them to submit, and I can return to the Queen's court. Sound good?"

All Ormond's hope drained away. Another pompous toff from the Queen's court who had not bothered to do his research.

"Very good, sir." Ormond pointed to the gates of the harbour. "This way to your residence. I have many people who wish to meet you."

"Oh, what a bore. I have just gotten off the ship, and my bones are creaking. Will there be wine?"

"My men have done their best to track down all the victuals you may require." Essex cringed.

"You make it sound like a camp. It better not be. Do you have continental wines here? You must do with a port so big. What else would you import?"

"We have continental wines."

"Good. I will need a large supply, for I have brought some of England's finest sons, eager to bloody their swords. They will need wine, for we mean to challenge the best they can put forward to a duel and will need something to celebrate with afterwards. I do so look forward to pitting my wits against these savages. You do have duels over here?"

"They have been known to duel but—"

"Excellent. I do so love a bit of sport. Now lead on, for the stink of the cow dung you clumsily left in my way still lingers. I desperately need a bath. You do have—"

"Yes, we have baths."

The Earl looked far more comfortable in his residence with a mug of wine and some of the local female gentry to regale with tales of his battle prowess on the high seas. The food, wine and company were the finest Ormond could muster in Dublin, for he wanted to impress the new Lord Deputy and encourage him to stay despite his reservations. He had arranged for the best staff in Dublin to service the house of the Lord Deputy. They would get him everything he thought he needed and an army of messengers and errand boys to get everything he did not. Still, Ormond was pensive even though he observed Essex and his entourage of thrill-seeking young lords from England laughing and joking with the local ladies.

Ormond invited the merchants' guild, acknowledging their role in supplying the army and providing loans in the absence of Crown grants. He knew the best thing for all sides was that the expeditions inland were profitable to the Lord Deputy and his officers, the local gentry and merchants, and the land dealers who followed in the army's wake. Captain Williamson, Cormac O'Cassidy, and Taaffe stood in the corner opposite the Lord Deputy and planned their introductions.

"If you thought it was a bonanza before," Captain Williamson said, "wait until Essex sets off. He's one of the Queen's favourite courtiers, and it's heavily rumoured that he may marry her one day."

"Rumours spread by himself, no doubt?" Taaffe said. "I am familiar with those tactics. Bingham was the master of it."

Captain Williamson became a schoolmaster with a wagging finger.

"No matter what you say today, do not mention your old master. He is persona non grata in these circles. His failed schemes ruined many a man's fortune in this room."

"What about me?" Taaffe protested. "You could get me stabbed by bringing me here. I've spotted three people I still owe money to, and the daggers for looks I have received mean they remember."

Captain Williamson grinned and put his hand on Taaffe's shoulder.

"You need to tough it out. You are a man reborn. No better man to do a dirty job for them. You now work for Cormac O'Cassidy, the famous rags-to-riches merchant who allows you the veil of his reputation. That is why you are here. To carve up the land in the trail of the Lord Deputy's glorious victory."

Taaffe's head dropped. Captain Williamson slapped him on the back.

"Let me introduce you. It is the manner of the introduction and finding out what the other person wants."

They worked their way through the crowd at a pace where Captain Williamson could observe his prey, assess his mood and choose his moment to strike. He waited until the Lord Deputy turned to greet the next group thrust in his face. Captain Williamson grabbed Taaffe by the elbow and dragged him forward. He caught the Lord Deputy's eye, smiled and moved forward. But then another hand lingered in front of Essex.

"You may remember me, Sir Warham St Leger? We served together a couple of times, even here in Ireland."

Essex's eyes rolled back as if he was searching the back of his brains for the man's face. Unsuccessful but overconfident, he tried to bluff his way out.

"Oh yes, we evicted those, Mac something or others from up in the north if I remember correctly."

"It was Wicklow where we served," St Leger said coolly, realising the Lord Deputy did not remember him.

Essex looked to Captain Williamson to give him an escape route.

"Are you with him?" Essex asked.

"He has one of my men with him," St Leger sneered. "A notorious land dealer."

"A land dealer?" Essex said, warming to the turn in the conversation. "Well, I may as well make the most out of this trip. Come over and speak with me."

Essex waved towards Taaffe, and Captain Williamson shoved him in the small of his back. Taaffe's legs felt like lead, for he had been suffering a crisis of confidence since being run out of Dublin town, and this was one way to announce he was back.

"What's your name?" Essex bent his ear upwards to the larger Taaffe.

"William Taaffe, sir. Ex-mayor of Sligo and now in dedicated service to Her Majesty's forces."

"Sligo?" Essex rubbed his chin. "I have several plots of land in this godfor-saken country, but Sligo does not ring a bell."

"He does his land trading all over," Captain Williamson said, "especially in Munster. If we could find out where your lands are positioned, he could greatly enlarge them, at rock-bottom prices, too." Captain Williamson put his remaining hand on Taaffe's shoulder and beamed like a proud father. "He also specialises in difficult scenarios such as land clearance."

Essex sized up Taaffe.

"You sound like a very handy fellow. Stay near me, and we'll see what I can arrange."

St Leger felt a pang of jealousy as his moment to reminisce and gain the Lord Deputy's favour disappeared. An accusatory finger was pointed at Taaffe.

"He used to be the lackey of Bingham."

St Leger grinned as that should have been enough to poison the well. Captain Williamson felt the sudden change in mood and knew he had to act fast.

"It's a wild country here, and you need men like Taaffe to navigate it. He was an excellent servant to Bingham, gaining much expertise in land dealing. But then he was equally as good a servant to the Crown when everything came out about Bingham's activities—indeed, he was the chief witness for the Crown."

Captain Williamson saw the smile rise on Essex's face again. He leaned in for the kill.

"But because Taaffe does a dirty job, he makes a lot of enemies. He could make you a lot of money if you took him under your wing."

Captain Williamson watched the idea take up residence on the Lord Deputy's face. Essex smiled.

"Taaffe, you can tell everyone that you have the protection of the Lord Deputy as long as the land deals keep flowing."

Essex winked at Taaffe, who bowed his head.

"Sir, you shall be the first to know."

St. Leger saw his opportunity slipping away and knew this was his last chance.

"Taaffe and his soldiers have been assigned to serve under my command", he said. "We shall give him all the support and protection he needs for as long as you should require it."

Essex gave a faint smile.

"Good. It will be just like the old days."

St Leger looked confused until he realised it was a throwaway comment. Captain Williamson stepped forward once more.

"Lord Deputy, while I have your attention, may I introduce you to Cormac O'Cassidy, one of the finest merchants in Ireland? He should be able to meet all your requests should you wish for anything and whatever your men would wish for, too."

Essex smiled as Captain Williamson led him away.

CHAPTER 23
HANG OR HIRE?

C ormac O'Cassidy poured another drink and gazed out his window at Dublin port below. The port was a hive of activity, with fresh ships arriving from English ports constantly. Their cargo consisted of scruffy young men hoping to gain fame and fortune in the rugged terrain of Ireland. Cormac grinned as he watched the bewildered youths waiting on the docks for instructions. None of them knew what awaited them, but Cormac felt no pity. His investments were so far-reaching that the naive youths standing on the dock would make him a fortune regardless of whether they lived or died. He turned away from the window and raised an eyebrow as if that were all the emotion he could draw from his face.

"I don't know whether to wish them success or ill luck. We make a fortune every time they send a new army over."

"Especially now," Captain Williamson said as he sat at Cormac's table and shovelled food into his face. "For this is the biggest army Ireland has ever seen."

Cormac's eyes turned back to the port.

"First, they march off the ships and take our kits and clothes. Then they eat our food and sleep in our tents. They fight the natives so we can maintain our lifestyles. They get wounded and end up in our hospitals. If they live, they get sent home with a few coins in their pockets while we swoop in like crows on a corpse and divide up the vacated land. How did you set up such a monopoly?"

"They took my arm," Captain Williamson said between chews, tapping the stump of the remains of his arm with his knife, "but I saw the light. Take who you know and add a dash of what you know. Once you get approved by the Crown and agree to give them a cut, they will always look the other way."

"Do you actually want this war to end?"

"All wars have to end sometime. You just have to make sure you have made it worth your while. When this is over, I want to retire to a nice estate—maybe in Munster, where fertile land is abundant—and settle down and let my peasants do the dirty work for a change. What about you?"

Cormac did not turn around to answer.

"Once I clear my lands and see those that murdered my family dead, I think I will be empty inside. The money I accumulate is only good for my revenge. Maybe I will restore my house to the state it was in before I lost my beloved daughter, and I may lie down inside it and die thinking of her and how I have avenged her death. Or maybe this window is the frame of the rest of my life, and I stand here perpetually accumulating money and asking you if Eunan Maguire is dead."

Captain Williamson shoved his bowl into the middle of the table for it to be removed by a servant's hand.

"He will be drawn like a fly to Munster, for that is where the MacSheehy believe their destiny lies. Unfortunately for them, it is in fresh graves dug beside those of their forefathers. Such is the reward for believing all those fantastic stories of chivalry by your ancestors. You sacrifice your life to find out they aren't true. Those like you and I, who used their brains and subterfuge, survive and prosper. The Lord Deputy means to march into Munster and douse the flames of rebellion. Taaffe and Shea Óg will track down Eunan Maguire and his uncle there. They have already perpetrated a massacre of their relatives on your estate, so they have made a down payment on your revenge and created a blood feud to draw them out."

Cormac turned and refilled his mug.

"As much as I don't care about the money, we have given them a lot. I expect more dividends from my investments."

"Don't you worry. The expedition to Munster will bring a glorious bounty. You may even get the head of Eunan Maguire."

"I should be so lucky."

Cormac O'Cassidy returned to his window frame once more.

The army camps around Dublin had grown into a sprawl, for there was no room in the city for the largest army ever assembled in Ireland. There was only room in the city for officers because of the amount of refugees that had fled there in the wake of the rebels. However, the morale in the camps should have been sky-high on the eve of perceived victory, but disquiet had been growing. A place where it flourished was in the camp of Sir Warham St Leger. St. Leger poked the fire to stir the flames of the fire alongside those of this soul.

"He may command the seas, but the cad has no idea about war on the land."

"Why do you say that?" Taaffe said. He extended his hands to reap the rewards of the freshly poked fire but recoiled at his master's anger.

"He sent half of the greatest army ever assembled in Ireland off to sit in castles on garrison duty," St Leger said as he gesticulated furiously in the direction he thought the Lord Deputy was camped. "The Irish shirk castles and walled towns if they can, for every fool knows they have no cannon. It would be better to send the men back to England than have them sit in a dump of a town waiting to pick up an illness. He should march north at the head of a glorious army and burn the rebels out of their hovels. But no. He has to march south for the glory of butchering angry farm boys."

Taaffe raised his eyebrows to Shea Óg.

"There would be a lot of money to be made from the ensuing land disputes after a rebellion. Many an adventurer spurned the romance of the clash of axes up north for the cold hard cash of clearing land in the south. And there they now sit in their estates in England, wealthy men indeed."

"We are soldiers, not mercenaries," St Leger said and turned when he remembered who his audience was. "How mistaken can I have been?"

"No offence taken," Taaffe said, with a smirk. "Sometimes it is a handy ruse to be mistaken for soldiers."

"When you serve under me, I expect you to act like soldiers."

"You took us on to act as land agents, and all those who watch our actions and sponsor us expect us to act as such."

"With your luck, Taaffe, you must have the protection of the devil himself. He must have convinced the Lord Deputy to hover over you like an angel."

"Just goes to show you, even angels worship money."

"All the same, all I expect from this campaign is for my men to end up in the infirmary. But they are more likely to injure themselves with their sharp weapons than for the rebel farm boys to lay a hand upon them."

A messenger ran through the camp, his face red with exhaustion and concern. "It is time to leave. The Lord Deputy has already set out for Munster."

St. Ledger got up and threw the contents of his mug on the fire.

"This does not bode well," St Leger said as he turned to dismantle his tent.

The army marched forward with relentless fury, leaving a trail of destruction in its wake. Clouds of thick, acrid smoke filled the air as forests and fields burned behind them. This destructive force advanced relentlessly like a ravenous beast, destroying all that lay in its path. The men were ordered to make examples of those who could be connected to the rebels to send a chilling warning. Frightened by this menacing presence, the rebels took refuge behind trees and mountaintops, lashing out at the flanks instead.

The army continued their march into Leinster, facing constant attacks from rebel forces. Whenever Essex tried to respond with force, the rebels ran away, forcing officers familiar with Irish combat tactics to beg the Lord Deputy to avoid pointless pursuits that would only lead to an ambush.

When they arrived on Ormond's land, two royal armies united there. Essex proclaimed that Cahir Castle should be taken as a warning sign for any rebel or anyone considering siding with them. No one dared challenge him.

The royal camp sprawled out like a web of chaos around the castle walls, tents, and siege weapons strategically placed to surround and contain it. Lord Cahir refused to concede and instead prepared for his grim stand as Essex's cannons began their booming bombardment. Three days of thunderous violence battered the walls until, finally, they collapsed, crumbling into a flurry of debris.

The rebels were taken captive and brought before the two generals: Essex, immaculately dressed in splendid courtier finery oozing superiority, and Ormond, heavily armoured, mud-streaked, and bristling beneath his helm. Without pause, Essex raised his cup of wine in a toast that mocked the fallen while Ormond watched on, barely hiding his contempt. The show was meant to display dominance, yet such arrogance would only spark resistance and hatred. They were supposed to subdue the insurgency, not incite it. Essex took another sip of wine.

"Bring out whoever the master of the castle is." Essex looked behind to see if his officers would heed his call. A snap of fingers later, a man soaked in blood and dressed in rags with his hands bound was cast to kneel in front of him.

"The lord of Cahir Castle," an officer said.

Essex swirled his wine around his mug.

"So what are we to do with you?"

Lord Cahir looked confused, but he assumed the Lord Deputy was asking him rather than the contents of his mug.

"I wish to recommit my allegiance to the Queen and pay any fine she saw fit."

Lord Cahir bowed his head to show contrition and calculate how he could afford the fine. Essex furrowed his brow.

"You nurture some extraordinary ideas yet kneel before me and expect pity. Do you think you can wreak havoc, defy the Queen, leisurely hold out your hand for the bill, and get a slap on the wrist? Off to the gallows with you. I shall take from your castle whatever I need to restore the Queen's peace."

The Lord Deputy's men lifted Lord Cahir up by the elbows as a wet patch grew around his groin. The soldiers muffled his protests. Ormond tutted and leaned over.

"Sorry, Lord Deputy, but it does not quite work like that around here."

Essex jerked back.

"What? Is a basic principle of the rule of law not exercised over here? You rebel, you hang. Before I return to Dublin, the woods will be full of hanging rebels. No wonder this island has been in chaos for so long."

Ormond leaned in, for he did not want the general populous to hear the basic level of advice he was giving the lord deputy.

"If you leave a trail of bodies, you just leave a recruitment poster for the rebels. It is better done with stealth, bribery, dividing the clans by backing a rival, giving them fancy titles and hereditary rule. Let them do the work and fight it out amongst themselves, and we step over the bodies and take the land. That works so much better."

It was Essex's turn to tut.

"No wonder you have had so much trouble for so long. You've had to wait for too long for them to kill each other, and the Spanish are offering better bribes. Still, let's play it your way, but not completely. I will have my ropes filled today. Anyone who will not turn or is useless to us shall hang." He tilted his head to the side, revealing a row of jagged teeth that gleamed in the waning sunlight. "Let us call this game hang or hire. I will be a good sport and give you that first man." Essex snapped his fingers. "Clerk. Estimate the damages Lord Cahir did and the losses we have taken to recapture his castle. Make that a price, then double it. Use that as the basis of the surrender terms he will sign." Essex rubbed his hands together. "I am looking forward to this game now. Send the next man out, and we shall decide whether to hang or hire."

A man with a sunken face, wide-eyed, with wild hair tumbling around his shoulders was thrown to the ground. His clothing was dishevelled and covered in grime as he knelt before Essex and Ormond, mouth agape in fear.

"Please, lords, sirs, whatever you may be. I was forced into this. I had no choice."

Essex waved away his protests.

"If only you curs could plead something original, then maybe I would listen. Captain, what is his story?"

The captain's face bore no expression as he read out the charges.

"Notorious cattle rustler and bandit. He claims to be Galloglass from the old families. Threw his lot in with Cahir when he declared for O'Neill."

"Not hearing any positives here or any scope for redemption. If we release him, we only make the journeys of poor travellers more dangerous. Definitely hang for me."

The man crawled forward on his knees and wrapped his pleading hands together.

"No, no. Please no. I can give you information about the rebels. You could crush the rebellion in a day with the information I could tell you."

Essex raised his eyebrow to Ormond.

"You would be taking his word for anything he promises. The man is not known to me."

"Then he shall curse Lord Cahir for absorbing all the doubt I wished to allow. Hang."

The man was dragged, kicking and screaming from the circle. Essex hooked his finger like death's scythe.

"Next."

A man with a long beard and unkempt hair stumbled forward, his hands bound before him. He wore a tattered coat and filthy pants dusted with dirt as he was pushed towards them.

"Do they all look like this?" Essex said. "Do they ever wash or just roll around the fields all day after their beloved cows?"

Ormond ignored him while the courtiers the Lord Deputy brought from England all laughed.

"I know this man," Ormond said. "He is Aidan MacSheehy, a man formerly in my employment."

Essex smirked.

"This should be an easy case. A definite hang if you don't want to look weak in front of your men."

"Don't be so hasty. I have a mission for this man. You need a bit of guile in these parts."

"Something that is not required on the high seas?"

"I do not point barbs at you, lord. I merely mean to act as your light in an unfamiliar land."

"Unfamiliar or not, do not let me think you are soft, or we may have a falling out."

"Fear not. I am as sharp and strong as an axe head. I merely advise upon how to best spend one's energy."

"I suppose I will extend you the benefit of the doubt, as you have always been a loyal servant of the Queen, if not one of her favourites. Especially from nobles that hark from these shores."

Ormond bowed his head with dubious intent.

"I am glad the Queen holds me in such high esteem, and I hope you also will in the future."

"Enough of this tomfoolery. Let us tell the man his fate instead of lobbing courtier compliments at each other."

Ormond got up and loomed over the prisoner.

"Aidan MacSheehy, you were wise enough to turncoat to me once, but even though you turned away from me, would you be so wise as to join me again?"

"My mind may be feeble, but my body strong. I command twenty men who will follow me. If I commit to you now, it will be the last time I turn my coat."

"Glad to hear it, but your men will have to make their own case, for as you can see, we have plenty of men."

"They will prove useful to you, lord, should you give them a chance."

"My concern is more whether you take your chance. I have a dangerous mission for you. However, it is either that or the rope. Which is your desire?"

"I pledge my axe to you, lord. You may do with me as you wish."

"Then it is settled. Hire. Send in the next man."

CHAPTER 24

ERRAND BOY

The woods echoed with the agonised cries of those whom the Lord Deputy had hung. Aidan MacSheehy watched and gave a morbid prayer of thanks that he had been handed a reprieve. The terms of his redemption were rammed into his ears, and the swinging bodies were pointed to as examples of punishment for failure or treachery.

Aidan MacSheehy was thrust onto a horse and sent on his errand. A day later, he arrived at the entrance to the rebel camp, but three armed guards blocked his way. His heart pounded against his ribcage like a drum as he knew that one wrong move could cost him his life.

"I have come from Cahir Castle. I need to speak to Murrogh at once." He hid his shaking hand behind his leg.

"How did you escape from there? We hear it was under siege by a huge English army?"

"It was. I am a spy for the rebels, so I have my ways and means, which I cannot disclose to you. I have a message for Murrogh, which I must get to him immediately. Show me to his tent, for this is of the utmost importance."

"How do we know you are not a spy for the Lord Deputy?"

"Murrogh will vouch for me. We share the history of the MacSheehy and our service to the Earl."

The guard looked him up and down and decided that if the worst came to worst, they could quickly subdue him.

"I will take you," the guard said. "You two stay here."

Murrogh sat outside his tent, polishing his breastplate while shouting instructions to some young recruits who were sparring before him.

"Keep your staff up. If you don't, he will hit you on the side of the head, and then you are dead."

The guard stood and waited for the opportune moment to interrupt.

"What?" Murrogh glanced upwards, his vision slightly obscured by the sun peaking out from behind a cloud.

"You have a visitor, lord." The guard held back the name to test his identity. Murrogh shielded his gaze to identify the person.

"Aidan MacSheehy," he growled. "What rock have you crawled out from under?"

"The rock of Cahir, lord," and Aiden bowed his head in deference. "It has fallen to the crown, and they have perpetrated a massacre on those brave rebel soldiers that held out until the end."

"Well, not all of them did, given you're here. Whose shilling are you taking now?"

"I think we got off on the wrong foot somewhere along the line. My name is MacSheehy, and I wish to fight for the clan."

Murrogh stroked his chin.

"You present me with a dilemma. Either you want to fight for the clan, which means the price on my head is too low. This situation is both bad for my ego and likely to do nothing to rally any true MacSheehy back to the cause. Or, the price on my head is high, which brings out the subterfuge in you. Which is it?"

"Can it be neither?"

"Will the tame wolf still bite?"

Murrogh picked up a blade from the ground and began to polish it, ensuring Aidan could see the sharpness of the edge.

"I can show you the bodies hanging from the trees, and you can see them with your own eyes. Then, you can decide what price lies upon your head. Let it not be said that we both served under Ormond, striding to preserve the clan for another day."

"The least said about our shared histories with Ormond in these circles, the better. At least the youth only have rumours and not memories. I will ride with you to see these bodies you claim to have seen. But I will first instruct my men to place the highest price on any of your relatives they come across should I not return."

"You will return to fetch them for revenge, and my relatives will remain unmolested."

Aidan bowed. Murrogh ignored him and called for his horse.

Murrogh surveyed the land around Cahir Castle from the advantage of a low hill. He saw the smoke rising from the castle, a black plume in an otherwise blue sky. The wind blew stronger, carrying a sour smell of char and timber as if all the trees in the area had been set ablaze. Murrogh turned his gaze towards the sky, but nothing stirred there except lazy white clouds. A crackle drew his attention back to the ground. Burning tree trunks littered the landscape, the charred bark still smouldering despite the dampness in the air. In the distance, a ferocious roar echoed through the valley, reverberating off nearby hills.

Aidan gestured to the smoke on the far-off horizon. "We can see that the English army is advancing through Munster and leaving a trail of destruction behind them, which may seem unpleasant," he said. "But what I must now show you is truly horrific."

Murrogh sighed.

"Lead on, for I cannot escape this day without my eyes being scarred."

They rode through the fields and woods, the sound of their horse's hooves muffled by the thick grass beneath them, watching for any movement that might signal an ambush. Nothing came but wear and tear on the men's nerves. They entered a circle in the woods, and Murrogh shielded his face.

"By God's eyes, what scene from hell do we have the misfortune to intrude upon?"

The foreboding canopy of the trees held an eerie yet familiar sight — a macabre gallery of former rebels, their skin stretched and taut against the branches, limp arms dangling below. Their faces were contorted in agony, eyes bulging from their sockets, tongues grotesquely extended from their mouths in a perpetual plea for mercy. The foul stench of sulphur and rot hung heavy in the air while a deep crimson oozed over the ground, pooling beneath each dead body. Their necks were broken and limbs twisted in unnatural poses, bellies sliced open, and entrails spilling out onto the parched earth. Blackened tongues lay motionless between swollen lips, stark against ashen faces drained of life-giving blood. Crows hovered above the corpses, sharp beaks like knives as they picked at the grisly remains. All around, eerily silent — only the mournful moaning of the trees and the haunting caw of birds echoed through the forest.

Murrogh raised his head from the crook of his elbow once more to lay sight on the bodies of the former rebels. He fell to his knees and swore vengeance.

"This abomination cannot go unanswered. Whoever ordered this is truly a devil."

Murrogh galloped back to the rebel camp, dispatching some men to bury the bodies and a priest to bless the ground to save it from being eternally cursed. He then went straight to the Earl's tent.

The Earl stumbled around his tent, swinging a wine bottle in his hand, cursing his luck and inability to escape the past. His father's wealth had been confiscated when he was in his youth. Once the Queen cut him off from his promised pension, he lived a life of relative poverty compared with the new landed gentry of Munster — not to mention the true poverty of the remaining local clans that now tilled his land. His situation seemed to have improved in reputation only since his new title commanded respect but no riches. He dwelt in a tent, wandering around Munster looking for the elusive wealth he felt should go with his newly found rank. Each time the flap on the tent door opened, he cursed; it was either a frigid blast of wind or someone asking him for something he couldn't — or wouldn't — give. Murrogh suddenly charged through the door and fell straight to his knees. At least he could always be counted on for some flattery.

"Lord, I have a heinous crime to report to you. One that cannot go unavenged."

The Earl's heart deflated. A freezing blast of air penetrated the door, a suitable topping for the pending bad news.

"Can you not take care of it? Is this not what my MacSheehy are for? Just tell me when the enormous battles are to be fought, or a siege is to be laid so I can make a speech, and I will gladly leave all the battles or the tit-for-tat stuff to you."

Murrogh bowed his head so his face would not give away his frustration.

"May I be so bold to say, now is one of those times when you need to lead, my lord. A great crime has been perpetrated against your people, and you must be shown to sympathise with them and avenge their cause. Anything less will be seen as a sign of weakness, and heads may turn to see if another, like your brother, should be the earl."

Murrogh raised his head to see the Earl's knuckles turn white.

"No one will challenge my commitment to the cause. Take your men and commit a deed that will make our foes think twice before perpetrating such a heinous crime upon my people again."

Murrogh stood up and bowed.

"What we shall do will live long in their memory."

Smoke climbed a ladder of pain into the sky. The ground shook with the thundering of hooves as Essex and Ormond rode to the rear of their column escorted by the Lord Deputy's bodyguards. A scout pointed the way to where the act of revenge had been perpetrated. They rode to a clearing in the woods where the ambush had taken place.

Essex took a step forward, his nostrils instantly assaulted by the rancid stench of death that permeated the air. The silence echoed all around him like a sigh held in the lungs. Overturned carts and dead bodies surrounded him. The carts had been looted, and the chests dragged off and prised open. Tattered clothes decorated the trees and drowned in mud puddles. They were strewn across the road, limbs tangled and separated from their bodies. A pile of clothes lay at his feet like great drops of blood staining the ground, flowers coiled up with them, escaping through holes in their coats as if made for beds to lie upon with unearthly maggots for bedfellows.

"They are truly cowards if all they have the nerve to do is to attack the baggage train and women and children."

But something brought Essex to his knees and a tear to his eye. He knelt beside a body and tearfully closed his eyes.

"My cook." His heart wrenched, for he took this as an attack on his person. He held the sides of his eyelids and the bridge of his nose as if it would hold back the tears. "The man was a magician in the kitchen, and all he got for his troubles was a knife in his belly from cowards and knaves."

Ormond stood over him, his face as grey as his hair.

"This is what it is like over here. A world of ambushes and tit-for-tat reprisals. I thought if we could get any good from your mass hangings it would be to draw them out. But if this is all they can manage, they must be weak. This is the act of bandits, not warriors."

Essex rose. His face froze in resolve.

"They are but cowards who think themselves men. I will resolve this once and for all."

Essex strode off towards his horse, and Ormond trailed behind him, wondering what he would do.

CHAPTER 25

THE FORBIDDEN FIGHT

T he night closed around the camp like a thick blanket of dread, the shadows seeping into every corner and crevice until the darkness seemed to swallow it whole. The yellow and orange flicker of flames illuminated the solemn faces of the rebels as they huddled in grim groups, conversation only carried out in hushed tones. Fear clung to their skin like a second layer, news of the hangings having spread like wildfire through the camp.

Suddenly, from deep within the darkness, a tall figure emerged, cloaked in black and with his face hidden by shadows. In his hands, he held a single white envelope, which he carried slowly and carefully across the camp until he came to a stop in front of Aidan Mac Sheehy.

The part-time rebel looked up, his tired eyes widening in surprise. He knew this messenger could only be coming from Ormond. With trembling fingers, he accepted the envelope, finding inside a single, white piece of paper and a letter with the wax seal of the Lord Deputy. His heart raced faster, his breath catching in his throat.

The messenger said nothing before fading back into the darkness just as silently as he had come. Aidan clutched the paper tightly in his hands, determination and resolve burning brightly in his eyes. The message written on it said simply. "Give this letter to Murrogh". So Aidan went into Murrogh's tent to give him the letter and returned to wait. Once Murrogh had read the letter, he stuck his head out from his tent.

"Aidan, Aidan, come here."

Aidan had somehow worked his way back into being trusted by Murrogh. Maybe it was because he reminded Murrogh they had been employed by Ormond, yet both of them had turned to the rebels, albeit at different times and for different reasons. But what made Aidan appear valuable to Murrogh was that he received a letter from the Lord Deputy through his intermediaries. More importantly, he had given it first to Murrogh so he could see if it was advantageous to pass it on to the Earl. But now, Murrogh wanted him to perform another duty.

"Go and find some red wax. I need to make it look as if the letter was unopened."

Aidan did not move.

"How will you replicate the Lord Deputy's seal?"

"Don't you worry about that. I will open the letter so no one will notice."

"Is it good news?" Aidan said, pointing at the letter.

"Excellent news for the MacSheehy. Now go."

The Earl summoned Seamus and Richard Tyrell to his tent to open the Lord Deputy's letter, for they commanded the bulk of the rebel army, and the Earl would, at the very least, have to consult with them depending on the letter's contents. As Seamus stepped into the tent, a chill ran down his spine. The room was dark and filled with shadows, and the faint glow of the candles did little to illuminate it. The air was thick with the scent of wine, which clung to him like a veil of uncertainty. It spoke to him of someone working up the courage to be bold and make a decision. He looked around the room, noticing the muted colours of the fabrics all splattered in mud and the array of mostly open bottles on the table.

The silence was palpable, and Seamus could feel all eyes upon him as he navigated his way through the room. He took up position in the corner of the tent, though he sensed this did little to ease the tension lingering in the air. He took a mug from the table and filled it. The lingering silence only nurtured his suspicion.

"What's going on here, then?" Seamus said. His eyes darted around the room like a scythe chopping down corn, for no one dared look him in the eye. "I see you have not acquired any guts even though you linger in the shadows." Seamus saw the flash of anger in Murrogh's eye and grinned. "How come you are at a loss for words?"

"I am not," Murrogh said through gritted teeth. "Nor do I disrespect the Earl."

Seamus took a swig from his mug.

"I will show respect when the Earl deserves it. We all know he is only Earl as long as I am here, for I represent the real power with the soldiers of the O'Neill. Now, out with it. Why did you call me here in the middle of the night? I would much rather be in other places, such as my bed."

"We are sorry the freedom of your own people is such an inconvenience to you," Murrogh said. "We have received a letter from the Lord Deputy, and the Earl will read it." Murrogh picked up the letter from the table and held it out for the Earl in defiance of Seamus. The Earl hesitated and looked to Seamus as if asking permission to take the letter.

"We have no authority to accept terms or declare a truce," Seamus said. "That is the sole preserve of the O'Neill."

Murrogh stood unmoved.

"The MacSheehy stand behind the Earl and his decisions."

"Do that," Seamus said. "See if I care. The northerners and I will sit back and watch you fight the Lord Deputy yourselves if you wish. I reckon you only have one battle left in you, given how you took casualties at Kilmallock Castle. You only survived because the Maguires came and saved you."

"You mock, yet you were too cowardly to fight."

Seamus threw down his mug and squared up to Murrogh. Richard put his mug down and rushed over to place himself between them.

"All we have between us is our family name and the past. Don't try me, for I may forget both."

"Our father would turn in his grave to hear you would fight your own brother. You chose Cian over me. After all I had done to protect and keep you safe, you chose him over me."

"For all his faults, brother, he did not slaughter the pride of his own clan or sell them out to the enemy. You did that all by yourself."

"I saved both you and your brother in the process. I tried to salvage as much of the clan as I could. No one else had the foresight to do that except me."

"I'm sure those you butchered in a field were glad to sacrifice themselves so you could live."

"Enough of this," Richard said. "We must put our differences aside, for the enemy is hard enough to defeat without us doing the job for him. Now let the Earl read the letter, and you can sort out your differences later."

Seamus sneered and backed away. He picked up a spare mug from the table and filled it.

"Since we are not here to explore my sordid family history, you may as well read the letter while we are all here," Seamus said.

The Earl emerged from the shadows paler than when he entered them. Unbeknownst to him, he was enmeshed in a family feud. But he wished to appease the glaring eyes upon him, so he held the letter up to the candlelight so he could see it better. He was about to read it out loud when he read ahead and realised what the contents were. His face contorted the more he read, and the more his face contorted, the more curiosity grew in his companions.

"What does it say?" Murrogh said.

The Earl held the letter out in front of himself and squinted to ensure the words said what they said. Seamus crossed his arms and drummed his fingers.

"The letter is mainly a long rant, but the gist of it is that we insulted the Lord Deputy by killing his innocent cook. Therefore, he wants to end the war as quickly as possible and challenges us to a duel. Fifty of his best men against fifty of ours in a field, and the loser withdraws permanently from Munster. He will take part with many of the nobles he brought from England, and he expects us to bring men of a similar calibre. If we wish to accept, send a letter to him in his camp, and we can name the venue where to fight the duel."

Murrogh's eyes lit up. He looked to the tent's roof and spread his arms like an evangelist.

"The hour of the MacSheehy's greatest victory is upon us. We can redeem the clan in front of the people of Munster, in front of our forefathers, in front of ourselves. We all can become Galloglass again. To take the head of the Lord Deputy in single combat would be the making of a legend."

Seamus turned away to shut down the conversation.

"You're not going," Seamus said.

"What!" Murrogh spun around to confront him.

"This is a trap. You would realise it if you were thinking straight. They will massacre you before you get onto the field, along with what they suppose is the leadership of the rebellion. Then they chase the remains back to their farmsteads and return them to work."

With a swipe as brutal as the descent of any axe, Murrogh's heart wrenched as he felt his dreams of redemption cut in two. He charged at the target of his fury, and his chest bounced off Seamus's. He raised his fist but thought better of it when they locked eyes.

"Do not deny us. The Earl can easily write to the O'Neill and have you removed. I will have you banished forever from Munster for being a coward."

Seamus smirked at his brother.

"Even if it were a real offer, the English would massacre your men, and the rebellion would be over in about fifteen minutes. Accept your lot, Murrogh. You no longer command Galloglass but merely farm boys."

Murrough went so red it was as if his head were about to explode.

"I can assemble fifty warriors," Murrough shouted, gesticulating as if possessed. "It would be like the tales of old, where fifty warriors held off the entire heathen army."

Seamus shook his head.

"More like the sad, cautionary tale of fifty hangings, swiftly followed by a dead earl."

No sooner had the words 'dead earl' settled in the air than a hand rested on Murrogh's shoulders.

"Maybe we should reconsider this. It may be a trap after all."

Murrogh could see the argument slipping away from him. He coughed as memories and emotions overwhelmed him. His finger trembled as he pointed it in Seamus's face.

"You haven't heard the last of this."

"I'd better have." Seamus stood out of his way to allow him an escape route.

Fáolán sat outside the tent, watching the shadows dance upon the canvas, waiting for his master. Murrogh brushed past him as he stormed out of the tent. Seamus trailed quickly after, and a flicker from the fire illuminated his wrathful mood. Fáolán jumped out of his seat to follow Seamus as if he were his dog.

"I take it they know about Black Mountain?" Fáolán said. It was more of a statement than a question, for half the camp knew the shouting had been so loud.,

"Just the pertinent facts, but my shame is out there for all to see."

A figure in the shadows stole into the night.

CHAPTER 26

THE DIE IS CAST

I t was morning the next day, and a haze hung over the rebel camp as a warm breeze blew in from the west. It smelt of the woods, the dampness of land, and men. The smoke from a dozen fires swirled in lazy coils and curled into the air. The assigned hunters brought back the latest batch of rabbits and squirrels. It was mainly allocated to make soup, with some of the larger specimens set aside for the officers, and the smell of roasting rabbit soon gained ascendancy in the air. However, a tasty prize had been reserved for Aidan MacSheehy.

"Here," the man said as he held a rabbit aloft. "Take it with two hands, as she is an awkward bugger."

Aidan reached for the rabbit and felt a significant gap in the fur. The man smiled.

"I got two Queen's shillings for this."

Aidan nodded.

"Did you open it?"

"Of course not."

"Then, as you have proved yourself reliable, there should be plenty more shillings from where that came from."

The man nodded and smiled again, then went on his way. Aidan stuffed the letter into his pocket and waited until he found somewhere private to read it. Once he had read it, he held it tight and went to find Murrogh.

Murrogh was sitting on the edge of a field watching his recruits spar before him, taking his frustration out on a stalk of barley he was chewing.

"Parry, parry. If you hold your stick out like that, you'll get your head knocked off."

He looked to see Aidan approach him with a rueful grin.

"Look at this latest batch we have received that claims to be related to the clan. They would not even have been horse boys in the old days."

"I can get you more men, men of experience," Aidan said with the letter hidden up his sleeve, waiting for the right moment.

"Are these men of experience trustworthy?" Murrogh glanced at Aidan, telling him he was not quite trusted yet.

"They can all fight, for they have been bandits in the woods for years. They may soon recall the discipline of the Galloglass training of their youth, but since they were turfed off their lands, they had little chance to use it."

Murrogh took the barley stalk out of his mouth and threw it on the ground.

"'Tis a familiar refrain you're singing. Many of the best men we get are from the woods, but they are not the Galloglass of old. They excel at arson, theft, and making examples of English tenants, but they have yet to be truly tested in a proper fight. I fear the day I lead a charge in open battle and have to look behind me to see if they are still there."

"What about the siege of Kilmallock Castle? Did they not hold their own then?"

"Those worthy warriors did hold their own, but most unfortunately, they gave their blood for whatever ground they gained. Most who survived ran away. Here I am now, once more in a field attempting to train the next generation of MacSheehy Galloglass, always with that nagging feeling: Will they be the last?"

"They may not be." Aidan reached into his sleeve and pulled out the letter.

Murrogh's face stiffened as he looked at the contents of Aidan's hand.

"Has anyone else seen this?"

"No. I brought it straight to you. I think like you do. This duel is the quickest way to end this war and restore the pride of the MacSheehy. But you must lead them out onto the field to ensure the MacSheehy rightly attracts the glory."

Murrogh took the letter.

"I have been training if that is what you are on about."

Aidan watched as Murrogh's face creased more into seriousness the deeper into the letter he got.

"He specifies where the duel is to take place," Murrogh said as he continued reading. "I know this place. It is open, preventing either side from going there purely intending to set a trap. I think he is serious about having a duel."

"By all accounts, the Lord Deputy is an English gentleman trapped in a gentleman's world and shuns any advice on the customs of these shores."

"Thereby, he has already ensured his downfall. He knows not that he is now in a world of beasts. Tell your contact we will be at the arranged place at the agreed time, adhere to his terms, and honour the consequences. He has my word as the head of the MacSheehy clan."

Aidan nodded and turned to leave.

"Take the letter and dispose of it well," Murrogh said, handing it back to Aidan. Aidan took it and threw it on a fire in the MacSheehy camp on his way to report back to his English masters. However, the flash of the red seal caught the eye of enterprising hands, who fished out the letter while most of the contents were still visible. The man rubbed those same hands together when he realised his catch was worth many a pretty shilling.

Murrogh had hidden himself away from the camp for days, burdened by the weight of his mission. His hands trembled as he gave orders to his novices on the training field, and sleep barely came anymore. In his head, it was either victory or death, a chance to redeem the MacSheehy from all their past suffering. He conducted trials without telling them what they were fighting for and, after much deliberation, chose fifty of his most skilled warriors. They trained separately from the others who couldn't make it, trying to build camaraderie between an unlikely group of misfits.

Finally, the day of battle had arrived, and Murrogh rose from his tent, having had little rest. His fingers clenched into tight fists as he issued the order to march.

With every step, opposing forces clashed in him: hope that he could accomplish this task and sheer terror at what lay ahead. He kept striding forward, determined to see his mission through until its bitter end.

He had to outwit Seamus, so he carefully plotted a confusing path through woods and valleys to the battlefield. His heart raced faster with every step, pounding like drums in his ears as he drew closer to his fate.

"You'll thank me for this one day," St Leger said.

"What? Thank you for putting me in harm's way with no discernible benefit to myself? I don't think so." Taaffe snarled as he stood with his arms out, getting measured by the Lord Deputy's armourer. St Leger did not need additional armour as he was already well equipped, so he supervised Taaffe in getting fitted for his. It was partly to ensure Taaffe followed his orders but mainly to watch him squirm. He hid his amusement at Taaffe's discomfort by covering his face with his hand.

"Why didn't you volunteer Shea Óg for this job?" Taaffe said. "It is far more his line of work than mine."

"Stop complaining. You will earn the Lord Deputy's trust and respect by taking part in a duel with him. Once he trusts you, then we'll all be richer."

Taaffe scowled.

"What if I die out there? We won't all be richer then."

"Stop complaining and put your energy into your training. If you are lucky, you could face off with Eunan Maguire and smash his head in. We would all be richer courtesy of Cormac O'Cassidy, your sponsor."

Taaffe wriggled as the sides of the breastplate chaffed his skin.

"I hate these things. Their weight saps my energy and reduces the swing of my sword."

St Leger smirked, enjoying this small measure of revenge on his underling, who had grown too big for his boots trying to get in with the Lord Deputy.

"You will just have to live with it if you'll excuse the pun. The Lord Deputy wants all fifty of his warriors dressed the same. It looks more impressive on the battlefield, or so he says."

"Surely he would easily have fifty men in his retinue that would love to participate in this duel without dragging me into it?"

"You should feel honoured. If I am going to do this, then you are too. Come on."

Now fully kitted out in his armour, Taaffe trudged after St Leger.

They arrived in the open area of the camp where Essex was fencing with one of his men. Taaffe looked on with surprise and jealousy, for the Lord Deputy was kitted out in a white shirt and blue breeches as if he had not yet gotten dressed. Essex signalled for his companion to stop the training when he caught sight of Taaffe and St Leger in their armour. He skipped over to them with the joviality of a teenage boy about to take part in his first duel rather than the duelling veteran he really was. He went over and slapped Taaffe's breastplate.

"There he is, the scourge of the Macs and Oes. I have told the boys here how many locals you have put to the sword. So we decided that you will be part of our sledgehammer that will charge the enemy and break them open, and then we'll charge in and cut down the scum. Sound like a plan to you?"

Essex's smiling face said there was only one reply.

"Yes, lord."

"Good man." Essex walloped him on his back plate. "Now I have some of the finest young men in all of England with me, and I have been promising them some sport for a long time, but the Macs and Oes do not want to play ball and keep running off into the woods. Will they show up this time?"

St Leger stepped in, determined to take this opportunity to raise his profile with the Lord Deputy.

"We have insulted their pride enough, and the leader of the MacSheehy is a proud man, if anything. Once we butcher his best men, all the memories of how we always defeated the MacSheehy in the past will come flooding back, and the province will fall. Today will be a glorious victory for you, lord."

Essex laughed.

"Good, let's get on with it then."

CHAPTER 27
THE TALE OF A FIELD

The Lord Deputy and his men spurred their horses to the appointed field, throwing dust clouds into the air. Ormond followed with a column of steel-clad warriors behind him. Essex leapt from his horse, his cape fanning out like a storm cloud. He thrust his hands on his hips and closed his eyes, inhaling the tension that thickened the atmosphere. A feral smile spread across his face as he revelled in the moment.

"Today is a good day for rebel scum to die, but not me."

He strode over to Ormond, who had also dismounted.

"So, have you ensured this is not a trap?"

"To the best of my men's scouting abilities, they have seen no sizeable rebel formations in the area, but I would suggest walking around the woods rather than through them to access the field—just to exercise some caution."

Essex laughed.

"I think your age has got the better of you and would have you become a hesitant old man. We must be bold and seize the moment, and the rebellion must be crushed."

Ormond nodded politely. He wondered how long this Lord Deputy would last. He had seen off many Lord Deputies in his career, and this one was the most reckless of them all.

"Only one rebel party has been seen in the area, and I assume they are the MacSheehy. I'm surprised they fell for your goading, but here we are."

"Here we are indeed. When victory is gained, I will ensure you are granted some handsome tracts of land. Then I suggest you retire and enjoy them and leave the fighting to the young men."

Ormond gritted his teeth.

"You are most generous in acknowledging my assistance, lord."

"Think nothing of it, I don't. Now let us go onto the field and wait for our foes."

Murrogh and his men marched in high spirits through the woods on the other side of the field. Aidan marched alongside Murrogh. The sweat on his brow was soon evident.

"What's wrong? Are you nervous about today? I have only asked you to act as a guide, not to fight. You can leave if you wish."

Aidan tensed up and sputtered, eager to impress.

"And have the men think me a coward? No, lord. For that would condemn me to be excluded from the MacSheehy forever. No, I may have a chill, for such ailments multiply in the camps of men. I could wield a sword if I had to, but your Galloglass will have won the day by the time I get there."

"I am only pulling your leg. You will not be needed out there today. How is the sky looking? Are we on time?"

Aidan looked through the woods' canopy and between the clouds at the scrapings of blue sky. A white fluffy blob obscured the sun, but it shone enough to give Aidan an accurate reading of the time.

"I think we may be slightly late."

"Then we should up the pace," Murrogh said as he signalled to his men.

"It is good to let your enemy stand in the elements as they wait for you to arrive," Aidan said, not masking his concern at the upturn in pace.

"We do not want them to leave and think we were cowards by not showing up."

Aidan smiled.

"If only our fathers could see us now."

Murrogh looked away, for he did not need the additional burden of estimating what the clan's glorious dead would think of his actions.

They turned a corner, and a solitary figure stood defiantly across their path. His men halted, and Murrogh pushed his way to the forefront of the column. When he saw who had confronted him, he seethed with fury and spat contemptuously on the ground.

"Murrogh," Seamus said. "Come speak to me commander to commander, and let us not have it out in front of the men."

Seamus was bathed in the shadows of the woods, and the thickets sprouted from every available space. It was difficult to estimate if Seamus was alone. The air swirled out of Murrogh's nostrils, spreading rage upon the already tense atmosphere. He stormed towards his brother.

"It is only because you are the emissary of the O'Neill that I did not order the men to shoot you off the road."

Seamus grabbed him by the elbow and dragged him around the corner of the bend. Murrogh wanted to shake him off but thought better of it, for he did not want to physically fight with another commander in front of the men.

"What the hell are you—"

But Seamus grimaced and thrust his face into Murrogh's. He signalled to Murrogh to look around him. Behind the thickets and just out of sight of his own men, the O'Neill shot smiled and raised their hands to salute him.

"I meant it when I said not to have this duel," Seamus said, his eyes protruding from his red face. "If you attempt to lead your men out onto that field, I will cut you down before you get there, and if I do so, I will spill far less MacSheehy blood than you ever did."

"Is this how it is to be? Are you a tool of the O'Neill now?"

"No, you fool, I am a tool of the rebellion, and as its tool, I have an obligation to keep it alive."

"You are a traitor to your clan," Murrogh said, prodding Seamus's chest. "This is the opportunity we have waited twenty-five years for. What would your father think of what you are doing now?"

"Do not bring our father, Cian or any of our forefathers into this, and I will not mention how you finished off the remains of the clan on the order of Ormond to save your own skin. We are here now and owe an obligation to our men, to the leaders of the rebellion, and to the people of Ireland not to throw away what freedom they have for your own foolish pride and sense of redemption. Now tell your men to turn around and go back to camp, for if I have to do it then they will never follow you again."

"Then your plan will be complete to take the MacSheehy from me."

"Your MacSheehy are farm boys who are an insult to the name, and I have far better men with their guns aimed at you. Now, make your choice."

Murrogh snarled at Seamus and shook his fists at the sky.

"God damn you."

He turned and walked back towards his men.

Essex stood in the middle of the field and scraped the top of his head with his hand. St Leger stood beside him, sweating in his armour as the weight on his shoulders grew and grew. He wished to edge away, for the more the day rolled on, the less likely it was the rebels would appear, and the Lord Deputy would then look for someone to blame. Essex now turned to him.

"They are not coming, are they?"

"They are cowards and liars, lord."

"First, they killed my cook, and now they are making a fool out of me. There will be retribution for this, mark my words."

Eager to take the opportunity to deflect any blame, St Leger ran after him.

"What would you have us do, lord."

"Make sure we take ten lives for each one we lost in the raid where the cook died."

St Leger saluted and hollered at Taaffe to follow him.

Freed from their armour to cause mayhem, St Leger and Taaffe unleashed a wave of destruction upon the two nearby helpless villages. Fire blazed through the homes, and cries of agony filled the air as the citizens were hung from the gallows in retribution as they felt the Lord Deputy's wrath. Murrogh watched in despair as pillars of dark smoke billowed into the sky, searing his mind with memories of his own cowardice. Filled with renewed courage, he declared that never again would he succumb to fear and let his brother stand in his way.

CHAPTER 28

THE HILL

Eunan trudged through the thicket leading up to Augher Castle, avoiding the main road, for he did not want any innocent well-wishers to disturb his line of thought. His throat was dry and tight as the fortification loomed above him and his chest tightened in anticipation of what might await him in the castle. He could feel the cold sweat forming on his brow, and he struggled to steady his breathing. The sun glared off its stone walls, forcing Eunan to shield his eyes. Though Eunan knew he had to go forward, his feet felt like lead.

He had left his ailing wife with child back home while his father-in-law still greeted him with the same contempt as always. Odhran's voice echoed in his ear: "Go on, lord," he said. "See if you have a child." Taking a deep breath, Eunan steeled himself for whatever awaited within the castle's walls. He fought his way out of the thicket and trudged up the hill. He could see faces looking out from the tower and then darting away, so he could only assume he had been recognised. He speculated who was looking down upon him, and a shiver went down his spine as he hoped his father-in-law was away on campaign. The door to the tower opened, and some of the women ran down the hill towards him. Their smiles bounced like the wildflowers bobbing in the long grass, so surely all they could bring were good tidings?

"Eunan, Eunan, come with us," they said as they took both his hands and attempted to skip back up to the tower. But the slope to ward off foe this time wore down friend, and they were soon reduced to a trudge.

They reached the door, and Eunan bowed to them.

"Thank you, ladies, for your kind escort, but I fear you have exhausted me when I have two flights of stairs yet to climb."

"You'll certainly need to save your energy," one of the girls said as she smiled coyly. She received a swift elbow in the arm.

"Shh, it's not your tale to tell."

Eunan squinted at them.

"I assume whatever I'm to be told is good, for there is a smile on every face and laughter in the air?"

"It's not our tale to tell," the girls said, skipping back into the fields, leaving Eunan standing in front of the door alone.

One of Cormac's constables opened the door, and the musty waft of the castle drifted up Eunan's nostrils.

"Come in, Eunan. The master will see you now."

Eunan entered the castle hall to see a faint smile dancing on Cormac's face. Was this euphoria personified in his father-in-law's restricted emotional range, whose normal mode was concern or, in Eunan's case, disapproval?

"Everyone else was banned from telling you either by word of mouth or stroke of the quill, for I wished to keep the pleasure all to myself."

Cormac reached down, took a mug, and raised it aloft.

"Eunan, you have a son. Maodhóg Maguire."

Eunan stepped back, and he heard all the air exit his lungs. He looked to the ground, and the periphery went blurry. He heard heavy breathing, and it felt like it came from the back of a cave. He felt two warm patches on his body. He began to sway.

"Now come and sit down here. It was a shock to me also."

Cormac guided Eunan to a seat.

"Now breathe."

Cormac bowed over with his hands on his knees, stared Eunan in the eye and began to breathe deeply with exaggerated noise for guidance. Eunan copied him, but his head gradually ceased to spin.

"Drink this." Cormac handed him some ale.

Eunan sipped slowly until his wits had recovered.

"When...when did this happen?"

"The boy is four weeks old. My spies, I mean informants, told me you were deeply engaged in the complicated politics of Munster, and it was best that you not be disturbed."

"You have spies watching me?" Eunan gripped the arms of the chair.

"Not spies as such and definitely not on you," Cormac said as he turned red. "We were never going to send an army south without a spy network to support it. You will always be mentioned somewhere, for you are the commander of the forces of one of our biggest allies. It was mentioned in passing."

Eunan shook the anger away, for even though he did not accept the answer, he knew he was not in a position to argue.

"We will discuss it another time," Eunan said. "Your son-in-law can report to you himself without the intervention of spies."

Cormac gulped and nodded.

"Now tell me about my son. Is he in good health?"

"Your son has been fortunate to get his mother's looks, but your constitution. He is well and is very capable of screaming the castle down should we hesitate with his food or do not accommodate him with a timely nap."

"And Sorcha?" Eunan could not maintain eye contact when he asked the question.

"Sorcha is... Well, Sorcha. Even through all the joy of achieving all she wanted to with the birth of her son she has managed to conjure up another set of illnesses that evade even the most expensive physicians her father's money can buy. She remains in her bed with her maids doing most of the attending to the child. We hope she will become fit enough soon to become the mother she always aspired to be."

Eunan leaned forward.

"My boy has a name?"

"That is a matter between husband and wife, not father-in-law and son-in-law."

Eunan sat back to take it all in.

"Can I go and see her?"

"She sleeps, but I'm sure she would not mind being woken for you. I will take you there when you finish your ale."

Eunan picked up his mug, downed the contents and held it upside down.

"Ready."

Eunan reached the top of the steps to be greeted by the sounds of a wailing child.

"My boy," he cried, running the rest of the way to Sorcha's door, which a guard blocked.

"Greetings, lord. Both mother and child await you." He went to open the door.

"Why is there a guard at the door if she is well?" Eunan said.

"Orders of the lord. You know what he's like with regards to his daughter."

Eunan gave a faint smile. His heart raced as the door gently swung open. He had to calm down, for overexcitement would just lead to disappointment. The door opened on his wife's pale face resting on her pillow as she gently snored. He searched the room for the source of the crying, and there, bathed in light and sitting on the window seat, was a nursemaid with her finger in a child's mouth. The child sucked at ease with the world, his bawling that made his father's heart race now consigned to the past.

"Do you want to hold him?" the nurse said.

Eunan's eyes lit up, his heart filled with joy as it attempted to pound its way through his chest, but his stomach was a pit of butterflies. There lay everything he ever wanted, but did he deserve it?

"If I take him from you, will he not cry out?" Eunan stuttered.

The nurse gave the smile of one used to the world of babies and their erratic reactions.

"He will be content in the arms of his father."

Eunan's mind raced to think of excuses why he should not take his boy.

"How do I hold him? What if I drop him?"

The nurse recognised the nerves of a first-time father.

"You support his backside like this, just like you would have done with your younger siblings."

"I am an only child," Eunan said, his cheeks now turning rouge.

"Then the same way you would hold your father's bastards," the nurse said.

"As I said, I am an only child."

"Oh, then you will both need my help. Here, take the child."

The nurse thrust the child into the cradle Eunan made with his arms. She saw the flash of panic in Eunan's eyes as his son whimpered.

"Here, let me adjust him for you."

She placed Eunan's hand on his boy's backside so one arm formed a cradle, and the other was laid on top, creating a blanket.

"There. How's that?"

Eunan stared down at his boy and welled up.

"It's perfect."

He gently swayed his arm cradle from side to side as his boy slept. He swore he would be the best father he could be and never treat his son as his parents had treated him.

"Would you like to sit in the window seat? Your boy likes the gentle breeze on his head."

Panic once more possessed Eunan.

"Will that not give him a chill? So many children die young, and it cannot happen to my boy, for I fear I will have only one."

The nurse smiled reassuringly again.

"The child must learn to live with the elements, especially in a cold and windy tower like this. He likes the breeze on his head, and so far, he does not take after his mother and her ailments."

"So you think he would be better off living by the lakes with me for his health?"

The nurse recoiled, for she knew she had to tread carefully.

"I could not say, for I am unfamiliar with the lakes and where you live. You would need to have that conversation with the master rather than the lowly nurse."

Eunan did not want to alienate his only source of knowledge of children.

"Excuse my rudeness, please. I did not mean to make you uncomfortable, but I fear I have the nerves of a new father, and words defeat rather than assist me."

The nurse heaved a sigh of relief.

"You can rest assured, for I have been assigned to tend to mother and baby for as long as I am required."

Eunan smiled.

"My stomach churns at the sight of my boy, but you help reassure me. I am grateful for your help. But I must ask now after my wife. How did she deal with childbirth, and is she any better now than when she was with child?"

"That is her tale to tell. Now, give me your son so you may wake your wife. I will feed and bathe the boy and return when you are done talking."

Eunan smiled at the boy in his arms and passed him to the nurse. He leant over and shook Sorcha's shoulder. Her eyes shot open, and she stared at the roof.

CHAPTER 29

JOY AND SORROW

"Eunan, my love. Is that you?" She stared at the ceiling, and her arms wriggled out from under her blanket. They explored the space above her head, tentacles seeking her husband's face.

Eunan reached out, plucked her right hand from the air, and held it to his beating heart.

"I am here. Can you feel me?"

Sorcha gave a faint smile and rolled her head from side to side as if trying to figure out where she was. Eunan broke into a cold sweat and fought back tears as his imagination raced as to what had happened to his wife giving birth to his boy. Surely it was his fault? The nurse came up behind him and placed her free hand on his shoulder.

"She lost her vision during childbirth, but it is slowly returning. Give her a chance, for everything she sees is a blur. She will wake up properly in a minute, and the fog will lift from her head. Hold her hand tight to bring her back, and I will return with the child in a while."

Eunan squeezed his wife's hand and brought it down to rest on the bed. Her other hand followed in the direction of Eunan's voice.

"Sorry."

Eunan smiled at the apology for the squished nose and smiled at his wife, who instinctively returned it.

"How are you?" Eunan whispered in her ear. "How are you feeling?"

Sorcha freed her hand from Eunan's grip and caressed the stubble on both his cheeks. She breathed through her nostrils into the heightened senses of her nose and smelt the land off him. She imagined where he had been, slaying their foes and keeping her safe in the four walls of the castle that had become her prison. Her husband's face was a blur, but the tuft of red hair was distinctive enough through the haze.

"All the better for seeing you, even though you are a blob of ginger."

Eunan smiled, and Sorcha lowered her hand to run the tip of her finger along his teeth, which were released from behind his gums by his smile.

"You still came back to visit your sick wife even though they need heroes like you on the battlefield."

Tears formed in Eunan's eyes.

"No one is more a hero to me than you, who blinded herself just so I could have a boy."

"I did it for you, for me, for my father and the O'Neills. That's a lot of responsibility on one wee sick girl."

Eunan laughed through the tears.

"A wee sick girl who is far braver than her husband."

"How so?"

"I can deal with a crazed man swinging his axe at me, but babies terrify me."

This brought a smile to Sorcha's face.

"Don't be silly. He is only a wee thing that needs feeding, sleep and his father's love."

"That's a lot of responsibility to heap on one young man's shoulders."

"Don't you concern yourself about that and leave it up to the nurse and me. You have a war to prosecute, and when we inevitably come to a truce in the winter, you can spend some time with your son and really get to know him."

Eunan's head bowed.

"I hope I will be a good father. Better than my own at least. I know you'll make a better mother."

Sorcha patted his hand and leaned into him.

"None of how your parents acted towards you is your fault. You're a grown man with a mind of his own. There is no need to live with your head in the past."

Eunan raised his head and smiled.

"I live with my head stuck in the past, and you lie there, trapped in your broken body."

Sorcha turned her head to hide her tears. She turned back when her mood recovered.

"So how long have you been released for? How long do we have together?"

Eunan let go of her hands and turned away.

"I am at the whim of the Maguire, the O'Donnell and their messengers as usual. Any minute a rider could tear past the corner of the woods and ascend the hill and I would be gone without the time to pack my bags or even say goodbye. We should live each moment as if it were our last, for at any moment, I could fall to the axe and you to what ails you."

Sorcha reached out and grabbed his hands with both of hers.

"Let us live as you suggested. Lift me in your arms and take me to the window, and let us look out onto the land as we did when we first met."

"Are you allowed to leave your bed? Will you be able to see anything? Will you not get possessed by a chill?"

Sorcha gave him a playful grin.

"Is making excuses living every moment as if it were your last? I think looking at a blurry bush or a mash of blue and white and trying to work out what time of day it is is far more like living every moment. Do you not think so?"

Eunan realised there was no point in arguing and slid his arms beneath the covers and beneath her body, lifting her off the bed. The covers fell to the ground, and he walked over and lowered her to rest gently on the window seat.

"Can you see the woods at the bottom of the hill?" he asked.

"My eyes may fail me, but in my mind's eye, I can see us strolling past the corner of the woods to the brook to dip our feet in the water. It feels so cold, but your smile warms me up, and in my embarrassment, I flick water at you with my toes."

Eunan looked out. All he could see were black clouds swirling overhead.

"You have far better vision than me," he said, and he did not spoil Sorcha's dreams by telling her what he could see.

Eunan sat on the windowsill, his boy nestled in the crook of his arm, and felt a sense of contentment and peace that had never before entered his life. The boy's breathing was soft and gentle. He was making tiny noises, so soft they were barely audible, like a bird fluttering its wings or a rose petal rubbing against another. For the first time in his life Eunan was truly relaxed, a feeling of security and safety that he had never felt before. He silently thanked the heavens for bestowing this gift of time upon him and his family.

Seeing his little one sleeping peacefully in his arms made his heart swell joyfully. He looked out the window and into the star-filled night sky, grateful for all the blessings bestowed on him. It had taken a while, but his dreams of having a peaceful and happy home were finally becoming reality.

His son stirred slightly, and he held him closer to his chest, savouring the moment. He had never felt so alive and full of hope. He smiled to himself and whispered a silent prayer of thanks.

Then, from beyond the windows, the sounds of war and distant gunfire invaded the room, and Eunan turned from light to dark. The sight of his little one sleeping so peacefully should have been comforting, but instead, it filled him with worry and dread. He knew all too well how quickly life can change and the fragility of those he loved most.

The tiny noises that his son was emitting made Eunan's heart swell with fear. His blessings were now upon the castle's thick walls, which would protect his son from his enemies down below.

He steadied his mind and vowed to do whatever he could to protect his little family, but he knew inside that sometimes it might not be enough. He tightened his grip on his son, savouring the moment, knowing that however much he wanted it to last forever, nothing ever did. He closed his eyes and whispered a silent prayer of thanks for the time they had.

"What do you think of this one?"

Eunan's head returned to the room, and his wife held out a yellow dress in her arms. Eunan cringed at giving his opinion because he was unsure how well his wife could see the dress.

"I have got to look my best," Sorcha said. "It is the baptism of our boy, and all eyes will be on me since I will be holding him."

"You look wonderful in whatever you wear," Eunan replied. He gave a reassuring smile and then wondered if his wife could even see his face the way she waved her arms around the room for guidance.

"This is not the time to placate me. All my relatives will be there. If I look ridiculous, they will know I am blind. I need help."

"Will the great Hugh himself be there?" Eunan asked, trying to change the subject, for advising women what to wear was definitely one of his weaker points. Anything he chose to wear came with a coating of mud.

"I suppose so. My father is kicking up quite a large fuss, so probably. But what do you care? You are the father, and your responsibility is to ensure our boy is brought into the faith, not an excuse to elevate your standing in the clan."

Eunan smiled.

"How little you know of these events. That is exactly what they are for."

Sorcha scowled and threw her yellow dress onto the bed.

"Do not mock me, the woman who has given you a child. How am I supposed to know about such things except for hearsay if I am trapped in my room ill all the time?"

"Let me help you, child." The nursemaid appeared from the corner of the room and held up a blue dress with a white trim.

"This is a nice conservative dress," she said. "Fitting the formality of the occasion. Needless to say, you will be in bed before the drinking and celebrations begin, so your requirements are for something less versatile."

Sorcha collapsed onto the bed, covered her face with her hands and cried. Eunan ran over to her, scooped her up in his arms and cradled her to his chest.

"It is supposed to be a joyous occasion. We can cancel and do it when you are better."

Sorcha sat up and dried her tears.

"That will be never. We must get the child into the house of God as soon as possible, for to wait would be to tempt fate to give him one of his mother's collection of ailments, any of which would probably kill him."

"You must not despair. The child has been healthy so far."

"So was I when I was young. Now look at me."

The nursemaid leaned forward and placed her hand on Sorcha's knee.

"I'm sorry, child. I would have chosen my words more carefully if I had known how sensitive you were feeling. Now, do you want to try on this dress and see how it looks?"

Sorcha nodded, took the dress and stood behind the maid. The same maid extended her arms out and gave Eunan an admonishing look for trying to make out his wife's body between the gaps. Eunan saw the pale white skin blotched with bedsores and the bones sticking out from her elbows, and he turned away voluntarily. She looked nothing like Cara, who had begun retaking possession of his mind.

"I am ready now," Sorcha said. The maid turned around and tied up all the loose strings so the dress fitted Sorcha's body shape.

"What do you think?" Sorcha smiled meekly and looked to her husband for approval.

"You look as beautiful as ever." A beaming smile backed up his words that only a husband could give to his ailing wife. Sorcha sighed and sat on the bed in a heap.

"At least that is decided. That's one less thing to worry about. Now, is there anything else you wish to discuss before I ask my father to finalise everything?"

Eunan hesitated, sat on the bed and looked at his hands. Sorcha felt the movement in the air and the atmosphere dip. She felt where he was and sat beside him. Her hands made playful little spiders which crawled down his leg and formed a cocoon around his cupped hands.

"Tell me what it is so we may resolve it?" she whispered.

Eunan looked her straight in the eye and saw the vacant look as she tried to focus on his face. His heart wrenched, for he did not want to hurt his wife any more than he could prevent. But he knew he had to be honest with her, for if she could not see his soul in his eyes, she would detect it, for spending so long in bed and listening to the doctors whispering about her, she had become very perceptive.

"I wish to know who named our child. I have never heard of a Maguire called Maodhóg and it is not a name in my family as far as I know. I don't wish to bring my boy back to Fermanagh with a foreign-sounding name and I, as the father, should name the boy. Nobody else."

Sorcha threw his hands away.

"Not even his mother? You should be more grateful to my father for all the kindness he has shown us and all the opportunities he has given you." She got off the bed and went to the door. "It is an old O'Neill name; some of our forefathers bore it, and they are embedded in the tapestries that adorn the walls of the O'Neill himself in Dungannon. Nothing would hold our son in better stead than to walk down the streets of Enniskillen bearing an O'Neill name. If you wish to assert your dominance over me and change the boy's name then there is the door. I'm sure you can easily find my father, and he will gladly argue with you on my behalf."

Eunan did not move from his seat.

"We are husband and wife and should discuss such matters together before making a decision. You should not run off to your father and ask him, for the boy is not his; he is ours."

"God forbid you ask your father, wherever he may be, for help. Whenever you think of him, you take to the forest to wrestle with your soul."

Eunan shot up from his seat and threw an accusatory finger.

"That is unfair. All I am asking is that I get to name my own son. I have compromised with you enough. Every time I ask if we can leave for Fermanagh, I get rebutted. It is not too much to ask that a husband can take his wife to his home."

Sorcha lowered her head, and her voice followed.

"If you wish to shout at your sick and blind wife, then I shall show you the door. The child will be christened tomorrow, and if you are to be his father, you should be there and be agreeable. Should you wish to return to Fermanagh, no rider will follow you to persuade you to return."

Eunan got up and walked out without another word.

CHAPTER 30

HOLY WATER

The castle of your father-in-law, Eunan decided, is a very poor choice of venue to argue with your wife. Paranoia may dictate that everyone is against you and listening around a corner to report back your every utterance, but paranoia would probably be right. Nor was it a great place to drink alone and drown your sorrows, for you could never be alone, and everyone would report back your melancholy. Nor was it good advice to sleep alone, for the only spare rooms available were down by the kitchen or out in the surrounding camp with the men, and they would be the last you would want to know you were arguing with your wife, for they would never let you forget it. Eunan instead went to the woods and spent his frustration punching a tree. He trawled through the significant people in his past and present to seek what they would do in a similar predicament. He settled on an image of his deceased mentor Desmond, the diplomat, and the one with the greatest insight into the minds of others and the motivations behind their actions. Eunan ruminated on what he thought he would say.

Eunan's feet dragged him up the hill and two flights of stairs as he made his way to his wife's door. He was not sure if she would forgive him or welcome him with her embrace as she had done so many times before. He hesitated in front of the door, his knuckles hovered above the wood, his heart wrenching as if it wished he was somewhere else. His duties as a husband and his duty as a diplomat for the Maguire clashed in his mind, making it difficult for him to decide which course of action he should take. He finally knocked, and entered.

He led with an apology and received a hug. Desmond would have been proud. But even in her warmth, he felt trapped. He put aside his feelings and the bedcovers and slipped into the warmth, allowing his wife to take up residence on his chest. Sleep quickly followed.

A knock was swiftly followed by the maid coming in and opening the shutters to the window. The sun tumbled in on the back of a fresh breeze. The dust swirled in the tempest of light. The smell of grass and flowers displaced the muggy air of the night. He should be relieved but instead felt more entangled than ever.

"Rise and shine, the both of you. It is an important day today. I'm so glad you both could make up last night, for it would have been a great shame and probably bad luck if you had your child christened under the cloud of his parents arguing."

Sorcha felt the breeze on her cheek, the gentle stroke of the back of unchafed fingers. Her eyes opened, and she looked to the ceiling. The periphery of her vision was definitely blurred, but she could see the light dancing on the ceiling. She threw her blankets off and felt the grooves of the rug on the floor. Cold penetrated her feet, but she felt confident about the approaching day, for the heightened sensation meant she was feeling a bit better. She smiled at the maid.

"Have the guests arrived?"

"They are making their way here in dribs and drabs. We are still waiting on the contingent from the Maguire."

Eunan opened his eyes and found the heat and weight of the blanket thrown over him to be oppressive. He felt the crisp air penetrate right down into his lungs and tickle some phlegm there. Sorcha immediately turned on him.

"I hope you are not going to be ill today of all days?"

"Can a husband not have a little cough in the morning without having to face a pack of wolves?"

"If you spoil today, there will be more than a pack of wolves hounding you," Sorcha said.

Eunan threw off his covers, riled by being needled by his wife's anxiousness so soon after he had awoken.

"If you think I will embarrass you, why don't you just have the ceremony with your father? I have already done my duty by siring the boy, and it seems obvious to me that neither of you want me around."

"Please, do not tarnish today of all days." Spittle flew to the floor as Sorcha tried to contain her anger. "You are the boy's father, and you entered into this marriage with open eyes."

Eunan sat and pulled on his shoes.

"Let us not get into what was and was not disclosed to me before you appeared in your veil. This is supposed to be the pleasant part of my life before I place myself back into the danger of fighting for your freedom. Let me offer you a gesture. I will agree to your O'Neill name. That is a big concession, a father abdicating the right to name his own child."

"We had to name him something during your prolonged absences. There is no point in writing to you to ask your opinion, for I would only condemn myself to a life of worry while waiting for you. Let me offer my own concession in return so we may have peace on our child's special day. When the war ends permanently, as in it is not a temporary truce, we will have a serious discussion with my father about moving to Fermanagh."

Eunan stopped buttoning up his shirt.

"Why cannot we decide that between ourselves?"

"Because such is your obligation for marrying the daughter of such an important man. Now hug me, tell me you love me, and let us be at peace for the rest of the day."

Eunan looked to the window and ground his teeth. Sorcha gave a coy smile and slowly raised her arms, inviting Eunan to embrace her. Her pale face looked so angelic with the sunlight behind her. He threw open his arms, determined to embrace the day.

Nestled deep in the rolling hills, beyond the sight of prying eyes and curious minds, the baptismal party gathered within the shelter of a nearby monastery. A place steeped in history and tradition, it had been used for centuries by this branch of the O'Neill family for all their religious ceremonies. Cormac stood at the head of his clan, surrounded by his sons and daughters and their children. Eunan held Sorcha's hand as they walked behind him, their fingers interlocked like the roots of two ancient trees that had meshed together over time. The couple glowed with a warm golden radiance, each grinning happily to each other with eyes bright like stars on a clear night. Maodhóg slept on Sorcha's arm, nestled against her chest.

Behind them came their guests from all the clans of the north. They wore fine woollen clothes dyed black, blue or brown with coloured trim, the most prominent being yellow, around their hems and collars, signifying wealth and status. Each man was accompanied by his wife, who wore a co-ordinating floral patterned dress under her coat, adding a hint of elegance to their outfits. They were not the leaders of the clan, much to Cormac's consternation, but the second tier of nobility that reflected Cormac's status. All of these were surrounded by Cormac's hand-picked men, standing watchful like sentinels around the holy ground.

The priests made a guard of honour to line the path into the monastery's chapel. They gave their blessings to all who passed, who in turn muttered prayers of thanks and gratitude. They entered the chapel, which could comfortably fit thirty people, so the immediate family entered, and the priests ran around to get seats for their esteemed guests who had to wait outside.

Eunan and Sorcha stepped into the chapel as their son, Maodhóg, stirred in Sorcha's arms. Like a window back to ancient times, the chapel was constructed, so it appeared to be carved from a single piece of bedrock. The walls were adorned with figures of saints, each in a valiant pose, frozen in time. The air was musty and thick with the power of centuries gone by, and the faint echoes of long-forgotten chants reverberated off the walls like whispers from another life.

Monks lined one chapel wall and began to chant when the child to be baptised entered the room. The Archbishop of Armagh stood at the altar, smiled, and invited them to sit just below him. The rest of the ceremony was a blur to Eunan; he did not like such ceremonies as he found them incredibly stuffy and did not understand all the Latin, so he had to rely on the interpreter to signal when they were supposed to do specific actions. When the holy water was poured over his son's head, he cringed at having no say as to the child's name. He noticed how wider his uncle's smile became when the child was named 'Maodhóg' as if he had won some victory over him. More Latin, spoken and sung, ensued before the ceremony ended, and they were invited to leave the chapel. When they came out hand in hand, the gathered crowd cheered, and Sorcha lifted the boy for all to see. Cormac then led the baptismal party back to Augher Castle, where the feast would take place.

The castle was too small to accommodate all the guests, so tables and chairs were assembled in its shadow. Sorcha hooked her arm into the crook of Eunan's elbow, and Eunan nestled the child into the cradle of his arms. With two bodyguards behind them and Cormac leading them and acting as a guide to introduce them, they went out to meet their guests. Eunan wore the same smile as one unknown person after another came up and shook his hand and gave something for the child to Cormac as a form of tribute. Sorcha followed with a warm smile when Eunan bent down and whispered in her ear who was in front of them. This all continued until they came to the contingent from the Maguire.

Cúchonnacht Óg stood up from his bench, smiled joyfully, and flung his arms open.

"Eunan, congratulations. Let me see this boy you have tried so hard to create."

Eunan smiled down into his arms and lifted the blanket off the boy's face so everyone could see him.

"He's certainly got your hair, but I hope the rest of him takes after his mother."

Sorcha looked vacant as she tried to settle her eyes toward the sound. Cúchonnacht Óg was a little startled. He knew Eunan's wife was ill but did not know the details. He looked around, a little lost, not knowing whether to mention it or keep quiet out of politeness. He decided to change the subject and turned to the host.

"Thank you, Cormac, for your hospitality. It is fitting that you have thrown such a wonderful event to introduce your grandson to the world."

"You're welcome," Cormac said as he raised a diplomatic smile. "Who are the two warriors you have escorting you? I certainly remember hosting them before."

Eunan turned his head, for his attention had been placed upon his friend Cúchonnacht Óg alone, and he had not noticed anyone with him. Feargal and Irial MacCabe stood up and smiled wryly towards Eunan. Feargal stuck his hand out to Eunan in front of his father-in-law, so he was forced to take it. Irial turned his back on him and paid attention to Cormac.

"I remember staying here. Your hospitality was legendary, and the training was even better."

Cormac smiled. He enjoyed talking with fellow military men more than anyone else.

"I'm glad we could serve our loyal allies, and your gratitude has surely been shown on the battlefield through our recent string of victories."

"Much of that is due to your brother's astute leadership."

Cormac was pricked with a pang of jealousy, for he did not want to talk of his brother and how great everyone thought he was to usurp his grandson's baptism.

"The child is too young to hear the talk of warriors on his baptism day. We can continue this discussion tomorrow if you are going to stay."

Cormac turned to move away, but Irial was determined to make a good impression.

"In my distraction, I did not see the boy's face." Irial stood in front of Eunan, who towered slightly over him.

"May I?" Irial said, gesturing that he would like to look upon the boy's face. Eunan reluctantly nodded, for his father-in-law was looking on, eager to meet the next set of guests. Irial lifted the blanket and gave a cursory glance at the child.

"Very nice."

Eunan glared at him.

"Like the hair. What is the boy's name?"

"Maodhóg," Eunan said as they tried to move on. Irial placed his hand on Eunan's arm.

"That is a name I'm not familiar with. Is it a common one around the lakes?"

Eunan shook Irial's hand off and went to walk away.

"No," Cormac said. "It is an old O'Neill name. Several of my distant relatives bore the name, and the legends of their martial prowess still live on."

"Is that so?" Irial said, growing more curious. "It is a fine name with a great meaning. Is it a favourite of yours?"

"Oh yes. It is seldom bestowed on boys these days, especially prominent ones. Everyone wants to call their boy 'Hugh'. But I favour the more traditional names, especially for those less prominent ones."

"I see," Irial said, having learned everything he needed to. I'm glad you got your wish. I'm all for traditional names myself."

"I always find that the tradition tends to be best. Now, I have no wish to appear rude, but we must meet the other guests."

"A thousand blessings and a good day to you all," Irial said as he bowed to them.

Eunan glared at him, and Irial smirked back. Sorcha turned and dropped something on the ground. Eunan had his hands full with the child, and Cormac walked off. Sorcha felt her way downwards, using Eunan's body as a guide. She patted the ground, hoping her palms could compensate for her lack of sight and locate the fallen object. For Irial, this was manna from heaven. He helped himself to the ground with the aid of his walking stick.

"Let me help you, dear," Irial said. "What have you lost?"

Sorcha hesitated.

"I'm not sure. It is one of the gifts for Maodhóg we received from a guest."

"Let me help you."

Irial saw the silver cross lying on the ground, glittering in the sun. He looked at Sorcha but said nothing while pointing at the cross. Sorcha continued fumbling on the ground. Irial grinned at Feargal. He moved the cross in front of Sorcha so it was in plain sight. Still, she continued fumbling. He had all he needed to know. He picked up the cross.

"Here, my dear. I think it is this you lost?"

Sorcha took the cross in her hand.

"Thank you."

"Come on, we have to go," Eunan said, itching to escape Irial and Feargal.

When Eunan and Sorcha had gone, Irial supported himself with his staff to climb back to full height. He turned to Feargal and laughed.

"Eunan Maguire is finished."

CHAPTER 31

PACK YOUR BAGS

The baptism celebration quickly faded into memory as the realities of child-rearing smothered Eunan's life. Sorcha's sight had not recovered, making her more reliant on her maid than ever. She waved Eunan away as she tried to limit her reliance on him, for she knew he would be gone soon.

Eunan succumbed to melancholy for the plight of his wife echoed the plight of his mother when he was born and he blamed Maodhóg as the perpetrator of Sorcha's blindness. But he tried to nurture the child unbiased by his wife's ailments. But this morning, as the shafts of sunlight came through the window and made patterns on the floor as clouds periodically disrupted their projections, Cormac knocked and invited himself into the room.

Sorcha lay in bed and meekly smiled at her father as he entered. Cormac scowled at the pained expression on her face. He looked around the room to see how his daughter was being looked after. Eunan sat on the window seat, making shapes with the shadows, and the maid sat in a rocking chair, cradling Maodhóg in her arms as he slept. Cormac bit his tongue as he looked at Eunan. He lay idly basking in the sunlight while his daughter languished in bed. But he held back his comments, for he as well knew Eunan would be gone soon. He pulled up a stool and took his daughter's hand.

"How are you feeling? How is the boy?"

Sorcha gave one of her resigned smiles, which she saved for him and his physicians.

"We are as well as can be expected."

Cormac edged a little closer to her. Eunan's ears pricked up.

"May we speak of your various conditions in private?"

"You can speak in front of both my husband and the maid, for as they look after me, I have no wish to hide anything from them. To do so would impede their efforts."

"As you wish. The physicians are as stumped about your general condition as always. The latest round of bloodletting yielded no results."

Eunan leapt from his perch on the windowsill. The memories of his trauma from his leechings on the islands in the lakes of Fermanagh overwhelmed him.

"Why are you drawing blood from my wife? She is a good person and does not deserve this."

Cormac sat back and crunched his face.

"Why do you act with such horror at the mention of the leech? Surely your physicians that travel with the Maguire army carry many containers of them? If not, how do they stem the flow of blood from an axe wound?"

Eunan took a deep breath and slunk back to his former perch. He berated himself for getting so agitated in front of his father-in-law.

"The leech has many applications for body and mind," Eunan said as he looked out the window, hoping his father-in-law would tire of cross-examining him. "The Maguires only use leeches in cases of extreme injury."

"The Maguire should have taken advantage of the superior knowledge of our physician when we trained together. An opportunity lost."

Cormac turned once more to his daughter and Eunan sighed in relief.

"Yet, here you lie, getting more and more sick. God, for some reason unbeknown to me, has seen fit to take away your sight. I mean to rectify this by getting the priest to bless you."

Eunan turned his face to the window to hide any smirks that may lurk on his face or a laugh that may slip out of the side of his mouth. But it was too late.

"Don't you turn away, boy," Cormac said as he raised himself from his stool. "Any curse brought upon this house could have been from you. I have no idea how you conduct yourself on campaign or on the battlefield, nor how God would view your actions or if anybody has cursed you."

Eunan flew off his perch on the window seat, incandescent with rage.

"She was ill before I married her and has grown steadily worse ever since. Whatever curse may have been put upon her was placed long before I met her. Maybe you should undertake the same self-examination you suggested for me to see if you did anything that may have warranted this as divine punishment."

Cormac dropped his daughter's hand on the bed and rose to meet his defiant son-in-law. Eunan's temper cooled as he saw the look on his wife's face and that this rupture with his father-in-law may lead to blows. Sorcha's fingers stretched out like spindly twigs, and red erupted on her pale white cheeks. A hiss came out of her mouth, a release of steam that could not yet form words.

"No." She bolted upright in her bed and held out her arms between the two men in her life. "If there is any curse, it is mine and mine alone to bear. Nothing has afflicted either of you, and the child is in robust health." She turned to Eunan. "Bow your head and receive your blessing. At the very least, it will stand you in good stead when you return to the war to have the grace of God on your side." She turned to Cormac. "My husband is a guest in your house and has been more than patient with you and me as I have lain in your house sick while he has a very good house of his own that I could convalesce in. Let the priest come in. We bow our heads and return to our duties, no matter what they may be."

Eunan backed away and nodded an apology to his father-in-law that did not quite make it into words. Cormac glared at Eunan, sat, and retook his daughter's hand.

"Now, Father," Sorcha said. "Bring in the priest, and let us argue no more. We have plenty of enemies beyond these walls that we can fight with instead of fighting each other."

Cormac nodded, went to the door and signalled for the priest.

Eunan enjoyed another two weeks with his wife and son before he was formally summoned to Cormac's private room by letter. He vowed to spend the last few moments with his wife, untroubled by guessing what his father-in-law wanted. He held the piece of paper in his hand as he looked down at his wife lying in bed. Her condition had not improved, and the consensus was that she would have sight problems now for life or maybe even be blind. Olcan and Sionn, their two Irish wolfhounds, lay at the bottom of the bed, half asleep with their ears pricked up, listening for anything that may endanger their mistress. Eunan walked around the bed, took his wife's hand, and shook it gently to wake her.

"My love, your father summons me by letter which can only mean one thing."

Sorcha opened her eyes to see the blurred hulk of her husband standing over her.

"You have to go, and I may never see you again?"

Eunan sat on the stool that was stored beside the bed for Sorcha's visitors.

"Don't be so pessimistic. Both of you will see me again."

He looked over his shoulder at Maodhóg, sleeping peacefully in his crib.

"I will see you again, and I mean that literally. This ailment is only temporary. I used to believe in such things as curses but no more. The next time I return, I hope to bring peace and end all of this suffering. Once that is done, you will be free of whatever afflicts you. You, Maodhóg and I will be free to move to my house by the lakes, and we'll be peaceful farmers with no more talk of wars or curses."

Sorcha smiled sweetly at him and took his hand.

"I will count down the days until you return and pray for you. I will tell Maodhóg a different tale of your bravery every night."

It was Eunan's turn to smile, and he gazed dotingly at his sleeping boy.

"He will grow up to be a fine warrior one day."

"Sure, he could hardly help it being half O'Neill and half Maguire," Sorcha said.

"He shall know peace," Eunan said. "Not just in his sleep, but the kingdoms will be settled and at peace."

"He may even grow up to rule one of the clans or both."

Eunan smiled.

"Let's not get ahead of ourselves and let our child be a child while he still can. Life can wait for him."

A knock came on the door.

"But my father will no longer wait for you. Kiss me and let it linger so I may have something to remember you by."

Eunan bent down to kiss her, conscious of the added pressure placed upon him. But when he removed his lips, his wife's lips remained puckered and frozen. He had succeeded.

Eunan slung his bag over his shoulder and walked down the castle's stairs to his father-in-law's room, still elated by his final kiss with Sorcha. Not even the gruff 'come in' could remove the smile from his face. Cormac was hunched over a table of maps, the array of candles projecting his distorted shadow on the wall.

"Are you glad to be leaving us?" Cormac said upon laying eyes on Eunan.

"Of course not, Cormac. I have just left your daughter a happy woman; her joy has rubbed off on me."

Cormac's face dropped.

"You haven't left her pregnant, have you?"

Eunan smirked.

"If there is one thing we agree on, the last thing I would want to do is to leave her pregnant for fear she would not survive. Even though it is a subject that should only be discussed between a man and his wife, she no longer talks about having another child. She is content the way she is at the moment."

Cormac breathed a sigh of relief.

"That is a good thing that she has seen sense at last."

But Cormac's face clouded over.

"But that is not why I brought you here."

"I know. The war. Where have I been assigned to? Am I off back to Munster?"

"I'm not sure about that. The summons I received was from the Maguire. Apparently, the O'Donnell is planning a massive raid into Connacht and has summoned his allies."

Eunan smiled.

"A more profitable raid then for the Maguire. Your brother monopolises all the spoils of Munster."

"To which he directs most to the pursuit of the war, in the buying of weapons for the various disenfranchised clans of Munster such as your uncle's beloved MacSheehy. The O'Donnell has not the vision to pursue such a strategy, which is hardly the fault of the O'Neill. He only wished to exert his clan's influence over their old lands in Connacht and then to sue for peace. It is a new era we aspire to, or else the clans will be gone."

"You think too little of your O'Donnell allies. The O'Donnell has been rigorous in his pursuit of the assistance of the King of Spain."

Cormac waved him away.

"No more talk of high politics. It is you I wish to speak about."

Eunan gave a little bow.

"I am at your disposal as always."

"I have been hearing rumours about your conduct in Munster."

Eunan laughed.

"I have many enemies, maybe even more than you. Most would like to plunge a dagger in my back, but the more cowardly would settle for rumours."

"Rumours are dangerous for a man. They plunge a dagger into the back of his reputation. Once his reputation is gone, he has nothing."

Eunan shook his head.

"I'm sure I'll be made well aware of all the rumours once I return to Enniskillen. You must remember that Munster is a very violent place, with atrocities carried out by both sides. Plenty of ammunition for my detractors who sit in Enniskillen to chew over and fantasise about while I do the fighting to keep them free."

Cormac held up his finger in warning.

"Still, watch your back. You are married into the O'Neills now, so do nothing that could reflect badly on us."

"I will do even better, father-in-law. I will win us a great victory that no one could help but talk about. That would drown out my detractors."

Cormac placed his hand on Eunan's shoulder.

"That would be a great blessing for us all."

CHAPTER 32

ONCE MORE INTO THE VIPERS' NEST

E unan rode with Odhran and the men from the MacCabes sent to fetch him. He was well used to the ride between Augher Castle and Enniskillen, but the trepidation grew with each trip. This time was no different, as the butterflies lodged in his stomach as soon as the O'Neill / Maguire border became apparent. Was he becoming more of an O'Neill? He spent so little of his time in his own lands since Dervella and Arthur were brutally murdered there. He had been so busy between his wife and the campaign in Munster that he had not arranged to visit his lands. His deceased mentor Desmond would berate him for neglecting his power base in that every vacuum breeds a rival, and if he lost his power base, he would lose his power. No matter what lay ahead for him in Enniskillen, he needed to get back to O'Cassidy house to secure his power.

"Rider ahead, lord," Odhran said.

Eunan looked through the rolling hills and saw more mounted MacCabes approaching them. He gulped and turned to Odhran.

"Stick with me. If I get arrested for any reason, ride to Munster and tell Seamus. If I see out the day a free man, ride to O'Cassidy house and make sure my interests are being looked after."

"I will, lord. But won't you need me by your side?"

"I estimate the Maguire really wants to see me if he has sent riders, and it is more likely because Irial and the rest have been winding him up rather than because he would like to see my face."

"Understood, lord. We shall wait and see what happens."

The Maguire sat in his ceremonial seat beside the embers in the grand fireplace in the great hall of Enniskillen. The fire was long since dead from the night before, and the Maguire fixated upon it lying in its decaying state, ready to be cudgelled to death by the poker when the servants came to clear the fireplace. Was the ember the remains of his relationship with one Eunan Maguire about to be cudgelled to death by his fellow MacCabes? It certainly sounded like that today, but the Maguire thought back to Devenish Island and how Eunan was one of the few people who stayed to defend him. He must launch some sort of last-ditch defence of Eunan now.

"I hear that the Munster campaign has been difficult for everyone. Massacres were committed by both sides. We have to judge Eunan Maguire's actions in that context."

"Oh, lord," Irial said, warming to his subject now, "I wish that was the basis of my critique, but it is far worse than that. His behaviour is a disgrace to the MacCabe and the moral standing of the men under his command."

"You do know, Irial, that I take into account the fact the injury he gave you forced you to retire. You do seem to have nothing good to say about Eunan Maguire."

"Would I be performing my duty if I refrained from speaking on a topic the Maguire should be informed about simply because of the potential for perceived bias? If I were coerced into silence, then Eunan Maguire and his trickery would have won."

"So what is the basis for your claims, Irial? Eunan will be here soon, and we need to get this out of the way so we can plan the next raid."

Irial pointed towards a seat.

"Do you mind, lord? Such tales, the likes of which I do not like to tell about my fellow soldiers, drain me. My legs are old and crippled, and I have to resort to my brains and my words to get young men to carry out my commands."

"Sit if you wish. I have no desire for you to feel uncomfortable."

Irial sat himself down slowly and deliberately to ensure the attention was all on him as Feargal and Fachtna looked on.

"I went as your representative to the christening of Eunan's child."

"I know that," the Maguire said. "What did you find that you feel such urgency to tell me?"

"The child of Cormac MacBaron was sick before she married Eunan Maguire. She has been sick for as long as anyone can remember."

"We know. Eunan's uncle Seamus and I had to negotiate hard for the marriage. Her father thought no one was good enough for her in her condition, but we managed to convince him otherwise. Eunan is doing the clan a great service in helping to cement the alliance with the O'Neills, and I will not see that put in jeopardy."

"That is why I tell this tale." Irial became quite animated, pointing at the Maguire. "She gave birth to Eunan's child, a hefty beast with a flame of red hair like his father. In giving birth to the child, the poor mother was rendered blind. She was so blind that she could not unhook her arm from Eunan's support while they greeted their guests. Indeed, I had to help the poor girl as she searched the ground for something she had dropped with only her hands for guidance."

The Maguire gripped his chair until his knuckles went white.

"As you said before, we all knew she was sick. I am no physician and neither are you. We don't know what caused this, and it is not to our benefit to speculate what it is and how it was caused. I want no mention of this to Eunan or the O'Neills. I do not want to put our alliance in jeopardy."

Irial leaned forward.

"But the men already suspect. Rumours abound that Eunan has taken up with a known witch and has fornicated with her. It is said she has cursed Eunan's wife, so he will abandon his wife and take up lodgings with her."

The Maguire gritted his teeth and subdued his growl in the pit of his stomach.

"Say no more of this and flog any man who repeats such rumours. I will speak with Eunan when he arrives and scotch these rumours once and for all."

"To forbid its discussion is to add fuel to the flames. The men will think Eunan is one of your favourites and you are protecting him. To be seen to be protecting him is to expose yourself to being dragged down with him."

The Maguire looked down and made a fist.

"We also cannot be seen to be abandoning one of our own over hearsay."

"Oh, it is more than hearsay, lord. Some of the men witnessed the witch both entering his lodgings in the evening and exiting in the morning. What else would the men think she was doing but casting spells?"

"It is up to you to discipline the men and ensure situations like these do not get out of hand."

"You will lose control of the men if rumours get around that one of their leaders is possessed by a witch."

The Maguire slammed his fist on the chair arm.

"You deal with the men and punish any who speaks of this. Leave Eunan to me."

Irial bowed.

"You are the one God chose to lead the Maguire and bestowed with his wisdom to lead us."

The Maguire waved him away as if he were swatting a fly.

"Send up Eunan Maguire."

Eunan climbed the stairs, and the guards opened the door to the great hall for him but stood in the way of Odhran, who was behind him. Odhran snarled and reached for his belt, but his weapon had already been confiscated. Eunan stretched his arm across Odhran's chest.

"Leave it. I'm sure these men will be good enough to feed you while I go and talk business with the Maguire."

"This way," one of the guards said, inviting Odhran to follow him.

Eunan straightened his shirt, composed what he would say, took a deep breath and pushed on the door.

The warmth of the blazing fire brought Eunan out in a sweat as he had been in the saddle and subjected to the northerly wind earlier that day. The room danced between flickering flames and looming shadows, lit by many candles, from the majestic, tall, fresh candles to those wicks that poked their heads out from a pool of molten wax. The Maguire squirmed in his chair as if it were covered in ants and drummed his fingers on the arms. Irial stood, his face devoid of all emotion except determination. Fachtna and Feargal stood in the shadows of the Maguire's chair, in the no-man's-land of whispering in his ear or slipping away unnoticed. Eunan bowed deep, for he thought he should start by showing respect, for he was short of allies in the room.

"My lord, you summoned me, so I am here to present myself and receive your instructions."

"Very good, Eunan," the Maguire said as he nodded to acknowledge the bow. "I have a new mission for you."

"What is your command?"

Eunan bowed once again.

"You are to lead the Maguires in the O'Donnell's raid into Connacht. See what booty you can get for us if they have replenished their lands after the last time we stripped them clean."

"It would be my honour, but why are all your advisers here, and why does Feargal not lead the men as he leads your Galloglass?"

The Maguire grimaced as he glared at Irial, for he knew what was coming next.

"Feargal has to recruit and train new men, and this raid is more expansive than any of the others, for the target is Thomond, and the O'Donnell wishes to destroy the Earl of Thomond's forces and hand the territory to one of his supporters."

"So my services are no longer required in Munster? There is still much to do there."

"There is a bigger plan, and we must assist our allies as they request. Now, can everyone leave so I may speak to Eunan alone?"

Fachtna left with a bowed solemn head. Feargal tried to hide behind Fachtna, and Irial struggled to contain his grin. Eunan gulped, for he knew something was up. The Maguire had his head in his right hand, and he raised it slowly.

"Eunan?"

He paused for what seemed an age. A drop of sweat rolled down Eunan's back.

"Do you have anything to tell me about your time in Munster?"

Eunan paused and looked up at the ceiling until he found an answer.

"It was a difficult campaign, lord. You would have to be more specific. I can give you a blow-by-blow account of our mission there if that is what you are asking?"

The Maguire gave Eunan a cold look.

"How is your wife?"

The new question took aback Eunan as he related it to the old one but answered anyway.

"As well as can be expected for a woman who is perpetually sick and has just given birth." Eunan braced himself. "Why do you ask these questions both together, lord?"

It was the Maguire's turn to hesitate.

"I hear your wife has gone blind?"

Realisation dawned for Eunan.

"What lies has Irial been bending your ears with? I saw the grin he wore when he left the room and how he paid attention to my poor wife as she struggled at the baptism. I knew there had to be mischief involved. I'm surprised he still has your ear."

The Maguire scratched his forehead more vigorously than if it were merely an itch.

"Irial is very experienced and also very influential. If he was not in the court, he would be off causing mischief elsewhere. I should have him near to watch him rather than have him in Castle Skea in cahoots with Connor Roe."

The Maguire leaned towards Eunan and beckoned him to come closer. Eunan took a few cautious steps and stretched his ear.

"He says you played house with a witch, and she possesses you."

Eunan roared with laughter, then was taken by a fit of panic. He hoped the tears from his original laugh would hide the now dominant look of fear.

"Who else are the protestant Scottish settlers going to cast as a witch than a rebel woman come to stir up trouble in their town? The woman in question was an agent of my uncle's, whom my men and I had to rescue. She is no more a witch than I am a demon or you a wizard. Whoever spread these rumours is mistaken. If done innocently they were probably drunk, if maliciously, they were agents of Irial."

The Maguire sat back as the tension melted away from his limbs.

"Be wary of Irial and his rumour-mongering," the Maguire said. "He is crafty and knows how to get the attention of the men and how to turn them against you. Have an exemplary campaign in Connacht, and keep your nose clean. The rumours will soon dissipate once the men meet with some success."

Eunan bowed.

"When my mission is complete, may I have some time to spend with my son?"

"I have no control over circumstances in these troubled times. I certainly hope you can, but we shall see."

"You will have my fullest efforts to bring glory and cattle in abundance back from Connacht."

CHAPTER 33

A RUDE INTERRUPTION

"WHY can't you make a bid to become the Earl of Desmond?" Eleanor Fitzgerald said to her husband, who looked pained to be once more the focus of her nagging. "You can use my status as the last proper Earl's wife, and people will support you. Surely you'd make a better earl than James Fitz Thomas Fitzgerald?"

"Oh please, woman. Stop nagging." Donough O'Connor Sligo held his ribs for they still ached when he moved suddenly. His wife's nagging was enough to make him writhe with irritation provoking his old wounds. "I have enough irritation attempting to persuade the Queen to give me back the rights to my family home of Ballymote Castle and to provide me with an army so I may retake it. Once that is achieved, and that is by far the more legitimate enterprise for us to pursue, we can turn to your business."

His red-faced wife leaned over and slammed her hands onto her hips.

"Oh, my business, my business. So it is my business to make you the most powerful man in all of Ireland while you sit and succumb to the pains of past defeats?"

"It is not like that and you well know it. There is no Earl of Desmond, and that impostor and anyone else who calls themselves that title will quickly hang from a tree."

"What about my son that rots in the tower? He is by far the most legitimate Earl, and I have spent the best part of my life fighting for him to have his inheritance. I am not asking you to be the earl, no, not at all. I am asking you to wrestle the title from the rebels, then petition the Queen to legitimise the title, and then abdicate in favour of my son. Then you will have all the resources you could ever desire to recover your beloved Sligo."

Donough gave a wry smile.

"How many nooses would I have to avoid before that sequence of events happened and I managed to ride the waves to succeed as you have outlined? Listen to yourself, woman. My plan is so much easier to achieve, and once that is complete, we can turn our attention to your son."

"Then what are you doing down here in Munster?"

What humour or amusement he could derive from this conversation went up in smoke. He longed to be back in Sligo if only to escape his wife's biting tongue. He gave a long sigh.

"You know why. Sligo is overrun. I need men to go back there with."

Eleanor gave a sarcastic grin.

"Yes, we all know your plan has flaws. Your next-door neighbours are the O'Donnells, and until they are subdued, your lands will know no peace."

"The least you can do is grant me respite from your tongue and allow me the space to think in the here and now. It is no good for us to bicker when work is to be done."

"Have all the peace you wish, but use it well, for this marriage was supposed to yield results, not measured in offspring."

Donough watched his wife's back as she walked down the corridor of her country house, which the rebellion in Munster had not spoiled. He looked out the window to the tenants working the land and bringing in money for the lady. The estate he sat within was small but well-formed, with productive land and an income large enough for them to live comfortably but not lavishly. Any other couple would be satisfied with their lot. However, both of them were tarnished with the blood of fallen Irish nobility with one head permanently in the past. The yearning drive to restore the historical lands of his ancestors was a burden on his soul. But with the right backers, he was sure he could succeed. Ireland was in such a state of turmoil that you could achieve almost anything with the right combination of might and luck. The question was, how long for? He sat at his desk and took out a piece of paper and a quill. He dipped the quill into the ink and wrote his umpteenth plea to the Lord Deputy for men.

Donough lifted himself into an upright position and held his lower back. Toiling in a field under the sun was no work for a nobleman of his age. But the rebellion had finally reached his wife's lands, and no matter how much they pleaded with the tenants and offered them better terms, they still all fled to join the rebellion. The harvest needed to be brought in, or it would get spoilt or stolen, and they would all starve. He smiled at the few remaining tenants who paused over their tools and smiled nervously back. He heard a noise over his shoulder, a weird animalistic squeal. He looked around and saw his wife running towards him, or indeed, the best run she could manage; it was more like the waddle of a duck, albeit an excited one.

"He is here. He is here. You have done it."

Donough raised an eyebrow. There was no way they had released her son and sent him back to Ireland. Where would be their advantage to that? It would be adding fuel to the already explosive fire of rebellion in Munster.

"The Lord Deputy is here."

Donough dropped his spade, ran past his wife, and returned to the house. He ran through it and flung open the front door. Indeed, there, sat upon a horse, his breastplate and helmet all covered in dust, sat the Lord Deputy. His officers, including several Donough recognised, flanked him. Behind him was a wall of pikes, with their spikes glistening in the sky above their heads. Donough stared, tongue-tied.

"Are you Donough O'Connor Sligo?" Essex asked. "Or if you are one of his tenants, please fetch him for me like a good man."

Donough froze and then looked to Ormond, who was sitting on a horse beside the Lord Deputy. He smirked, and Donough knew he would not get any help from him.

"I am him you seek," Donough stammered.

Essex glanced at Ormond.

"I am told you are one of our great supporters in Connacht but fear I have found you in humbler circumstances."

Donough went red.

"I am and I am not. Sorry, I mean, the rebellion has taken many of our tenants, and there are no idle hands with a spoiling crop.

Essex now glared at Ormond as if he had been duped to pursue a fool's errand.

"Indeed. I hope the faith the Crown has placed in you was astute. Aren't you going to invite me in, for we have business to discuss?"

Donough began to shake and look around for anyone he could order to arrange some seating and some drinks for his esteemed guests. His wife arrived at the doorway with inflated red cheeks, doubled over to catch her breath, and looked up to see the Lord Deputy and her hyperventilating husband.

"At once," she cried and ran off towards the kitchen.

Essex smirked at Ormond, a satisfied smile that showed his position held real power in the land. He jumped off his horse and signalled for Ormond to do the same.

"Come," Essex said, putting his arm over Donough's shoulder and steering him towards the house's entrance. There is no need to make a fuss of me. We are but two soldiers in the field."

They walked into the house, but Ormond scowled, as age had robbed him of his flexibility. He had to signal for one of his men to help him down. Once his feet hit solid ground, he hurried after the Lord Deputy.

Eleanor threw a cloth over a table, rinsed out a couple of mugs, and invited Essex to sit.

"Please, this way. Welcome to our humble abode. We don't have much since the servants ran off, but we do have this one bottle of Spanish wine we can share with you."

Ormond entered the doorway to the room. "We won't ask where you got that from," he said with a smile.

Essex held out his mug.

"Indeed, think of us not as drinking the last of your wine but as opening up the opportunity to get an endless supply of wine."

Eleanor fluttered around the table like a plump bird filling everyone's mug, attempting to spread cheer as the foundation for her to talk up her husband.

"My husband will do whatever job you wish. If you want him to be the English Earl of Desmond, he can surely do that. He's a great leader of men. The Battle of the Rain wasn't his fault at all. In fact, he was commended for his actions that day."

Donough gave her a deathly stare that frightened her off into the next room. His hand shook as he raised it to propose a salute.

"To the Queen, and to freeing all her loyal subjects from the oppression of these brutish Irish lords."

Two mugs met his in the air.

"The Queen," they all said in unison.

Donough took a swig from his mug in an effort to swallow his nerves. But they returned in a gentle wobble in his voice.

"Please ignore my wife. She got a bit excited by meeting you, Lord Deputy. She has always said you'll come and save us."

Essex took a swig from his mug,

"You and every other loyal subject of the Queen. That is why we are here."

Donough gave a nervous smile.

"And we are very grateful. More wine?"

Essex held out his mug. He paused, looked at Donough and put his hand on Donough's shoulder.

"We came here to meet you, for we have a mission for you."

"A mission?" Donough's eyes lit up at the indication that the Lord Deputy thought him somewhat important.

"Yes. I need you to go back to Sligo and be our eyes and ears for the activities of the O'Donnell."

Donough's shoulders slumped, for he thought he might have been given an achievable mission instead of one that almost certainly ended in his death.

"Sligo, at this moment in time, is beyond saving. All my old allies have turned to the O'Donnell, and all the English settlers have been driven back to the Pale. I no longer have a support base there and would be, at best, easily driven away by the O'Donnell."

"We have come here to call upon stout-hearted men to do their duty for Queen and country," Ormond said as he held out his mug to be refilled. "If you do not have the heart to do it, we'll have to disappoint your wife's hospitality and tell her we need another to lead the troop of men we mean to send back to the wilds of Ireland. She may even think it may be worthwhile to swap out her husband for her son in the Tower of London."

Donough had spent many years in an English prison; the prospect of a return to jail made the offer to go to Sligo seem enticing.

"How many men do you have to offer me?"

"That's the spirit," Essex said, punching him on the shoulder. "I have one hundred men I will assign to you, and Clifford will see you all right for whatever else you may need."

Donough smiled to cover the thoughts of being set up for failure. One hundred men in Ireland would quickly become fifty on the journey alone, whether from desertion or illness. Never mind how many he would be left with at the first sign of combat. But Donough knew he should just nod along, and soon the Lord Deputy would be gone, and the failure to carry out his instructions would be lost in the chaos of Ireland. But his nerves got the better of him.

"I had to flee Connacht, swept out by the tide of rebels, and Clifford can only hide behind the walls of Galway and the like. How is he supposed to break out if he does not have the means to do so?"

Essex leaned in to whisper to him.

"When I finish with the rebels in Munster, I will turn to Ulster. I will attack from the Pale and Clifford from Connacht. We will crush the rebels between us."

Essex looked so convinced, and his hand gestures played out the plan with such conviction that Donough did not have the heart to say it had been tried before, which led to his current injuries.

"That sounds like a great plan. Do you want to finish the wine?"

Essex held out his mug and grinned. Donough knew his fate was sealed.

CHAPTER 34
DIVIDING THE SPOILS

S everal days later, Donough found himself on the road to Sligo with one hundred men. His wife had already deserted him and fled back to their house in Dublin, where she said it was the only place she felt safe on this wretched island. The men he was given were all from Connacht, either loyal natives or English settlers keen to return to their lands. It was like being given a sword of water to defend oneself from one's enemies. How long would these men stay loyal before they would desert? Did they accept this mission for the sole purpose of going somewhere they could easily switch sides? At least the English settlers may prove loyal because they could not quickly disappear into a hostile land.

They marched silently through a countryside deeply scarred by the enormous rebel raid that had just passed through it and currently resided in Thomond. The number of refugees on the road and those farmers who had taken to the woods to become bandits were a lot fewer now as the land had become noticeably depopulated because of the constant war. As Donough rode, the images in his head of the glorious past reigns of the O'Connors became somewhat tarnished by the devastation around him. Was this the prize for the eventual winner? Was all of this worth it for such pain and destruction? He shook his head, for he was already on the path to war, and the only way out he could see was on the tip of a sword or the end of a rope. He noticed the men steadily becoming more nervous as they advanced into Connacht.

"The quicker we get to my castle, the sooner we'll all be safe," he said to the men.

"How do you know you still have a castle?" asked one man.

"I have it on good authority that Collooney Castle still holds. Once we are there, I will send word to Galway, and Clifford and his army will come. Then we strike north and crush the rebellion."

The men murmured, and Donough tried to keep his nerves in check.

"But we are only one hundred," said one man eventually.

"The castle walls are ten thousand men to us for the rebels have no cannon. We only need food for one hundred, and Clifford will come and save us."

The men began their muttering once more.

"Come on and quicken the pace," Donough said as he pointed northwards. "We are nearer the castle than the safety of the Pale. The quicker you march, the sooner you will be safe."

The muttering subsided, and the pace doubled.

Several days later, Donough looked down from the castle walls across the surrounding lands. Collooney Castle was built on a prominent hill with a commanding view of the countryside as far as the sea, the perfect place to spy on the enemy. His fingers drummed the top of the castle wall as he saw the herds of cattle being driven north past him. His captain came and stood beside him.

"Does that mean Clifford is coming and drives all before him, lord?"

Donough considered his response. He had received no messengers from Clifford nor saw any of his men. On the other hand, he managed to retain most of the one hundred men given to him and wished to keep it that way.

"Tell the men, first we'll see the rebels, but do not despair. The governor of Connacht chases them north, and peace will soon be restored. They will be able to return to their homes shortly."

The captain hesitated.

"Are you sure you want me to tell them that?"

"Carry out my instructions. Tell the men whatever it takes to keep them on the walls when the rebels pass."

"I bow to your superior wisdom."

"Remember who is in charge here and keep a cap on your insolence."

Within a week, the rebels had returned from Thomond, but instead of being chased up north as Donough had told his men, they threw a siege around the castle, for it was the last one in Sligo to hold out against them. The men were unhappy, but Donough was relieved, for at least they stayed. Donough summoned his captain once more.

"Send word to Galway that we're besieged. Clifford can crush them beneath the walls of the castle."

The captain nodded and left. A siege was no time for insolence.

The O'Donnell sat in his tent, elated as he summoned his clan subordinates and allies for a conference. His raid to Thomond had been his most profitable yet. An achievement, considering his other raids had stripped most of Connacht. It was his first raid as far south as Thomond and the lands there were plentiful. He even managed to appoint someone, the O'Brien, to establish a rival to the Earl and a rallying point for rebels in the region. Now, no lands in Ireland were untouched by the rebellion.

His prominent men in the clan and allies were all buoyed with the expectation that the spoils would soon be allocated, so all were eager to please the O'Donnell and assure themselves a generous share. Eunan entered the tent, took whatever hands were thrust in front of him, and embraced anyone he knew well. Feargal was more cool towards him, for Eunan had excelled in the campaign once more, elevating his status within the Maguire clan. The Maguire himself had joined them, having extricated himself from the politics of Enniskillen. He reserved his warmest embrace for Eunan.

"I am so jealous of you," the Maguire said. "You are free of the obligations and administrative burdens accompanying my title and can lead the men into battle."

Eunan let go of the embrace and bowed his head.

"What you do is far more important than what I do. You lead the people through the worst of times and plot their path to a better place."

The Maguire smiled in the face of flattery.

"The people now need to see leadership from the field. They need to see me out there, and we must end this perpetual war so they can sow their crops and end their unceasing famine."

Eunan gave a congratulatory grin.

"When we return with our haul from this raid, they should have plenty to eat. There will be milk and cheese aplenty with beef for feast days."

The Maguire looked over his shoulder for prying eyes.

"I would temper your expectations and see how the O'Donnell makes the cut. Along with all of his success and conquests comes the responsibility of feeding many mouths and inspiring true loyalty from the clans who have turned to join us."

Eunan frowned.

"He cannot forget those who supported him all along."

The Maguire slapped him on the shoulder as he moved on to talk to the next person.

"Have a drink and relax. You have earned it. You'll have plenty of worries when you leave this tent either way."

Eunan stuck out his mug when he saw a soldier pass with a bottle, and the Maguire disappeared into the crowd. Eunan began to fret that his men would not get rewarded for his efforts and that the people on his lands would endure further unnecessary hardship despite his efforts on the battlefield. But he was tired after his long ride, and his mind could only see gloom and darkness. He needed his bed.

The O'Donnell's steward called for silence. The O'Donnell stood in front of everybody dressed in a white shirt with the widest smile anyone could remember him having. The drained mug of wine he held out to be filled may have had something to do with it.

"My friends," the O'Donnell said, arms outstretched to welcome everyone in, "we have roamed in Connacht further than we ever have before and mostly unopposed."

A huge roar erupted in the tent, and wine spilt freely as mugs were thrust towards the roof.

"We almost have the whole of Ireland under our control."

Whatever wine remained in mugs after the last salute now spilt onto the floor.

"However, we must temper our excitement. The Lord Deputy roams Munster with one of the largest armies ever to march on Irish soil. But the wily O'Neills have him running here, there and everywhere, refusing to engage him."

There was another roar and the O'Donnell's men distributed more wine to the crowd.

"The English can hide in their castles and roam the fields, and we can avoid them, but that cannot last forever. Therefore, the O'Neill and I have once more written to the Spanish King requesting cannons and a large army to land on these fair shores and drive them out for good."

Wine spilt down Eunan's shirt as the wine fell generously from nearly every mug.

"Unfortunately, if we wait for a large army to join us, we must make provision for them once more."

The room went silent; everyone deflated into themselves once more, and the wine stayed within the confines of their mugs.

"Therefore, I must requisition half of all the cattle taken and half of all non-perishable food and keep it in storage until we receive word of the Spanish King's plans."

Murmurs blazed across the room as if a rebel had set an English settler's field alight.

"My people starve, and what crops they have rot in the field as my men go out and fight for you," one chieftain said but hid in the crowd's anonymity.

The O'Donnell searched the crowd for the dissenting voice, but those not brave enough to speak up at least hid from view those who were. As the murmurs spread, the O'Donnell knew he needed to appease and not punish the dissenting voice.

"Those who have been allied to the O'Neill and me since the start of the rebellion know the O'Neill is a canny negotiator and ensures there is a ceasefire around harvest time. It suits both sides. What do you think will happen to the largest English army to roam these lands when winter comes? If they do not rebel, they will starve or desert to us. That is why, besides denying them a set-piece battle they could win and end the war in one decisive blow, they deny them provisions. We can win a war of attrition but cannot, yet, win a set-piece battle."

"We have heard these promises before, and they never came," another voice said.

"You must have faith, faith in God that he will deliver us from these heretics. Both the Spanish and the Pope have sent soldiers before and have reassured us they will do so again. But rest assured, what food we can spare will be divided according to contribution and population size so all our clans can see out the winter."

The crowd again broke out into low-level murmurings. O'Gallagher, who had stood behind the O'Donnell, watched the reaction of the crowd. He stepped forward and raised his mug.

"TO THE O'DONNELL, THE REBELLION AND FOR GOD!"

O'Gallagher stared down the crowd, daring them not to join in the salute. One by one, the mugs rose until it became an irresistible wave.

"THE O'DONNELL, THE REBELLION AND GOD," the crowd echoed back.

The O'Donnell stepped forward and gestured to the crowd to be silent.

"We will now lay siege to the O'Connor and once he falls, all of Sligo will be ours. Then we move on to Galway and return to Thomond and all of Connacht will be ours."

The crowd roared, and more wine was distributed. It would be a long night.

CHAPTER 35
BAITING THE TRAP

News of the siege of Donough O'Connor Sligo in Collooney Castle quickly spread across Ireland and to the ears of the Lord Deputy. Essex wrote to Clifford in his Galway base and ordered him to make all haste to relieve the castle. He emphasised that O'Connor Sligo was a key ally and should the castle fall and he be killed, or worse, switch sides, then all of Connacht was in danger of falling. Once in receipt of the letter and cursing the resources he was given, Clifford sent appeals to the earls of Clanricard and Thomond and the other remaining loyal allies to send as many men as they could spare.

Within weeks he had assembled a force of fifteen hundred men and two hundred horse, a substantial army comparable to that which took the field at the Battle of the Yellow Ford. However, it was the usual mixed bag of quality that plagued all the English armies: a core of experienced English fighting men and commanders were surrounded by raw English recruits and wavering Irish. But Clifford was confident of success, having thought he had learned the lessons of the Battle of the Rain. He considered himself a lucky commander, for in the Battle of the Rain, he had been blessed with luck to extract his army from the battle intact.

He had a second force set sail from Galway under the command of Tibbot na Long Burke. This was supposed to sail along the coast of Connacht and land in Sligo, outflank the enemy, and the two armies would relieve the castle and then strike into Tyrconnell.

Clifford split his own force into three columns, front, centre and rear, with an experienced commander in charge of each. The plan was for the columns to stick closely together, force their way through the Curlew Pass, the main geographical obstacle in their way, and then on to Collooney Castle. The defeat at the Battle of Yellow Ford had been seared into the memories of the English officers, who were determined not to repeat their mistakes again. They marched along the road at a good pace, and scouts searched the nearby hills for the enemy. The scouts returned as Clifford sat outside his tent with his commanders, planning the approaches to the castle. Clifford waved the scout forward.

"Speak with haste, man, for as you can see, you have the army at your mercy in front of you."

Clifford looked down at the map of the terrain before him and smiled, showing that his words were in jest.

"The enemy is sparse before us in the hills. The O'Donnell and the bulk of his forces are still at the castle and would take some time to get here. The rest of the opposition comes mainly from the O'Rourkes, who would want to avoid a direct confrontation should you pursue your objectives aggressively."

Clifford clapped his hands together for good news had been in short supply lately.

"Then that is what we'll do. Push ahead past the hills, and all that will lie before us is the castle."

"The men would not like that," one captain said. "They have been marching all day and want their dinners."

Clifford laughed.

"They shall have dinner aplenty once we clear these hills, and O'Connor Sligo sorties from the castle to catch the O'Donnell in a pincer. The beef from recaptured cows will be all the tastier after our glorious victory."

Clifford folded the map.

"Go back to your men and draw them up in formation. We press through the hills today."

The captains muttered their protests but obeyed all the same.

Hardly had they left when news of the army marching from Galway arrived at the O'Donnell's camp. The forces assembled around Collooney Castle by the O'Donnell were slightly larger than the Crown's, but he had to maintain a siege and keep away the relieving forces. He did what he could with the resources available, but it was evident that taking the castle quickly without enduring crippling casualties was not possible. Thus, the O'Donnell decided to keep his siege in place and sent the Maguires to help the O'Rourkes guard his flank against an assault from Galway. Eunan was delighted with his new mission.

The south Fermanagh shot emerged eager to do battle, their bullet pouches fully stocked. This gave them the means to engage in a prolonged battle, without the need to risk charging forward and endangering their skilled comrades due to limited ammunition. Behind them marched MacCabe pike with their tips shining in the sunlight. After the Battle of the Rain, they had replenished their numbers, but most recruits were inexperienced and did not match up to the standards of MacCabe Galloglass from earlier days. Feargal personally took charge as they needed to deliver well in their upcoming encounter to enhance his reputation and remain within the Maguire's good books. Meanwhile, Eunan rode confidently ahead with Odhran beside him, having no such concerns.

"What news do you have to bring me of O'Cassidy house?" Eunan said turning to his constable. He had not yet had the time to receive Odhran's report, for he had just returned to the camp and joined up with Eunan and the men.

Odhran paused and looked away to measure his words, for he did not want to say anything negative to his master on the eve of battle.

"Not all the news I have is good."

Eunan grimaced.

"Go on, you may as well tell me. I feared the worst anyway."

"The lands lie idle, and most tenants have fled to the islands. The English lash out from the Pale, and the end of their range is your lands."

"I knew Dervella and Arthur held those lands together, but I didn't realise it was by that much."

"It is worse," Odhran said.

"How so?"

"The attacks are rumoured to be sponsored by your ex-father-in-law, Cormac O'Cassidy."

Eunan turned to the other side of his horse and spat, carefully directing it so he would not hit any of the men.

"I curse the day I let Cormac O'Cassidy walk away. I was too soft and too naïve to think that I could win his daughter over if I showed clemency and left her father alive. Both were stones in my shoe until the day she died, and her father has been a spectre over me ever since. But all that is for another day. I will return to O'Cassidy House and fix it before returning to Augher Castle. We must clear our minds of such stresses and concentrate on the battle ahead."

Eunan turned to Odhran and raised his finger.

"Not a word of this to the men."

Odhran nodded.

"They will loyally follow you home when the campaign is over."

One of Eunan's scouts ran back to the south Fermanagh shot's encampment on top of the hills.

"The English are almost upon us," the messenger said. "They attempt to rush the pass."

"Men, grab your guns and as many bullets as you can fit in your pockets. We're going hunting."

Several minutes later, Eunan was hugging the tops of the hills so the main body of his men would remain out of sight, with only a few scouts shouting where the enemy was located on the other side. Eunan chose a hill that he could easily charge down and retreat up, and he hid over the brow of the hill to wait for the trap to be sprung.

Brian Óg O'Rourke and his men were all over the mountains, for it was in the northern part of his territory and was a favourite hideout and ambush site for his clan for generations. The road through the pass had been barricaded, and his men lined the hills in ambush positions. They had been waiting for the English army ever since they left the town of Boyle. They were well equipped since the O'Neill had been generous with his distribution of weapons, especially muskets, and Brian Óg's men had quickly become acquainted with them. However, there was a certain what-if bitterness in the O'Rourke's heart that if the clans from the north had extended the same generosity to his father then he may not have faced exile, trial and execution at the hands of the English. If was a bitterness that always resided in his heart and gave an edge to any negotiations with the northern clans.

The O'Rourke ordered his men to fell trees and place them on the roadside and created a barrier across the road hidden deep within the hills and not readily visible to the enemy. He also placed musket men behind the barrier and roaming shot and javelin men along the route to harass the English army until the trap was sprung. He sent word to the O'Donnell to send his forces.

The O'Donnell's men began to arrive in the mountains and took up positions behind the main barrier and along the route of the English army so they could harass them as they made their way to the barrier. Eunan and his men were given the signal to begin their attacks.

Clifford rode ahead of his men to the base of the hills and saw little opposition. The sun appeared out from behind a bank of clouds and invited him forward. He rode back to his men and saw discontented faces. It was time to spur the men onwards.

"Men, I know I have driven you hard on this hot August day and that I promised you rest. However, we must take an opportunity where it presents itself. If I let you camp and eat here this night I would be negligent. The enemy would be on the hills and taking pot shots at us by the morn."

He looked at the faces and saw his words were beginning to gain some traction.

"However, if we camp on the other side of the hills, then it is we who have the advantage this evening and the enemy would not dare approach us. What do you say, men? Will you follow me to victory?"

The men gave a half-hearted cheer. Clifford went red and stared down his commanders. His commanders then started roaring their support and walked along the ranks of their men to ensure they also joined in. Once the roar gained some volume it spread like wild fire down the ranks. Clifford waved his sword in the air and pointed it at the hills. The men marched on with renewed vigour and enthusiasm.

They marched through the hills unmolested until they came across a barrier of freshly felled trees across the road. A small number of rebel shot peppered the front ranks with bullets but few met their mark. A couple of volleys and the rebels were dispersed, and Clifford ordered his men to clear the road. The brief skirmish only served to encourage their confidence.

They marched further into the hills and began to notice the felled trees along the sides of the road. The men began to look nervous but Clifford just spurred them on, confident they could overcome any resistance given they had encountered little so far. The rear of the final of the three columns entered the hills. The road now passed between two bogs with a wood on the fringes of one of them. Concentrated fire now came out of the woods and Clifford ordered some of his men to clear the woods as the rest of the army marched onwards.

CHAPTER 36
THE BATTLE OF CURLEW PASS

Eunan sat alone on the top of the hill, hidden behind some trees, and his men sat below him at the bottom. He listened to the drums of the English army as they marched past on the other side of the hill. He turned to Odhran who now lay beside him after returning from inspecting the men.

"Are they ready?" Eunan said. "Have they sufficient bullets for a sustained firefight?"

Odhran smiled the confident smile of youth not yet jaded by the experience of battle.

"They have full pockets, and we have riders on the hills with bags full of bullets if we need them."

"Good. Now, remember my instructions. Only fire volleys until I say otherwise and concentrate fire on the nearest large block of the enemy to maximise the damage."

Odhran saluted him.

"Just like we practised." He turned and waved to the men and signalled them to move to the crest of the hill.

Eunan signalled to the men to stand behind him as he was the first over the top of the hill. He rounded the crest of the hill and crept his way down from tree to bush to tree again so he could get a better view. It was a crisp day, warm for that time of summer, and Eunan could certainly feel the discomfort of sweat beneath his armpits.

The sky was a sheer blue with wispy white clouds casting passing shadows on the ground as they flew overhead; whatever cloud formations had been there earlier on had been blown away. Eunan could see far across the countryside, but all he had to do was look to the bottom of the hill to see the lumbering snake of the English army slithering amongst the hills below him. He could see the front of the army make its way in between the two bogs, but his position was near the rear of the army and the baggage train. His mission was to force the army further into the trap while not allowing the discipline of his men to break down and for them to forget about the battle and just loot the baggage train.

Eunan snuck a little further forward to see what troop types were before him. The musket men had been deployed on the flanks for the firefight that had broken out at the vanguard, which could be heard all the way to the rear had put their commander on alert. There were not many of them, and they could be easily driven off. The main body of men were pikemen who were sitting ducks for his marksmen. The English cavalry, the units he feared the most, were in the vanguard, attempting to pick their way through the bogs to get some space to mount a charge should the enemy be foolish enough to appear. The rebels shadowing the army had not yet started concerted attacks as the O'Rourke wished to ensure the English were fully in the trap first. It looked good enough to him, so Eunan went back over the hill to order the attack.

Clifford's heart raced as the firefight at the vanguard intensified. He spurred his horse forward, bellowing out orders. But as his men desperately fought against the overwhelming numbers of O'Donnell's rebels, their ammunition began to run low. The rebel forces now surrounded them on three sides and unleashed a hellish wave of musket fire.

"They fight like cowards!" Clifford yelled defiantly, sword held high. "Drive forward, men, and we can sweep them from the field."

The Irish lines wavered under the ferocity of the English onslaught, but they dug in their heels and began to make a stand. So many men had arrived that they could now send in a fresh volley of shots each time one was expended, and soon enough, they found themselves with a new strength and a renewed sense of purpose. The waves of English shot slowly began to waver as they ran out of ammunition, and with no other choice, the pikemen broke ranks and ran down the valley. The musketeers were left exposed to the fire of the enemy, and chaos ensued as they fled from the field. All around them lay corpses of those who had bravely charged into battle — it was Yellow Ford all over again; Clifford had failed to heed the lessons of past battles, and now he was paying for it in blood.

Eunan and his men raced down the hill, using the sparse cover of trees, bushes, and rocks to keep out of sight. Eunan peered over a rock at the English army marching in perfect order just beyond his men's firing range. He watched as their musketeers faced forward, away from the sound of battle, while the pikemen behind them provided an easy target. Clenching his axe above his head, he bellowed out:

"THE CRY OF THE MAGUIRE!"

His men sprang up from their positions and formed a line with lightning speed. The English musketeers heard the cry over the roar of distant fire and began to fire off random shots at the now visible enemies — too few bullets to cause any actual damage.

"FIRE!"

Eunan roared through gritted teeth as his men let loose a deadly volley, granting no mercy to those who dared stand in their way.

The Maguires opened fire with a thunderous roar, shredding through the pikemen below them. Bodies flew left and right, clumps of flesh and bone ripped apart by the volley. The men below desperately tried to form ranks, but their efforts were for nought as another volley careened down towards them.

They were riddled by a hail of bullets, leaving behind a mass of bodies strewn across the ground. Men dropped their pikes and ran in a wild frenzy, but the carnage continued as Eunan kept firing without mercy.

The bullets thundered through the air, tearing through the soldiers as if they were made of paper. Blood and screams filled the air as smoke blanketed everything in sight. The rebels' shouts echoed off of the hills around them, bellowing out from every direction. Eunan held up his axe one last time; "TO ME, MEN!" he shouted, more determined than ever. As he plunged forward, he could feel the heat from burning gunpowder that hung like a fog around him.

The smoke devoured his vision, and Eunan could hear the thudding of his own heart in his ears. Men fell around him, their bodies convulsing in pain as they coughed up blood. "RETREAT!" he roared through gritted teeth, struggling to maintain control of his troops. The men flocked to him, seeking shelter from the endless volleys of English muskets that were driving them back. Eunan counted their numbers with trembling fingers, a euphoric high coursing through his veins as he realised how few they had lost.

"Three," he exclaimed triumphantly, raising his fists to the sky in a manic frenzy. "We only lost three! Think of how many we've felled! The Maguire will be proud of you boys — as am I!"

The soldiers fell into formation before him, some grinning through the pain while others winced at their wounds. "Are we charging?" one man asked eagerly, looking at Eunan like a boundless ball of energy balanced on the edge of exhaustion.

"How many bullets have we left?" Eunan demanded, scanning the faces of his troops for answers.

The men fished in their pockets and most could come up with the best part of a handful. Odhran came and made himself known by slapping Eunan on the back. He held out a sack so Eunan could see the top of the contents.

"Dip in here," Odhran said as he invited the men to place their hands in the sack. "This is the last of our bullets. The riders have gone to fetch more."

Eunan stood in front of the men and extended his hand as an invitation for them to fill their pockets with bullets.

"Lest you forget, but I shall say it again if I have not said it many times before," Eunan said. "Each of the lives of my men is precious, and take this to be true no matter what you hear my detractors say. We enjoyed great success with the bullet today, and we shall stick with it. We shall volley until we are out of bullets and then see where the battle takes us. There are many Galloglass armed with the axe that will revel in the charge. Eat what food you have and refresh yourselves with ale and water. Then we shall form a line and engage with the enemy once more."

Clifford stood amongst his fleeing musketeers, a rock in the stream trying to stem the momentum of the water.

"Stand and fight! Stand and fight! Do not let our courage be lost today; we can still push forward!"

The commander of the vanguard shuffled up, his body bleeding heavily from wounds in his leg and shoulder.

"If we pull back now we can still save most of the army," he said, trying to avoid Clifford's gaze.

"No retreat! You must throw all of your men into one final attack," Clifford commanded sternly, his face twisted with a fervour like wild fire.

"My men won't listen," the commander despaired, defeated.

"Make them listen. That is what it means to be a leader."

The commander turned to his sergeants, desperation in his voice.

"Turn those men around. Charge at the rebel barricades ahead!"

The sergeants grabbed any soldier they could find, urging them to lift up discarded weapons as they ran past. Clifford followed suit, rounding up more men until there was a mob ready to follow him. He held his sword aloft, casting its shining blade against the dark sky.

"Look at me here! Let no man say I did not put myself in danger as I asked of you! Now charge forward, men, and drive these rebels away — FOR THE QUEEN!"

A thunderous roar filled the air as Clifford charged into the smoke-filled battlefield, sword held aloft. Men followed behind him, propelled by their loyalty to their leader and their Queen.

CHAPTER 37

THE LAST CHARGE

B rian Óg O'Rourke's jaw tensed as the smoke billowed up from the bottom of the hill, filling his nostrils with the stench of death. He held a miniature crucifix tightly in his pocket, its cold metal reminding him of the last time he had seen his father alive. His head pounded with rage at the thought of how these same allies had not come to aid his father against the English oppressors.

A man staggered through the smoke, cloaked in blood and dirt. "The English are counter-attacking," he cried desperately, "this is our last chance!" Brian Óg surveyed the row of men behind him — all that remained of his father's MacDonnell Galloglass, those who had stayed loyal when he had been left alone to fight the English in Breifne. Armed only with their traditional armour and battleaxes, what chance did they stand against muskets and pikes?

"The men are champing at the bit," a constable who came up and stood beside him said.

Brian Óg put his hand on the constable's shoulder.

"I will speak to them."

Brian Óg held out his hand to his horseboy to receive his axe. He turned to address his men.

"You have always served my family well. I remember the sacrifices you have made for both myself and my father. I treasure each one of you. But I also remember you are Galloglass and fighting for glory and livelihoods. Then I give this to you as your shot of glory to go down in the annals of the O'Rourkes.

The enemy lies in disarray below us. The MacDonnells can smash them from the field and be legends for all eternity. Are you with me, men?"

The men roared back and shook their axes in the air.

"DEATH OR GLORY, FOR BRIAN O'ROURKE."

"FOR BRIAN O'ROURKE."

The MacDonnells charged into the smoke.

Clifford thrust his blade through the acrid haze of smoke, aiming at every soldier he saw fleeing.

"The enemy is the other way! Cowards shall find no quarter with me!" he bellowed.

With a sudden resolve, they turned and ran into the smoke to ensure their commander could not see what they did next.

"Where are the cavalry? Where are the cavalry?" Clifford shouted behind them, but his plea was rendered mute by the din of battle as gunfire echoed in every direction. He heard the thundering clamour of men charging each other, yet all he saw was an impenetrable blur of fire and smoke. Suddenly, he felt a thud in his chest, which knocked him off his feet. His lifeblood draining out from his wound, he felt his energy seeping away while his hearing dimmed into a dull buzz. Out of the fog of war, an axe came hurtling towards him, and all he could make out were its sharp edges gleaming like silver in the sunlight.

Brian Óg O'Rourke brought his axe down time and again with a fierce passion, feeling the spatter of hot blood on his face. Each swing was an act of vengeance for his slain father, whose spirit he felt watching him through the smoke of battle. He met little resistance with each strike as the enemy fled in terror until a single man stepped forward to bar O'Rourke's way. Filled with rage, he shouldered them aside with enough force to send an ordinary man flying. The enemy continued to run in all directions, causing Brian to roar in frustration as the heavy weight of his armour kept him from pursuing them. Finally, O'Rourke held his axe aloft above his head, its sharp blade dripping with the blood of justice. In a voice filled with fury and victory, he said, "I have done something small to avenge the massive wrong done to you, Father." At his cry, the remaining MacDonnells cheered and surrounded him, patting him respectfully on the back.

As the men devoured their meals, the acrid scent of gunpowder burning in their nostrils, Eunan and Odhran slunk down the hill like predators stalking prey. Their breaths came in short gasps as they darted from rock to rock, fear pressurising their chests. With adrenaline coursing through their veins, they finally found refuge behind a boulder. From there, they watched the battle raging below, terror gripping and rooting them to the spot. Through the thick smoke, Eunan pointed out the enemy's position.

"I think they're breaking. We must get back to the men now."

"How can you tell?" Odhran said. "I can only make out occasional masses of men between the smoke."

"The musket fire sounds more dispersed and sporadic now. My bet is they have run out of ammunition. It is up to us to ensure no bullets are passed from the baggage train to the men at the front."

They abandoned the rock and any attempt to conceal themselves and took to their heels.

Eunan raced towards his men, his feet pounding the ground in heavy thumps that shook the earth beneath them. He stopped before them, huffing and puffing with his hands pressed onto his knees as he tried to catch his breath.

"Men," he said between breaths. "The climax of the battle is upon us. If you want to be greeted as heroes when we return to Fermanagh and for the people to open their doors to you and welcome you in, then the time for action is now."

"Lead us," said one man who stepped forward. "For the glory of the Maguire and the good of Fermanagh."

"Then form a line, and we shall charge down the hill. Look around and pick something memorable about the landscape that will lead you back to this hill. We'll assemble here after the battle."

The men quickly stowed their food and grabbed their weapons, frantically cocking them and filling each chamber with a cartridge. Eunan roared a rallying cry as he formed the men into an unwavering line. An unstoppable force, they descended upon the fleeing enemy below. With every step forward, Eunan was determined to meet their adversaries with an ironclad resolve, bullets be damned. Nothing could slow their momentum as they marched forth in unison towards certain victory.

"FIRE," Eunan cried as soon as they were within range. "Stay steady and reload." Once the men were ready, he yelled "FIRE" again. No longer would he be known as the butcher of the Battle of the Rain. He would gain the men's respect by leading by example and preserving their lives.

Brian Óg O'Rourke's men surged forward with a primal ferocity, rallying around him as they regrouped. The English cavalry had remained unscathed by their gunfire and counter-attack. The rebel shot also rallied after being dislodged from some of the hills by the cavalry charge and now began to concentrate their fire on them. Shots rang out, bullets whizzing past the riders as the vanguard of the English, who the encircling rebels had trapped, desperately attempted to escape under the cover of mounted men. Bravely, Brian led his men into battle, fighting through the enemy lines until they stopped over Clifford's dead body.

"Take him to the rear and guard him with your lives," he commanded. "He will come in useful later."

The English horse galloped forward, their hooves thudding like thunder on the ground, until they formed an ironclad wall of steel trapping the O'Rourke and his men like rabbits in a snare. Brian planted his axe into the ground before them and braced himself for the impact.

"Men! Hold fast! For if we survive this charge — our victory is certain!"

The horse boys ran up and down the hill, frantically tossing handfuls of bullets to the musketeers so they could volley into the enemy ranks before they escaped. But everywhere Eunan looked, he saw the overheating or explosion of guns and the subsequent injuries to the musketeers, who immediately dropped their weapons at the first sign of danger. Eunan had lost more men to injuries due to weapons malfunction than to the enemy so far that day. Odhran had taken charge while Eunan snuck up the valley to evaluate how many more of the enemy would be running past to see if the army was in full retreat. He went to fetch his master after he had been gone for twenty minutes. Eunan lay behind a rock, spying up the valley.

"Look," Eunan said, pointing. "The enemy attempts to rally behind their cavalry. But look how our shot surrounds them. What a wonder the musket is. I was brought up a Galloglass but most certainly will not end the war as one."

"I would not be so hasty, lord. The men can no longer volley, for though they may have bullets, their guns require repair or rest."

Eunan smiled and took one of his throwing axes from his belt.

"These may see some action after all," he said as he admired the sharpness of the blade. "I have had these a long time and think I shall get some blood on them today."

"The men have an assortment of weapons, but if we charge the enemy, we will lose some of them."

"Some may die for glory today, but I will ensure their lives will not be lost in vain."

Eunan ran back to his men, who stood, their muscles strained, waiting for his instructions. Eunan stood panting in front of them and pointed down towards the valley.

"I could stand here and compose another speech, but the sight below you should be motivation enough. The enemy below is beaten, but we can charge down, rout them, and become heroes. Are you with me, men?"

"YES," they roared in unison.

"Odhran, get the horse boys to arm the men with whatever they can. We have no time to waste."

Brian Óg grasped his axe tightly, the sharpened metal of its blade cutting into the palm of his hands. He wanted to make sure he could feel if he was going to become a martyr and join his father in heaven. He could almost feel the terror of those oncoming horsemen, smell their sweat and hear their pounding hooves as they barrelled towards him. His father and brother flashed through his mind as a single bead of sweat rolled down his spine. Steeling himself with their memories, he tensed his body as the enemy charged.

The ground trembled beneath him, and Brian Óg closed his eyes with one last breath, praying for salvation.

Clenching his jaw, Brian Óg faced the onslaught, knowing full well that in moments, the first wave of horsemen would be obliterated by the force of his men's charge. Then, something inside him stirred — it was courage, or maybe it was rage — and with a strength he hadn't known he possessed, Brian Óg reached to the ghosts of his past and shouted "God help me", as if beckoning divine intervention.

The ground beneath him shook as a great crash filled the air, and then came smoke. He opened his eyes and felt the discomfort of a wet patch around his groin. He found himself standing amidst a field of mangled corpses and groaning horses, blood splattered across his chest and legs but somehow still alive! Somewhere far off, another explosion rang out. He realised it was the sound of the volleying of Irish muskets, and they had shattered the charge before impact. Brian Óg felt a surge of power run through him. God had answered his prayers. With a battle cry, he charged forward, slashing and slicing any hapless soul who stood before him until none were left standing and the English army scattered in fear.

Eunan wielded the six-foot Galloglass axe in his grip and felt its power grow with each rotation. He admired his weapon, and it felt balanced in his hands. The horse boys had assembled an impressive arsenal to arm his men; now, it was time for a reckoning. Eunan swept the axe above his head, bellowing as loud as he could:

"THE CRY OF THE MAGUIRE! FOR THE MAGUIRE!"

Fury burned in his heart as his men raced down the hillside towards their unsuspecting enemies. Most of the enemy turned tail and fled, while those who remained were cut down mercilessly by Eunan's axe. Blood flew everywhere with each mighty swing, drenching him from face to chest. Stragglers cried out for mercy, but they found none here. Eunan was a force of nature, a dealer in death that could not be impeded. Men fell left and right until only the Irish remained victorious over the dead bodies of their enemies. Heaving one final breath, Eunan raised his axe, and they retreated back up the hill, bruised and bloodied but alive to tell their stories.

CHAPTER 38

THE FEAST

The O'Donnell's heart raced in his chest as his fury drove him relentlessly around his tent. He had missed another glorious victory, one that could have secured his place in history alongside the great O'Neill. The bards and poets were already singing songs of triumph while he was left with nothing but a swirling tempest of envy and regret. How many victories would he miss before he was no longer remembered at all? The thought made him shudder with dread. Would he be remembered in history as the man who could have been great if only he had arrived on time? He must seize this moment, find some way to claim glory for the O'Donnells and displace the O'Neill as the pre-eminent force in Ulster. In a rage, he summoned Eoghan McToole O'Gallagher, hoping against hope that his right-hand man could offer some solution to this unshakable feeling of failure.

"Get the best cattle from my herd and the finest wine we recently got from Spain. Then spread the word that the O'Donnell is to have the finest celebration of the victory at Curlew mountains."

O'Gallagher froze as he determined what his master was up to.

"What if the O'Rourke is celebrating himself in his own lands?"

"Spare no expense, do not shirk at any bribe. All celebrations must be held under the tent of the O'Donnell."

O'Gallagher spent lavishly, twisted many arms, and adjusted the spoils of the battle until everyone was happy to show up and have the battle celebration under the tent of the O'Donnell.

The raging fires of the O'Donnell's feast lit up the night sky like a beacon, spreading from one horizon to the other to display the victorious might of the O'Donnell's army. The smell of roasting cows wafted through the night air, summoning man and beast to raise their noses and admire the feast. The bards and poets flocked from Tirconnell, chasing their master's coin to witness and immortalise the moment. Their words were needed to ensure that the memory of this grand victory was credited to the O'Donnell and was etched into history as so for all time.

Eunan and his men arrived at the feast, and Odhran walked beside him with his head held high. Instantly recognised, Eunan was welcomed at the top table while his men were escorted to the section reserved for the men of the Maguire. He demanded Odhran join him at his side, claiming him to be his loyal right-hand man and secretary should any business need to be done. A chair was hastily arranged as Eunan approached the top table where the Maguire rose with pride, extending his hands in greeting towards his commander.

"Eunan, come and let me embrace the hero of the Maguires."

Eunan made his way past the table, to the other side, past his fellow Maguire commanders and into the embrace of the Maguire. A wave of clapping broke out at the public display of affection for one of the victors of the battle. A strange calm came over Eunan as he rested his head briefly on the Maguire's shoulders. The Maguire broke the embrace and held Eunan at arm's length. He then took Eunan's arm and held it aloft to the jubilant crowd. Eunan beamed as he looked out onto the sea of ecstatic faces. The Maguire held his arm aloft and moved in a short crescent so all could see the victorious Eunan. The Maguire let go of his arm and invited him to sit beside him. Feargal grunted, for he was not forewarned that he would have to give up his seat to his underling. He told a passing servant to prepare a seat for him next to Irial among the MacCabe leaders at the Maguire section of the table.

Eunan sat, and the rosy glow of being acknowledged in front of the entire O'Donnell army settled on his chest. He sat down and his mug was immediately filled. His head swam with a multitude of emotions. He took a swig of his wine, which went straight to his head. Amongst the swirl of alcohol were the memories of those who had slighted him.

He thought of his mother in her little cart, her spindly useless legs hanging over the sides. She wore her usual scowl as she scolded him for whatever he had done that was not good enough. *I showed her.*

He thought of his father. The man who had coldly handed him over as a hostage to the Maguire Galloglass while all the other fathers wept for their sons. *I showed him.*

In his mind, his birth father was a giant ginger ogre who greedily ate and drank, while his parents were stuck serving him for eternity. *Serves them all right.*

"More wine?" asked a smiling girl. Eunan snapped to and nodded towards his mug.

He watched as his mug was automatically filled, and a plate of beef and bread was placed before him. The only work he would have to do tonight was lift his wine and food to his mouth and pull down his pants to piss. He began to swim in more emotional depths as he took another swig of wine, and the easy emotions of hatred and revenge melted away as more of his emotional range became exposed.

His mind then switched to Desmond. Desmond was the first person to believe in him, the first person to give him a chance. If it were not for Desmond, what he taught him and who he introduced him to, he would not be here today. He owed Desmond his life. He felt his throwing axes on his belt — the gift from Desmond that he went nowhere without, so he would be reminded of him always. His head hung as he remembered how Desmond had sacrificed himself at his trial and how Desmond had turned a hopeless situation into a triumph. He took another swig of wine and drifted further into melancholy.

He saw the dead bodies of Dervella and Arthur and imagined himself holding them to his chest with tears streaming down his face. Today may be great, but he still had scores to settle. Then he thought of Seamus, and his mind tipped over into stormy seas. His emotions about Seamus were as tumultuous as the ferocious Atlantic Ocean they took to when Seamus came to rescue him. He received a punch in the shoulder.

"Hey, don't fall in your mug there," the Maguire said, the beaming smile having not been diminished even by a degree. "The O'Rourke is about to be presented to the O'Donnell."

Eunan smiled back and realised what he felt when the Maguire had embraced him. Acceptance.

The grimmest faces on the top table belonged to Feargal and Irial, their eyes burning like hot coals. Feargal's men had hardly blooded their axes in battle, only managing to make it to the end of the fight because they were positioned at the rear of the O'Donnell army. Irial had been forced to attend the feast by the Maguire, who insisted that this day was a pivotal moment for his clan. But Irial's presence was not an act of worship for the glorious victor. He had no intention of bowing down to Eunan Maguire. Leaning in close, he whispered to Feargal, his voice dripping with venom.

"That witch he has taken up with sure has some magical powers."

"How so?" Feargal said.

"His wife has been struck blind, so she no longer presents as a rival, and somehow Eunan has taken over this day, the victory of the O'Donnell."

"My gut wrenches just as yours does at the sight of that impostor taking the glory. What did he do in that battle exactly? Not get all his men killed? If we look on the bright side we are down to farm boys to be the next MacCabes so at least we do not have to go on a recruiting drive. But to be fair to the Maguire, he needed to be seen as contributing to the victory and Eunan's was the most prominent Maguire unit to take part in the entire battle."

"Such is the downside of your plan, to put him in harm's way, but he survives and accumulates glory."

Feargal turned away and sneered.

"He will get his comeuppance one day."

"Well, maybe I will have to intercede so that day comes all the quicker."

"Don't let me stop you. If you wish to take the dirty work out of my hands, I am more than willing to give it to you."

"Then it is done. I assume I can resume an active rank in the MacCabe once again?"

"If the Maguire gives you permission, then who am I to stand in the way?"

"Leave the Maguire to me. Now let us resume watching this pantomime where the O'Donnell attempts to claim glory from a battle he did not even attend."

Brian O'Rourke was directed to the rear of the celebrations. MacSweeney Galloglass cleared a path for him through the crowd to the top table with the O'Donnell. He stood at the base of the cleared path and refused to move. The O'Rourke was not best pleased to be made a show pony by the man who had given sanctuary to his half-brother and the next with the strongest claim to be the O'Rourke. Especially when this brother had once been in the pocket of the English and was used as a puppet to replace his father. O'Gallagher grabbed him by the shoulders when he saw his doubts.

"Take the plaudits, put the past behind you and make up with the O'Donnell."

"But it was my victory, not his."

"You know how the clan system works. He may not have been there himself, but he supplied plenty of men and weapons for you to win it."

"The spirit of my father won it. His spirit came to me when the English cavalry tried to ride me down. He came and protected me. I remember how others, such as the O'Donnells, failed to protect him."

O'Gallagher stood in front of the O'Rourke to block any prying ears.

"You may not have your advisers here, but take this as good advice from me. Go and take the plaudits from the O'Donnell, and do not insult him. Bury the past deep in your heart and do not speak of it until you are alone with the O'Donnell and are at liberty to speak freely. Do not throw away the most significant victory the O'Rourkes have had in God knows how long just to prolong a bitter squabble about the past. Now get up there and shake his hand in front of everyone."

The O'Rourke snarled at O'Gallagher and felt for his dagger.

"That would not only throw away the victory but be the end of the O'Rourkes. Do you really want to do that?"

The O'Rourke glowered at O'Gallagher.

"You know I'm right. Do I have to march you up there, or will you go willingly?"

The O'Rourke turned, grunted, raised his hand, and smiled, and the men around him clapped. He walked up the cleared path and O'Gallagher followed behind him slowly with two bodyguards of his own to ensure everything passed peacefully. When he approached the O'Donnell, the MacSweeney braced themselves and went for their weapons when they saw the O'Rourke was still armed. The O'Donnell raised his hand and smiled, and his men stood down. When the O'Rourke reached the top table the O'Donnell embraced him. He let go and then raised the victor's hand in front of the crowd just as the Maguire had done to Eunan. The O'Rourke smiled, kept his mouth shut and took the applause.

CHAPTER 39

DRUNKEN FOOTBALL

T he feast, which began early in the afternoon, stumbled and fell into the evening. Eunan looked at his plate and his mug being refilled and wondered if the supply of refreshments was endless. Several bards had taken to the tables beneath him and, much to his embarrassment, composed songs about his bravery. He would have given any amount of money to make them stop, but the Maguire found it hilarious and encouraged them to continue. They crept ever forward with their rhyming couplets, and Eunan cringed back into his chair.

"ENOUGH."

All eyes switched to the top table as a drunken O'Rourke flailed his arms around to get the O'Donnell's attention. Eunan took advantage of the Maguire being distracted by throwing his old meat bones at the bards to drive them away.

"I forgot," the O'Rourke said, wagging his finger at the O'Donnell. "I have a present for you."

The O'Donnell was equally as drunk and roared laughing at the O'Rourke's antics.

"Get the bag," the O'Rourke roared at his men, who looked back at him in confusion. "You know, the bag."

The O'Rourke made as many frustrated gestures as he could that would provide meaning to the men but not give the game away. At last, one of them remembered and ran into the crowd.

"You shouldn't have," said the O'Donnell as he waited for his present.

"I should have, I did, and you'll like it," the O'Rourke said as he flopped back into his seat. He drummed his fingers on the arm of his chair and berated himself for not bringing the present to give to him when they shook hands to celebrate the victory. His man back ran through the crowd with a sack in his hand. The O'Rourke scowled at his incompetence as he saw a wet red stain on the sides of the sack. But the O'Donnell had become distracted again, and the O'Rourke leant over, grabbed the sack and hid it under his armpit, out of the view of the O'Donnell. With the sack firmly under his armpit he took one last swig of wine and attempted to creep behind the chairs of the top table and over to the O'Donnell. But as people tried to get out of his way and some ended up getting in it, he stumbled and fell onto the table. The O'Donnell turned around and laughed.

"At least you weren't trying to stab me in the back. Here, let me help you up." He reached down his hand. A red-faced O'Rourke held up his.

"God damn it," the O'Rourke said as he got up and realised he had got blood from the sack all over his coat.

The O'Donnell grinned.

"Is that what I think it is?"

The O'Rourke grinned back and nodded.

"You present it, then. It is your prize," the O'Donnell said.

The O'Rourke picked up the sack and climbed on the bench and stood on the table. His men rushed to support his wobbly legs. He struggled to maintain his balance and the sack hit the table with a thud.

"Give it here," the O'Rourke called to the man who retrieved the sack.

"COME ALL YE REBELS AND LISTEN TO ME," the O'Rourke called out to everyone at the feast. Every head turned in his direction if only to see if he could manage not to fall off the table. The O'Rourke looked around and saw all eyes on him.

"WE WON A GREAT VICTORY YESTERDAY, THE GREATEST SEEN BY ANY CLAN HERE SINCE..." He paused to look down to see if anyone could give him a date but they all looked away. "ANYWAY, IT DOESN'T REALLY MATTER. ASK ONE OF THE BARDS OR THE PO-

ETS, THEY'LL KNOW, THAT'S THEIR JOB NOT MINE. IT WAS THE GREATEST VICTORY IN ALL THE NORTH, GREATER EVEN THAN YELLOW FORD." The crowd heaved a collective sigh for something that could be taken as an insult to the O'Neill. "DO YOU KNOW WHY?" The O'Rourke thrust his hand into the sack and pulled out the contents. "BECAUSE I GOT HIS HEAD. BY GOD'S BLOOD I CUT CLIFFORD'S HEAD OFF!"

The crowd roared and threw their mugs in the air. The O'Rourke stood bow-legged and raised the head up in victory. The O'Donnell was elated at the sight of the head and scrambled on top of the table to be seen beside the head and the O'Rourke. The table wobbled under the weight of the two men, the wine spilt, and the O'Donnell slipped. The O'Rourke felt his balance going.

"HERE'S A LITTLE TREAT FROM ME. YOU CAN PLAY FOOTBALL WITH THIS."

He kicked the head out of his hands and into the crowd. He slipped on the wet table, fell backwards, and the table collapsed beneath him. O'Donnells and O'Rourkes alike rushed to assist their clan leaders to their feet. The O'Donnell got up relatively unhurt and dusted himself off.

"BRING ME THE HEAD," he roared into the crowd. O'Gallagher and some MacSweeneys waded into the crowd to retrieve the head. They wrenched it back from some angry O'Haras who were about to use it as a football as the O'Rourke instructed. O'Gallagher strode through the baying mob and handed the head to his master. The O'Donnell took the head, looked into the eyes of his former adversary and laughed.

"I've got a much better use for this head. Saddle the horses. We must get to the castle before nightfall."

The O'Donnell and the O'Rourke mounted their horses behind each of their respective clan's best sober riders and made for the gates of Collooney Castle. They pulled up out of gunshot and arrow range and got off the horses.

"Don't look, don't look. The O'Rourke has to go do something undignified." He held his stomach as his men helped him off his horse. He ran behind the horses and out of the range of the back-kicking hoofs and threw up.

The O'Donnell laughed even though his stomach barely felt any better.

"It is good the men see you are human after all. Now come, we have business to attend to."

The O'Donnell waved the O'Rourke forward and walked towards the gate. O'Gallagher ran after him. He tried to grab the O'Donnell's arm, thought better of this and with a little spurt, ran in front of him.

"Let me go to the castle under a flag of truce. Not for glory, lord, but because the men in the castle are without honour and would strike you down if given half a chance, no matter the circumstances."

The O'Donnell sighed and held up the sack.

"You are right. My mother would kill me if I placed myself in such reckless danger. Make the truce, place the head and give them my offer. They are safely tucked up in their castle and we can wait until morning should they not see sense."

O'Gallagher called for a horse and took a white handkerchief out of his pocket. He mounted his horse and rode slowly towards the castle gate with the white handkerchief clearly visible.

"That's far enough," came the cry from the parapet.

"I have a present for the O'Connor that he really should see. It could end all of this amicably."

"What is it?"

"It's in the bag. If you let me ride up to the gate I will leave it there and ride off. No tricks. Show it to the O'Connor. Then we shall see how it goes from there."

"Leave the sack and be on your way."

O'Gallagher did as he was told and rode back to join the O'Donnell. He slapped O'Gallagher on the back.

"Let's get back to the feast before our friend here, the O'Rourke, sobers up."

The next day, the castle surrendered.

CHAPTER 40
TROUBLED DUBLIN

By this time, the campaign in Munster had petered out as Essex left most of his force there, and he marched back to Dublin. The force he returned with was a ragbag of horse boys, the sick and wounded, while only the minority of the army was fit and well soldiers. Every step they took towards Dublin stripped them of their strength through desertions and the further spread of illness. The largest army ever sent by the Queen was now broken and wasted. Riders came from Dublin with messages from the Queen. Essex kept the contents of the messages hidden, but the Queen was not shy about bad-mouthing Essex in her court. Rumours spread around Dublin about how angry she was with him at having squandered her army and having the mere taking of one castle to show for it.

Essex secured himself in Dublin castle and called a council of war.

Captain Williamson stood at the window of Cormac O'Cassidy's house and stared out over the docks, a sense of dread permeating the air. The pristine morning sun struggled to push away the darkness as it crept across the horizon, a vain attempt to bring hope amongst horror. Gone were the days of ships filled with soldiers, now replaced by jetties overflowing with food, guns, horses, and pikes — enough to rearm an entire broken army.

"Even in defeat we become rich," Captain Williamson said as he poured himself a mug of wine.

"There is only one thing that drives me," O'Cassidy said, "and that is getting revenge for my daughter's death. Our arrangement goes well, but I have paid a lot of money for the head of Eunan Maguire and still have nothing to show for it. Is there any news on his whereabouts?"

"His newfound fame means he cannot hide from me. If you hadn't changed sides, he would have been quite a catch for your daughter."

"Don't insult my family like that, even in jest. He is a thorn in both our sides. What plans do you have to deliver him, or else all of this money, this house, is useless to me. My life is unbearably lonely without my daughter."

"Don't worry. The Lord Deputy has called a council of war. Rumour has it he will march on Ulster."

"Given the large influx of orders I've received, the army is an utter shambles."

Captain Williamson turned from the window.

"I will hold my remaining hand up and be the first to admit there have been mistakes. But the Lord Deputy is still one of the Queen's best men for all his obvious faults and lack of experience on this island. Once we are in the north, we can dispose of Eunan Maguire."

O'Cassidy gave a wry smile.

"I hope you are right for all our sakes."

It was supposed to be a secret but the Lord Deputy announced loud and clear to all the land that he was back in Dublin for a council of war. He threw the most lavish parties Dublin could cater for to both impress the local gentry into supporting the ongoing war, and to make up for the fact that he was no longer in the Queen's court. Her letters to him, although never subtle, became more and more blunt, questioning what he had done with both the army and the budget given to him. She ordered him to take the battle to the O'Neill on pain of being recalled in disgrace. He summoned his best officers and spies.

Essex sat liberally drinking wine as his underlings unfurled several maps of Ireland and its provinces on the grand table in the hall of the castle. The officers stood on the wings of the room whispering and giving darting glances to the maps, hoping this conference would not be concerning itself with assigning blame. Only after the wine and accompanying food had been distributed evenly along the table did Essex invite them all to sit. Captain Williamson and St. Leger sat towards the end of the long table, glad they were out of immediate range should the Lord Deputy choose to victimise anyone in a fit of anger. Essex took one last sip of wine, stood up and placed his two hands on the table and leaned over. His reddened cheeks gave away his stress.

"The Queen has set me the task of restoring order to this wretched country, and I have marched south, and none of the rebel cowards had the nerve to face me in the field."

He looked at the faces of his audience to see if anyone would contradict him, but just like the rebels they turned away without the heart to tell him for the umpteenth time how things worked around there.

"However, the rebels still lurk in the bogs and forests, and it is illness that would stop our men from driving them out, not any actions of the rebels. What weak constitutions must our soldiers have to be so unable to fight off the ailments that fester on this island? Therefore, we must cut off the head of the snake. Does anyone have any good suggestions for a course of action that would bring this wretched war to an end?"

Again all heads looked downwards.

"What am I supposed to say to the Queen about her military representatives in Ireland if none of them have the guts to speak up?"

Essex slammed his fist on the table. Ormond lifted his head slowly, for if anyone should speak up it should be him as the former head of the Irish military.

"The more an army traipses around Ireland, the more it attracts illness and fever. If you take a butcher's boy from Bristol, put a pike or musket in his hand, and get him to wade through a bog barefoot, it is not long until he is lining up outside the physician's tent claiming double rations. You have got to consider that we have suffered two serious defeats, in Connacht at the Curlew Pass and in the Wicklow mountains."

He looked at Essex's reaction to be met with a face of granite. He had started so he may as well tell the whole truth.

"Our men melt away, many to the rebels. We may have just marched around Munster but the army is spent."

Essex stared blankly in front of him. He came to and looked at the faces around the table to see if they agreed with Ormond. Most evaded his stare.

"Thank you for that, Ormond, the pessimistic opinion of an old man not far off his grave. When I see her next, I will tell the Queen that you revelled in telling me what I could not do but had very few answers when asked what I could."

Ormond made a fist and released it when he remembered where he was.

"I have tried to tell you many times, both through subtleties and being more blunt, that things do not work around here like they did in your previous theatres of war. They will not oblige you and line up in front of you for a pitched battle like the Spanish. The land and sea are worlds apart when it comes to war. There is no such thing here as a gentlemen's duel. They revel in the ambush. They know the English are easily worn down by illness and have great difficulties with resupply. Most of the time, they wait until you beat yourself and ambush you when you are down. You must deprive them of their means to wage war to win against them."

Essex shook his head and smirked.

"I'm sure all the men who are sick and those that died wished you made me understand that before now," Essex said.

He took the corner of the map of Ulster and pulled it towards himself.

"So please correct me if I am mistaken or suggest fighting the incorrect form of warfare, but I take it we must defeat the enemy in Ulster?"

"We do," Ormond said.

"I take it from our previous briefings there are three ways into Ulster?"

"Please elaborate," Ormond said.

"A landing by sea into Lough Foyle, an attack from Connacht, and a thrust here from the Pale?"

Ormond sighed, for if he had heard these plans once, he had heard them a thousand times.

"You would be hard-pressed to persuade our men to leave their forts in Connacht, never mind forming a coherent force, and it would be lunacy to expect them to invade Ulster — their morale is so low. That is to say nothing of the task of finding someone to sacrifice their reputation to lead them.

"As for a landing in Ulster, if you want to own the responsibility for the worst defeat of an English army in Ireland, go right ahead. The army is spent, and even if it managed to get there, it would be annihilated. If you must do anything, a march on Ulster is your only choice. We could, at most, assemble two thousand men, which should be enough to put the enemy off directly attacking us. Then you need to achieve something before the army peters away."

Essex raised his head.

"I will bring this to a head either way with a march on Ulster. Then you all can have your wretched island back. Now leave me be and summon your men."

Everyone shuffled off towards the door, glad they had avoided the wrath of the Lord Deputy.

CHAPTER 41
MEETING IN THE RIVER

"What's he doing here?"

Eunan looked downwards from his horse through the trees and into the gully below. Around him was his father-in-law, the Maguire, his brother Cúchonnacht Óg and Feargal MacCabe. Bodyguards formed a ring around them. In the river at the bottom of the gully sat the O'Neill on his horse with the river swirling up to the horse's knees. Opposite him was the Lord Deputy in full battle armour leaning over and whispering in the O'Neill's ear. On both sides of the river sat the respective advisers, and a ring of guards who closed off the area so neither side could attempt any tricks.

"Is he allowed to do that?" Eunan said.

"The O'Neill does as he likes," Cormac said with a tinge of resentment.

"He means the Lord Deputy," the Maguire said.

They all politely laughed as Eunan's marriage was the glue that held them together.

"The Lord Deputy, on the other hand, cannot do as he likes," Cormac said. "They are very particular about noting things down, who said what, while we do things on a nod and a handshake. It's because they answer to the Queen and her court, and if you think a clan house is a pit of vipers, it is nothing compared to the court."

"Have you been there?" Eunan said.

"My brother went there many times in his youth when he was trying to become the O'Neill. He understood how it worked and how he could make it work for him. I went with him a few times, mainly to make him look more powerful than he was. But it is not a place for warriors like me. I would be too quick to resort to the sword and would probably have died at a much younger age in one of their duels. I doubt you will ever see the inside of the Queen's hall unless you did something really bad and were dragged over there to be put on trial."

"There's still time for the lad," the Maguire said as he slapped Eunan on the back.

"Well, I only hope my brother can get us a winter's truce and not give too much away as to have the O'Donnell complaining again," Cormac said. "Either that or press our advantage on to Dublin, but he's far too cautious for that."

"Look at what's happening below," the Maguire said as he pointed into the gully.

The O'Neill and the Lord Deputy shook hands, and both climbed up their respective banks of the river. The O'Neill's Galloglass immediately swarmed around him to protect him from treachery. He rode up to his brother and the Maguire. He made sure the English could not see him before he burst out into a broad smile.

"If I can get him to put quill to page with all the things we have agreed just there, then I have won a greater victory than Yellow Ford without a shot being fired."

Cormac slapped his brother on the back.

"I always knew you'd see us right. I'll get the secretaries to work, we'll get the harvest in and then make another plea to the Spanish King."

The O'Neill winked at him as he rode past.

The weeks dragged by like a noose tightening around the neck of the Lord Deputy. The ink had barely dried on the truce when news arrived at the Queen's court of the successful negotiation. The Queen unleashed a crushing avalanche of anger and disgust at the generosity of the terms given by her agent. Furious letters poured in, each accusing the Lord Deputy of gross incompetence and failure in Ireland. Those once in his favour now cast him aside with contempt.

Terrified of punishments to come, he summoned his remaining captains to Dublin Castle. No longer was there a sense of false bravado as before. Instead, a deep dread permeated the air. Outnumbered and outmatched, the greatest army ever seen in Ireland was reduced to tatters.

Ormond sat at the head of the table while Williamson lurked in the shadows. He clenched his fists tightly, yet still, his hands trembled uncontrollably. All across Ireland and England, he could bend reality to his will. Yet here he was, an old man robbed of control of his own body.

Finally, the Lord Deputy rushed into the room. His coat was unbuttoned and he hurriedly threw it over a chair as if unburdening himself of a heavy load.

"Good evening, gentlemen. Thank you all for coming. I leave you with your country in a state of peace, better than when I arrived here. It is for you to do with as you will; as you often reminded me, only you understood how it worked and would not explain it. I am forced to return to the Queen's court to defend the peace I won, for the court is full of men who know less about Ireland than I do. I leave the Archbishop as the Lord Deputy, and Ormond oversees the army. I wish you good luck, gentlemen, in all your endeavours."

With that, Essex rushed out, leaving behind him a room full of dropped jaws. He took to his horse and boarded the first boat to England in Dublin docks.

CHAPTER 42
COMING HOME

E unan was granted leave to spend with his wife, and because his father-in-law knew of his whereabouts, he could not take a detour back to his lands. He feared the worst, for his lands were within striking distance of the Pale, and he no longer had Dervella and Arthur to look after them. With the amount of raiding being done by both sides, he may not have much to go back to if the war did not end soon. Expecting a prolonged absence, he reluctantly tasked Odhran with inspecting and protecting them.

Eunan galloped up the hill to Augher Castle, fear rising in his chest at the thought of what he may find when he arrived. As he approached, he saw a figure in his wife's room run from the window. His heart leapt. She must feel better if she could see him from that distance. He had thought of his son every day, how he had his hair and eyes, how he was a miniature him bouncing on his knees. He felt a little guilt for whereas before seeing his wife would have dominated his thoughts as he rode up the hill, this time he only thought of his boy. But someone else had re-invaded his thoughts: Cara. He thought of how beautiful she looked on Devenish Island and how she had been there for him at his lowest ebb before he was put on trial. He dismissed the doubts that it was all a distraction set up by Seamus. The night they had in Munster had certainly distracted his thoughts, but in a different way than Seamus had intended. He needed to banish Cara from his mind once more and think about his wife and son. But in his deepest, darkest thoughts, he began to resent Sorcha.

Eunan's heart sank as he saw Cormac step out of the castle. He remembered that fateful day they had parted company when the Maguires went home after celebrating the truce. He had been overjoyed believing he would be free from his father-in-law's smothering presence, yet now here he was again.

Cormac waved to him, but Eunan could feel him judging every move and every decision he made. His father-in-law searched for any mistake, any sign of weakness, so he could swoop in and take over again. The pressure was unbearable, and it only worsened whenever Sorcha fell ill. Whenever Eunan thought he was making progress, there would be another setback, and Cormac's controlling grasp would tighten even more around her and their son.

Despondency enveloped Eunan as he understood that nothing would ever alter with Cormac. He only wanted to have a relationship with his son without his father-in-law continuously watching over them.

But he had considered all the permutations on his ride to the castle. He had no one to look after the child at O'Cassidy house, his home in south Fermanagh, for Dervella and Arthur were now dead. He would have trusted them with his child's life but no one else. The Maguire would never release him from his bond to lead his men — well, at least not for the duration of the rebellion and long into the peace afterwards. Therefore, he could not look after the child himself. He could not give the child to the Maguire, for that would be akin to handing Irial and his ilk a hostage, something they could always use to control him. He could ask Seamus for a solution, but Seamus was not exactly child-friendly, even to those he was related to. Therefore, he was left sticking his hand out to his father-in-law as the best guardian for his child.

"It is good to see you again, Cormac," Eunan said as he withdrew his hand as it was not met. "I hope all is well with my wife and child?"

Cormac sighed and looked down to the ground.

"It is very much the same, he is healthy, she is poorly. He yells the place down for her, but the nursemaid soothes him as Sorcha lies in bed. One can only hope she brightens up at the sight of you but I wouldn't put money on it. You can go and see her and we shall talk afterwards."

"These words may tumble out as clumsy, but I am tired after a long ride. I know you are her father, but I am grateful as to how you look after them."

Cormac laughed.

"Not many a young man of your age would express such sentiments. They'd want to be out sowing their oats rather than having to look after a sick wife after coming back from campaign. We may have our differences, and I suppose fathers and sons-in-law always will, but you have a good heart. Now go up and see them before she gives me something else to worry about."

Eunan smiled, entered the tower and climbed the stairs to see his wife and child.

Eunan put his ear to the door to listen for any sounds from mother and child. It was silent except for the low hum of a children's song used to lull them off to sleep. He opened the door as quietly as possible, remembering the nuances of the squeaky door depended on how you opened it. It had always really annoyed Sorcha and Eunan took it as a good sign that the aural annoyance of the door had been fixed.

He stuck his head around the door and the scene was much like what he left behind. His wife was in bed, smiling meekly at him. She raised her hand to say hello. The room smelled musty and of a baby that had freshly soiled himself. The nursemaid was bent over with her back to Eunan, changing the boy. It all seemed so domestic. Eunan felt in the way and that he did not belong there. It was all right for his father-in-law to visit occasionally, for he was the grandfather who was there to protect them overall but with few domestic obligations other than to play with the boy when he was not crying. What was he to do? He was the father but he seemed to have no role. His own father never wanted him and as a father he wanted to be the complete opposite to that. Desmond was the closest thing to a father figure in his life, but God forbid imagining him looking after a child. That was one task he definitely would have assigned to Arthur.

Cormac only wanted him to visit briefly and not interfere. Was he supposed to play nursemaid to both his wife and child? Not knowing what to do, he floundered in the doorway and finally decided to pull up a stool and speak to his wife.

He took her hand and caressed it and leaned in to whisper.

"How are you feeling, my love?"

Sorcha broke into a faint smile and Eunan could see the effort her facial muscles had to make to achieve even that.

"Maodhóg has a fair pair of lungs on him. My father can even hear him from the bottom of the hill. He is like you. The nursemaid feeds him more and more every day. He eats until the nursemaid is in fear that he will throw up or he will soil his pants in a most unpleasant way. He grows so quickly that if you leave him even for a few days, as my father tells me, he is barely recognisable."

"That is very nice for you all," Eunan said, feeling more of an outcast than ever. He let go his wife's hand and sat back on his stool.

Even in her diminished state, Sorcha would sense something was wrong.

"Go and hold your boy. See how he will smile up towards you if you go and hold him."

Eunan looked over his shoulder at the nursemaid. She smiled back.

"He's ready for you now." She held out Maodhóg, all wrapped in blankets."

Eunan hesitated and Sorcha took his hand and shook it.

"Go on, he's your son."

Eunan got up and tiptoed over as if the boy could turn on him at any moment. The nursemaid slid Maodhóg into his hands. Eunan squeezed his eyes shut.

"You have to have your eyes open at a minimum to look after a child," the nursemaid said in her most soothing voice. "Here. Let me show you how to hold him."

Eunan opened his eyes and his boy wailed up at him.

"See, he can feel how nervous you are. He needs reassurance as he is just a child."

Eunan tried to hand the boy back.

"Let me," the nursemaid said. Instead of taking Maodhóg back she pulled Eunan's arms into a cradle and placed Maodhóg inside it.

"See. You need to be calm and gentle. The boy is still young and can pick up an anxious father."

"I don't think I'm cut out for this," Eunan said as he blushed.

"You'd be surprised how many fathers I have heard say that," the nursemaid said. "But all it takes is practice."

The nursemaid pointed towards the window seat.

"Go sit there with your son. Rock him gently and he will soon settle into your arms. He needs to get used to your smell and your touch as you are his father. The bond will grow from there."

"But will he not get ill from the draught?"

"Go do as you're told," Sorcha said. "The boy has a constitution like you, not me."

Eunan went and sat on the seat by the window and made a shallow rocking movement. The boy soon settled as the nursemaid had said. After a few minutes Maodhóg fell asleep in his father's arms. Eunan, stiffly upright for fear of dropping the boy, found a deep well of satisfaction staring down at the sleeping boy. He felt like a father.

CHAPTER 43
BUBBLING BROOKS

E unan now got to spend several blissful months at Augher Castle with his wife and child. The war seemed far away even though a minor level of violence and raiding rumbled on in the background to the truce. Even better was that Cormac left to do his brother's bidding for long periods. They more or less had the castle to themselves except when Sorcha's siblings would come to the castle. But Eunan did not care. Even the Maguire left him in relative peace with only the occasional despatch and he heard nothing from Seamus.

Sorcha began to feel better immediately once she knew Eunan would stay for an extended period of time. She was soon out of bed and looking out the window with him. She soon had the energy to mind Maodhóg herself without the aid of the nursemaid. Eunan had been building sympathy for her, for even he considered Maodhóg a handful. Often, he roared down the room when he soiled himself or wanted more food, and he wriggled like an eel to free himself from even the firmest grip.

As Sorcha gradually improved, she begged Eunan to let her leave the castle and told him he should come with her and spend a little time down by the brook in the valley by the castle as they used to. Eunan finally relented and they left Maodhóg with the nursemaid, and strict instructions to watch them from the window and if she saw them in trouble to call the guards. The maid handed them a bag with a blanket and shawl for Sorcha so she would not catch her death from the cold.

Sorcha struggled down the stairs refusing all help from Eunan. She made her way to the main door of the tower, using her hands to support herself on the wall. Eunan opened the door for her, and she supported herself between the two doorposts. She closed her eyes and breathed in the fresh air through her nostrils.

"You don't know how long this has been," she said. The cold air seared down into her lungs, and she was soon bent over, coughing and spluttering.

Eunan bent over her. His hands shook, and tears crept into the corners of his eyes.

"Are you all right? Let's go back in for the chill of the wind will be the death of you."

Sorcha grabbed the knob of the door and pulled herself upright.

"I have long been acquainted with the spectre of death and it is not going to stop me now. You don't know what it's like to be trapped in the prison of that bed with a roaring child that you can't comfort. Nothing will stop me from going out today, not you or all of my father's Galloglass."

Eunan stood back to let her breathe but with his arms extended out to catch her if she fell. But Sorcha stood propped up in the door frame and let the air into her lungs. She let go of the door posts and stepped forward onto the grass. An untimely stumble had Eunan reaching out to grab her elbows. Sorcha staggered and waved him away.

"Let me walk, man. Let me feel the air on my skin and the grass on my knees. If I fall and graze my knees, all the better, for I will have lived."

"But you have Maodhóg and me to think about now. You cannot throw your life away on a whim."

Sorcha turned and ignored him.

"Take my arm and help me down the hill. If I stumble, pick me up. Bring me to the brook where we lay and made sweet love so I may lie there again. I have longed for your return and that is what I have dreamed of."

Eunan looked to the ground.

"It can't be like the last time."

Sorcha snarled at him.

"Even I realise that. If I was with child once more, it would be the death of me."

"Don't speak like that, don't speak of death."

"I would have thought a man of your occupation would be familiar with death and all its guises."

Eunan scowled.

"Whatever the folly and beliefs of my youth, I do my best to keep everyone in my charge alive, especially my wife and child."

Sorcha reached out and took his hand.

"Take me to the brook, and we can talk about love, life and the future there. I need to be assured that you have a realistic outlook on life."

Eunan gulped but took her hand and helped her down the hill.

Eunan led his nearly blind wife as she stumbled through the woods towards the brook. Sorcha became weaker and weaker until she could barely lift her leg over the branch Eunan had warned her of. Her head sagged, her breathing became heavy and Eunan could see she was a spent force.

"Shall we turn and go back while you can still walk?" Eunan said. He stopped and pointed back to the castle, inviting Sorcha to come with him.

"No, no. Come with me to the brook. Carry me if you have to. We have to go there."

Eunan cursed and looked to the sky.

"What is your obsession with the brook? It will be the death of you."

"At least I'll have a nice memory to slip away to."

"Don't be so morbid. I forbid you from going to the brook. Turn around now before I go over there, pick you up, and carry you back."

Sorcha collapsed and fell, but before Eunan could get to her, she had hauled herself up into a seated position. She cocked her head back and laughed.

"You forbid me!? You forbid me? If only my father could hear you say that."

Eunan gritted his teeth and held out his hand.

"Come back with me now. Let's hear no more talk of your father. I am your husband, and I am telling you to go home. You are ill and do not realise what you are doing."

"If you are my husband and you love me, you'll bring me to the brook. I have dreamed about going back there with you for so long. Help me with this last wish."

"Last wish?" Eunan stood and knitted his brow. "Does that mean you will never ask me for anything ever again?" He looked at Sorcha to see how his attempt to lighten the mood had landed, but her half-blind eyes were looking into the forest as she tried to find a route to the sounds of the brook.

"If you are that insistent, I will take you. But you shall dip your feet in the water for a minute and not a moment more. You need to be back in your bed. God only knows what your father will say to me after this debacle."

Sorcha beckoned him forward.

"Never mind my father, it is just you and me now. The brook is over here. I can hear it here and here." She pointed to her ear and her heart.

Eunan shook his head at such folly but knew once his wife got an idea in her head, it was very hard to dislodge. It was easier to facilitate her until her desires had played themselves through. He took her by the hand, pushed every branch out of her way, and warned her of every gnarly root. The sound of the brook came ever nearer, and Sorcha became more elated the closer they got. Eunan lifted one last branch.

"The brook is in front of you, my love. There are no rocks or roots in your way. Go dip your feet in the water, and then let us be on our way. You'll catch your death of cold being out here for too long."

Sorcha just stood there and felt the moisture of the splashing brook on her face and the cold breeze that licked her cheeks. She felt every frailty in her bones, but she felt alive.

"The brook," Eunan said. "It's in front of you."

Eunan extended his arm so his wife could follow it. She sat down on a dry tuft of grass, took off her shoes and dangled her feet in the water.

"Is this what you wanted?" Eunan whispered sweetly over her shoulder.

She smiled faintly, splashed her feet and fell backwards on the grass. Memories flashed into Eunan's head of the last time they had been there. The sun shone in her hair, and she laughed with youthful innocence. But all this was quickly replaced by her pale face. Her pale face! Eunan's eyes bulged as he held his wife's face. He had not noticed the colour in her face drain away as her feet stopped splashing.

"My love, are you all right?" His voice became a rasp, for he did not know what to do.

"I'm sorry, my sweet husband, but I have a confession to make."

"What is it? You can tell me anything."

"Prop my head up and let go of my face. I fear you may not like it, but it is what I wanted, which may limit your objections."

"I would never oppose anything you truly wanted to do."

Eunan's hands began to shake, and he clasped his eyelids together, for he was determined not to cry in front of his wife.

"Make my pillow, and let us talk."

Eunan fumbled through the bag and pulled out the blanket and shawl. He gently lifted his wife's head, placed it on the shawl cum pillow, and threw the blanket over her.

"Now tell me your confession," Eunan said.

Sorcha smiled meekly up at him as his face loomed over her.

"Do I look pretty?"

"Always."

"Bend over and lend me your ear. I have a secret to tell you."

"I would prefer it if you would tell me such things in front of a roaring fire in our room, but since we are here, I will indulge you. What is your secret?"

"The physician told me I was going to die."

Eunan's face froze, and when his brain began to function again, he shook his head and laughed.

"I'm sure he didn't say that in front of your father or else he would have found himself thrown out the window of your room."

Sorcha scowled.

"Do not mock me when I pour my heart out to you."

"I'm not mocking you. I'm concerned about you lying here on your back in the cold. Any physician can tell you that a person in your state is going to die. It is whether announcing it in public would make it more believable."

"Shut up, take my hand and listen."

Eunan was taken aback, for Sorcha had never spoken to him like that before. He frowned, but it dissipated when he saw how frail and fragile his wife looked.

"The times you brought me down here to the brook are some of the most pleasant memories I had in my short life."

"Don't speak like that, love. You have plenty of life to live yet."

"Remember I asked you to hold my hand and shut up?"

Eunan nodded and agreed to be quiet. Even if he had to bite his lip he would be silent.

"For years I have been confined to my bed. All I had was a distant window and the ceiling to play my memories upon. When you would go it seemed like an age until you would return and all through that time, I would dream of you holding me in your arms down by the bubbling brook."

Eunan was becoming more perceptive to his wife's needs. He lifted her into his arms and rearranged her blanket so she would not be cold. Sorcha nestled in his arms, and he bent down and kissed her.

"This is what I always dreamed of, dying here in your arms. Look after Maodhóg, don't fight with my father. He will provide the boy a good home until you are ready."

Eunan bent down and kissed her on the lips again, determined to stay silent in the face of what he deemed to be his wife's dramatic fantasies. But when his lips met hers, they felt strangely cold. He saw the peace on her face and the goosebumps on her cheeks.

"Sorcha? Sorcha? I have indulged in your dramatics for too long, and now it goes beyond a joke."

Eunan studied her face, but she did not move. She must have had so much practice playing dead lying in her bed that she had now perfected it.

"Sorcha? Get up now. This is beyond a joke."

But still, she did not move. He shook her but to no avail. He shook her with slightly more force but enough to annoy her. Nothing.

"Sorcha? Stop it. You are seriously worrying me."

Sorcha's eyes were firmly shut.

He lifted her body up. The blanket snagged in a branch and was ripped off her body. He began to run through the forest towards the castle.

"Help! Help! I fear my wife is dead."

But nobody came.

He stumbled out of the forest and fell to his knees at the bottom of the hill. The nursemaid saw him through the window and sounded the alarm.

CHAPTER 44
TELLING TALES

The sky above Augher Castle was lit by a hundred torches, flickering in the wind as if they wept for the daughter of the master whose passing had brought them there. Torches burned, lighting the night with a sombre orange glow as musicians played mournful tunes and poets shared stories of the afterlife. Every note or rhyme seemed a reminder that death is always close by, even amidst life's joyous occasions. Cormac had refused to wait and let the whole of Ulster pay their respects through a wake, instead arranging a small private burial with only his closest family present. But he still planned a feast to celebrate her life, inviting all the chieftains of the North and prominent Maguires to fill his castle.

Eunan was not sure what to make of it all. On one hand, he felt grateful for Cormac's magnanimous gesture. On the other hand, he couldn't help but feel put out by how little he was included in the preparations. The mournful music of the pipes filled him with sadness, reminding him of his lost wife, yet at the same time arousing both guilt and anger for how indifferent he had been to her suffering in life. He maintained a stoic composure until it all became too emotional and wiped away his tears with a rough sleeve, only to be met with a slap on the back from a welcomed guest.

"You've been through a lot," Seamus said. "If you told me I could have helped but then again, I'm not much good at the emotional stuff. I have a rock in my heart ever since my dear Dervella died. I've been barely able to feel. But I had to come once I heard about your wife's funeral."

Eunan coiled his arm around Seamus's shoulders.

"Thanks for coming at such short notice. How can the Earl cope without you?"

"Oh he does just fine without me, or so he thinks. I'm sure he is delighted to rid himself of the bee in his ear who tells him everything he does is wrong and has to blackmail and threaten him to get him to do the right thing. I'm sure he does not miss that at all."

Eunan laughed, glad of the distraction from the funeral.

"And how goes it with your brother?"

Seamus turned to him and laughed and put his hand up to gain the attention of one of Cormac's servants.

"Even here at the top table you have to hail for assistance," Seamus said.

The servant came and nodded.

"Fill our two mugs and leave the bottle. You look like you will have a busy day, and we don't have the patience to wait for you to quench our thirst."

The servant nodded and went to retrieve a bottle of wine. Eunan looked at Seamus, still expecting an answer. It was Seamus's turn to laugh.

"If God had known what evil lay in my father's sack he would have cut off his balls and cast them into hell."

Eunan smiled and pointed at himself.

"I know you would have shrivelled in hell with all the other evil sperm, but what about me?" he said.

"Ah, you would have crawled out from beneath some rock regardless. You'd find yourself a nice shaded spot and wait your turn to impregnate an innocent young woman. Hard to kill, you are."

"So what of your brother, the MacSheehy and the rebellion down south?"

Seamus sighed and looked into his mug.

"The curse of Black Mountain still blights the province. Nobody has the stomach for a fight anymore. The memories of the massacres, being forced off the land and the mass starvation are all too raw. The only ones not blinded by those memories are the farm boys. You'd be lucky if they survived long enough to be useful."

"And your brother?"

"You're insistent, aren't you? Are we not supposed to be cheering you up at your wife's funeral? Why are you so chipper even though your important relatives watch your every move? Are you back to being a regular ol' Maguire now?"

"The father-in-law has always been far keener on Maodhóg than me."

"Sure he's way better looking and even with the screaming and all, he's far less of a pain in the arse than you."

Eunan raised his mug to Seamus who met it in the air.

"His great-uncle is always going to be biased."

"There's got to be some good in all that MacSheehy blood flowing around. So what will you do with Maodhóg when you go off on campaign next?"

It was Eunan's turn to look into his mug.

"If I could prise him out of Cormac's hands then I'd not be sure what to do with him except retire from the Maguire's service and raise him at O'Cassidy house."

Seamus shook his head.

"There's no chance of the Maguire letting you do that."

"I could leave him in the care of the Maguire in Enniskillen."

"That would be like presenting a kidnap victim to your enemies."

"How about I bring him on campaign?"

"I can really see you nursing Maodhóg before tucking him under your arm to lead the next charge."

"Then what?"

"Don't protest too much, but enough to show you care when Cormac takes the boy."

Eunan's head fell.

"It is just like that night when my father gave me to the Galloglass."

"Yes, it may be so factually, but you are looking at it through the eyes of a scared, lonely boy. Look at you now and look where handing you over to the Galloglass got you. The first thing that happened was you met Desmond."

Eunan smiled.

"That is the wisest thing I ever heard you say."

"I say plenty of wise things. You never listen."

Eunan opened his mouth to reply but was interrupted by the Maguire approaching him. The Maguire stuck out his hand.

"I am sorry for your loss," he said in a low, hushed voice. "Please ask if there is anything I can do to help, especially for the boy."

Eunan bowed his head.

"Thank you, lord. I need to make arrangements for the boy."

"You leave it to me. I will make him my ward and bestow on him my protection."

Eunan bowed his head and shook the Maguire's hand.

"Thank you, lord. I gratefully accept."

"That is a wise decision and saves me some embarrassment."

"How so?"

"I thought you were going to ask me for some time to yourself, but it is good that you take your frustration out on the enemy."

Eunan knitted his brow.

"We move south with the O'Neill any day now," the Maguire said. "He is going to inaugurate the Earl of Desmond and the other clan chieftains of Munster who have chosen to side with us. You can support me on the move south. The south Fermanagh shot will be much in demand."

Eunan tried to hide his emotions, for he was not expecting to return to war with the truce holding. He thought he might get some time to spend with his boy. But he bowed his head, thinking it was the right thing to do.

"I will be there, lord. As will the men of south Fermanagh."

Eunan nodded and disappeared into the mass of people offering their condolences.

Eunan began to feel sluggish and rested his elbow on the nearest table.

"I'd lay off the ale if I were you," Seamus said as he requested a servant to refill his mug. "It would be terribly ungrateful of you to throw up all over the horse you expect to carry your fat arse all the way to Munster."

"The horse will be fine," Eunan said. "She'll have had fatter drunken arses on her before than me. You for instance."

Seamus smirked.

"Have you been practising? That was almost funny."

Eunan was about to reply when one of Cormac's men tapped him on the arm.

"Your father-in-law wants to speak to you privately before you leave."

"Can't you see I'm talking?"

"Given the master's mood, now would be the best time."

Eunan slammed his mug on the table and sloped off after the guard.

The guard opened the door to the room, and Eunan saw the shadows on the wall dancing in the candlelight. The dancing stopped when he saw the scowl on his father-in-law's face.

"Come in and sit down," Cormac said, pointing to a seat. I'm sorry to have this conversation on such a sad day, but circumstances leave me with little choice."

Cormac poured wine into two mugs and passed one to Eunan, who raised it in the air.

"To Sorcha, may God rest her soul."

"To Sorcha," Cormac said as he mumbled his reply, his mind occupied by other matters. "I saw you spoke to the Maguire. Did he tell you of our arrangements?"

Eunan tried to look as innocent as he could after several hours of drinking.

"Only that we are moving south with your brother. Is that what you mean?"

"Kind of." Cormac looked troubled and sat in front of Eunan. "Unfortunately, there are several matters we need to discuss, but not all of them are pleasant."

"I am a commander in the Maguire and used to having unpleasant conversations."

Eunan smiled, trying to give some reassurance but none of it fell onto Cormac.

"The Maguire has made Maodhóg his ward and therefore has his protection. You should be honoured your clan leader would do that for you."

Eunan smiled again.

"I am, and he also held Sorcha in high regard."

"Then I can only assume he has left it to me to tell you."

Eunan tilted his head to the side. He could guess what his father-in-law was going to say but it was a modicum of revenge to watch him squirm so.

"I am to mind the boy until you can look after him yourself."

Eunan looked suitably shocked so he could keep up the ruse.

"Who is to be the judge of when I am ready?"

"It will be made in agreement with the Maguire who will act as ward. Your child will be well looked after here. He is not a hostage. Given your position, that is a blessing. You can visit him anytime and spend as much time with him as you like. However, I would advise you to build up your own lands and your own defences. You have not spent much time there recently. Security is the key to bringing up your boy. Always remember he is an O'Neill and, therefore, has many enemies as well as friends. We may all have to wait for peace to achieve security, but in the meantime, he will be a lot safer here."

Eunan began to get angry, for he was tired of his father-in-law lecturing him, and if there was one good thing to come out of all of this, he would see a lot less of him.

"So, are we in agreement?" Cormac said.

Eunan paused because he did not want his father-in-law to feel like he had gained any type of victory over him.

"It is what Sorcha would have wanted and I can abide by that. May I leave my dogs with the boy, for he has become quite attached to them and them to him?"

"Of course, we must make the boy's stay as pleasant as possible and make the castle seem like his home."

Eunan raised an eyebrow.

"Is that it?" Cormac asked.

"It is. Thank you for being so kind to both myself and my son."

"So ends the pleasant part of our conversation."

Eunan froze. What else could there be? Cormac stood up and began pacing the room.

"It has come to my attention that certain rumours about you have been circulating around Enniskillen. Is there any truth in them?"

Eunan laughed nervously for such a question out of the blue unhinged him.

"You know I have so many enemies there it would be impossible to memorise everything they say about me. You must tell me who told you and what the rumour is."

"I would not normally name my sources but my son Rory is well disposed to you being in your debt for saving his life."

Eunan did not see his father-in-law as naive, but he always had a blind spot for his son. Rory had always come across as jealous of Eunan, so there was no surprise at the source of the rumour. The surprising aspect was that Cormac gave it any credibility.

"Tell me the rumour," Eunan said, the agitation grew in his voice.

Cormac stopped, made fists with his hands and turned to face Eunan.

"He told me you had taken up with a witch in Munster after saving her from the fire, fornicated with her, and then she laid a curse on my poor Sorcha so she could have you. She blinded my child and then killed her and now you return to Munster to be with her."

Eunan laughed.

"I am not such a prize that a woman would go to such elaborate lengths to have me."

Eunan stopped laughing when he realised he laughed alone. He saw the anger blazing in his father-in-law's eyes.

"These are obviously lies, campfire stories made up to slander me. I will find the source of these rumours, extinguish them, and restore Sorcha's good name."

"So my daughter's blinding had nothing to do with your actions?"

Eunan jumped out of his seat and made the sign of the cross across his chest.

"I swear and may God strike me down if I tell a lie. It has nothing to do with me."

Eunan could see the flames of anger in his father-in-law's eyes diminish.

"I will believe you and grant you any doubt, if only because it is my daughter's and your wife's funeral. But you should be grateful you have such good friends in the ranks of the Maguires."

Eunan did a double take.

"How so?"

"Irial McDowell MacCabe has said he will go down to Munster personally and finish the witch's punishment and be rid of any rumours or curses she may have bestowed."

Eunan's knuckles went white as he gripped the chair. He had to save Cara. He composed himself to tell his father-in-law what he wanted to hear.

"Then we must all make haste to Munster to restore order and to quell any smear on Sorcha's good name."

"I knew you would see it my way," Cormac said. "Go pack your bags for you leave at sunrise."

CHAPTER 45
THE CLOUDS GATHER

An immense horde of O'Neills descended from Ulster in a storm of raging violence and vengeance. They were determined to wreak havoc on all who opposed them, laying waste to any and all Leinster clans still loyal to England. Ormond and his dwindling force could do little more than follow behind as the O'Neills left destruction and chaos in their wake. The Maguires joined the raid in full force, Irial, Feargal, and Eunan at their head.

They set up camp by Inishcarra on the banks of the River Lee, sending out word to all would-be clan leaders to declare allegiance to the O'Neill in return for his protection.

Seamus had made haste from Sorcha's funeral back to Munster, arriving several weeks ahead of the O'Neill. He led his own men in a cordon around the camp — fighting off numerous battles along the way. His forces weathered the illness and disease that commonly plagued armies in Ireland, yet Seamus struggled against desertion more so than enemy combatants. Formerly loyal men from Munster had begun to use this opportunity to seek out leadership roles within their clans, informing Seamus of their plans before they left or defected entirely. Though he had expected some treachery from his followers, the O'Neill leaned into it, allowing such transgressions with no harsh punishments to spread his rebellion far and wide.

The O'Neill camp was hastily erected, each clansman knowing they were at risk of attack from Ormond. Eunan rubbed the back of his neck as he surveyed the camp for potential weaknesses. He noticed Irial sitting beside a crackling fire with Feargal and Cearbhall, the two most fearsome MacCabes in all of Ireland. As Eunan approached, his heart raced, his muscles stiffened, and he felt the adrenaline pulse through his veins. He saw Irial's piercing eyes lock onto him. Trembling under his gaze, Eunan felt his soul had been laid bare for all to see.

"Eunan," Irial said as he raised his hand to signal to him. "Who are you looking for? Come and sit with us, and we may be able to help you."

Eunan cursed at being caught but raised his hand in salute for he could not openly reject the request in front of the men.

"Sit," Irial said and pointed to an empty spot by the fire.

Eunan nodded and sat. The wind reverted to its favourite direction, and Eunan was overwhelmed with smoke. He coughed and spluttered and tried to wave the smoke away in vain.

"Manoeuvre, manoeuvre," Feargal said as Irial roared laughing at the entertainment. "You are supposed to get out of the way and not just sit there and take it, just like you did in the Battle of the Rain."

Eunan ground his teeth for he hated being mocked, especially in public.

"That battle only had one hero and that was me," Eunan said as he got up to find a seat out of the smoke.

"That's because everyone under your command was dead," Irial said.

"Then those tents are occupied by ghosts," Eunan said pointing at the tents of the south Fermanagh shot. "Where is your friend Connor Roe on the O'Neill's great raid? Off in the Pale selling himself to the English?"

Irial attempted to rise and retaliate against Eunan's insult, but Feargal held him back with a firm arm.

"Easy now, boys. There'll be plenty of English for you to take your frustrations out on soon enough."

Irial snarled, shook off Feargal's arm and sat down again

"Who were you looking for, boy?" Irial said as he taunted Eunan. "You can't put a curse on me as you did your wife."

Eunan leapt out of his seat and threw himself across the fire and landed on Irial. He began throwing punches, but the stunned Irial could not reply in kind. Several MacCabes launched themselves upon him and dragged him off. Irial lifted himself up to his elbows and spat on his hand. He watched the blood trickle down through the saliva.

"So what are you going to do about this?" Irial said, turning his wrath on Feargal. "He drew blood while assaulting the Maguire's military adviser in front of the men. It cannot go unpunished."

"You are a coward, Irial," Eunan said as he struggled in the grip of four MacCabes. "You insult a dead man's wife and the daughter of a prominent O'Neill, provoking an attack and then hide behind the law."

Feargal stood between them and noticed how riled the men were getting, already splitting into different factions.

"There'll be no punishment handed down on this occasion, but if you don't keep your temper in the future, Eunan, you'll be up in front of the Maguire."

"He assaulted a cripple," Irial shouted at Feargal.

"Your mouth certainly isn't crippled. I can't defend you if you provoke an attack on purpose."

Irial cursed and then turned back to Eunan, brushing himself down after being unhanded by the MacCabes.

"You can search all you want but you'll never find her. Once she is gone, all of this will disappear for you." Irial drew a circle with his arm.

"Don't provoke me, old man," Eunan said, shaking his fist at Irial. "And stop spreading lies about me."

Irial held out his arms to draw more attention to Eunan.

"Is that a threat? Look, everyone he threatens a cripple. What Galloglass threatens a cripple?"

Feargal grabbed him by the forearm.

"Come on, there is a time and a place for this and this is not it."

Feargal dragged Irial away, and Eunan went to find Seamus to find ideas about making discreet inquiries about Cara.

A day's notice was given to all of the arrival of the Earl of Desmond, for he was afraid of being intercepted by superior English forces despite being reassured that Ormond and the bulk of the English army were in Leinster and the English in Munster remained in garrison. The circle in the middle of the O'Neill camp was designated the inauguration ground, and seats were arranged for the O'Neill and the other northern dignitaries. Seamus was sent to escort the Earl to the camp because he was familiar with him.

Seamus marched out with three hundred men to find the Earl. The sun shone through the boughs of the ancient oaks, casting beauty and dappled light onto the lands below. The fresh air hinted at woodlands, a tang of decaying vegetation, and a chill of pine. The grass was a lush green, and the forests were full of giant oaks whose friendly branches hid the mysteries of what lay beneath. The wind's whistle through the trees was an eerie chorus, followed closely by the munching of the forest's wildlife. The sky, now a deep navy blue, had been a brilliant hue of orange and red when the sun first peeked over the horizon. But the day was slowly fading and soon dusk would settle in, bringing a chill.

As the shadows stretched and the night grew ever closer, a lone figure emerged from the forest.

"Who goes there? These lands are claimed by the Earl of Desmond."

Seamus did not look impressed.

"Boy, go fetch your master for he is not the Earl until the O'Neill says he is. I am here to bring him to his destiny, be it Kilmallock Castle or the noose."

"I am not a boy but the heir to a great tract of land by the sea taken from me by my uncle."

"Then you will be in good company at the inauguration surrounded by your fellow petitioners with an axe to grind but not the skills to wield it. Now bring me to your master for mine is not a patient man."

The boy cursed for he thought himself disrespected but bowed to the superior show of force.

They marched through the shadows of the woods, conscious they were always under prying eyes. But Seamus did not care. They were far too well armed to be attacked by bandits and he noted that the Earl's men must not have improved in quality if they could not even show themselves to a friend.

They eventually came to a clearing where the Earl was camped. It was like a camp for vagrants rather than a military camp. The Earl had acquired such a following of disenfranchised civilians, forced to flee their lands because of never-ending war, that the camp had swelled to many times the size it should have been if it only consisted of his soldiers. There were makeshift tents, huts and carts randomly scattered around the woods and their clearings with spindly peasants stripping the leaves off bushes which had been long shorn of their berries. Children poked their dirty faces from amongst the spokes of carts and begged for any food the soldiers could give them. Seamus and his men tried not to show their shock at the scene, but the stench of human sweat, dampness, and faeces was so bad they could not help but pull faces if only to relieve their nostrils.

Memories flooded back to Seamus of the last glorious earl he followed as a boy. He had been that boy pressing his face amongst the spokes and begging for food when a new group of strangers arrived. All the worse, he was a boy of privilege, the son of a prominent Galloglass who would be entitled to the best food, and he was also of the age where he could hunt for himself. But such had been the devastation wreaked by Ormond over Munster that the column that followed the earl rapidly diminished through death and starvation. But at least when the last of the Galloglass took to the Kerry mountains with the earl to make their last stand there was more to eat — if only because the people had abandoned them.

Seamus's mouth went dry and he could not spit out the foul taste of the air. He took a swig from his water bottle only for the children to run out of their hiding places and mob his horse, begging for food or water. He took what little bread he had out of his satchel and threw it to the children.

"This is all I have. Now leave me alone so I can see the Earl."

But they left him alone to fight it out for crumbs of his bread which disintegrated as little hands grabbed at it and pulled it apart. Seamus looked up and away. He must succeed in bringing the rebellion to Munster so all this could end.

Murrogh saw Seamus approach the Earl's tent and signalled to his men to block his path. Seamus sneered as he saw the odd assortment of morion helmets, chain mail, swords and axes that came to stand in his way. The old faces below him snarled while the young betrayed their nerves.

"The MacSheehy have fallen even since the last time I saw them," Seamus said as he looked at the scowling Murrogh. He smirked at those below him. "How many of you actually have MacSheehy blood in your veins?"

"They could have MacSheehy blood on their blades if you come any closer," Murrogh said, trying to bolster his men's fluctuating courage. "Men, here is the traitor I told you about sitting on his lofty horse. My own brother is too good to join his own clan and fight for the Earl. A man who turns his back on his past and for what? He has not even told me what his price was to turn traitor. But I'll wager it'd not even be thirty pieces of silver for he has killed for far less."

Seamus's face hardened and he pointed at the men below him.

"This rabble may bear the weight of the armour of a Galloglass but that is where the resemblance ends. Anyone who stands in my way will be protecting the perpetrator of the massacre at Black Mountain. Don't force me to clear the way and don't dare resist me for the O'Neill will not take well to the murder of his men the day before he is supposed to inaugurate the Earl."

Murrogh came and stood behind his men directly in Seamus's way.

"Make way for the men of O'Neill," Murrogh said to his men.

His men parted and he stood in front of Seamus.

"I have what your nephew wants and it will be the end of you," Murrogh said as he smirked at Seamus.

"I could ride my horse over you and it would be the end of you. I am only prevented from doing so because our masters are allies. You had better make your master a useful ally of mine or your protection will cease and I will be under no such obligation. Now pack your things and follow us for the inauguration will be tomorrow."

"Mark my word, there will be a reckoning," Murrogh said, wagging his finger at Seamus.

Seamus ignored him and ordered his men forward.

CHAPTER 46
THE INAUGURATION

The O'Neill sat in a large wooden chair looking suitably bored. The chair was elaborately decorated with dragons and crosses, holy saints and scribes all carved into the larger expanses of the backrest and arms. Two cushions were strategically placed so the O'Neill could comfortably fit his large form in the chair and remain seated for long periods. His was the biggest chair specially made for the occasion, as the earldom was an English creation with no traditional inauguration site. Beside him sat the Maguire in a hastily constructed chair, for he had not prepared like the O'Neill. The other clan leaders made do with what their men could find for them, most not taking the inauguration that seriously as the O'Neill was the only person worthy of impressing. The O'Neill's Galloglass created a path for those who were to be inaugurated to march up, and the O'Neill ensured there were enough men on parade to impress any wavering potential allies.

Seamus stood with the mercenary captains as they smiled and made small talk. Seamus felt he should join in, for it was always beneficial to know who was paid to be on your side and their price. The man beside him was barely out of his twenties, with a scraggly beard, the main growth being on the chin and the moustache. His long, unkempt brown hair poked out from below his morion, and his breastplate appeared new, as if freshly off a Spanish ship. The man smelt of gunpowder, sweat and leather. But what left the biggest impression on Seamus was the man's steely eyes and the meanness of his grin. Seamus extended his hand to introduce himself and his grip was like iron, Seamus felt like his hand would break. The man appeared friendly, but the look in his eyes was aloof. He looked at you, sizing you up. His eyes told a story, of things he had seen and done, of things he had endured, of things he had survived.

"Dermot O'Connor Don," he said as he took Seamus's hand. His voice was deep and commanding, and Seamus felt it in his chest and ears. This was someone to keep an eye on for all sorts of reasons.

"Seamus MacSheehy. What offer of cattle and coin has you here?"

Dermot laughed.

"Is it that obvious?"

"Not many O'Connor Dons in Munster, especially in such shiny armour."

"Well, now you have one more. Munster seems to be where the money and action is these days."

"You'd not be far wrong there. Are you staying or just here on a brief excursion with the O'Neill?"

"Staying, apparently."

"How many men do you have?"

"Five hundred good Connacht men."

Seamus smiled.

"You're the prize, then."

"What?"

"Whoever pledges the most to the O'Neill gets you to enforce the claim of the pledger on his clan."

Dermot laughed again.

"Sounds like my career as a mercenary rolled into one."

"And mine."

"Who do you hope gets you?"

Seamus sighed.

"I've been here a while. I have the misfortune of being assigned to the Earl of Desmond himself. Never has the fate of so many been placed in a bigger fool."

Dermot roared laughing.

"Why don't you just ignore him? I hear they call him the straw earl?"

"Or the puppet prince if you're being generous. The rebel alliance down here is a fragile one of the reluctant or the greedy. I have to bide my time, bite my lip or rest my axe in whatever order keeps the alliance together. Such is the fate that awaits you."

"I always believe in the power of the axe." Dermot's condescending grin suggested that such talk made him think Seamus was old and past it.

"Don't get too smug, son, or place too much weight in the persuasion of coin. If you do, you'll never make it to be an old man like me."

Dermot stuck his hand out.

"I'll heed your advice and look out for you on the road."

As Seamus turned to watch the inauguration his instinct told him he would have to watch out for that young man.

The Earl of Desmond was announced and a polite round of applause rippled around the onlookers. The Earl and his escort passed beneath the canopy of oaks that lined the road, their old and proud trunks and branches reaching out to the sky as if pleading with their gods for the Earl to keep his promises. The birds sang to the earl as he passed, a fine melody that spiralled up to the treetops and then fell back down in droplets of song to the ground hoping they would bestow upon him both good luck and virtue that he would live up to the promises of his inauguration. But their melody seemed to falter as he passed. The Earl was a man who made promises with ease, but kept them only when they suited him.

The Earl wore a fine blue cloak, white shirt, and yellow breeches. He waved to the crowd as he passed and they politely cheered to show support for the title of Earl of Desmond rather than support for the man himself. He had begun to wear his hair a little longer and his beard was a little more unkempt but this spoke more to his desperation to fit in with the locals than any genuine desire for camaraderie. But it did not work for his tall, lank frame and mannerisms set him apart from being one of the people and the best he could settle for was old English lord.

Behind him marched Murrogh and the MacSheehy Galloglass. Murrogh exuded pride as he puffed out his chest and gave a beaming smile and saluted the onlookers. At least he resembled the locals, but those locals hiding in the woods were bandits rather than those who toiled the fields or were their clan overseers. His Galloglass marched behind him, a collection of old men from the last iteration of the MacSheehy Galloglass, their weathered faces betraying years of struggle and hardship, or young boys caught up in the excitement of a rebellion. They were lucky if they had a decent weapon or a full set of proper-fitting armour. It was nothing Seamus had not seen before but it was all the sadder for it was his own clan and reviving that clan was what had motivated Seamus through the hard years since he was banished from Munster. Seamus couldn't help but feel a bone-deep ache at how far his beloved Galloglass had fallen.

The Earl bowed before the seated O'Neill who acknowledged his arrival with a wave. The O'Neill rose and gave a speech which barely registered in Seamus's ears for it was clear the O'Neill knew nothing about the man knelt before him and they were just meaningless platitudes floating away in the wind. He was giving the Earl numerous opportunities to disappoint his reluctant followers.

Murrogh stood behind the Earl and beamed pride at the position he had attained for himself, as this moment was the pinnacle of his success after years in the wilderness. The O'Neill was handed a crown by one of his attendants and he placed it on the head of the new Earl. It summed up the whole ceremony perfectly. A random crown with nothing to do with the title, placed upon the head of an unworthy man in front of a shambles of badly equipped old men and boys.

There followed a series of ne'er-do-wells, pretenders and hard men who carved their kingdoms out of woods and mountains and those who had turned coat with their castles. They pledged men to the cause in the hundreds and some even in the thousands with very little supportive evidence by way of an entourage or other means. Most came with pleas that if the O'Neill gave them support then they would topple the current incumbent at the head of the clan and then once placed as head, support the O'Neill with the men pledged. Seamus and Dermot O'Connor were certainly the prize since they were the most capable warriors the O'Neill had in the province. Dermot was given to help Donal MacCarthy Mór and Seamus to assist Florence MacCarthy. Neither looked enamoured at their newly assigned roles but realised it was temporary.

The inauguration feast began, and Seamus went to sit with Florence MacCarthy to assess the man and his task. Meanwhile, Eunan sat with the Maguires and the MacCabes in particular. He used Odhran as a buffer between himself and the leaders of the MacCabes, for neither side had done anything to initiate a reconciliation since the fireside incident with Irial.

Eunan grew suspicious as Murrogh came to lean down and whisper in Irial's ear. They both laughed and Irial raised a mug to Eunan's prying eyes as Murrogh left. Things grew ever more tense as the ale was drunk and the Maguire went to sit with the O'Neill. Irial was getting especially drunk.

"Hey, boy."

No one replied for everyone thought Irial was asking for more ale.

"You, boy." Irial picked up a chicken bone from his plate, dipped it in gravy and threw it towards Eunan. It landed in Odhran's lap. Both he and Eunan turned to see the source of the bone.

"You, boy," Irial said pointing at Eunan. He grinned when he got Eunan's attention and gravy dribbled down his chin. "Sorry to hear about your wife's death."

Eunan's body tensed for what he perceived would be the follow-on insult.

"We may have been able to save her if we'd have got here quicker."

Eunan was confused but assumed it was a ruse.

"If we'd have got here quicker we'd have burned the witch and saved your wife. Alas, all you'll be left with is one dead witch and one dead wife."

Eunan flew at Irial. Along the way he barged past Odhran and Feargal, knocked Irial off his seat and punched him in the face. Three Galloglass set upon him and dragged him off. Irial rolled on the ground beside him holding his nose and Feargal stood over him, his fist threatening and his veins bulging from his neck.

"That is it. You are going before the Brehon for assault when we get back to Fermanagh. Throw him in the jail until we take him before the Maguire."

The three Galloglass picked Eunan up and dragged him away.

CHAPTER 47

BAITING THE BEAR

Eunan found himself once more on the back of a cage cart waiting for what his enemies in the Maguire passed off as justice. At least they gave him the respect to throw him in a cart by himself and not with the criminals or English soldiers who refused to desert. *They will pay for this when the south Fermanagh shot hear of this, never mind Seamus, the Maguire or my father-in-law.* He was an important man now, too important to be put on trial for defending his honour and the honour of his dead wife. But darkness fell, and no one came to rescue him. Never mind giving him food or water.

They had taken him to a cage cart in an opening in a wood. He could see campfires in the distance, and he reckoned this must be the outskirts of the camp where Feargal thought no one would find him. He sat on the floor of the cage, wondering which would come first: food, rescue, or his murder. As the light faded, he drifted off to sleep.

A tap came from the bottom of a bar of the cage and then a whisper.

"Eunan."

Eunan jolted and tensed up and studied the shadows without letting on he was awake.

"Eunan, down here."

Eunan turned around and looked beneath the rim of the cart. Two mischievous eyes came out of the dark.

"Fáolán? Is that you?"

"Not so loud. Have they told you what they are going to do to you?"

Eunan stooped and put his face to the bars to limit the risk of them being overheard.

"No, nothing. They are not going to try anything here. I need you to get the Maguire to release me."

"Seamus will do his best but with no guarantees. He found out Murrogh has Cara."

Eunan furrowed his brow.

"Why would he have her?"

"Any friend of Seamus's is an enemy of his."

"And any enemy of Eunan Maguire is a friend of his. Somehow, he is in cahoots with Irial. These fights have started because Irial had been taunting me about what he would do to Cara."

"Seamus wants you to leave this to him. Your enemies have spread their lies as far as your father-in-law. It would not take much for the poison to sit on his ear and slide into his head. You risk everything by going to save Cara."

Eunan paused, but he could not control the rush of feelings in his weakened state.

"I owe her so much. I don't think I would have made it through my trial if it was not for her. This is her trial, and I must stand by her."

"So, shall I tell your uncle he has the answer he'd expect from Eunan Maguire?"

Eunan wavered. He knew Fáolán was mocking him, and he would tell him he was a sentimental fool. He thought about where such sentimentality would get him.

"Tell him if he does the honourable thing and rescues the girl who did his dirty work for him and if the Maguire will no longer have me, I will join him here in Munster. I will unite with him, and we will dispose of Murrogh and form the MacSheehy once again."

Fáolán hesitated.

"Are you sure you want me to tell him that? Talk about getting his hopes up. He'll never forgive you if you renege on your word."

"Remember, I said if the Maguire would no longer have me. If he understands that, there will be no disappointment, for I will be a renegade, and I may still be afforded the protection of my father-in-law one last time and be banished to Munster."

"On your head be it making rash promises to Seamus MacSheehy. Don't go anywhere."

Eunan shook his head.

"Your jokes don't get any better."

Fáolán waved goodbye and was swallowed by the dark.

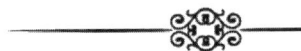

Dawn broke, but Eunan was still trapped in the cart with no food or water. The cart creaked beneath Eunan's feet as he rocked back and forth, tapping his fingers on the wood. He hummed a tune to keep himself entertained. The cold air was like a thousand needles piercing his skin, making him shiver uncontrollably as he huddled in the cramped space. Frigid fog covered the landscape with an eerie mist, making it impossible to see beyond arm's length. He heard nothing but the soft pitter-patter of rain on the cart. He watched in terror as moisture condensed and trickled down the sides of the cart, forming small pools of icy water around his feet. Every breath felt like he inhaled blades of ice that cut through his lungs, leaving him gasping for air. The damp air carried disease, and he couldn't afford to get sick, not when his life was already on the line. Though despair weighed heavy in his heart at the thought of never seeing his son again, he found comfort in the silence — time to reflect, time to regret. As he waited for whatever fate had in store for him next, part of him hoped for a quick end rather than a slow, painful death from starvation or sickness.

When the clouds parted, lifted the fog, and the sun shone between the trees, Eunan heard the sound of men talking and the flapping of leather against chain mail, and he knew someone was coming for him. He sat up straight and cleared his head of any cobwebs of the past from which the spider of doubt might crawl out and steal his confidence. From around the corner of the trees came the bottom of a staff and then the grinning face of Irial.

Eunan's heart sank into his stomach as he faced off with Irial. The cold of the morning had sapped him of his strength and resilience. Eunan's mouth dried up. He swallowed, his tongue sticking to the roof of his mouth. He tasted bile in the back of his throat, hot and bitter. He wanted nothing more than to vomit all over the ground. Irial cackled maliciously at him, showing the gaps between his brown rotten teeth. His face was lined deep with wrinkles as the crow's feet tightened their grip on his features, stretching from his eyes to the edge of his grizzled beard. Irial threw back his head and let out a roaring laugh so deep it sounded like rolling thunder reverberating through the clearing. The trees quivered in fear, and all that could be heard was Irial's raucous laughter.

"Today's the day I deal with Eunan Maguire forever."

Eunan searched his mouth with his tongue to find the saliva to speak.

"The Maguire will never let you put me on trial."

"Don't tell me what I already know," Irial said. "But I know where your weakness lies."

Eunan stood up. His bones creaked as he lifted himself up. He stepped to the front of the cage and took hold of the bars.

"Yours is your arrogance and belief that you are so important to the Maguire that you can do whatever you wish."

Irial stood and swayed back on his heels and grinned.

"Then we have finally something in common for I could say the same about you. But I am not so foolish as to think the Maguire will accept what I say willy-nilly. No, I mean to provide him with evidence."

"What evidence? What deed do you think you have over me? It is surely not the assault, for such things are a regular event in the camps of soldiers. He will dismiss that out of hand but take up the issue of my imprisonment with you and deal with it most harshly."

Irial reached behind his head and rested his white ponytail on his shoulder.

"This white hair is not just a sign of age. It is a sign of wisdom. Here's what's going to happen. You will stay in that cage and wait for the Maguire to summon you, for he will. I, in the meantime, am going to fetch the witch you have been cavorting with and torture her until she tells me every last thing you and her did and what spell she cast upon your sadly departed wife. Once she has confessed and the Maguire and your men are assured everything she says is true, she will burn, and the Maguire will come for you."

Eunan's eyes bulged as he stretched every sinew, shaking the bars of his cage as hard as he could.

"You'll never get away with this. The Maguire will see through your lies."

Irial laughed.

"Would you bet your life on it? Before she dies, your witch will sing any tune I wish her to. She will say whatever is necessary to convince the Maguire of your guilt. I want to say it was nice to know you, but it wasn't."

"You'll never get away with this. I should have killed you when I had the chance."

Irial turned his head around his shoulder as he walked away and smiled smugly at Eunan.

"You never had the opportunity to kill me, nor will you ever. Goodbye, Eunan Maguire."

CHAPTER 48

KNIFE OF HOPE

With a fierce intensity, Eunan slammed his body against the iron bars of his cage, causing them to rattle and shake as if an earthquake had hit. He screamed and shouted in rage and desperation, knowing all was lost. With a sigh of defeat, he slumped down. His throat was tight with thirst, and he thought that if he just licked the droplets of rain off the bars, it may bring some relief, yet he knew it would poison him even more than his current anguish. Lost within himself, he dropped into a corner of his cage and covered his head with his hands. His mind tumbled through melancholy, brought on by his inability to save Cara. All of the women he had ever loved or been with were now gone, lost to him forever through death or soon-to-be-inflicted horrific torture. How could one man be so cursed? He stayed in that position for hours, letting himself drown in despair.

"Eunan."

Eunan jumped from his slumber, his eyes wide with guilt and surprise. He looked in front to see if anyone had seen him jolt, and he turned to the bushes to find the source of the voice.

"Eunan."

Fáolán's face appeared amidst a clump of bushes.

"Guards surround the perimeter of the woods. Seamus will try to rescue you, but you must be prepared to defend yourself should the guards come for you."

"I have nothing but my bare hands but that should ensure I take one or two of them out before they get to me."

"Can you hide a knife on your person?",

"They stripped me of my coat so the elements would do their dirty work, so I have nowhere to conceal anything."

"Let me see if I can hide it in the cart itself."

Fáolán crept out from his bush and crouched beneath the cart. He examined the bottom of the chassis for any weaknesses he could exploit to free Eunan and, when unsuccessful, switched to finding somewhere to hide the knife.

"Put your hand here. Can you reach the knife?"

Eunan stuck his hand through the bars and searched the underside of the cart floor with his fingers.

"If needs be, I could reach it, but I would have to see them coming."

"I think that is the best we can hope for. I will tell Seamus you are ready. He will wait for the opportune time to strike, for he does not want to provoke a fight with the Maguires. I will try to come back to protect you should they try to kill you in the rescue attempt."

"Thank you, my friend, but please hurry. Cara's life depends on it."

"Yours too."

Eunan's heart pounded in his chest as he sat in the corner of the cart, desperately trying to anticipate a rescue attempt. He heard the shouts growing closer and closer and knew it was only a matter of time before he was found. With tense fingers, Eunan reached for the knife beneath the cage floor and prepared himself for whatever fate lay ahead.

Suddenly, two Galloglass burst into view, their chain mail clanging and their morions gleaming under the dawn light. One had a bloody shoulder, but both carried battle-worn axes pointed directly at Eunan. He scrambled desperately to look for any sign of help from Seamus or anyone else - but no one came. The Galloglass advanced rapidly on the cart, one jabbing his axe forward to keep Eunan back while the other scrambled up the side of the cage and began fiddling with the lock on the chain. Eunan could almost taste his imminent freedom — or death.

"Sorry, lord," the Galloglass, fiddling with the lock, said. "Feargal's orders. Any rescue attempt, and we were told to kill you."

"That is if I don't kill you first," Eunan said, and he thrust his hand between the bars of the cage and grasped for the knife. His fingers grazed wood and thin air as he realised he had dropped it during a half-asleep practice session. With no weapon to defend himself, Eunan retreated to the corner of the cage, extending his arms as if daring the enemy to come any closer. The lock clicked and the chain clattered onto the ground. The man swept his six-foot axe around the cage, blocking any escape from Eunan as he advanced with menace.

At that moment, there was a cry from outside, and over the Galloglass's shoulder, Eunan saw a spurt of blood. The Galloglass fell to his knees, leaving Fáolán standing behind him, his face dripping with fresh blood and a feral smile spread across his mouth. Seamus and his men burst through the trees and charged at the Galloglass.

"Careful there, fella," Fáolán said to the remaining Galloglass. "Drop your axe and run into the woods, and no one will be any the wiser you were ever here. For if you kill Eunan, we'll all hack you to bits, but not only that, we'll find your family in Fermanagh and hack them to bits, too."

The colour drained from the man's face, and the axe shook in his hand.

"How do I know I can trust you?"

"You don't. But you know what will happen if you don't have a little faith."

The man looked at Fáolán and then at Eunan.

"I guarantee you safe passage if you tell no one what happened here today," Eunan said as he nodded at the man reassuringly.

The man hesitated, then dropped his axe and ran down the stairs and into the woods.

"Leave him," Eunan shouted after him. He climbed out of the cage and embraced Fáolán. "Now we must save Cara."

Eunan looked over Fáolán's shoulder to see Seamus smiling at him, and Odhran was beside him, holding the reins of two horses. Eunan let go of Fáolán and walked over to Odhran.

"You don't have to do this. Even if we succeed in freeing Cara, we must throw ourselves on the mercy of the Maguire and hope he sides with us instead of his military adviser and the head of his Galloglass. Even if we win, you may find yourself banished forever."

"One must follow one's conscience and let God sort it out."

Eunan put his hand on Odhran's shoulder.

"You are a good man and a faithful servant. I am lucky to have you."

"Don't worry, we didn't kill any Maguires to rescue you, aside from the body at your feet," Seamus said. "But they'll have word to your master soon enough, and he'll come after us. As far as I know, Murrogh has Cara imprisoned near here. They mean to take her back to the village where she was first condemned as a witch and carry out her sentence there. It is less than a day's ride away. We may beat Irial there if we are lucky and have fewer men to kill to free Cara."

"We have been in worse scrapes before," Eunan said.

"Not one where it is more or less lose, lose."

"What's the worst thing that can happen if we all live? We all become Mac-Sheehy?"

"Then we would have an even harder task to restore the clan name after the way Murrogh has tarnished it."

Eunan slapped him on the back.

"Let us mount our horses, cast our fate in the air and begin our rescue mission. At least we will die Galloglass."

Seamus laughed.

"Knowing your luck, Irial will think of a way to throw you out of the MacCabes after you die."

"Then I will die a MacSheehy like my father, his father before him and his before him."

Seamus smiled, for at least some family honour had been restored.

"Then let us go forth and die if that be our fate."

CHAPTER 49

THE CHASE

The Maguire stood in his tent, giving instructions in a low, steady voice to Feargal and Cearbhall as they mapped out the strategy for the rebellion in Munster and plotted their return to Ulster. A guard coughed as he entered the tent, his eyes wide with urgency.

"What brings you into my tent unannounced?" the Maguire snarled at being rudely interrupted.

"I have a man who says his message is private and of the utmost importance."

"Can he be trusted?"

"He is one of your own guards."

"Bring him to me, but be vigilant."

"He is unarmed, lord. I searched him myself."

The Maguire nodded his approval.

The guard escorted in the man who had been guarding Eunan. He bowed sheepishly to the Maguire. The Maguire saw the fear in his eyes as he looked at Feargal. The Maguire placed his hand on his belt in case he needed easy access to his knife.

"Leave us," the Maguire said to Feargal and Cearbhall. They left the tent only to be recalled by an irate Maguire a minute later.

Feargal bowed his head when he saw how angry the Maguire was.

"I have a man who claims he was guarding Eunan Maguire and that he was assaulted by Eunan's uncle," the Maguire said as his tone became a guttural growl. "Do you know anything about this?"

Feargal went red-cheeked.

"Alas, the vendetta Eunan Maguire pursues against Irial continues and gets out of hand. He once more assaulted Irial in front of the men, and I had to apprehend him so we could bring him before a Brehon."

"Why didn't you tell me this?" the Maguire hissed.

"I was going to tell you today after we had discussed the campaign."

"Where is Irial?"

"Lord, there is a rumour that Eunan has taken up with a witch who cursed his wife, leading her first to go blind and then to die. Several men claim to be witnesses to the fact that Eunan has fornicated with this witch and wishes to take up with her."

"I have heard these rumours, some whispered into my ear by Irial himself. I put it down to malicious gossip."

"Alas, it is more than gossip. I fear Eunan has gone after Irial. Whether or not to save the witch is a question one can only ask Eunan Maguire."

The Maguire's head dropped, and he sighed deeply.

"Eunan, Eunan, Eunan."

He raised his head and put on his clan leader mask again.

"Get my horse and call out your men. Whatever the story is, it must end here. Eunan will face the Brehon with the charges to be decided by both what happens and what we learn on this day. I am sorry it came to this, men, but justice must be seen to be done."

"At once, lord. I will summon the men and bring you Eunan Maguire."

A hand-picked escort of five men mounted up, and the Maguire turned to take his weapons.

"Are you sure, lord, you wish to take such a small escort with you?" Feargal said. "There are reports of enemy scouts roaming around these parts."

"I want to bring Eunan in peacefully, not start a war. I will be back in a couple of hours. Fetch me a Brehon so we can have this trial here and now and settle the price Eunan has to pay."

"At once, lord, and good luck."

CHAPTER 50

REVENGE REARS ITS UGLY HEAD

Taaffe sat and poked the fire, then spat into it to alleviate the boredom. Whatever morale there had been in the Munster army had deserted and fled back to England on the same boat as the previous Lord Deputy. The new Lord Deputy Charles Blount, or as he was better known, Lord Mountjoy, started by imposing discipline in the ranks by attempting to stop thieving and to stem the levels of desertion. A new Governor for Munster, Sir George Carew, had also been sent but had not yet left Dublin. But all that meant nothing to the ranks. It was just going to be the same old same old — the Lord Deputy would flounce around trying to provoke the rebels into a set-piece battle while the rebels melted away. Then the Lord Deputy's army would be eroded by illness and desertion, he would get sacked or resign, and the whole drama would start again.

Being in the army and reporting to a commander had proved very difficult for Taaffe. He was terrible at taking orders at the best of times and often clashed with his commander St. Leger. The pickings from land deals had also been slim as they now mainly stuck to the borders of Ormond's lands, which were definitely not for sale. The richest pickings were in the west of the province, where there was the most friction between the old clans and the old English lords. But he would have to get through a couple of counties of rebels to investigate, and with the army in such disarray, there was little chance of that. So he sat and poked the fire hoping for a change of luck.

Shea Óg came and approached him. Shea Óg had it a little better under St. Leger than Taaffe, for St. Leger did not attempt to keep him under such a tight rein. St. Leger saw Shea Óg and his men as cut-throat mercenaries, an ill-disciplined rabble that was beyond taming. Therefore, he kept them as his scouts or men to do the dirty work while pocketing a regular payment from Cormac O'Cassidy for the privilege. But there was one obsession that all except St. Leger held.

"There seems to have been a sighting of Eunan Maguire nearby here. Do you want to investigate?"

Taaffe was unmoved. He did not even look up from the fire.

"Did you just get another letter from O'Cassidy promising more money?" Taaffe looked up and smirked as Shea Óg stood over him.

"This sounds like a reliable sighting," Shea Óg replied. "The man has set eyes on Eunan Maguire before and is normally steady of judgement and not greedy."

A wet blanket of melancholy and defeatism refused to lift itself from over Taaffe.

"Well, we've had so many false sightings before. I don't know if I could be bothered."

"If you don't make an effort, we'll never free ourselves from this never-ending mission," Shea Óg protested.

"I think we should saddle up. I could do with the exercise." St. Leger strolled over and grinned, for he had overheard their conversation from a distance. "I have always wanted to meet this Eunan Maguire, the subject of such obsession. I'm sure he is just another dirty bandit like the rest and won't seem so frightening when swinging from a tree."

"I am not afraid of him," Taaffe said as he lifted himself up. "I don't see the point of going on a wild goose chase when there are so many rebels about."

"I, for one, could do with the exercise and you lot could do with the practice. Now let's saddle up and chase down this bogeyman that obsesses you all so."

Taaffe picked up his saddle and cursed. If there was anything worse than knowingly going out on a wild goose chase, it was going on a wild goose chase with St. Leger.

CHAPTER 51
PRAY FAST

I rial and his men cautiously entered the village of the witch, but quickly sensed an oppressive wave of fear emanating from the ruins. The air felt thick and still, like a stifling blanket over their shoulders. The once blue skies had been swallowed by clouds of swirling darkness, and the desperate howls of dogs seemed to echo in all directions. A gentle wind whistled through trees that trembled with invisible terror. Though there was no sign of immediate physical danger on this desolate street, a looming menace lingered in the background.

The English settlers were nowhere to be seen — only the Irish remained, living in ramshackle huts after being driven away from their homes. Their clothes were worn and tattered, their eyes hollow with despair. Irial squinted ahead at what appeared to be the largest house in town. He assumed it must be occupied by Murrogh. Its walls were weathered with age, its windows shuttered, and its roof thatched. Wooden planks creaked and splintered underfoot while crumbling plaster flaked from the stone steps leading up to the door.

As they approached, two Galloglass warriors stepped forward to guard the entrance. Irial slowly dismounted from his horse before them and stood tall with staff in hand. His heart thudded faster in anticipation as he steadied himself. Even he had begun to believe the stories of the witch. He adjusted his cloak before staring at the ancient house and asked: "Is this where the witch resides?"

"Are you the men from the Maguires come to rid themselves from the curse?" said the guard.

Irial's lips moved, but his stony expression did not as he tried to steady himself. He was about to meet the witch he used as a cudgel to beat Eunan over the head.

"We cannot undo all the damage she has done but only hope to release the souls she has condemned to purgatory, if not hell."

The young guard smiled.

"She's ready for you, but she's a feisty one. She's spouting all kinds of curses at us. Some of the boys are afraid of her, so they had to lock her in the pig pens out the back so no one could hear her curse and come under her spells."

"Everything will be cleansed and equilibrium restored when we have finished with her," Irial said.

"Where is your priest?" the guard said. "This witch can be much trouble."

Irial turned and signalled to his men. A nervous young man barely out of his teens dismounted, bowed his head and came to stand behind Irial. He took a set of rosary beads from his pocket and muttered barely audible prayers as fast as possible. Irial smiled.

"See? He's a fast prayer, the fastest I know. If anyone can protect me from the witch, it is him."

The guard glared at him, for he could not work out if Irial truly believed that or if he was mocking him.

"That's not how my mother told me prayers worked."

"Your mother is not a priest."

Murrogh came out of the house with several men, beaming from ear to ear. He walked over and embraced Irial, who was surprised at such a reception.

"One witch's death will be the making of both our clans," Murrogh said.

"One witch's death will mean less evil in the world and us being brought closer to God," the priest said.

Both Irial and Murrogh glared at him, but he did not notice, for he had already dropped his head in prayer.

"So what is to be done?" Murrogh said. "Have you baited the trap?"

Irial smirked.

"His uncle should have freed him by now, for I made it deliberately easy for him to escape. He is so arrogant he will not realise it. I expect them to be not far behind us."

Murrogh slapped him on the shoulder, almost knocking him off his unsteady feet.

"Then I will ride out and lead them away to give you time. Make the witch confess, and we'll have constructed a trap neither of them will wriggle out of."

"Then saddle up and bring the witch to me."

Murrogh signalled to his men, and they brought the horses while others went into the house to fetch the witch. Irial's heart twitched, and his body tensed. Was this the power of the witch taking possession of him? Maybe the men's tales had been right.

CHAPTER 52

LAYING THE BAIT

Murrogh and his men rode determinedly towards the hillock between two small woods, knowing that Seamus and Eunan would have to pass through if they would ever approach the village. With each beat of their horses' hooves, Murrogh's mind raced back to memories of his youth. Pain and guilt surged within him from his brother Cian's reckless behaviour, and he felt hopeless for Seamus, who did not possess Cian's strength or battle wits but had an uncanny ability to sense danger. He was a very different man from the one who presented to him today, but anyone who witnessed the clan's demise had been brought up to expect the worst. The shadows from deep within his heart seemed to grow ever more powerful as he swore revenge upon those who brought ruin to his clan.

Suddenly, one of the scouts galloped back, and the time for Murrogh's redemption had come. No matter its effect on his immediate family, he was prepared to do whatever it took to revive his lost clan.

The scout hurried back to his master with the taste of news on his lips.

"I saw them amongst the many patrols the O'Neill has sent out. Both Eunan Maguire and his uncle were among the party."

Murrogh smiled.

"So, which of you volunteers to play the part of the witch, don the blanket, and ride on the back of my horse?"

There was silence as all the men looked away.

"I guarantee it will be the safest spot, for if they pursue us, they will not want to shoot the prisoner they came to free."

Still no volunteers. Murrogh reached into his pocket.

"How about I throw in this bag of coins?"

One man put up his hand.

"No, no, you are too large. No one would mistake you for a dainty witch, and the horse could not take both our weights."

Once one man was spurned, more suitors volunteered. Murrogh pointed to a small man at the back.

"Come, you'll do. The horse could put up with you."

They waited until the party of rebels came over the hill and was within hearing distance.

"I HAVE YOUR WITCH, MAGUIRE," Murrogh bellowed across the countryside. "COME AND SAVE HER BEFORE SHE BURNS."

He watched the almost instantaneous reaction. The rebels dug their heels into the sides of their horses. He gave a smug grin and raised his hand.

"Follow me, men, just as we rehearsed."

They took off as fast as they could into the woods.

CHAPTER 53

THE TRIAL

Irial's guards entered the house and dragged Cara down the stairs and outside into the street. She was a shadow of her former self, having been constantly beaten, prodded and starved over the long period of her captivity. She gave a few kicks and punches but was resigned to her incarceration ending in her death with rescue a dim fading dream. The guards threw her to the ground in front of Irial. She may have been a heap of dirt, rags and bones, but the men still backed away from her and her perceived power. She lifted her head up, her hair a patchwork of shaved parts, clumps of her once luscious black hair, scabs and bruises.

"I came here a rebel just like you, to tell the clans they could be free, just like you. Yet, here I am, all battered and broken just because some rich Englishman slandered me as being a witch, and you take up my title with vigour and enthusiasm for your own malicious purpose. What is that purpose? Surely some of you rebels must have a thought in your head and compassion in your hearts? I lie before you victimised purely for being a woman."

Irial's eyebrow twitched, and he paused momentarily, for even he was touched by such an eloquent plea. But he regained his thoughts and turned to the men who also seemed to sympathise with Cara.

"See, men? See what spells she can still weave with only her tongue? If our fellow rebels could not resist her spell and restrain her, imagine how powerful she would be before you if you were not already under her spell."

The men took a step back in fear of Cara, who struggled to lift herself to her feet. She stood up and swayed a little until she regained her balance.

"So why am I here?" she said to Irial. The contempt on her face only hardened his heart. "Is it to get a suntan, or are you going to be the one who is brave enough to kill a wee woman?"

Irial knew which crowd he was playing to and once more turned around to address his men.

"See how she taunts me? Any good Catholic woman would be on her knees praying to God to forgive her sins and to ease her way into heaven, but not this witch. She still breathes hatred even though we have diminished her powers."

"So what is it to be?" Cara said. "What are my crimes? Tell everyone how little old me, sent on a mission to spread the rebellion, ended up being a witch and possessing a man twice my size for no material gain for myself. If I was such a clever witch, how come I'm standing here as a pawn for your purposes?"

Irial now grew tired of such a spirited defiance. The men tiptoed from side to side the more their unease grew and doubt festered upon their faces. It had to be now while he still had the advantage. He thrust his accusatory finger into Cara's tired, blotchy face.

"You bewitched one of our great commanders, turned him into a fool and then blinded and killed his poor wife while they still have a babe in arms. I have witnessed it."

Cara wearily shook her head.

"I did no such thing. In the recent past, I would have been a war wife to the soldier in the field," Cara said. She swayed from side to side as she was growing faint, such was the efficient manner that Murrogh's men starved her. "I bet all of you would like a war wife in Munster and go back to Fermanagh to the wife and children?"

No man would face her to deny her suggestion.

"Enough of this," Irial said. He threw his hands to the sky, and his eyes bulged. "The more we listen, the more she weasels into our brains. It is time to condemn her and free Eunan Maguire and all the men who witnessed her evil deeds and fell under her spell. It is time to let the witch burn in the middle of the village."

The men set upon Cara and dragged her towards the fire before she could get a fist or a foot in.

CHAPTER 54
THE MORE THE MERRIER

E unan pointed to the figures on the hill. Sweat poured from his brow, his heart pounded in his chest, and his finger shook.

"They look like Murrogh's men, and it looks like a prisoner is riding with Murrogh."

Seamus squinted.

"How can you tell from here?"

"Because his eyes work properly," Fáolán said with a laugh.

Seamus scowled.

"I want to be sure we chase the right riders, for Cara's life is at stake. Is there any way we can tell?"

"Not from here," Eunan said. "If we ride towards them, we may get a better look."

They proceeded at a steady trot so as not to draw attention to themselves but at such a pace that they could break into a gallop if required.

"I HAVE YOUR WITCH, MAGUIRE," Murrogh bellowed across the countryside. "COME AND SAVE HER BEFORE SHE BURNS."

Eunan turned his head towards Seamus

"What more do you need?"

Seamus nodded, and they both kicked their heels into the sides of their horses.

Murrogh had set the trap perfectly, knowing that Eunan would have to tire his horse by riding down into a dip and up a steep hill before even attempting to catch up. Murrogh charged headlong into the dense woods with reckless abandon, following a path he knew like the back of his hand. Eunan and Seamus pursued him at full gallop, mercilessly hammering their horses' flanks as they thundered towards their quarry. Suddenly, without warning, Murrogh came to a stop. Seamus saw it coming just in time to slow his mount, but Eunan was too late to react. The path ahead narrowed precipitously, hemmed in on both sides by unforgiving rock faces. As Eunan tore towards the narrow gap, rocks suddenly rained down from above, pelting him and his horse unmercifully and nearly causing him to lose control. But the worst was yet to come. Sacks filled with a vile-smelling sludge were hurled from the trees overhead, bursting open as they struck branches and drenched their hapless targets in thick brown goo.

"Urrgh, pig shit," Eunan said as he held out his arms and tried to shake the loose excrement off.

Seamus laughed, as did Fáolán and the more experienced men who had held back from the tightening of the road.

"It seems my brother has a sense of humour after all. That was the perfect opportunity to kill us and blame an English patrol. So, obviously, he has planned something far more devious and wide-reaching than having us murdered. Let us see what he wants. Ah, look, he waits for us once more."

Murrogh appeared ahead of them.

"WOULD YOU LIKE TO KNOW WHAT IRIAL HAS LINED UP FOR YOUR LITTLE WHORE, MAGUIRE?"

Murrogh grinned but Seamus did not have to see it through his bleary eyes, he could hear it in his brother's voice.

"Where he takes you leads to folly, Eunan."

"The only reward for a faint heart is Cara's death, and I won't have that on my conscience. Now, who is with me, men?"

Fáolán shrugged his shoulders at Seamus.

"You've rode into worse, and you were old."

Seamus grinned back.

"Then let me be a fool forever."

They thundered after Murrogh.

Eunan's steely gaze never faltered as he charged through the thick woods, splattering mud and dirt from beneath his horse's hooves. Branches scratched and clawed at him, but the howling in his heart kept him going, pushing back the pain that threatened to slow him. The thud of his own heart seemed to match the rhythm of the hooves, no matter how hard he pushed them. A symphony of terror followed behind him, the clatter of blades drawn and cries of rage echoing through the trees. Nothing could stop him now. Murrogh maintained a steady lead, manoeuvering down winding trails according to plan.

Seamus galloped ahead of Fáolán with his arm outstretched towards Eunan's men. They eased their horses to a trot while keeping their quarry in sight.

Fáolán's brows furrowed deep with determination.

"I thought we were going to follow Eunan?"

"The route seems too perfect," said Seamus as he studied the road ahead. "If we are being dragged into an ambush, then we can ride to the rescue by hanging back."

"You're the lord," Fáolán said as he turned his head to hide his disapproval.

"I am indeed, and you all put your lives in my hands, and I'm determined to protect them. Now ride on."

CHAPTER 55
THE CROSSROADS

T aaffe held the reins of his horse to drag him from the tufts of grass he was replenishing himself with after the afternoon's leisurely ride. He looked at St. Leger and cursed to himself as he watched his master diligently survey the land. They were tucked beneath a grassy knoll, and St. Leger contemplated which direction to take next. Taaffe turned to Shea Óg, laid out on the grass, eyes shut, chewing the end of a piece of grass that lazily hung from his mouth.

"This is a waste of time," Taaffe said as he cursed and spat on the ground. "This patrolling is a fool's errand and a waste of the talents of a man of my expertise. I should be taking back the land and reallocating it to good English settlers. I'll never be able to pay off my debts and step back in Dublin without the escort of some bodyguards at this rate."

Shea Óg opened his eyes and smiled.

"Why don't you sit down here and take the weight off your feet and the worry off your mind?" He patted down a tuft of grass beside him. "There'll be plenty of time for that when the new Lord Deputy settles in. For now, let St. Leger exhaust himself, and you relax."

Taaffe sighed but decided the freshly patted down grass was the most comfortable place to spend the afternoon.

"TAAFFE. GET UP HERE," St. Leger hollered down the hill.

"This better be good," Taaffe muttered. "I was just about to get comfortable." He climbed up the hill and stood beside St. Leger. His commander pointed into the woods.

"There's a commotion from there amongst that clutch of trees. Can you hear it?"

It was not hard to hear, for thundering hooves rolled towards them.

"I can hear it but cannot tell if they are friend or foe," Taaffe said.

In front of them was a break in the woods where the road passed. A group of horsemen burst out of the woods, through the clearing and onto the road, passing through the woods on the other side.

St. Leger jumped and instinctively drew his sword.

"Were they rebels?"

"Looked like it to me. But we weren't sent out here to chase down any rebel patrols we may come across."

"Don't forget who the commander is here," St. Leger sneered. "Bring the horses."

His men jumped up and mounted their horses below the hill, bringing St. Leger and Taaffe's mounts up.

They heard the thunder of hooves through the woods again, and a group of horsemen broke out of the woods. Taaffe's face lit up.

"Christ, I am redeemed," Taaffe cried. "That's Eunan Maguire."

St. Leger thrust out his sword.

"After them, men."

They thundered towards Eunan and his men, and their screams caught Eunan's ear. Eunan slowed his horse to see who was charging after them.

"It's the English," he cried. "This is Murrogh's trap."

Eunan pulled on the reins of his horse and turned and charged down the left turn of the crossroads to leave the pursuit of Murrogh to Seamus. St. Leger and his men thundered after them.

CHAPTER 56

THE TWO BROTHERS

S eamus and his men barrelled through the crossroads, leaving only dust in their wake. He had lost sight of Murrogh and Eunan, and the guilt weighed heavily on him. He pushed forward recklessly, desperate to make up for lost time. Fáolán followed close behind, skilfully pushing his horse as far as it could go without faltering. Seamus seethed with rage inside, blaming himself for letting Murrogh out of his sight. As they burst from the woods, Murrogh was perched atop a small hill, surveying his pursuers with an air of superiority. Seamus and his men skidded to a stop, the dust swirling around them like an enraged tornado.

"Did anyone catch sight of Eunan on the way here?" Seamus said.

All the men shook their heads as they caught their breaths and steeled themselves for a fight with Murrogh and his men.

"I think we lost them," Fáolán said, but he bowed his head so Seamus would not see his disapproval of his actions.

"Well, Eunan is big and ugly enough to look after himself. Wait here while I see what Murrogh really wants."

Fáolán dismounted and took Seamus's axe from him.

"I'll keep it safe for you. Are you sure it's not an ambush?"

Seamus looked around and saw that the path to the hill Murrogh was sitting on was relatively clear.

"He is a fool but not that much of a fool. He could never openly kill me as long as I have the protection of the O'Neill."

"Good luck, then. The men and I will sit here until you give us the signal."

"If something does happen to me then ride as fast as you can to the O'Neill and tell him. May my death not be the final nail in the sorry coffin of the MacSheehy."

"We'll bring pride back to the clan yet, despite all that has happened," Fáolán said.

Seamus nodded, undid his sword belt, and handed it to Fáolán. He began to saunter across the dip between the hills, thinking a show of confidence would give him the upper hand. He hoped Murrogh would have the honour to dismount and meet him halfway in distance and differences. Seamus held his hands up in the air.

"Come, brother. Let us discuss this together like men," Seamus called across the valley. "I am unarmed, and either of us falling this day to some foul treachery would mean the end of our clan, and neither of us wants that, no matter its sorry state."

Seamus fixed his gaze on the hill before him as he increased his pace. Murrogh dismounted and assisted the blanketed figure in dismounting. He gave his weapons to one of his men and slowly walked down the hill towards Seamus.

The clouds swirled overhead as blue became subsumed by deep gunmetal grey in an endless cycle of birth, death, and rebirth. They locked gazes, each face a crimson mask of rage. The clansmen seethed with hurt and indignation at the other's betrayal. Thoughts of retribution coursed through their veins like venom. They stopped ten feet apart, and the tops of their morions now pinged beneath gentle raindrops. The smell of heather mixed with the sharp taste of bile in their mouths. A tightness gripped Seamus's stomach as he felt the coming violence and looked to the heavens for a sign to quell the coming storm. His hands shook, but as he stood transfixed, he could not run. He swallowed hard, for even with his decades of battle experience, no one could trigger him like his older sibling.

"Brother," Seamus said as the past with Murrogh flew in front of his mind's eye. "How have you come to conspire to bury the last of our clan's reputation this day?"

Murrogh laughed.

"I conspire at nothing. I was merely carrying out the business of my, I mean our, master, the Earl of Desmond, when you took it upon yourself to pursue me under the threat of violence. What mischief do you plan to do unto me and my men to finally destroy the last of your clan, which seems to have been your objective ever since you placed your sorry feet back on Munster soil."

"Who is that on the back of your horse?" Seamus said as he pointed to the figure standing on the top of the hill, still covered in a blanket. "You have kidnapped a loyal rebel and are bringing her to her execution."

Murrogh threw his head back with a mocking laugh.

"I have done no such thing. Look." Murrogh turned and signalled to the person beneath the blanket to drop the covering to the ground. The blanket was discarded and the man hidden beneath laughed and gave Seamus the finger. Murrogh's men on the hill laughed alongside him and made mocking gestures at Seamus. The veins in Seamus's neck bulged.

"So where is the girl?" he growled at Murrogh.

Murrogh grinned back at him.

"I don't mind the Maguire's business for them. I only manage that of my clan. If they want to set fire to a witch, then it is none of my business as long as they do not disturb the Earl's peace."

Seamus went for his belt, but his hand only met thin air. Murrogh laughed.

"So that is where we are at, brother? The good of the clan did not last long."

Seamus ignored Murrogh's goading.

"Where is Eunan? He was hot on your heels and is now nowhere to be seen."

"Who do you wish to know is where because you can't save both."

Seamus grimaced and made a fist for he would so like to smash Murrogh's face in. But in this instance, he knew his brother had all the cards.

"May your withholding of this information not portray you or your master in a bad light in front of the O'Neill. Tell me where they are and restore some kind of trust between us for we are the last of the true MacSheehy Galloglass. If you are to do it for anyone, do it for the memory of your dead father to whom you promised to look after your younger brothers."

This only encouraged Murrogh's grin.

"It was worth it just to see you squirm, for in Munster, you are nothing without the O'Neill's protection. The village where your witch is on trial is half an afternoon's ride west from here. The last I saw of Eunan, he was being pursued east by an English patrol. So, decide who you are going to save. The girl is further away but will not see the afternoon out without your help. Can Eunan fight off the English as they drive him to their camp? That is the choice I leave you with, for I must return to my master and continue our mission to liberate these lands. The next time I see you, I expect you to be at least grateful for the information I gave you today."

Murrogh turned to leave.

"I will prove you had a hand in whatever comes of today and I will have my revenge for that and all you have done to the clan," Seamus said.

Murrogh laughed over his shoulder.

"How is your revenge on me going? Don't stand around thinking of an answer, for the more you procrastinate the greater the chances both will die."

Seamus cursed, clenched his fist, and turned to the east and then to the west.

"May God grant me wisdom even though I do not deserve it."

He paused, looked at his brother's back, then turned and ran up the hill. No divine insight came to him, for if he considered himself a tool of any other being, he would be one of the devil. He pointed in the direction he considered best.

"That way, men, and make all haste."

Seamus mounted his horse and rode at full pelt in the direction he had indicated.

CHAPTER 57

THE FINAL FIRE

"Time waits for no man and God does not wait for a witch," Irial said as he spread his arms to rally the men. Trees felled from the local forest had been built up around a pole to which they meant to tie Cara and set her on fire. The sun dipped behind a billowing dark grey cloud rolling in like a pestilence from the heavens. The guards shook as they held Cara and they looked at the pyre, which was to be her destiny. Her brown dress was nothing but tattered rags now, barely clinging to her trembling form. Suddenly, she felt a hand slip something into her pocket.

"This is from Seamus MacSheehy," whispered a voice behind her. "It will make your passage easier should you need it."

She squeezed her hand in her pocket and felt the vial roll between her shaking fingers. She desperately wanted to be saved instead of facing a painless death. But the cold presence of the vial made her realise that rescue was an impossible pipe dream. A fiery heat bloomed on her chest, quickly followed by a chill that spread all over her body like spiders crawling over her skin. She could feel every blade of grass pricking against her bare feet, and the rough fabric of her dress itching against her flesh. Tears streamed from the corners of her eyes but with one swift movement Cara had managed to slip the vial from her pocket into the side of her mouth and used her tongue to position it, waiting for the right time to set free its contents.

"Take her," Irial ordered.

The guards clamped their iron-like grip around Cara's arms and dragged her towards the pyre, each step only causing more desperate screams of curses and promises of bloody vengeance to spew from her lips. They bound her wrists painfully tight behind the stake, so tight it was as if they would cut off the circulation in her arms. But Cara had a plan. She stilled herself, knowing Irial wanted to see her suffer, and kept her head bowed in defiance, never allowing him the satisfaction of hearing her cry out.

A rainstorm began to pour down but Cara kept her mouth closed. She knew that any suggestion of pleasure would bring forth a beating from the guards.

"Do you have any final words, witch? Do you wish for the ear of a priest?" Irial mocked with a malicious glint in his eye.

Cara met his eye.

"If I were to confess to anyone, it would be to you. If you wish me to whisper Eunan Maguire's secrets in your ear then come forth and if what I tell you is juicy enough, maybe you could see if you could set me free?"

Irial looked nervously to the men. He could see the doubt and fear in their eyes at being in the presence of a witch. But he could not be seen as being weak.

"I will lend you my ear as an act of God's charity to ease your soul into a place that is not hell. But any of your tricks or spell casting will make your passage all the worse, let me warn you."

"Come and hear my last prayer," Cara croaked, "and bring me some water for it would do either of us no good if I come to face God and I cannot recite a word of prayer because my throat is parched."

Irial looked to his men and put out his hand. One man rushed to him with a water bottle. He mustered all the courage he had and stepped forward towards her. Strides of steel punctuated by a walking stick. A head held high. He held out the water bottle with a trembling hand.

"Why are you still afraid of me?" Cara said. "Here am I bound and about to be set alight and you still quiver beneath me. Come closer, give me water and let me whisper my confession in your ear."

Irial clenched his fists, anger coursing through his veins. How dare this witch look down on him like that in front of his men? He could feel their judgemental eyes upon him, the fear and doubt ingrained deep within them. He would be a laughing stock for eternity if he showed even the slightest hint of weakness. But he could still not bring the bottle to her lips.

"Come closer, for I can't drink the water from there."

Irial tutted and reached out with the bottle of water. Cara clenched her teeth around the vial and spat its contents right into Irial's face. He recoiled, clutching his face in agony. Dropping his staff, he sank to the ground, shrieking as he tried to wipe away the poison on his skin. His men rushed over to help him stand up.

"Light the fire," Irial rasped, pointing vaguely at where he thought the pyre was located, his eyes blackened and streaming with tears.

"Free me now, for this cruel death will gnaw at your souls until the day of your judgement," Cara cried.

A sombre-faced man with a fire torch appeared and, disregarding all of Cara's pleas, thrust the rod several times into the bottom of the pyre until he was certain it had caught. Flames sprang up, defying the rain. They quickly licked around Cara's feet, and her mouth felt parched as the oxygen near her was drawn away by the heat. She leaned back against the pole she was tied to in an effort to get some respite for her lungs. The ground shuddered beneath her feet as darkness began to overshadow the sky. The wind accelerated, further fanning the flames. The logs popped and cracked as they were piled on top of each other, followed by a dull thud as each one jumped and smacked into its neighbour. A strong smell of burning oak from the fire and bracken from the woods filled the air. She could hear the men nervously moving around her. The smoke carried a heady, intoxicating scent which made their eyes sting. The heat became unbearable and she lost all her strength to fight. She screamed at the top of her lungs.

The men wiped Irial's face with a damp cloth, trying to clean away the poison that had seeped into his eyes. His heart raced as he thought of never being able to see again. Over Cara's cries, he heard the sound of horses galloping, creaking armour and angry shouts in the background. Desperate, Irial grabbed a nearby water bottle and doused his eyes with its contents. Through the blurriness, he could make out the silhouettes of people moving around him and the changing light outside. One shadow came into clear view, pushing past the other shapes.

"You'll pay for what you did today," came an angry voice.

"And who exactly will make me pay?" Irial said. "Here I lie blinded by the witch and all I can think of is I did the people of Munster a favour by ridding them of her vile influence."

"She was under the protection of Eunan Maguire."

Irial laughed.

"So that's what you call it? Who are you to threaten me, a servant of the Maguire carrying out his business?"

"Fáolán MacSheehy."

"I may not recognise you but you are as unwanted here as you were in Augher Castle when Eunan brought the MacCabes there. Now be off with you before my men string you up for interfering in the Maguire's business."

"You haven't heard the last of this."

"Oh, I have, for Eunan Maguire is next."

Fáolán shook off the grabbing hands of Irial's men and walked off cursing. Cara still screamed and Fáolán took an axe from one of his men and put her out of her misery.

"Goodbye, friend. Your kindness will not be forgotten and your death will be avenged." Fáolán and his men took to their horses before Irial's men could turn on them.

CHAPTER 58
A BURST OF LIGHT

E unan gritted his teeth as he felt his horse start to tire. He clutched the reins with a tense grip, desperately urging it onward to outrun his pursuers. His heart raced as he shot tumultuous glances over his shoulder and saw their determined faces getting closer. He felt the earth trembling beneath him as they shook their reins and spurred on their horses. With one last ditch effort, he kicked at his horse's sides with all his might, willing them both to escape.

Odhran pointed to a fork in the road. He was behind Eunan and had to strain his voice to be heard.

"TAKE THE RIGHT TURN. I KNOW THIS WAY."

Eunan pushed his horse through the dense forest as a cold sweat poured down his face. He stole a glance over his shoulder and saw Odhran's desperate face, mouthing something he couldn't make out. The trees blotted out any chance of seeing how close their pursuers were but Eunan felt they were near. He ducked just in time to avoid a low hanging branch, barely missing it, while one of his men was not so lucky and cried out from behind him as he fell. Now, only four were against an ever-growing number of enemies. Despite being outnumbered and exhausted, he was confident in handling whatever came their way using only his throwing axes. With a flick of his wrist, Eunan pointed the way forward and spurred his horse onward with what little strength he had left.

The rebel horses galloped through the woodland path following Eunan's lead, their hooves pounding like the drums of war against fate as death followed closely behind. The trees around them seemed to loom larger, towering over them like mountains around a tiny glen, while a single sliver of light above them sent shivers down Eunan's spine, a warning more than a sign of hope. In the shadows, he could just make out the shapes of those chasing after them, looming closer and closer with each stride.

They burst from the woods like a wildfire, their horses' hooves churning up clods of earth and sending them hurling through the air. The looming, tumultuous clouds had already swallowed the sun. They began to slow as the ground became soft and covered in dense, knee-high grass, which restricted their movement. Eunan glanced behind him. The English patrol was still among the shadows of the trees but closing in quickly. Ahead, he saw a small group of men tending to some grazing horses, indistinguishable from friend or foe due to the chaos of war. His heart quickened when he spotted a familiar face amongst them, Hugh Maguire. He signalled his own men to part and make way as the Maguire mounted his horse and took hold of his lance. With a great wave, the Maguire signalled to his men and with one deafening roar, they began their charge. Fear pulsed through Eunan's veins as he prepared for battle.

CHAPTER 59
THE DUEL

S t. Leger leapt from the forest like a wolf pursuing his prey, his band of men following close behind in a howl of thundering hooves. As they charged into the wide-open field, St. Leger's hand flew up instinctively when he caught sight of two groups of armed horsemen blocking their path. St. Leger's heart raced, his eyes flicking back and forth between the two groups of mounted men standing before him. Every muscle in his body tensed as he tried to discern whose side they were on, but the heavy silence over the field only fuelled his growing sense of unease. His fingers twitched on the hilt of his sword.

"THAT IS THE MAGUIRE CHARGING AT US," Taaffe shouted.

St. Leger saw one group of horsemen turn their horses and begin to build up speed, lowering their heads before they charged. He saw the other group pull around their horses as if they were about to join in. St. Leger pulled on his reins to steady his horse.

"You have to forget your vendetta against Eunan Maguire. We have other business to conduct here."

Taaffe rode up beside him and pointed at the group of horsemen now charging them.

"THAT IS THE MAGUIRE, THE REAL MAGUIRE!"

The Maguire was now eating up the ground between them.

St Leger took his pistol from his belt and held it aloft.

"FOR THE QUEEN, MEN. CHARGE."

The axe in Eunan's hands felt like ice as he watched his clan leader charge towards the enemy. Eunan had by now pulled his horse around and his heart clenched as he realised what his reckless actions had caused. With a cry of rage, the Maguire lowered his lance, steered his horse towards the leader of the enemy and sat forward to brace for impact, leaving Eunan behind to writhe in torment and agony.

"WITH ME, MEN," Eunan shouted as he raised his axe above his head. "WE MUST SAVE THE MAGUIRE."

St. Leger and his men charged forward, lances lowered, and let out a cry like a pack of bloodthirsty wolves baring their fangs. The Maguire's eyes fixed on St Leger's head as he held his lance steady and aimed at the target. St Leger discarded his lance and brought his pistol up, taking aim at the Maguire's chest. The sound of the gunshot echoed through the air as a line of crimson splattered from the Maguire's chest and across his face. But the injured warrior refused to let go of his lance, gripping it with every last bit of strength. His horse collided with that of St. Leger and the two riders fell towards each other. The tip of the Maguire's lance pierced through St. Leger's face, ripping off an entire side with a sickening crunch.

St. Leger flew backward off his horse, thrown with dizzying force. The impact sent the Maguire flying too, as he was already unbalanced from the impact of the bullet. He thudded on the ground before raising his arms to protect himself from his own horse trampling him as he panicked. The horse galloped away into the open fields, his bloody hooves wiped clean in the long grass leaving the Maguire in a mangled heap.

Both sides then collided, for even though their masters had fallen the momentum drove the rest of them into each other. Howls and shrieks filled the air as weapons penetrated and bodies fell to the ground and they suffered the same fate as their masters. Some weapons were deflected and rode the wood and steel of a shield until their owners fell to the ground as they lost their balance. The other men clashed their swords and lances briefly but quickly disengaged for their focus was no longer on fighting each other, but on attending to their injured leaders. They drew their weapons to their chests and backed away while not letting their enemies out of their sight. Shea Óg rushed to where his own leader lay and saw his face was a mess of raw flesh and oozing blood. Shea Óg's mind flew to when Seamus had horrifically scarred him and pity pulsated through his body. He tossed St Leger over his horse's back and remounted before fleeing into the woods.

But Taaffe was far from done. He had been thrown off his horse by the sheer force of the Maguire's charge, but had found his feet and his weapon too. He was all too familiar with taking down other Irish riders who rode with no stirrups and he grabbed at any rebel within reach and pulled them down and stabbed them. He barely noticed that the two sides had disengaged and when he did, he started to back away. Was he the only one who knew how to conduct a blood feud? He spun and looked for his next victim hoping it would be Eunan Maguire.

The Maguire lay on the ground, holding his chest and groaning in agony as the blood spurted from his wounds. His limbs were mangled by the sheer force of his own horse and his face was a sickly white in the luscious green grass as his life drained into the Munster soil. He raised his hand above the tips of the grass and cried out for help.

Both Eunan and Taaffe saw the hand tremble in the crisp air. They both hesitated to see who was nearer the Maguire, but stole a glance to their men to rally them to the charge. Eunan raised his axe.

"THE CRY OF THE MAGUIRE!"

The men roared behind him but the words lingered in the air with a special poignancy as if this could be the last cry for this particular Maguire. That is, if he failed to save him. The man who had been Eunan's great friend and protector. The man who the whole north looked to after the O'Neill and the O'Donnell to lead the rebellion. His life was now in Eunan's hands. He swallowed hard and dug his heels into the sides of his horse.

Eunan surged forward with a strength he did not know he possessed, and his men followed suit, driving the English back with axes and swords drawn, taut muscles and determined eyes.

"Secure the Maguire!" Eunan yelled above the chaos as his steed galloped towards where the Maguire had fallen.

But before Eunan could close the gap between them he felt his own body flying backwards as an invisible force toppled him off his horse. His back shuddered on impact and Eunan groaned as he was winded. He regained his senses and his eyelids darkened. He opened his eyes and found himself looking up into the face of an old adversary. Taaffe sneered with malicious intent.

"You don't know how long I have waited for this, Maguire," Taaffe snarled.

Taaffe thrust one arm forward to overcome any defence Eunan may put up and jerked his other arm back to ensure his dagger would get the purchase to pierce armour and leather, flesh and bone, and put this feud to rest forever.

"Don't talk. Do," Eunan spat back, thrusting his foot with all the strength he could muster, ramming his heel right through Taaffe's knee. Taaffe collapsed like a puppet whose strings had been cut, writhing on the ground. Seizing the opportunity, Eunan scrambled to his feet and drew out his throwing axe from his belt. He pulled his arm back as Taaffe raised his as his last line of defence. Taaffe's eyes were blinded with tears as he fought the desire to cry out for mercy as he thought his time of judgement was upon him. His father appeared in his mind's eye to damn him to hell and to ensure he knew the way. However, the din of battle intervened as another group of men on horseback thundered out from the nearby woods with a blood curdling roar. Protect the Maguire. Eunan turned his head. Were these friend or foe? Protect the Maguire. Could he get to the Maguire on time? He recognised Seamus as the lead rider. Seamus and his men pulled up to survey the melee they had missed so they could identify which group of men were the enemy they should attack. Eunan turned back to take care of Taaffe only to see he had disappeared, leaving nothing but crushed grass where he had lain. The blood feud would not end this day.

CHAPTER 60
ON BENDED KNEES

E unan sprinted towards the Maguire, his feet pounding against the ground and his heart thundering in his chest. In what felt like an eternity, Eunan finally reached him. He pushed past the guards surrounding him and saw that the Maguire was still breathing, though barely, with a spark of life still flickering in his eyes.

"Secure the area and make sure no one lies wounded nearby that would seek to do harm to the Maguire."

The men nodded and left Eunan with his chieftain.

"You are going to see another day," Eunan said as he smiled and tried to provide reassurance. His hands trembled and the tears welled up in his eyes, but he had to put on a brave face for his friend and leader. The Maguire tried to mouth some words, but whatever their meaning was drowned in coughs and splutters. "You don't have to say anything. Let me make you more comfortable as the men fetch your horse."

Eunan placed his hands beneath the Maguire's upper back and gently lifted him so his upper body rested on his thighs as he knelt down to make the Maguire more comfortable. The Maguire's teeth chattered so Eunan undid his body armour and took off his tunic to provide his chieftain with a blanket of sorts. The Maguire's chest heaved up and down with the hum of a wheeze as he struggled to fill his lungs with air. He rolled his head to the side to cough up blood with alarming frequency. Eunan felt his heart sink as he watched the life slowly fade from the Maguire's body. The smell of blood, urine and faeces mingled in the air around them made him want to gag. Eunan's hands trembled as he held the Maguire's head in his lap. The Maguire's eyes glazed over, almost lifeless. The howling wind seemed to be mocking him, throwing its gusts at their broken forms as if to remind them of their impending doom.

The Maguire's lips moved slightly as he croaked a word from between parched lips. "Water."

Eunan reached for the canister on his belt, his trembling fingers barely able to hold it steady enough to pour water down the Maguire's throat. The Maguire held up his hand and Eunan stopped pouring. Eunan examined the Maguire's face and eyes to see if the water had led to any improvement. It only made the Maguire cough up more blood over Eunan's legs. He breathed more deeply and pulled himself up and patted Eunan on the face, leaving behind a patch of blood.

"Forgive me for doubting you and the many wrongs I have done you as a consequence."

He paused to cough up more blood and then to clear his throat.

"Do not let the Maguires fall into the hands of Connor Roe, for that will be the end of us. Do not fight my brother to become leader but support him as he has always supported you. Please do not destroy my legacy or my place in the annals of the Maguires. Give me your pledge so at least I can die in peace."

Eunan could no longer hold back his tears and they fell on the sallow face of the Maguire. He reached out to grasp the Maguire's hand to make his pledge. The Maguire's arm fell limp on the ground.

"I have made far more mistakes than you, lord, and you are the better man for the mistakes you have made. I could never fight your brother for the only person who has done more for me was Desmond."

The Maguire reached up and tried to grab Eunan's hand, but he had so little energy left that his arm fell once more to the ground. Eunan placed his hand on the Maguire's and listened.

"Fight for the rebellion, fight for me. For if we lose this war, we never will be free."

The Maguire's breath became shallower and he looked up and into Eunan's eyes, hoping to receive his pledge.

"You have my word, lord. Your place is assured in the clan tapestries, and many a free young Maguire will look up at them and recite the songs and poems of your glorious death."

Eunan sniffled and raised his eyes to the sky for he did not want the Maguire to see him crying. He smiled up at the dark rain clouds and looked down when he could not hear a sound. The Maguire was now still, his eyes transfixed by the sky. Eunan closed the Maguire's eyes as he was gone. He wept bitter tears.

Why did the Maguire have to die and not him? Why would the Maguire leave him alone like this with the fate of the clan on his shoulders? Where had all his loved ones gone? Desmond, Dervella, Arthur and now the Maguire had all been taken from him. How could someone so young bring so much death to those he loved? It had to be him. He had to be cursed. His mother was right to damn him so. Sorcha loved him and he resented her for her illness. Now she was taken from him. Was this a punishment from God for carrying the bad blood of his father in his veins? How could he carry on? He thought of the one person he loved still alive. He must save Cara. She must live. But all he could do was cradle the dead body of the Maguire in his arms.

A hand came upon his shoulder. He could feel its warmth, for amongst the tragedy, his body had gone numb from the cold.

"I'm sorry for your loss and the great loss of the clans of the north and the rebellion," Seamus said. He hunkered down in front of Eunan to speak directly to him. "We need to leave. The enemy has only retreated into the woods, and God only knows how many more of them and their allies lurk there."

But Eunan could only rock up and down upon his knees, cradling the body of his dead friend. Eunan shook his head as a single drop of rain struck his cheek, and he came to.

"What about him? I cannot leave him to be savaged by crows or worse, for his head to be on a spike outside Dublin Castle."

Seamus stood up to survey the landscape for their enemies.

"Throw him over your horse and we'll take him back to the O'Neill's camp. It is at least half a day from here and the sun has not long left in the sky this day. Here, let me help you."

Seamus signalled to his men and they brought a horse and held it by the body of the Maguire.

"We need to go," Seamus said.

He signalled to his men again and two of them came and stood over the Maguire. A noise came from the woods. Seamus was now on full alert.

"Let there be no more rebel bodies here today. Get to your feet and let's go."

Eunan held up the torso of the Maguire and Seamus took his legs. The two men gently lifted the body onto the back of the horse and made sure he was secure. Eunan then waved them all away.

"I will lead his horse."

Eunan took the reins and started back towards the camp. Seamus directed some of his men to take up the rear to protect Eunan and the Maguire. They got beyond a set of low hills in the distance and were then out in the open with no enemy in sight. Seamus dismounted and went to walk alongside Eunan. Eunan kept up a brisk pace with his eyes firmly on the horizon, determined his old chieftain would get a proper Maguire burial on Devenish Island back in Fermanagh. But something weighed on Seamus's chest that compelled him to confront Eunan, even if it was dreadful timing.

"Your leader is dead, along with your wife. You now have nothing up north, and the clan of your forefathers need you. We can retrieve your boy, for he will be part of the next generation. Will you now stay here with me?"

Eunan looked away and over his shoulder to see if they were being followed. He turned back but looked at the ground for he had little emotionally left to give.

"I'm sorry if I led you astray but everything has changed now. The Maguires need me more than ever, and I have pledged. I must bring the Maguire north, bury him, and see that his brother is made leader of the clan. Then I will bend my knee and offer to do the new Maguire's bidding."

Seamus furrowed his brow.

"Is that wise with all the enemies in high places you have there?"

"This fight is my destiny, and I have pledged. The least you can leave me with is my honour."

The colour drained from Seamus's face as he looked away.

"So be it. You were always a man of honour. But it is a dark and difficult path your honour brings you down."

Eunan looked up and gave the best smile he could. He reached out and placed his hand on Seamus's shoulder.

"As difficult as the one my uncle is on. I leave it to you to restore the family name and honour. You are more than capable of doing so."

Seamus looked to the sky as if someone was looking down upon him.

"I will do it for Dervella. Now let us make haste for we are vulnerable out in the open."

Eunan bowed his head to do battle with his inner demons once more. It would be a long journey home.

ABOUT AUTHOR

If you enjoyed this book, please leave a review on the retailer where you bought it.

For maps, character bios and more information about the period, please go to https://www.crdempseybooks.com.

Join C R Dempsey's mailing list for news on new releases, monthly updates, offers and insights.

*QR code for the C R Dempsey
newsletter mailing list.*

C R Dempsey is the author of 'Bad Blood', 'Uprising', 'Traitor Maguire', 'Breach of the peace' and 'The Curse of Black Mountain', five historical fiction books set in Elizabethan Ireland. He has plans for many more, and he needs to find the time to write them. History has always fascinated him, and historical fiction was an obvious outlet for his accumulated knowledge. C R spends lots of time working on his books, mainly in the twilight hours of the morning. C R wishes he spent more time writing and less time jumping down the rabbit hole of excessive research.

C R Dempsey lives in London with his wife and cat. He was born in Dublin but has lived most of his adult life in London.

C R can be found at:

https://www.crdempseybooks.com/,

https://www.facebook.com/crdempsey,

https://www.instagram.com/crdempsey/,

CLANS AND MILITARY FORMATIONS

Clan structure

Irish clan structure came from ancient times. Clans were kinship groups that would have various septs beneath them. Therefore, there were usually various family branches, each with different strengths of claim to be the clan leader. The clan leader is usually referred to as being 'the' and then the clan name (e.g. 'the Maguire'). Within this system, you could have septs with a different surname that would still be part of the clan (e.g. Keenan Maguire).

They used a tanistry system to elect their leader, so to be elected leader, you had to galvanise support amongst the men eligible to vote. This inadvertently created several different power bases, and therefore rivals, within the clan. After being elected, and during the normal course of events, it was usual for the clan leader to demand the eldest male children of his rivals to be handed over for lengths of time as guarantees of loyalty.

These clans usually had subservient clans, outside their internal sept structure, that paid tribute to them. The example in the story is that the Maguires switch between paying tribute to whoever was the dominant O'Neill and paid tribute to the O'Donnells for a period.

Gallic military formations

At the time of the outbreak of the Nine Years War, except for the O'Neills, the fighting formations of the Irish were at best outdated, but in truth obsolete. The main European fighting formations were pikemen and shot. The main Irish battle tactics were the ambush, to which their soldiers were suited. They were not capable of facing the English in a pitched battle. Hence the urgency of O'Neill and other leaders to train their men in the use of firearms, import weapons from the continent and Scotland, and get as many Spanish trainers as they could.

Below are the main troop types of the Irish clans at the time of the outbreak of the Nine Years War:

Galloglass – mercenary soldiers usually Scottish or from Scottish descent. These were heavily armed mercenaries who used long axes with curved blades. The main Irish houses usually had clans of Galloglass that worked for them permanently. A Galloglass leader was called a constable, a formation of Galloglass a battle and a Galloglass usually had the support of a horseboy or Kern and this was referred to as a spar. Galloglass got paid around three cattle per quarter.

'Cogin and livery' (referred to in the book as 'coin and keep' for simplicity sake) – the clan leader would hire Galloglass, and to share the burden of paying for them, he would assign them to different areas. The population assigned would be responsible for the payment and upkeep of the Galloglass for a time period at the discretion of the clan leader.

Redshanks are 'new Scots' or Scottish mercenaries hired directly from Scotland, usually on a seasonal basis. They were called Redshanks because they went barelegged. They were usually armed with swords and bows. They normally got paid the same as Galloglass, around three cows per quarter.

Kern – traditional Irish light infantry. They were usually not armoured and supplied their own weapons. The weapon of choice was the dart. They also used javelins, swords and bows. Their main uses were to support the heavier armed Galloglass, capture and herd cattle away from enemy territory, and against the English, they were used for lighting attacks and harassment. They usually got paid around one cow per quarter.

Horseboys – Galloglass usually had horse boys to support them. When they fought, they normally functioned as light infantry armed with javelins.

Horsemen – these were usually the nobility of the clan. They rode without stirrups, which potentially made them unstable when facing heavier English cavalry, and were usually armed with javelins.

Shot – these were armed with muskets. The Irish lords tried to retrain their Galloglass and other experienced soldiers to become either shot or pike as fast as circumstances would allow. The amount of shot the Irish armies could field would depend on the clan. The O'Neill formations were mainly armed with shot while the smaller clans were not.

Pike – there is little evidence that the pike was widely available to the Irish rebels. These formations also did not suit the Irish style of ambush warfare. Again, mainly the larger clans such as the O'Neills would have had the most pikemen.

The Irish formations were supported by experienced Irish mercenaries who had fought mainly with the Spanish army in the Dutch Revolt. These men would have been skilled in modern European warfare and made a vital backbone to the Irish military formations.

English military formations

The English forces in Ireland usually came from four sources: Irish conscripts (mainly from the Pale), Irish allies, raw recruits from England and veterans who had served in France, the Scottish borders or the Netherlands. There was much changing of sides between the Irish on both sides.

Shot – the English were mainly armed with calivers but also had a small number of muskets. The men armed with calivers, the lighter of the two guns, were mainly used for skirmishing. The muskets were used to support the pike as the muskets were heavier and less manoeuvrable.

Pike – Pikemen were the core of the army. They had a ten to fifteen-foot spear, a helmet and breastplate armour and were mainly used for defence. They could also make a very effective charge.

Horsemen – these were comprised mainly of Irish cavalry. They were more heavily armoured than the Irish cavalry and were armed with a lance, sword and occasionally a pistol. They were the most feared element of the English armies. They were mainly used for skirmishing.

English system of government in Ireland

Lord Deputy – the representative if the Queen and the head of the Irish executive under English rule

Irish Council – the executive branch of English rule in Ireland

Lord President (Governors) were the English military leaders for the various provinces of Ireland with wide-ranging powers.

London Privy Council – the body of advisors to the Queen

ACKNOWLEDGMENTS

Thank you to all my family and friends and all of those who helped to create this book.

Special thanks to Mena (endless patience and support), Eoin (advice and inspiration).

Thank you also for the professional support of:

Book cover: Dominic Forbes

Editing: Robin Seavill

Both these individuals can be found on www.Reedsey.com

Printed in Great Britain
by Amazon

49791168R00192